SO MANY WAYS
TO SLEEP BADLY

SO MANY WAYS TO SLEEP BADLY

Mattilda Bernstein Sycamore

City Lights Books
SAN FRANCISCO

Cover design: Stefan Gutermuth
Book design and typography: Gambrinus
Editor: Robert Sharrard

Special thanks to Ralowe T. Ampu, for assisting with the physical, emotional, and creative labor of this book. And to the most brilliant team of editors that money can't buy: Kevin Killian, Brian Pera, Jennifer Natalya Fink, D. Travers Scott. To the confidantes who delivered feedback and/or fever: Chris Hammett, Reginald Lamar, T Cooper, Tony Mueller, Andy Slaght, Lauren Goldstein. And thanks to Dodie Bellamy's workshop for thoughts on the earliest chapters.

For tangibles and intangibles: Jessica Hoffmann, Kirk Read, Katia Noyes, Felicia Luna Lemus, Thea Hillman, Killer Nepon, Eric Stanley, Grant Donnelly, Sarah Schulman, Stephen Kent Jusick, Gina Carducci, Jason Sellards, Perverts Put Out, Rhani Remedes, Gina de Vries, Jen Cross, Ananda LaVita, Jason Devastation, Steve Zeeland, Socket Klatzker, and everyone at City Lights.

To everyone I've misrepresented. And everyone else.

Library of Congress Cataloging-in-Publication Data

Sycamore, Mattilda Bernstein.
  So many ways to sleep badly / Mattilda Bernstein Sycamore.
    p. cm.
  ISBN-13: 978-0-87286-468-9
  ISBN-10: 0-87286-468-5
  1. Gay men--Fiction. 2. San Francisco (Calif.)--Fiction. I. Title.

PS3619.Y33S6 2008
813'.6--dc22

                                        2008020489

10 9 8 7 6 5 4 3 2 1

City Lights Books are published at the City Lights Bookstore,
261 Columbus Avenue, San Francisco, CA 94133

Visit our Website:www.citylights.com

For JoAnne, 1974-1995

For San Francisco, or what's left of it

CONTENTS

HOUSEPLANTS

⊙　　⊙　　⊙　　⊙

The sky is pink and moist, branches are shaking but if I listen hard enough I can hear this guy's teeth going clack-clack-a-clack. He lives in Burlingame, drove up here 'cause he's tweaked—and for me, of course—standing in the dark, waiting to unzip his pants. In yoga, the carpet smells rotten like an armpit filled with dark green mold, the instructor shouts KILL KILL KILL. Sure, it's yoga, but it's Bikram Yoga, they turn the heat up to 120 degrees and the instructors wear microphones like Janet Jackson.

Afterwards, I'm waiting for the shower and some guy steps out with a dick like a bowling pin, Rolling Pin Donuts, sending me back and forth from Collingwood Park to Dolores Beach with no luck either way, it's too late at night for cruising. But Rolling Pin's been gone for years, what gentrification does to an already gentrified neighborhood.

The shower is cold enough that maybe I'll stop sweating, outside there's a guy I'd kill for, maybe I already killed for him but it got me nowhere. Either he's Italian and plucked or French and radiated, but cute faggots can't talk to cute straight boys in locker rooms, so I'm just studying the curve of his spine and all that's around it.

He's one of those guys I hate to want, end up hating myself but downstairs I catch him eyeing my abs, field goal. Mostly, though, in this world where everything's wrong, the women are eyeing me and I'm salivating over Mr. Buff 'n' Tough: fancy yellow sneakers, over-dyed jeans too loose at the ass, powder blue vintage T-shirt my favorite color and then the kicker is the runway hairstyle halfway between mod and '50s 'cause of the part.

Outside, I'm so high from yoga that the stoplights are telling me things and the buildings are extra-sharp against the dark sky, night-time breeze and the tweakers are staring at me. If there were mats out here, I'd somersault all the way home. Instead, I go to Scottie's house to look at photos. He lives on the seventh floor of a six-story building; his apartment was once a speakeasy. He took the photos on his roof, but with the topiary bushes I look like I'm in an Eng-lish garden—well, there's the Transamerica pyramid in the background, so okay it's Egypt. Or Vegas, Shirley Temple's still alive! Singing Britney Spears covers in a room so smoky you can hardly see her hair.

Chrissie calls from Ryan's house, reading a feng shui book while Ryan's out doing eBay errands. Who's Ryan? The boy Chrissie met three days ago—party play poppers porn. Selling everything off for better feng shui, okay. Chrissie says I'm twenty-seven. I need to fig-ure out what I'm doing with my life. Honey you're twenty-nine. Magdalena says Chrissie's thirty, but Chrissie says it's the drugs.

This happens every day: I think about cocktails until I can't think anymore, then I think some more and finally I think well maybe just one. But one's too many because cocktails open up my nose for line after terrible white line—vacuum cleaner, Colombian cartel, I could put up a Missing Nose poster, but what would be the reward? Every day I wonder when I'm getting the goddamn thinking-but-not-drinking prize, the announcer shakes my hand until my wrist falls off, oops—well here's some more money to fix that. But who's killing my houseplants?

Chrissie's doing more eBay errands, a photo crew over the house to take pictures of the merchandise: bloody noses and cuts and bruises, no sores 'cause they're just not as marketable. Chrissie's taking the power back from the corporations—she's gonna make a fortune off her own misery. But why do I go to the Power Exchange? The best part is the ride home, cab driver says well at least you're smiling. Plus, the woman at the entry desk all frisky—still actually enjoying her drugs, but it won't be long, honey, it won't be long. Ping-pong, beer bong—same old song—flip-flops on an escalator—come rain or come-stain.

At yoga, I concentrate so hard on one guy's freckle that I build a house there: Park Place, Boardwalk—why can't I remember any of the other properties? My sister and I always claimed to like the yellow ones better; we wanted to be rich but not too rich. Chrissie wants to go to a vegan potluck, but what kind of people will be there? Vegans, she says. The problem is when it's pouring out and I jump into a cab, get inside and the entire cab smells like the driver's breath. What is wrong with his liver? But rain is so much better when you're in a car, the pretty patterns on the windows, neon through mist and oh these comfortable seats. Though I'm worried that sex will never again change my life.

Gina says I'm listening to music she'd dance naked to, as a joke. The elevator up to my apartment is so slow, motor struggling against all that fucking gravity. Get me some full-spectrum light bulbs!

Living in a bubble, Hubble Telescope, who are all these people? At first I catch each cockroach between a glass and a sheet of paper, runaway floor, swoop and out the window. But there are always more, flushing them down the drain I'll do anything to avoid bloodshed. But soon I see them crawling out of my speakers and unfurling dangerous flags, one of them grows so big it takes up half the kitchen, excuse me I need to do the dishes.

Needless to say, I'm back out in the rain. A trick who surprises me, I could suck on his armpits all night, though would that give me strange wrinkles? After a good trick, there's always a tough one—this couple with neck problems: they look like two versions of the old English schoolteacher plus Fabio. Then there's the trick who leaves me standing outside his house in the freezing cold, the house is sealed like a fortress: a neo-Orientalist masterpiece, with a huge door made out of an entire cherry tree. How many times can I ring the bell? Waiting for a cab to rescue me, I dream my revenge. Turning that house into Pick-Up Sticks in a tornado, but wait—she's no Dorothy.

Cold is so relative. Here it's fifty degrees out and I've got on a wool coat, scarf, and mittens but I'm ice. Some guy walks by in a T-shirt—what a crazy bitch! I'd sell my matchbox cars for her cha-chas. Leave it to me to take the Mission bus in rush hour, fifteen minutes and we've only gone four blocks. Stalled in front of the Sony Metreon, I'm an economic downturn waiting to happen.

The ringer on my phone mixes so well with the music that I decide to let it sing. Frankie Bones is bringing me everything I've ever needed—oh these bleeps and clanks, that hard hard bass, the building frog sound and I am so far into the ceiling I can't even tell there's a floor. The frog runs into a toy car horn, I can hardly breathe and all that pounding bass, windshield wipers, rattlesnake— oh faster faster and higher and this is the steadiness. Where I forget about everything else, all there is in my life is that horn, oh that muted twisted horn, that Merlin melody child's piano in a wind tunnel—don't ever fucking, never fucking leave me.

Here comes the melody, rushing into a chain-link fence, shake that fence! Oh shake it shake it SHAKE it! It's all about the finger piano swing song in the background, and no way is that a broken air-raid siren turning into a trumpet and giving steam-heat radiator whistle, six miles high and then what on earth? It's just everything speaking back and then in and then out, here comes the march and where oh where could we possibly go from here? All that I need is in the vocal: put your head in the speaker. Come closer.

ROACHES

⊙　　⊙　　⊙　　⊙

This trick sold his house today; tomorrow he's moving to South Africa. Tonight he's smoking crystal. Broke up with his lover of ten years and so they sold everything: San Francisco, Miami, somewhere else. While I fuck him, his legs push against me with so much force that it hurts my back. He's one of those tricks who thought I was shorter, from the one-column-inch photo in the paper. We're both allergic to the same lube, plus latex—lucky for him, I've got polyurethane condoms and oil. He pays me one-forty-eight plus two dollars in quarters.

Outside, everything's cardboard, reflecting and absorbing the floating 2 a.m. light. I feel so calm, must be the crystal in the air—the dangers of secondhand smoke. At home, the oven's still on, but the roaches don't look dried out at all. Can I fall asleep without eating first?

Rue wants to jump off the Golden Gate Bridge, but when did she get into extreme sports? Zan and I go to American Rag, where they've got a ratty peach cardigan with hand-sewn patches made of

old sheets—peek-a-boo, I see brown spots! $52.95—what a steal—
I mean deal, 'cause if I'm gonna steal it's not gonna be that.

Zan finds black corduroys to replace her black corduroys. Outside, there's a truckload of pine trees—what a feast for the senses!
Twenty Shopping Days Until Christmas. Miss Thing, Miss Thing,
lost her diamond ring—see, diamonds aren't forever. Rue says it's
not your business what other people say and think of you—how
postmodern!

Zero calls from Provincetown, she's moving to the West Coast in
the spring, or is it the fall? She's deciding between Santa Cruz and
San Diego. Are you kidding? Rue says what's the difference between
a Mormon and a punk? Well, punks have better clothes, and the
music's different.

Once, I tried to get into the Mormon Temple. Benefits: healthier,
softer skin and hair. On the bus, this guy watches me eating beans
from a plastic container—right on, he says. He's a yum-yum treat,
shaved head and cute piercings, do you want to sit down? Damn—
he's getting off at the next stop, five seconds longer and he could
have been fucking my face. The girls next to me want to know
where the fabric store is, we just passed it but it's closed.

Actually, the girls have been talking about the fabric store since I
got on the bus—do you think it's open? They seemed excited by the
possibility that it might not be open, I wanted to let them ride that
possibility. Yum-yum asks them what they're looking for—but he
doesn't know about *that* kinda thing. Pop quiz: is he cuter now, or
was he cuter before?

Rue says pigeon beans don't taste like pigeons, and he's right.
Another interview with Hilary Swank, still recovering from playing
Brandon Teena: these are my tits, this is my husband, these are my
tits, this is my husband. At yoga, I turn the cord of lights across the
ceiling into an elongated trapeze, I'm flying 'round and 'round so
fast that my body becomes a blurred circle of enlightenment. Afterwards, I'm a little tired. Zan and I go to a butoh performance called
"Cockroach," it's nice to see that roaches are so artistic.

When I wake up and my stomach feels like it's in my back, which
way does my head face? All this rain, pain, serotonin drain. Imagi-

nary mice crawling across the floor, what happened to the imaginary cats? My ears are so clogged with wax—if Drano doesn't work, I'm gonna have to call the plumber.

When I come, it shoots from one room to the next, if only someone were here to watch. Afterwards, I'm so bored. Is it time to go back to bed yet? At yoga, the heat is way too high; I get a rash by the corner of each eye like I've been crying. When I turn from my stomach to my back, entire waves of sweat roll off. The instructor is Julie the Cruise Director with a fascistic streak.

I realize it's Saturday, people go out on Saturdays. I watch them through my windows, it looks like it's raining out but it's not. I make toast, this bread's better than the one I ate before. The trick who left me waiting outside his house calls: sorry about that—do you want to come over? As long as you pay me for last week. All he's got is a hundred in cash, but he can write a check, his checks are good.

I just love the way a night of sleep makes my whole body hurt—new day, new promise! But wait, Cristian Vogel's taking me somewhere, I guess the bitch did name the album "All Music Has Come to an End," so I should have expected something frantic. I put on Bernard Badie's "Love Explosion" to relax, but what was I thinking—oh how can I even begin to describe this rat-a-tat-of-course-I-look-gorgeous-no-matter-what-I-fucking-do beat? Legend in a box—I could play this song over and over, and just walk around my apartment for the next few years.

Of course I can't ever seem to get out of the house before 4 p.m., though at least today there's some sun—I stare at the tops of buildings, hoping sunlight will reflect off them and regulate my pineal gland. I've been up for three hours, I need a nap. I go shopping—everything's ugly. My shoes are too small. I go into the plant store—full-spectrum lights don't work.

This trick could be fun, except he's so nervous that I can't stay hard, and his crotch smells like rotten eggs. I wake up holding my head and thinking let's engage, let's engage, let's engage. When my mother says you need to go to the root of your problems—get me a shovel! Lilie says: I like when you talk about incest because you can laugh about it. I go to the bookstore to look for *Disco Bloodbath*.

Chrissie says I've got these pictures of you in drag taped up on one side of the bathroom mirror, and on the other side are these pictures my mother sent me of the countryside in upstate New York—I look at you and the countryside in the mirror every morning when I'm brushing my teeth, I talk to you both and we collaborate on how we're gonna take over the world and things.

The skin underneath my fingernails starts itching, are there lice in there? Drugstore Price Wars, I just want the fucking photos they lost. Everything that itches: gums, eyes, thighs, nose, scalp, urethra, toenails turning yellow then black. Eating toast again, something's burning, that eternal question: cultured pearls or fresh-water pearls? In my dream, Rue's having a birthday celebration in Torino, but why Torino? Honey, she's thirty-five, she wants something special. Luckily, it's only a four-hour drive and the party's at 8, we don't have to leave before 4. What's four hours from Torino? I need a map. Milan? No, that would be awful. Okay, Reno—of course Andee keeps telling me London is the answer—bitch, I'm not moving to London just so it'll be easier for you to visit me.

At yoga, there's a new instructor who's calmer, but I want to kill the guy next to me for breathing too loud. It always gets dark when I'm there—outside, the windows start floating. Afterwards, I watch the red Christmas lights by the Rendezvous—how pretty! It's a good thing this guy's dick is beautiful, because he's—well, you know. His dick is my world for fifteen minutes, throat massage; oops that's my esophagus. His rhythm is pump pump pump slide BOOM. Whoops—there goes some part of me, good thing I've got so much saliva it's like I'm rabid.

A straight orgy on the TV? Afterwards, he asks me if I had stuffing for dinner. He's calling attention to my breath. I don't say anything about the mood lighting to hide his wrinkles. Full moon, everyone's saying honey it really makes me crazy. What about the day before the full moon? No big deal. I'm finally on my way to get cocktails, but then I need to eat. Then I'm on my way again, I go down in the elevator, but come back up. Yes I'm ready to get smashed, obliterated, destroyed and then demolished, vomiting out taxicab windows and waving hello and then taking another swig.

Or skip that part: three cocktails and then line after beautiful white line, hello Dolly.

Luckily I get a trick—that's what I need, more tricks to keep me out of trouble. An outfit change and a six-block walk to the hotel, and I'm ready for—well, money, of course. He's a nice guy, even though his breath is a different story—I love grabbing his hard-on through his old vintage jeans, the way it keeps guard on the left side. My favorite part is the orange shower curtain; the light shines through it like the-sun-will-come-out-today, dammit—fucking today. Right now, as I'm standing and wetting myself.

Drying off, I notice a woman watching me from the restaurant next door. Then I get contact solution at Walgreen's and the night has turned to practical necessities instead of an ambulance ride to detox. In the dream where I always find my father, he makes a toast to me—to my beautiful wife, miss Mattilda, the apple of my life! If I wasn't dreaming, I'd be dead. Zan says he was having sex and he couldn't stay hard, where was the hundred dollar bill? At yoga, I notice the ceiling fans for the first time, turning and turning without effect. When I was a kid, I wanted to be a mouse, crawling beyond power.

Later, I wanted to be fifteen and sheltered by a force field, flying around with mysterious best friends, solving the world's problems. Brodie and I go to a performance about 9-11. This one actor talks about running into a homeless guy after the Towers went down, and how could he be so insensitive as to ask for change at a time like this? We rush away after 15 minutes, pull open the door and we can't get through because there are so many people. Oh no—we're backstage.

I've run out of passionflower tincture, so I can't sleep. Who says herbs aren't addictive? The roaches are all over the counter—what a nice new tablecloth! I make toast, which tastes freezer-burnt. They need to pass a law that says it can never get dark before 8 p.m.—I really need my sunshine. Rue says pretty soon you'll be a house-plant, and he's right, I'm stretching out to the sun from behind closed windows, though at least I have a little more mobility. I can wipe the come off the floor, though immediately I feel so exhausted that I can't do anything else but put on Frankie Bones and breathe deeply, hoping for air.

Days when I never wake up, just walk around delaying sleep. This guy on the Geary bus says you don't know where Geary Street is, do you? Nope. At 1:30 a.m., I finally get a trick—I was about to go to the Power Exchange but I love hotel lobbies late at night, the shelter of the chandeliers, wondering what the security guards think of me so I yawn, pretending I'm just so used to all this money. Then the hallway that goes on and on, I want to run back and forth! The trick's nervous, he keeps saying I just didn't want to deal with the bars, you know what I mean.

I say: I'm the last person you need to explain this to. The toiletries all have pictures of the lobby and I think of starting a collection. I used to collect crystals from hotel chandeliers. Afterwards, everything's crisp—it's the last moment of my day. Outside my building, the same hooker is working, but is her hair wet, makeup smeared, or is it just the light? I want to invite her up for tea, but I'm worried that she wouldn't understand my attempt at solidarity.

Whole Foods on Sunday: this woman screams at her kid in the stroller—SAY APPLE. At the fish counter, a woman in fur wants to know which fish is the least fishy. There are so many different kinds of roaches. There are the tiny ones, or are they babies? The short, fat, dark ones. The big, long brown ones are the scariest and the fastest, reaching their heads out from around corners.

Obviously, I'm trying to get around talking about my nerves, winding around my body like an electrified fence—turn it down, turn it down! Tendons betray me, pincushions for the air and everything beyond it, weighing down on me, just me, why me? Outside Bagdad Café, this guy grabs his boyfriend and points at some muscleboy—look at those fucking lats, he says. I go inside to use the bathroom, then sit on the bench outside Harvest Market and watch the gays go by—there are so many ways to wear khakis! This woman tells me she went to see a psychic, the psychic told her someone's after you, give me your refrigerator.

I like the way this trick's whole body clenches then releases every time my dick goes in and out of his ass. I hold his neck. The shower's fancy for a motel, tiles on the ceiling and a light inside. Afterwards, I go for a walk and I realize I'm in the urban suburb at the bottom of Russian Hill—big guys in suits, smoking cigars. A gym called Gorilla Sports inside an old movie theater. Two guys walk by singing a cute song—I hate fags, I hate fags! The women with them giggle, hee hee hee.

Two-thirds of the way through yoga and I'm still energetic, yes this is the answer and then boom the exhaustion hits me, I almost fall asleep during final relaxation. I realize the sky is the deepest, brightest blue at dusk, so who needs daytime? In the locker room, two white guys talk about traveling to Vietnam, how beautiful it is, how nice the people are. Then one of them says he was in the infantry during the Vietnam War.

I'm saved from runaway desire until I see this other guy's back, just let me grab on and stay there—a koala bear in a tree, how cute! Andee calls from Berlin, he went to Greifbar and everyone was so drunk they couldn't even stand up. He says we never got that drunk, did we? I say no, they need to learn a few tricks from their New York sisters—it's time for lines! Then at least they can say: you gotta bump?

Times when the lines were cut with too much laxative, on my way from the bar to the after-hours, I'd have to shit in the street. Andee says everyone in Berlin goes to the sun box, it helps with seasonal affective disorder. You mean the tanning salon. Does it help with four-seasonal affective disorder?

Another annoying call: what service do you provide? A hot dog and a hernia, honey, pass the ketchup. At Magdalena's birthday party, everyone's sweet and cuddly—though Zan keeps throwing weird shady comments out of nowhere. Something like: watch out for Mattilda, she's got lots of STDs. Then she wants to hug me and pretend we've been boyfriends since we were nineteen. We were boyfriends when we were nineteen, but that was almost ten years ago.

This straight-acting boy who I'm practically drooling over goes to bed. Let me be clear here—when I say I'm drooling over the straight boy, I mean that the drool piles up inside my mouth, choking me. No one notices. Rhania drives me home, a puddle forming in my lap—is that a hole in the roof, or are you just happy to see me?

Rue has pneumonia, that's why she's been vomiting for four days. I'm worried about her, but I'm also worried that I'm gonna get pneumonia too. Fatigue and horniness fighting it out in my head, and—as usual—fatigue wins big. Brodie invites me to a going-away party for people I don't know, but I'm going away to Diamond Heights. Sure, the views are good, but what a hideous neighborhood—the dark years of architecture, after the U.S. saved the world. The trick will call me a cab, and the cab will take six hours to find the place, small talk will get so large that neither of us will be able to move. That will be the going-away party.

There's a big ditch next door to my building, where they tore down this huge laundromat but left up the façade. I throw my rotting food down there so the roaches don't get it, figure it'll biodegrade faster anyway. In the big room at yoga, I can hear the fluorescent lights humming or maybe that's the heat, boiling our bodies into all these weird positions. After class, one guy asks—is there a specific temperature the room's supposed to be? Good question. Downstairs, someone's talking about the owner's new Porsche, or is the Mercedes SUV new and the Porsche old?

Ms. Diamond Heights wants to watch *Will & Grace*, but I'm worried she doesn't think the meter's running. I get all romantic and seduce her: let's go into the bedroom. On a bathroom break, I notice an hour's passed—I say how 'bout if we just relax and come when we're ready, you can pay me 250. Suddenly this bitch gets uptight. Before, we'd been exchanging porn talk and pulling back and forth and back from coming, not yet. It was fun, I was turning it out, I was feeling it, he was feeling me, I figured I'd give him a nice deal and we'd relax into searing orgasms.

But no—Ms. Diamond Heights of the three-bedroom house, views of all San Francisco and artifacts strewn about like knick-knacks—Ms. Diamond Heights who told me she bought the house three years ago at the height of the market, Ms. Diamond Heights can't afford more than 150 because she's losing her technology job. I tell her she can come all over me, but then I figure I might as well come too, even though I was fantasizing about a bar pick-up. I hate bars. I can't even remember the last time I picked someone up a bar. I know I'll want to kill Diamond after I come, but this is still before.

It's one of those orgasms that could be amazing, but it arrives when I'm trying to prevent it. Then Diamond comes on me, and I want to kill him. Luckily the cab shows up quickly, but one of these days, honey, one of these days. Miss Scarlet. In the study. With the lead pipe. After the chiropractor, my jaw aches and I just want to lie down and die. Wait: here comes a toothache. I love healthcare practitioners. This trick has the ugliest apartment I've ever seen in my life, so many cigarette burns and wax stains in the carpet, it's two choices: stick to it, or fall through. Of course he has a waterbed. Limo after limo on Polk Street—or even better, the fake cable cars with loads of screaming drunken straight guys—where are all these wonderful citizens going? I refuse to take another nap—so sick of that bed, sick in the head. Tonight's solstice, another excuse for everyone to get fucked up. It's the holidays, right, the holidays—oh the holidays. Tell me where it hurts and I'll get the make-up, break-up, this is a fucking stick up! Just stick it in. Next season's look: I killed my best friend.

I'm worried that when I push food down the drain, I'm not only clogging the drain, but also feeding the roaches—burnt beans and rotting grains, a feast for their senses! I actually make it to the solstice party at the Fourteenth Street House for the first time ever, it's so crowded that people are standing in line. They send twenty of us around the block so we can get some cardio.

There's a cute boy in line and that's the boy of my night: Jeremy. We make out—he has such nice big soft lips. He's aggressive and almost frantic, grinding down on me—his favorite position is to pull one of my legs up and push his dick between my leg and my asshole, fun. Everyone's crowding around us but we're alone, together, opening our eyes every once in a while to look around: bigger crowd.

Jeremy keeps teasing my asshole with his dick and I keep switching positions and then we slow down, oh it's such pressure between our lips and the magnetic pull as his dick brushes my asshole so gently, and then the head is inside, I pull away. Don't want to get fucked without a condom in front of all these people—what a bad example—and maybe I don't want to get fucked without a condom, period. But then I'm sitting on his lap again, his dick pushing inside me, he's grabbing my chest all over like he's holding me in and damn I can't stop from shooting, he shoves his dick in farther and leans forward to catch some of my come in his mouth.

What a fun discovery—holding hands, we explore the house but mostly each other. The highlight is later, sucking him off upstairs while the hippies are pounding on their drums, sweat pouring down my face I almost don't know where I am except head resting against his leg, dick pumping my mouth and he's moaning moaning moaning come into my throat it's like I'm being cradled there in his lap with something nice to suck on. I sit up and spit come into his mouth, what a messy concoction! We find vegan sushi, and it's the best thing I've ever tasted.

LEARNING

⊙   ⊙   ⊙   ⊙

It's the morning of Christmas Eve and the marquee at Frenchy's says COME SEE OUR HO HO HO'S, but what about me, discreetly plying my trade from only a few hundred feet away? I go to yoga and there's hardly anyone there, the employees want to leave. The instructor says let's get cocktails!

I get home, and I'm ready to throw all my dishes out the window and listen to them smash. Maybe I should go back to the yoga studio and throw a brick through the window. But that would hurt my hands.

I need exercise, but everything except Bikram fucking yoga destroys my fragile fragile body. I'm so angry, screaming hurts my throat and pounding my head against the wall hurts my neck—what are the other options? Taking a plane somewhere would destroy my digestion, should I just turn up the music and see what happens? Last-minute Christmas sale: I need a body that doesn't hurt so much.

Midnight and I have a manic moment, must be all those gifts piled under the tall tall tree, oh everything smells like gift-wrap and pine, oh how I love the smell of pine! And the reindeer flying through the window—oh shit, now there's glass everywhere. I throw together a Christmas wig anyway, purple hair tied in big messy ponytails, toilet cozie doll on top with a garland of plastic poinsettias. Then it's Christmas and I'm a gingham catastrophe—dress and oven mitts that match, or clash, depending on your opinion. And who asked for your opinion? Christmas stockings over my shoes, makeup smeared everywhere, red lipstick and green glitter and don't forget white, oh it's a white white Christmas!

Magda comes over to do her makeup and then we rush off to the Castro Theatre for *Female Trouble*. The movie's gorgeous, but awfully long. Our bathroom photo shoot is the highlight, Magda on the toilet and I'm sprawled on the floor. Then we're in the Badlands bathroom with the boys complaining—we thought it would be fun to terrorize them, but we were wrong. Later, we're at the Stud and fags are just gaping at me like what on earth, or worse—they're saying: you go, girl! That's what straight people say. If only these girls would learn. Pick something—anything—and learn it.

The day after Christmas and there are still no evening yoga classes, my trick has eyebrows like Dracula or at least someone from Transylvania. He's from L.A. Wants me to stab him with a fake knife, push it into his belly and there's a website for it. When he comes, I see two strands of saliva between his upper and lower gums like fangs.

Of course I shouldn't tell anyone this, but I've been thinking about Jeremy since the day we met, kissing those yum yummy lips and then collapsing in his lap, take me into your arms! He comes over and I'm nervous, we drive to the beach in the rain, the waves are frightening in the dark but I love all the air. That's why we're there; Jeremy thinks it's funny and we hold hands, which makes me giddy. We walk towards the ocean and I'm trying to piss when the tide comes in—rushing backwards, I trip over Jeremy and fall flat on my back. The water pours over me and I can't stop laughing.

Jeremy's surprised that I'm not more upset—he says: I'd be cursing and yelling—but I just think it's funny, I mean I think it's funny because I'm with Jeremy. And I'm glad he has a car, otherwise I'd probably get sick out in the cold, waiting for the bus.

I'm soaked and sandy and freezing; we head to my house. I get undressed and we make out but I'm nervous, I need to eat. I eat in Jeremy's lap, he holds me but I'm still nervous—I don't know what to do with all this vulnerability rushing inside me. I thought I didn't go on dates because I didn't meet the right people, but maybe this is why—we take a shower and I'm almost shaking, Jeremy says is it because we had such a great first time? We go to a cheesy but glee-fully stylized movie that's somehow beautiful, it's about how tiny miracles change people's lives so easily, and how you have to go after what you want, which is probably what you need. Jeremy and I hold hands, I kiss his neck.

Back at my house, Jeremy's tired because he went out drinking the other night and ended up doing coke then crystal. I wonder how often that happens. Jeremy wants to know what I do for a living—I've already told him I'm a whore. No, really, he says. I guess he's used to a more respectable crowd, but he recovers quickly—I'm a total slut, he says—it's not much different. I say: you have more fun. We kiss goodbye, I feel calm with anticipation.

A few days later, Jeremy and I are jerking off in his car, cops bothering the girls working the street and I hate the fucking cops. We drive around the corner instead of going upstairs. I love Jeremy's expression when he comes, a baby ready to cry. I'm pushing Jeremy's head to my dick—desperate for release I say please—and when I come I'm screaming, the windows are fogged.

I'm so excited about yoga but then I get scared, almost like with Jeremy but he holds me. This yoga beats me—turn the fucking heat down or I'm gonna vomit! Afterwards, there's a long line for the showers and one guy's practically doing his laundry in there, I want to smack him. The owner's telling someone about installing a private shower for himself and I want to smack him too. Smack smack smack and they all fall like dominoes. Yoga is so relaxing!

I want to go to the tops of tall buildings and look at the views, but Jeremy wants me to go to Oakland in the rain. I bring him ginger and ganmaoling tablets because he's getting over a cold, I don't want to kiss but I want to kiss. It's so easy and smooth until Jeremy says why fight gay landlords who evict tenants with AIDS when you can fight the Christian Right? He thinks mainstream gay people aren't the real enemy—I'm suspicious that he's on their side.

This is the point where usually I'd disengage, but this time I want to see what else is possible. Jeremy says I really like you. I like him so much and I'm scared I mean I'm not scared—at least, not when I'm with him. On my way home, the Seventh and Market 24-hour check-cashing place is jammed and the cops drive up and arrest two black guys who are just standing there. The cop car drives off and then this one white guy chases after the only other white guy there with a baseball bat—racial profiling is so effective! The 19 bus stop has moved, so I miss two buses in a row.

I dream that it's sunny and warm out; I can sit on the fire escape to get tan again. I wake up covered in sweaty sheets, but it's still cloudy out. Rue's sick again, body giving out. Chrissie says girl, I need someone to open me up—it's been a hideous afternoon, give me a razor blade. She's running around my house, filling a vase she got at Goodwill with batteries and pens: art. Benjamin calls to figure out which New Year's party to go to, I want to go back to bed. Chrissie says remember when we used to get high together, why don't you just do a bump?

Chrissie better be kidding. I make my eyebrows into glitter catastrophes, one pink and one green, then a mini glitter moustache and sure I just happen to be wearing pink and green too. Chrissie's shaking on the sofa and then trying to shit, over and over again—too much crystal or not enough alcohol? Too many edges giving me too much pain, she says. We go to a party that's so boring I'm already figuring out how to say goodbye. I flee to the party on Haight Street—three parties actually, which is what I need to hold my attention. I get all sweaty from dancing, but the highlight is when Brodie shows up and we take over a carpeted back hallway, synchronizing our eyes and steps and breath. It's our fucking runway—turn, burn, shake it out and learn! Everyone's confused; they don't know what to do about our glamour.

Jeremy makes a late appearance and I sit on his lap, makes me all happy but he's still getting over his cold, and the coke he did earlier didn't help. At home, my back hurts so much that I'm stretching until 5 a.m., then a bath and finally bed at 6. Waking up and the full-spectrum fluorescents are way too bright; oh no it's my own special hangover, courtesy of everyone else's smoke. Rue comes over, but he's still recovering from pneumonia—he says I've counted the times I've had drinks and it's 4,000. Magdalena comes over for tea and that cheers me, 1 a.m. and it's time for my hour of energy before I'm ready for bed.

But whoops—2 a.m. and I've got a trick, off to Diamond Heights. This trick likes straight porn, a gang-bang where all the guys take their turn at her pussy lips just opening up to say hello. Or her asshole, wow she's relaxed. The trick wants me to tell him his mouth is just like a pussy, pussy mouth, and when he's rubbing my balls and chest and sucking me off—yeah, relax bitch, yeah just like that, nice and slow, yeah keep your mouth right there when I shoot, yeah take it all—and the screen's just one big maze of cocks and chests and hands, and somewhere a woman.

Kayti calls, I can't believe her rent is $2,000 for a one-bedroom in Gaithersburg, Maryland where we took karate together when we were thirteen. She went to the doctor and her white blood cells were so low it looked like she had cancer. The doctor said no that's normal for someone on all these psych meds for so long. So she stopped the meds and now she's just a little anxious about someone's baby on *Friends*. But can you believe she reads all the books on Oprah's Book Club?

Apparently, someone vomited at the 11 a.m. yoga class on New Year's Day. Leaning back into camel pose, the vomit splattering all over someone's face—happy New Year! Waiting for the bus and this guy says to me: I had a seizure, went to the hospital and had two more, then in the cab home I had another seizure—so I had to go back to the hospital. At Sixteenth and Mission, there's a pregnant woman screaming at the cops: I didn't get any fucking presents! A better-dressed crackhead with a bike saves her—that's my sister, I'm taking her home. The 22 never comes, so I take the 49 back home, sweet home, so sweet the roaches are getting bigger, but I love watching Jeremy's eyelids flutter and droop, he's so cute in bed. In the middle of the night I kiss his neck, he reaches for my hand. I can't sleep but I feel good beside him. In the morning, he forgets to kiss me goodbye and I have his cold. I try to sleep all day. My trick fucks my armpit.

Every surface in my apartment becomes a desk: floor, table, kitchen counter, sofa, bookshelves, bathroom sink, and yes, even the desk. Jeremy takes me to the Powerhouse and actually it's fun, they play Stacey Q's "Two of Hearts" and I'm living for it, then we're in the backroom, I'm on my knees sucking his dick, he's smacking my face with it and everyone's getting excited. This one guy wants to taste but damn his breath smells.

At my house, Jeremy and I play this game. I say, when I fell on the beach, that wasn't the water I fell in but your come, right? Jeremy nods his head. But how'd you get such cold come? Two gallons of ice cream. Two gallons? For each meal. What flavor? Strawberry. But how'd it get so salty? Strawberry miso.

And I'm hard, pushing Jeremy's head to my dick and then he falls backwards into the bed—sailor, you look unsteady. Jeremy wants me to brush his teeth—I've got an extra Brillo pad to remove that tartar. He says would you mind sitting on it? He means his dick, not the Brillo pad. I ask him when he's gonna come in my food, vegans need more protein! In the morning, we make lentils but I can't wake up. Jeremy plays Bach and I do my stretches. Later, my trick is even joking like Jeremy, he says you need some lube for that car; park it in my garage. While I fuck him, I hold his head like I hold Jeremy, manufacturing intimacy and it works.

NPR says people in Afghanistan are struggling to stay alive by eating grass, while the U.S. plans to bomb Somalia. I struggle to get out of the house; Kayti calls to ask how to get to the point where you don't care what other people think of you. I tell her I have to think about it. I get a trick at the Fairmont, balcony that stretches on and on, but I'm still fucking sick. Sleep can't even be a nightmare anymore because I can't sleep. Just keep waking up wired. The fire alarm goes off, I get back in bed.

All day I'm exhausted—until 3 a.m., when I'm ready to start an art gallery, write three books, call everyone I know, and run naked through the streets in search of a hard cock. Nuclear neighbors: do you have a light?

Ten minutes before the hooker clinic opens, twenty people are already in line. It's a fun crowd, mostly Filipina transwomen and one butch white guy with two girlfriends. Oh, wait—maybe they're girlfriends, and he's flirting with them. But already I'm too late to see a doctor about my never-ending jock itch. Back to City Clinic, where the doctor clearly thinks whores are vectors of disease— excuse me, can you please eat my shit? Allison calls to say we should be on *Survivor* together; the brother-and-sister team, or not *Survivor*, another one like *Survivor*, but it's a treasure hunt where there are teams. But they'd pick you for *Survivor*, she says—they like interesting people.

Jeremy and I duck behind a stairway on Minna Street before he catches the last BART, I like the way he reaches his hands under my clothes to rub my chest. He comes in my favorite briefs, I turn around so he can grab my thighs as I shoot for the gold—look how far I got, look how far! Jeremy says you were saving up for me; funny thing is that I was.

The soundtrack of my destiny is just shake and break, take those steps every step counts. Feeling every beat, cold hands but honey oh the heat, the heat. Watch out world, techno before food and I'm oh-so-manic, no need to panic 'cause it's all—lovely. Okay, time for toast—then the depression's back. I put Fugazi on, what was I thinking? Immediate images of staring through the vertical blinds into the yard as a teenager, huge tall pine trees and could I live inside one? I call the phone sex line over and over, everyone's saying they're twenty-nine—which means forty-five, and everything else I say is a lie too! Or party/play—no thanks, I'm not horny anyway.

This trick calls to say he's on his way, and then doesn't bother to show up or cancel. Guess he got scared away by the hookers outside. Magdalena reminds me of the time she got drunk and slapped Jake in the face, then chased Andee down the street screaming: SAY THAT YOU LOVE ME OR I'M GONNA BEAT YOU UP! She says I just realized how scary that must have been for him.

I hate it when my meditation goes the wrong way; I open my eyes and everything's worse. I'm so depressed that peeling the price tag off the dishwashing liquid feels like the most satisfying thing I've done all day. When I wake up in the morning—it's not fucking morning, bitch, it's 2:30 p.m.—all right, when I wake up, all I want to do is piss and shit and vomit. Then get back in bed. Later, I dream that in place of my eyes is nothing but raw flesh and rivers of blood, sometimes I'm wearing a mask to keep it all in, but it still hurts.

THE FUTURE

◎   ◎   ◎   ◎

The energy is exploding upwards through my head, and for a moment I can't see except this beauty, expanding inside and out of me. I want to lie on top of today's yoga boyfriend, namaste, tongue wrapping around tongue, hands on his head we're grinding and squeezing sweat all over rubbing and dammit his cock into my mouth, thickness feeding me his hands on my head his come tastes like butter, pushing him down we roll around until rug burn overwhelms us. The instructor says if we could just harness this energy and make fuel for our cars, we'd have a perfect world.

At dinner, Rhania's adding red and white to her eye makeup while I'm shitting because my digestion's too sensitive. Rhania walks me home and the kids downstairs see us kissing goodbye. I go in and one of them says you're embarrassed, I can tell because you're red. He's right: I'm embarrassed because Rhania's wearing fur.

Daddy Scott, who lives across the street from me, calls me up for a trick with another whore, Davey—it's the three of us on the guy who's a 911 operator. Daddy Scott's got an electric dildo that fucks the trick in short motions that make him howl. Davey comes over to my place afterwards and I get all excited, playing music for him and talking about clubs I should just throw already, but for some reason Davey goes home to bed instead of just seven-and-a-half—or okay, maybe eight—steps to my bed.

I want to cuddle with Jeremy but he's not answering the phone, really I'm worn out but also still high from last night's sex with him, the orgasm that went on and on while Jeremy kissed me and held me all over. I want that high to continue, I want to overcome the brain-numbness so I can live in that soft space between my head and the sky.

I go on a detour to the Power Exchange. There's this blond guy on the bench by the entrance with his hand on his crotch, a welcoming committee. Upstairs, the music gets gorgeous—so much space and why won't the girls dance? And that's when I fly upwards, laughing and smiling and cackling for every tweaker who looks at me with double question marks in his eyes. Let's throw down a couple of definitions. There's high hypoglycemia, when I've finally started a group scene at the Power Exchange—I mean, these girls stuff their entire faces through glory holes, but they're too scared to do anything in public! This one shady bitch—high hypoglycemia is pouring lube all over her hair. Low hypoglycemia is when I keep thinking why am I here why am I here why am I here, but I can't do anything about it because I'm so fucking hypoglycemic. There's a porno with this guy doing anal sphincter exercises, and I notice the fly on his ass.

In the laundry room, a woman asks me if my earrings mean I'm a member of some group, do you need the piercings in order to join? Do you mean a cult—why of course! She asks me if I eat Filipino food, they have Filipino food in the basement every Saturday. I'd really love to say yes and be her neighbor, but I can only picture a tableful of meat and allergies. I've seen them setting up before. I tell her I work Saturdays.

Speaking of work, Chrissie's back in the business—she calls me from Union Square, hello Fairmont! A trick comes over to deliver just what I was craving last night, a hot load in my throat—tastes awful but oh the feeling, once in a while I love my job. Funny how the guy won't kiss me afterwards, honey it's your come.

Speaking of come, Daddy Scott has this barebacking video on, one guy has come oozing out of his asshole and someone else shoves his dick through the come and starts pounding away. It freaks me out but turns me on: the abandon. The next day, this hot couple hires me—two super-friendly preppy guys from New England, staying in a fancy bed-and-breakfast in an old Victorian in the Mission on a corner once known for gangs. But this place has lace curtains and armoires. It's some kind of kept boy situation—while I'm sucking the older guy's dick, the kept boy starts teasing my asshole with his dick—which is way too long—but pretty soon it's inside. I can't believe it—I've hardly been fucked at all this year, and it's suddenly so easy, even with a condom, a non-latex Avanti condom, product placement at it's finest.

Except that after I come, the guy thrusts a few times more and then he shoots, the condom breaks and for some reason I don't really freak out. What can you do? Then the come might be oozing out of my asshole like in that video, I can't tell for sure because there isn't a camera there. Chrissie arrives at my house with a can of Dust-Off, just as depression enters through my sinuses. Every ten minutes, she takes a sip through the straw until she's got her pants down, leaning over the toilet to piss while talking to the bathtub. Huffing and puffing and she would blow the house down if I let her—maybe I should—would it do me some good?

So much air outside, encircling my headache but failing to enact justice. Three annoying tricks in a row—if only I could stay hard! The cab driver says: I like to go to a good movie alone first, then lie to my friends and say that I haven't seen it yet. Are dust mites the root of all my problems, burrowing into my sinuses until I can't do anything but dig? It turns into an excavation—entire lost cities—see, what an advanced civilization! Jeremy says as long as you don't wake up with roaches in your nose.

When Jeremy comes over, at first I wonder who is this new person in my life, a few moments before I feel comfort. At dinner, I'm remembering how nice it is that Jeremy always wants to share, I mean he can eat practically anything on the menu. And usually I don't even try sharing with other vegans. I mean I can't even digest raw vegetables—let alone fried foods, sugar, tofu, fake meats, night-shades or refined oils. But Jeremy actually gets excited about shifting his options and then when he pours soup into my bowl or passes the stir-fry it feels so intimate. Later, I want to say I love you—just casu-ally—but can that be casual? I say I'll get some new pillows for you, I mean I'll get some new pillows for you to use. He says what's the difference? I'm laughing. All this work not to feel too vulnerable.

My trick says: do you like music? Too much conversation, I get on my knees and suck, suck, suck—watching him close his eyes and sway. On the bus, one obnoxious straight guy says to the other: so man, have you tried Viagra? On the radio, a seventy-five-year-old woman talks about selling her house to pay for arthritis meds.

At yoga, the sun is a spotlight, photoshoot, Kraftwerk in my head: "she's a model and she's looking GOOD." Sun sparkles off my sweat, better than glitter, and the shadow of the ceiling fan cre-ates a strobe. If only they'd open the window and let me breathe. Downstairs, the owner is flirting with every longhaired woman. He must be in his forties or fifties, but he's wearing a frat sweatshirt. Telling some blond woman with overly plucked eyebrows: you just need to keep coming, keep coming. Yeah, so you can buy another Porsche.

Late-night expedition: I just need to get rid of one more black-head, one more before I go to bed. Jeremy calls and says I heard your voice on the answering machine and I got all excited—that gets me excited, 3 a.m. and I'm playing dancing games, head peering out my window, and is it kind of warm out? I go outside, the rain feels so good. When I wake up, I'm still happy until everything floats away, fuck it's a new day.

Later, Jeremy and I are hugging and hugging, he keeps telling me how hot I am in my magenta pants with yellow plastic floral belt, orange floral print T-shirt and a necklace made of huge clear plastic beads and a piece of a chandelier. It's so refreshing that Jeremy gets all excited by my queeniness; faggots are usually so afraid of fag-gots. When sex is on the agenda, I've learned to channel a masculinity that isn't exactly shutting off. I mean I can still experi-ence all the sensations in my body.

That sounds awful—let's get back to Jeremy—we go to the Berkeley Free Clinic to get HIV and STD tests. There are forty people waiting. On TV, there's a fascinating history of diseases. Then it's a movie where a guy is about to get his finger chopped off. Jeremy and I race up the Oakland hills in his friend Sarah's BMW, searching for a place to watch the sunset. But it's wall-to-wall mansions—blocking the sun with money! We race down and then up to the Berkeley hills, finally at dusk we arrive. The sun's beneath the clouds and it's freezing out, but the air is amazing, it actually smells like trees. I piss and someone probably watches. In the car, I'm grabbing my crotch and Jeremy's head, he says we're gonna get arrested. Ten feet away in their own car, a straight couple pretends not to notice, the guy is looking for his heart in the gravel.

I know it's a relationship, because we've reached an impasse: my asshole. Jeremy wants to fuck me, but there's so much locked in there—I'm Cinderella in yellow gingham, pounding a frying pan on the washing machine. As long as I make noise and jump up and down I'm all right, otherwise I feel shards of glass poking at the pulp where my eyes used to be. Inside the washing machine, I'm a squashed frog, pulpy goo, and outside I'm a cat inside Cinderella's head. I just want Jeremy to pet me. He doesn't know all this yet.

Jeremy and I are making out on the street, hard-ons and all, and can you believe the homeless woman with the white wigs says *disgusting*? I mean, honey's in the Castro practically 24-7. Jeremy takes my hand and says gay is *good* as we round the corner like we're in some 1970s documentary, I mean we're actually both wearing clothes from around that time period, the glittering dome of City Hall in the background. Jeremy catches the BART, at home I get sky-high wired and horny too—I love it when I actually have a libido for more than five minutes, not just craving sex to crave feeling.

Now I know what mood I need for the Power Exchange: it's like I'm on speed except I'm not gritting my teeth. I hook up a four, five, six–some and I'm grabbing everyone's necks and chests and asses. I fuck this one guy after asking for a condom, it's fun and then three guys argue about who gets my come. Afterwards, I'm in such a great mood, it's another window into how I could feel, everything in my head so expansive oh open all the windows, keep them open it's time it's fucking time. 3:27 a.m., January 30, 2002, and I notice that the stamp on my hand from the Power Exchange is a peace sign.

Where's Chrissie? Last I heard, she was turning a trick and then buying three quarters of crystal to treat her friends who've been treating her for the last few years. On self-immolation: Mike Tyson is barred from boxing in Nevada! Jeremy and I have these abstract discussions that usually I'd hate—college shit—I left college for a reason. The worst one is about the meaning of art. Jeremy believes in the classics, the European tradition, as in the Renaissance and everything's been downhill since. No, wait: he's all about the nineteenth century; maybe everything went downhill later than I thought. The worst part is that he believes in standards of greatness—there's been no great art since 1950, he'll say, and I'll get caught arguing with him.

What about Eva Hesse, I say—I've just come from her exhibit of infinite textures in repeating plastic forms. Not *her* exhibit—she's dead and that's why SF MOMA's giving her a show. But Jeremy hasn't seen it.

What about contemporary Iranian cinema, I say—Mohsen Makhmalbaf or Abbas Kiarostami? But Jeremy doesn't know if he's seen their movies. What about Mike Leigh—did you like *Secrets and Lies*? It was okay.

I try my favorite authors—David Wojnarowicz, Rebecca Brown, Robert Glück. Jeremy hasn't read them. I scan my bookshelves. What about Jean Genet or James Baldwin? Okay, Jeremy says, maybe 1970.

Then Jeremy wants to talk about the democratic process—the what? That's how I know I'm falling in love, because I can tolerate these silly conversations. But even without the falling part, I want to say I love you like with all my close friends, but I'm worried he'll get scared. And maybe I'm scared, a wolf ready to bite off my head and will Jeremy sew it back on?

We're making out at a party, I'm ready to get on my knees but Jeremy's uptight around his friends—they might think he's a slut! And this is the high fashion set; some cheap-looking new carpeted flat on Mission with a bunch of '80s runway casualties hanging with the mods and suburbanites. Every time the music starts to sound okay, it ends up turning into a dance remix of a rock or pop song: "Another One Bites the Dust," "Paint It Black," and something that sounds like Bon Jovi. Jeremy and I are slamming each other into the walls, and the buttons of my sweater keep coming undone. One guy asks for more tongue and I ask for his, but apparently he's lost it. I lose my mittens and Jeremy finds them—how romantic!

Jeremy goes home to do K and I go home to wash the smoke out of everything. The next day's good news: endless scenarios run through my head about what to do if I test positive, wait stop the cameras I'm dying. But the good news is there are no white lines in this fantasy—just crying, food, and shopping. Jeremy's so nervous he's shaking, and I just want to hold him all day, night, and right through to tomorrow—forget about the earthquake, at the clinic it's duck! Duck. Goose.

Luckily we're just ducks in this game. Jeremy says I don't have much stress in my life and it was just so hard waiting. I don't know what he's talking about: no stress? We look for music, Jeremy's Bach and my electro. Later, we go to Steamworks, where the sauna's too hot for Jeremy, but I like the eucalyptus—or wait, is it Pine-Sol? Afterwards, I'm hugging and hugging, the feeling of Jeremy's skin. He says I feel like I'm coming to a new period of calm in my life and you're part of that.

Jeremy holds me so tight while I'm on my knees sucking this guy's cock, wanting his come but mostly wanting Jeremy to keep holding me. We get a five-way started in a room—every guy is kissing me too softly and I get way too hypoglycemic, my body shuts down and I panic. Jeremy's a raging ball of non-stop arousal and I'm scared in the cheesiest way, what if he doesn't love me? Looks like he's about to fuck this one guy and I'm jealous, but if I don't eat I'm gonna cry. I whisper: I'll be right back, wait for me to fuck him. Then I say it out loud: I'll be right back.

The guy who was in the TV room when we arrived is still sitting there, and I still can't decide if he's cute. I'm having problems digesting my food; I just feel so edgy, rushing to shit again. Then I'm heading back to the room and Jeremy finds me, he says I missed you.

We go back to the TV room so I can eat more, and I get all teary-eyed, I say: I keep wanting to say I love you, but I stop myself 'cause I don't want to scare you. Standard TV-movie fare. Jeremy says I love you too and the clouds clear in the background, my hair blows in the gentle breeze, light reflecting off three small tears. But wait: we're at a sex club, glaring fluorescents and a chain mesh wall behind us.

Jeremy fucks me on the floor in the video room, it's easier to relax if I'm watching someone else getting fucked—we're in this together! Hardly anyone watches, what a weird crowd. We're a bad example, without a condom—well, it's on the floor next to us and when we come, on that floor too, Jeremy's tired and I'm ready to go dancing. In the morning, I sit in the sun on Jeremy's roof, a view of everything. We go to a movie in which time slows down, a man steals clocks; a large fish in the kitchen swallows the man's father, reincarnated as a roach. Everyone loses their luggage or acts like it. At the end, time and everything is a giant Ferris wheel spinning backwards. Jeremy says I can't imagine you not being in my life, and the Ferris wheel is my eye spinning around into the beauty of the future.

WHAT IF EVERYONE LIVED IN A TWO-MILLION-DOLLAR HOUSE?

⊙   ⊙   ⊙   ⊙

The yoga instructor says we'll all have Tina Turner legs when we're sixty. At Whole Foods, a woman rolls around an entire cart filled with Smart Water: she's gonna be very smart. 2:30 a.m. and this trick comes over two hours late, I fuck him for so long and so slowly that I'm actually aching to come yes I do mean aching. Pushing slower and slower, I was gonna save myself until tomorrow's trip with Jeremy, but if I don't come now, I'll come as soon as Jeremy touches me. The trick says he's milking me with his ass, and there it goes and sure my orgasm's all right, but I wanted to be screaming. The trick slides off—you really gave me a workout—and I'm left with this piece of plastic digging into my dick.

Jeremy and I drive up to Guerneville, weird it's so small and the redwoods are so tall. Everything smells like air, I mean like the redwoods. We find the vegan restaurant and then Jeremy wants to tour the bars. At the Eagle, they're playing Paula Abdul, which is the highlight. We walk over the river in the cold, but we can't find it, hurry back to the room to jump in the hot tub. But first a sexual distraction, no wait that happens earlier, when Jeremy wants to fuck me harder and I feel like I'm turning a trick, but are the neighbors enjoying the show?

The hot tub is locked and we're freezing, Jeremy sucks me off and then we lie in bed for thirteen hours. I sleep for about ten minutes. The best part is laughing at who-knows-what at five in the morning. Next day it's warm and I'm wrecked, we drive to the coast, where Jeremy finally shoves his come down my throat and sure I choke, he says sorry, but honey I need to choke.

Let me paint a picture: cliffs towering above us and the sun in our eyes, the warmest day so far this year and here I am on the wide-open stone-covered beach sucking Jeremy off and choking, yes choking, I said choking on all that come sticking in my throat. Then Jeremy's holding me and we're snapping pictures—porn shoot—damn, I can't remember anyone else who made me pant. Okay, so my last boyfriend situation ended eight years ago—that was Zan, he gave me my first incest flashbacks. I mean, he held me when I started to panic, an extra dimension of terror in the room and I did-n't know what it was. Zan had already dated an incest survivor, he held me and I felt like a little kid, just losing it, trying to figure out what was real. With Jeremy, I'm ready to feel like a little kid again, not just the pain but the potential.

We drive down the coast and jump out of the car to watch the sunset. Jeremy's kicking sand into the saltwater creek and I'm worried that he's damaging the ecosystem but oh it's so nice when the sun sinks into the ocean, all those pinks and oranges and reds. Jeremy and I sit down on a piece of driftwood and stare at this celestial magic trick, the colors in his face too. Even though I haven't slept, everything feels softer like I'm in a space I never want to leave, a space with Jeremy, until he declares that there's no good art any-more because now anyone can make art—oh no, it's one of those conversations. We're in the car and Jeremy acts like we're fighting except when I ask him why he's so upset, he says: I'm not upset. But he still sounds angry. I feel like my mother when I ask him to breathe, only my mother never said that, to my father or anyone else. And never breathed.

Back at home, Jeremy pulls down my pants, and I love it. A message from Andee: I think it's February, I'm just calling to see if your phone rings, because mine still does. The yoga room smells like bacon; I want to leave. Then hot chocolate, which is okay, and then back to the usual rotten sock smell. Zan calls from New York, he went to a *Hedwig* party and someone punched a hole in the wall. On the way to dinner, Gina and I pick up the pictures of Jeremy and me—I think the photo guy's looking at Gina to see if she's Jeremy. The ones of me sucking Jeremy's cock are so hot—I look great in that position. Then the sun shining down on us and we're smiling, it's so sweet, I look at the photos over and over again until Gina calls to say are you still looking at those pictures?

I'm trying to stay connected to the air around but mostly above me, the sky pulling me into alignment. I have a boyfriend, shouldn't everything be okay now? I just want to lie down and stay there, falling deeper into the bed floor ground earth until I dissolve. Or freeze—this is a stick-up! Where is that sky, clear blue the color of that fate I can't hold onto, a robin's egg falling falling until splat!

I'm trying to pull the wax out of my ears but the doctor already took it out. I still can't hear a thing. He said it's your jaw, take a Motrin twice a day for a week and you'll be fine. I said all that will get me is a stomachache, but he didn't laugh: he was the doctor and that was my prescription.

Jeremy calls and says I love you, not just I love you too and I'm jumping up and down, back flip, triple sous-cous or some other ice-skating move I can't even recognize, I had to look up the spelling of that one but oh what a feeling feeling feeling, stay on the ceiling. Andee calls: I think we're on different time schedules, no that's time zones, right, time zones. She says: some of these people in Berlin—I mean I like living here and all, but some of these people, I don't think there's a word in English for them. Or in German. Maybe that's what I need to do—think of a word—I'll think of a word, and then I'll call you back.

Jeremy's excited about the bathrooms at SF State—so many cocks to suck, so much come on the floors! He's a grad student there now; studying linguistics because it seems easy and he can get financial aid so he doesn't have to work for a while. I like that he doesn't take it too seriously, and that he doesn't want to work. I'm walking home from my trick and there's a guy grabbing his dick, pretty soon I'm grabbing it too, and then I'm on my knees in the middle of the tourist district—snap a shot of this! The guy comes; his dog licks it up. I ask him if he lives with his boyfriend.

Walking home again and now I'm so much happier, thinking of the silhouette of the guy grabbing his crotch—really. Looking back and yes really, then we're grabbing each other's crotches until I get on my knees on the hard, yes so hard lovely cement. Rewind, rewind, rewind. Once a night on the cold warm streets inhabiting someone else's desire would heal me.

Jeremy makes me do it; he makes me hook up over the internet. I hate the internet, but he keeps saying it's so easy. It's so easy. He hooks up with someone practically every day, sometimes before or after me and sure I'm jealous but I know it's irrational to think Jeremy's gonna leave me because someone else lives for him to pump that asshole like bread—you know, something easy to digest—but still I worry that I'll be dumped for that talented individual's special hole. Of course I don't say anything. I'm a whore—I'm not supposed to get jealous.

I hook up with this guy Jerrold, who isn't hot and rushes me out as soon as we come, why did I come? The next day, Jerrold emails me and says: I'm really nervous, there was precome on the outside of the condom, when was the last time you were tested? I email him back: don't be ridiculous, we used a condom, relax. Then it's Valentine's Day, my first time celebrating it, or at least the first time in years. Jeremy and I get it on in the botanical garden, then he fucks me at the top of Buena Vista Park, I love listening to the trees shake in the wind, they make screeching sounds like some kind of mysterious bird. Later, we try something new: the bed. I shoot all over and Jeremy says don't rub it in. We both like the covers untucked.

Jeremy says: you are my restaurant—what a hungry hungry hippo! Rue notices my new laugh, like a soft hum—is it because of Jeremy? Rhania leaves a message at 6:45 a.m.: I found someone you should start a club with. I call Rhania when I get up. She says: my father came over to give me a computer and I spent the whole time cleaning my room, do you think he noticed anything? Last night this guy gave me a chunk of glass and said hold this for me, I kept giving it away but I still have a big chunk left, though at least I don't have to work tomorrow—or Tuesday.

Sucking Jeremy's cock at the Powerhouse and everyone's cheering him on: give him your load, make him eat it, give him your load! They always love it when he starts smacking my face with his dick. Afterwards, I feel so glamorous. Andee says: diamonds? Well, it came in a Tiffany box, but I think it's cubic zirconium from the Quality Value Channel. Andee says Tiffany—as in, "I think we're alone now . . ."

Andee's been reading *Dracula*, and seeing the undead everywhere. At yoga, I'm lusting after this Abercrombie model; I just want to wax his car. Later, when he pulls on the jeans, I realize he's the same Mr. Buff 'n' Tuff from way-back-when, I died for him and it got me nowhere. I thought he was Eurotrash then, but turns out he's got a New York accent; he seems as dense as a fence, but maybe I'm a fence sitter.

It must be the acupuncture, because I'm all the way to Union Square before I realize I need to eat, no I can't just walk off this crazy wired energy. Okay, let me eat. Plus it's Jeremy's fault for getting me all sketched-out by being so wishy-washy, complaining about his plans to have sex with Mitch and Len, and then still choosing to hang out with them over me. I say who am *I* going to have sex with—all dramatic to hide the fact that I feel dramatic. Really I just want a ten-hour hug. At least Rue's home, I say I feel so edgy, falling off.

Meanwhile, I haven't come in a week, so my trick is hilarious, I have to rush to the bathroom three times to piss so I don't come. Jeremy and I are having our relationship conversation later on—I'm saving my come. The trick says: you remind me of my dog. Jeremy and I talk about our biggest fears—Jeremy's afraid of losing his independence and I'm afraid of abandonment, is this a gendered relationship? Plus it's like I'm the therapist, asking: what does that mean, losing your independence? Jeremy doesn't want to feel obligated to call me; he just wants to call whenever he feels like it. I tell him I freak out when he doesn't call me back; all I need is a quick hello. Jeremy doesn't really agree to this, but he doesn't say no either.

We talk about boundaries, Jeremy's never been in a non-monogamous relationship and I've never been interested in monogamy. Not that Jeremy's interested in monogamy; he's excited that he finally doesn't have to lie. Actually we have the exact same issues—I don't want him to sleep with my close friends, he doesn't want me to sleep with his—no problem, we each make a list, plus we agree that if we go out together, we go home together. Perfect.

Then Jeremy says would it bother you if I jerked off with someone in the bathroom right before meeting you, and then I didn't want to have sex? I guess that's what happened today. I call Rue for sleeping pills; can I just borrow a few and then give them back? My mind is a racehorse on the wrong steroids, without injection tranquilizers to cushion my demise, rise and shine! My digestion doesn't work, I tried a lobotomy but now I can't feel anything.

Rhania says: I'm getting sick because I've been crying, it wasn't the crystal binge; it was those damn tears. I take Jeremy to see Alvin Ailey and damn it, just the hand choreography in "Revelations" is enough to make me cry, except that I'm holding it in while Jeremy holds my hand as I go from hot to cold to hot. There's an incest flashback waiting in the ceiling but I don't quite go there. Afterwards, we're waiting at Cha-ya, the vegan Japanese restaurant in Berkeley, and Jeremy's hungry, I'm grinding my dick against his leg and he's embarrassed. The angry hippie crew watches us as we take a seat. What's wrong—is there heroin in my hair?

On the highway, Jeremy wants me to jerk off and how did I get so hard, his fingers pumping the edge of my asshole, I want him to fuck me *now*. I don't say anything because Jeremy's in a rush to get free drinks at Moby Dick, but I should probably take advantage of moments like these when I'm actually craving it. Jeremy's going to New York where he'll be fucking this other guy named Jeremy who told Jeremy—I'm resisting calling him "my Jeremy"—anyway, this other Jeremy told Jeremy he was the best sex of his life. This other Jeremy is pussy-boy city and Jeremy loves that, but wait—Jeremy loves *me*, filling the holes in my other relationships. My asshole is less important, even if pulsating with symbolism.

Oh, the Power Exchange—well, the good news is that I get there by 12:30 and leave by 1:15. I dream about pissing in the pool at my grandmother's apartment building. On the bus, this guy says I like your outfit; it looks like you escaped from a circus. At the beach, the almost-full moon is surrounded by a circle of light and clouds, Jayseh says that means there's gonna be a hurricane. But we don't have hurricanes here. Jayseh says I grew up here, and that's what I learned in school—there's gonna be a hurricane somewhere.

Zan calls to tell me this boy responded to his ad on gay.com with pictures of Jeremy fucking him. I get this shot of sadness and damn is that jealousy again? I need to clear that shit out; bring me the goddamn Dustbuster. Or never mind, I need something with super-high suction power, the thing that sucks all the water out of a swimming pool. Zan says how about my mouth? But girl, I thought you were a top.

Zan and I go to Buena Vista Park to look at the full moon and it's the closest I've felt to him in a while, like neither of us is on guard because we're focused on this simple act of beauty in the sky. Later, he sends me the pictures of Jeremy and the gay.com boy. The boy's ad is all about needing loads of come up his ass, I think he's the dancer that flew to Hawaii to marry his boyfriend, then called Jeremy to say: I'm in love with you. One of the pictures is a huge blow-up of Jeremy's cock in the guy's ass, without a condom, the other picture shows Jeremy fucking him. Jeremy never mentioned the barebacking part. I can't tell if I'm turned on, all I know is that I need to come immediately, it's almost like spitting it's so fast.

My grandfather is dying, and my grandmother says when are you going to make up with your father? After two months of asking for a rent reduction, I get a rent increase in the mail. I call the building owner and at least they offer me $125 less—a $900 Tenderloin studio, what a bargain! Rue calls, slurring his words, to say: I took five Ativan and my legs are made of tube socks, everything is tilting off my desk, the desk is bending, no it's breathing—the ceramic pot is nudging the computer mouse like she wants to have sex with it.

My next trick tells me he didn't find out about masturbation until he was twenty-three, and then he became compulsive about it. He would do coke and look at *GQ* or *Exercise for Men Only*, and jerk off all day. It took him another twelve years to realize he was gay, he says the wires were all wrong. Then another twelve years to have sex. It's been eight months of hiring escorts and finally he's okay, he lives in a two-million-dollar house. He doesn't look okay.

At home, I can't understand the words to the music, but it better get me out of this cranky mess in my head. Ten, nine, eight, seven— go to heaven? Eating a pear on the fire escape in the sun, the pear's too sweet and the sun's too hot. How did I get so dehydrated: six glasses of water on the counter and I drink them all. But wait a second—I only have four glasses, plus the one I use to catch roaches, crawling up and down the walls as soon as the light goes out. I tell Rue I need another 45 minutes after I'm already an hour and a half late to meet her and Jupiter. Jupiter says who does she thinks she is, Billie Holiday?

I write my dying grandfather a letter: I'm learning that everything can be as comforting as it is scary. Lauren, the receptionist at the chiropractic office, has a dream that she's taking care of elephants— elephants in a loft, elephants in an elevator—it's stressful. At yoga, the instructor talks about crushing garlic with her hands. I slide right into camel pose: back arched, ass tight, chest up and belly forward. All of the sudden, my hands reach my ankles. Later, from my window, I watch the cops pull over a car, question the driver, then let him go and arrest the passenger. It's one of the women who works Geary and I feel so powerless. She stands tall.

Rhania's starting the Society for Cutting Up Boxes, but outside it's grey—whatever happened to summer, spring—whatever that was? Jeremy's back from New York and what is it about this boy— I can't stop hugging hugging *hugging* him; Jeremy's best New York story is some guy he meets at The Cock, who takes out a stack of pictures on the subway and says I'm a model—this is me with the editor of *Vogue Homme*, this is me with David LaChapelle's assistant, this is me with Christy Turlington's publicist. Then he tells Jeremy about the house he shares in Brooklyn Heights with three other models—his bed is so big he stores things on it, and he doesn't even notice them. But why is he getting off in Williamsburg? All the cool people go to Williamsburg on the weekends.

This guy calls me three nights in a row to ask me the same questions. Before he hangs up, he always asks: so, there's a chance you won't get fucked? If only I were a machine, my asshole swallowing each cock and push the button, next, grunt, next, grunt. Someone else calls, it's two guys and they want me sucking both of their dicks. Well, that's better! Though there's a third guy tweaking in his room, he's making the decision—he'll call me back. I knew it was too good to be true. Now I'm wired.

Jeremy and I are so horny for each other, he's getting ready to fuck me but I'm not ready—I'm not hard, I'm scared. I go to the bathroom to shit, when I come back, I say I just had a mood swing. We lie in bed and talk. I'm such a good facilitator, even when it's my own pain—help, brain drain! Jeremy wants everything to be easy; he thinks talking won't get us anywhere because no one ever changes. He says: I'm used to everything going my way. Well, congratulations—you're a white man. I would say straight, but the context would be strange.

Maybe Jeremy's been reading too much turn-of-the-century European literature. Inside I'm vanishing, breathe, outside I'm calm. I just don't understand—we're so excited by each other, holding hands is a celebration. One small conversation and Jeremy's saying maybe we're not compatible. How do I get beyond his fatalism and into the beauty when we talk through our skin, eyes steady?

Jeremy: I'm worried I'm not turning you on. Me: what do you mean? Jeremy: you're always moving my hands. Me: but that's how I let you know what I want. Jeremy: I'm not used to that. Me: what do you want me to do instead, should I stop and tell you what I want? Jeremy: no that would ruin it. Me: if you don't want to talk about sex, and you don't want me to show you what I want, then how can our sex get better? Jeremy: I just want it to be easy. Me: It is easy. I just want to feel more comfortable, like I can stop and talk if I'm having an incest flashback and you'll hold me. Jeremy: I don't know if I'm willing to do that.

Jeremy is holding me, or maybe I'm holding him. At least he's talking about his fears too, not just mine, piling up like trash in a windstorm—there's always more. Oh Jeremy Jeremy Jeremy, just the sweat on your hands is enough. He says: maybe you're just a top—doesn't he know that I don't believe in that shit? He says: if it's too much work to get fucked, then maybe it's not natural. I get dramatic, I say: if I believed in natural, I never would have gotten anywhere.

I go home, and sleep so badly it's worse than fate and destiny put together. When I'm telling Zan about Jeremy and me, he says oh no you're giving me flashbacks of Franz. Franz is Zan's ex-boyfriend with masculinity issues. Jeremy calls and says: I'm just a big baby, I can't handle anything, I'm sorry. My stomach feels better.

There's a preppy blond white woman playing violin on the corner of Polk and Geary, right in front of the homeless shelter. I can't imagine she's getting much change. I end up getting a trick and then Jeremy comes in my mouth, his come tastes weird and strong. He says maybe it was the hamburger I ate at Fuddruckers—bitch, spare me the details. I go out and dance so hard that I'm covered in sweat, and then I dance some more. The show ends and I'm still dancing, this random woman and I are twirling around the floor and damn I need this. After I swallow Jeremy's come, he admits he's scared, but the two aren't related. Jeremy's scared of getting too involved, scared of hurting me.

I'm scared when we don't resolve things. Jeremy's scared when we talk about talking; I'm scared when we don't talk, when getting fucked becomes a desperate show of bravado. More fear: Jeremy feels guilty about being a slut, and I guess that's another difference between us—anonymous sex is new and exciting for Jeremy, *he's* new and exciting for me. My grandfather dies, I wash my sheets with my underwear and everything is stained yellow.

I don't feel sad until I call Rose to see how she's doing. She's struggling for words—this is so hard on your father. My father: the monster devouring my sleep. Spring roaches are smaller—how cute, I should start a petting zoo! One day out of the hospital, and maybe my grandfather was ready to die, but Allison says he was so bitter; it was such a horrible place to be. Rose says I wish you could be here, which means: you can't be here.

HOUSES

◎   ◎   ◎   ◎

Chrissie shows up with Forrest and another can of Dust-Off, crooked glasses and a safari hat. She's mid-eighties Banana Republic, Meryl Streep in *Out of Africa*. We get to the Fourteenth Street House for Tuesday Sucks, but Chrissie's banned because she got too drunk and caused a scene or something. There's too much chlorine in the hot tub, and I'm somewhere between calm and bored.

The next day is another day of shitting. It's sunny out but freezing. At midnight, I take two herbal sleeping pills, plus passionflower and a Vicodin—I can't possibly deal with being awake. I lie in bed for at least two hours before drifting away. Then I wake up with a back spasm and horrible stomach pains. Poison?

I remember what I mean when I say valerian and poppy give me incest flashbacks: I don't literally have memories, but everything becomes a flashback. Taking an elevator, trying to get into Belgium with my sister, but the border is a mental ward, *je parle français*, but it's too late. Did they shave my head for this bed?

Socket and I watch *Trembling Before G-d*, the movie about

Orthodox Jewish queers, and it's a vocabulary lesson for wayward Jews: *frum* means Orthodox, I wonder if that's where frumpy comes from? The Jews who are still practicing have their faces obscured like crime victims—it's hard not to laugh when they're crying, ghosts of rebellion. Jeremy says where were you fleeing to Belgium from—Germany? And everything goes to my head, mostly tears, which don't quite emerge—they stay stuck behind my eyes, blurring my vision anyway. Another Holocaust dream, always had them as a kid: joining the resistance, fighting the evil—my father—waking up in terror just as I was about to die.

I just want to keep touching Jeremy. In bed, I stare at the red light bulb in the ceiling lantern while he takes a nap, hand between my legs, my hand between his hip and belly and wow I feel so calm. Someone breaks into Jeremy's car and ruins our perfect day, right after Jeremy says nothing bad has ever happened to him, which is still mostly true I guess. I go across the street to see Rhania and Benjamin's bands, afterwards I feel like I'm going crazy but it's just hypoglycemia, honey—haven't you learned your lesson?

So much come on Jeremy's face, he says how long has it been? Nine days. He can't imagine, with all those trips to the S.F. State bathrooms he comes at least twice a day. The funny thing is that I still feel horny afterwards, phone sex line at 4 a.m. for this guy who says he wants someone to eat it, yes I want to eat it, yes yes yes YES. But he doesn't want to respond; I eat toast.

My mother calls to say that the flowers I sent Rose are the most beautiful flowers she's ever seen, well then I guess they were worth eighty dollars. Florence calls to say each individual rose was in a plastic tube of water and Rose was touched. No matter how exhausted I get, there's that little voice in my head: keep going, keep going! That's why I'm toasting to toast at 4 a.m.—to calm the voice, not just for more stomach pain.

I should carry a notebook for the funny things Jeremy and I say to each other. The grammar show on NPR is hilarious, is it *take* it all, bitch or *bring* it all? But maybe this flower legend is going too far: my mother says Rose told her every other arrangement pales in comparison to my roses, rising through the ceiling like hot air balloons. When I talk to Rose, she'll probably say the flowers are dying because you won't talk to your father—poor little boy hasn't been the same since his daddy's death, why you treat me so ba-ad? After yoga, I stare into space for an hour—all I can feel is my sinuses throbbing. I call the phone sex line to wake myself up with desire; it doesn't work.

Is yoga fucking me up? Songs of beaten and broken flesh, but dammit the calm moments are worth anything. But oh this fucking headache, it's so exhausting just to change the radio station to escape spoken word. Rhania says she's moving to the East Bay, needs to live alone, find more purple dresses.

I guess I could go out—is that what people do when they're exhausted? If I'm not horny, why do I keep thinking sex will rescue me? Though I like the guy on the phone sex line who says he loves sucking it down, but he's on the Peninsula and *I* love sucking it down—we could fight. For the right of way—hey, blue jay! My sinuses are opening up a new store: victimless crimes, elevator alarms, and used battery acid.

This woman in the car better be on acid, otherwise she's got no excuse. Trying to impress the fags by talking about big dicks, honey you're tacky. Then she's screaming because she can't breathe. Whining *I just need to get fucked*. She makes a big deal about not getting dropped off on the wrong side of Market Street. On Geary, all the working girls are lined up against the wall—my building, I guess— four cop cars, this is awful. In the morning, it's spring again.

Why is every day one of those days? On the radio: wild daffodils are much more delicate and they flutter in the breeze, growing on mossy stones—unlike the somewhat more stiff garden varieties. While these failures are widespread, they are not deliberate. More rain is expected in the hard-hit areas where sometimes people let down their guard. Rick calls to tell me about Hong Kong: everywhere people are jumping off buildings. Mothers carry their children out the window with them, policemen run up gambling debts and it's the honorable way to go—they have guns so they can just shoot themselves. Thousands of Filipino maids meet on street corners on Sundays, their one day off.

Rick wanted to get some of the chocolate tofu at the market, but it was congealed blood. He says everywhere there were carcasses, everywhere, and the air coming out of the Holland Tunnel in New York was like a fresh breeze compared to the air in Hong Kong. The bar where Rick worked only paid $1,000 a month for 54-hour weeks, but the gay bars were fun, and China was another world.

I go to a trick, guess he's in another world because no one answers the door. Of course I take a cab home—Rue says I turn tricks to pay for my taxi habit, but see—I proved him wrong: I don't even turn tricks. In the morning, my sinuses explode. Volcanic eruptions of blood up to the ceiling and then back down on my face, a fountain, but I've always hated horror movies. What else is above or behind those juicy eyeballs? Smashed TV screens that my head peeks into like a hand, broken glass scraping at everything ouch ouch ouch ouch OUCH. On the way to yoga, I drop my keys down the elevator shaft.

For once, yoga gives me energy and I keep it. Then Sara, the building manager, gives me free replacement keys instead of charging $150 like she's supposed to. She says: the way that I look at it, we're already paying more than enough to live in substandard conditions. Watching the sunset on the Geary bus, all my senses feel activated, though Rue says: first I'm depressed, then I'm obsessed.

I try to avoid the obsessed part because it's too exhausting. Alex goes to the Lexington and someone's handing out pieces of Brie with American flag toothpicks. Someone else comes up to him and says: have you seen the new Grand Marshall? Turns out it's a party for the trannyboy who I guess just got chosen Grand Marshall. Alex says: I thought they only had Grand Marshalls in the Klan.

Sometimes when Jeremy's sleeping, he makes these little shudders, but one of them's bigger, is that an earthquake? In the morning, I watch Jeremy's eyeballs move under closed lids, crisp thick eyelashes, pouting lips—last night he said I didn't think my life could get any better, but now I lost my job so I have two more free days! If I dream his world, will my headache go away?

At the Odeon, Jara says who's your friend? Oh, my boyfriend? Jara's scandalized, well you know: once every eight years. You mean he's your second? Well, that too. Jeremy wins the Longest Pubes Contest, even though I'm embarrassed because he's so drunk. Then he heads out to some party in the Castro. I don't want to go, but when he leaves I feel sad. He's loving me so much, pulling my shirt up to rub my belly and then kissing me and even saying it, oh how sweet! But he wants to party and I want to go to bed. Why do I get so scared?

Sushi and Magdalena can't find the car, but it's nice standing on the hill watching each of them walk in a different direction. And watching the angles of the houses against the sky; the air is fresh. Sushi asks what I do when I'm not sleeping or dancing. Magdalena says: she's setting a good example by loving herself. That's the highlight of my night. Driving up Mission, I'm just staring out the window at the bright lights and storefronts, trying to lift all that light inside.

Magdalena's working at a Montessori school, one day Sushi drops her off, Magdalena's boss is upset and Magda can't figure out why. Finally, the boss says: you know I like the way you are with the kids, but I deal with some very conservative parents—it's not my business how you lead your life, but next time, could you get dropped off around the corner? Magdalena doesn't get it. The boss says: you know—the mobile home, the pit bull.

The mobile home, the pit bull. Jeremy doesn't call in the morning, I decide it's crystal or a car crash. Or he's still fucking some boy, fourteen hours and going strong. I leave a message: are you at the End Up? He was joking about it earlier—I have nothing to do for a week, might as well stay up.

Jeremy calls. It was three awful parties, coke and then a sex party, he says you should've come with us—you were so sexy last night, I wanted to hump you—you're always so sexy. And I'm not sketched out anymore, see it's just when I don't know what's happening that all that fear builds inside me, searching for a way out. Now I just need to deal with the sinus headache, the exhaustion, and the depression—laundry in the dryer. Trying to locate my anus—oh, that cut-up thing.

Jeremy kisses more with his tongue when he's drunk. Otherwise, he waits for moments of abandon. Tonight, we're going grocery shopping and then we're gonna cook together. The shopping is the fun part, later I'm getting a cold and Jeremy's ripping holes in my sweatpants, I say wait until I get a new pair and you can tear them off me. If I'm getting a cold, why do I have to wake up wired at 7 a.m.? Fuck it's bright; I need curtains.

My father's fingers are in my asshole, cut open and blood pouring out—he's trying to pull something out of me, I'm a dead chicken with its head cut off. Running into the fireplace until I'm burnt to ashes, floating up and escaping through the chimney, a charred bird. Karen, my new therapist, says remember your body was powerless but you were not—I'm not so sure that I agree with this rather contestable claim, but somehow it makes me feel better. Rhania says: do you ever feel like you're in touch with something extra, and if you get too in touch, you won't be able to go back to being out of touch?

Benjamin calls to give me the sex party update: the coke was great, everyone wanted John but he only took off his pants, Jeremy's a great cocksucker and his ass was tasty. Jeremy never gives me the details—Benjamin says that's so bourgeois; she likes that word. I get a grapefruit seed extract inhaler, haven't been able to use the neti pot to clean my sinuses since some yogi died of a brain infection. Rue thinks I'm crazy, but there are roaches in my forehead—they climbed through my eyes and settled behind them, nests of fury.

I want to go to the Power Exchange with Jeremy, but he just took a Vicodin—he says: wait for me and we'll go tomorrow. If I said that to him, he'd run out the door. Did I mention that I fought the cold and won? I decide to stay home and make sure. It's become clear during the Pope's busiest week that his mobility is seriously impaired. Jeremy and I drive down the coast to look at the Montara Point Hostel. It's cute, but they make you leave your room by 10 a.m.—forget that shit. The sand is coarse—Jeremy's right, it doesn't get in my clothes. We're a spectacle for the other tourists. Jeremy says I'll take you for a ride, and pulls over into a ditch. Santa Cruz is a suburban blight; I can't believe there isn't something we're missing—why would anyone live here? At night, we discover the beach: okay, that's why.

We walk out to a lighthouse and play our favorite game. Do you like light? Yeah. What color? Green. What about blue? Yeah. Red? No. How come? Too red. And I'm sucking Jeremy's dick. The sign says DANGER SUDDEN WAVES CAN WASH YOU OUT TO SEA EVEN ON CALM DAYS. But the real danger is my come-shot— two weeks' worth and Jeremy's scared, I make him take some of it anyway, but honey don't spit that out when you can spit it into my mouth. Afterwards I'm so high, I can't open my eyes.

Do you like houses? There's one with a staircase down to land-scaped gardens—on the fucking beach! It must cost millions for that simple pleasure of sand in your toes every morning. Zan's mother has a stroke, Zan says now I have to visit my horrible family. The tricks decide I am a whore, after all. Number one asks me if I do this often. Two plays "Will You Still Love Me Tomorrow?" while rub-bing Aveda body polish on my back—it's supposed to feel like an orgasm but it hurts. Number three says your mouth is eternal. Num-ber four smells like stale sweat, I mean really stale. Number five wants me to dress him up in something sexy—two nights and I've made about as much as the rest of March. Jeremy calls from down the street at the Gangway, but I need to go to bed.

Do you like lighthouses? Not when it's so bright outside, today I feel like either I'm still sleeping or I didn't sleep at all—what a delightful combination! Andee calls to give me the Berlin update: when Larry King asks Liza how it feels to be back in the spotlight, she says Larry, it's a long way back from encephalitis of the brain. Elton John on what he wants to get Liza for her wedding: a hetero-sexual husband. Jeremy goes to the 12:30 a.m. show of *Panic Room* with Jodie Foster, it's the worst movie he's ever seen—he calls to tell me the plot from beginning to end: Evian, booby-traps, and an Upper West Side townstone, or is it a brownhouse?

Do you like brown houses? Three more tricks: first one wants to fuck me, second one has six cats, third one lives in a brown house with Jodie Foster. In between my tricks, Jeremy and I go to Cha-ya and Aquatic Park. There's no one at the park, guess we have to get it started. With the fog rolling in, it's a vibrant landscape in some dusty museum, look at the way the colors shine through the canvas—but wait, there's the highway just across the blue lagoon. I'm sitting on an overturned tree, it's all about the wind rushing up my legs as I'm sucking Jeremy's dick, damn it he gets me so excited when he says with so much eloquence and charm: you want my load? Honey I want everything, piling up in my stomach like glue.

I still want to hug Jeremy for ten hours, but we go to a bar and he licks the salt off my neck and pulls a lime out of my mouth with his teeth. The trick with the brown house says I like that you're not jaded. At Aquatic Park, Jeremy opens his coat over my head while I'm sucking his dick, all that warmth. Back home, I'm calm in my exhaustion, for a change. Chrissie says I called you because you're not drama—are you ready for drama? The light in the bathroom was off and then it went on, there are three men in the bathroom closet waiting for me, I went to the door to check it and it locked by itself.

Chrissie, how long have you been awake? Three or four days, I know that's what's wrong with my life but my illness is not turning lights on. I'm standing here with the knife, Mattilda—will you call me tomorrow? Chrissie, maybe you should take a cold shower— remember that time when we were outside the Hole in the Wall and I could feel my head cracking open, slipping into death, and cold water brought me down?

Chrissie says: I'll try it, but call me tomorrow. I say: I'll call you tomorrow. My three-hour trick is so nervous—the military in the English countryside, operations on his dick when he was born and he says it looks weird but it works okay. It looks like somebody smashed it with a hammer, over and over again until it gave way. He has two holes in his dick; I wonder what the second one is for. Next trick at my house says interesting view, are there many sirens? How does he know? Fire after fire—is the whole city burning down? Then I realize he means police sirens.

WINGS

◉ ◉ ◉ ◉

Every time I open my eyes, I'm staring at one of my trick's moles—
why are there so many? He wants to know if I've eaten caper
berries, everybody's eating caper berries this season. They look like
tadpoles. I taste one—it's crunchy and tart, really tart. This season
is gonna be a good one.

Jeremy calls, he says someone asked about Mattilda and I just
said everything's perfect, it's what I've always wanted. It makes me
so happy when he says things like that, how can I even worry? I
meditate to Mistress Barbara's pounding non-stop techno assault—
when I get up, I'm ready to do cartwheels. Later, I jerk off for the
first time in I-don't-know-how-long, it feels like months. I mean
really. It's much better than trying to hook up on the internet with
someone I'm not gonna be attracted to anyway, who says things like:
dude sup dig yr profile man wanna hook?

I go out to get groceries at 1 a.m.—everyone's outside and I've
got that calm sweetness pouring in through my eyes, yes oh yes I can
actually feel joy. Until this one guy swivels around his head to stare

at me with such an off-centered confused and dazed, vacant—surprise! No, really—surprise.

Back home, I'm allergic to the Oriental wrap that I bought as a late-night treat. Everything itches. I'm over the fucking electro revival, Miss Kittin can overdose. I have so many books that I'm never going to read, so much awful music. Next morning I wake up to a trick downstairs—shit, I rush to open the door but oh no it's rejection, first thing in the morning he says I'm sure you're a nice guy—wrong! Chrissie leaves a message: oh I hate your fucking answering machine, bitch—oh—stop it why are they here? Get away from me! I've got a present for you.

A trick comes over to fuck my face and I'm actually loving it, could come any second and oh the beauty of just holding it in and holding down my not-quite-act: desperate for his load! And then he comes, three four five streams all over my face and I'm rushing to the bathroom to snap a picture—my new art project. Then my eye swells up—dammit I can't be allergic to come! Um, what happened to your eye, buddy? Dude I got punched in the face, it fuckin' sucks.

Something amazing is happening to me. I walk into the Pilsner to piss and they're playing Steely Dan, I mean Carly Simon, but it just sounds *great*, I want to dance around the room with my hair flying around in circles. Wait, it's Sinéad O'Connor—well, same thing. The point is maybe six years of being macrobiotic and five years on and off of acupuncture, four years more or less of fighting candida and exercising regularly plus a year of physical therapy then seven months of chiropractic, therapy on and off forever, two years of no drinking or drugs, plus all the yoga, meditation, supplements and just plain learning to listen to myself and my body and everyone and the air around me—maybe all that's finally getting me somewhere, though my shoulder still hurts.

Are the liver detox pills working? Is it all about Jeremy, nothing compares to you, opening me up like Sweet Valley High in elementary school? It's all here inside me, hummingbirds waiting inside purple flowers. But where's Jeremy? It's his birthday and I've prepared the gifts, I've made a special dinner. Maybe he decided to stay for his last class, or maybe he got really involved in the bathroom—

there he is on my cellphone, sounds so sad oh honey of course I didn't forget, damn it the phone cord's unplugged. So glad I gave him my cellphone number, mostly I just use it for work.

Jeremy arrives, I'm hugging him to make him feel better—the flowers, Nina Simone, seaweed soup and rosemary red lentils, and yes the gifts, arranged with shiny silver notes between them. I fucking love having someone to love, can't you tell? Jeremy's so happy about everything—the earrings, shower mirror, *Anal Pleasure and Health*—he loves the food, he loves me, he loves me yes he loves me! Did I mention the earrings? Sparkly geometries, thick hoops like your mother wore in the eighties but they're not really hoops because they don't go all the way around, blue shiny grapes, dangly pink hearts, and porcelain roses. Jeremy said he wanted tacky earrings—these are the best tacky has to offer and he's smiling and laughing, oh I want to look at them again!

Jeremy's red lips that get more and more chapped, why do I worry so much about getting hard? Nina Hagen really shakes it out in "Spirit in the Sky"—who doesn't have a friend in Jesus? But "Universal Radio" is a dance floor danger zone, those beats are unavoidable—I'm standing barefoot on top of Jeremy's shoes as we glide across the floor, my come down his throat in three gulps but wait there's more. He says I can't come, I've jerked off six times in the last two days. On the roof, it's warm, we can watch everyone in the ugly apartments next door that look like '80s condos—oh there's Bree on her laptop!

Rue makes me a mix CD that's almost all country, old country I guess but whatever it's still country. My cellphone's vibrating in my pocket, but wait I'm not carrying it—hooker! My trick wants to know where my boyfriend is—he's at home. The trick looks both ways—here? No, silly—at his house. The trick's more relaxed but confused, dense as a fence—no, that's a brick wall, honey. Rhania calls, oh did you say hello? I only slept three hours last night; I was having a Mattilda moment. I'm at work, I just put the baby to sleep but now it's awake again, okay bye.

Jeremy has crabs and I call craigslist for come on my face, anything else and I'm not really attracted to them, but I'm always ready for that subtle stickiness, that glimmer and shimmer, that gooey authenticity. Then the photo op—see, I do have a sense of history! Later, Jeremy helps me clean up the box of papers that's been decomposing on my floor ever since I moved in—his suggestion—that's love!

Domestication.com—where is it? There's a sign for a permit hearing posted on the demolished building next door, am I going to have to move out? I call Zan: it's a good thing I have this boyfriend 'cause no one else calls me back. Zan calls back: you never come to anything in the East Bay. I call her: I know you expect me to feel the vibe, but someone's gotta call and tell me if something's going on. Zan calls back: I'm quitting school, so you'll see me more often.

I've heard that one before. Before bed, I drink the water that the flowers were in, with the mysterious white powder mixed in to preserve them. It doesn't taste weird, but both of my ears close up—something's bubbling over! In the morning, I piss in a glass, it feels kind of safe. It's a beautiful day out, but my sinuses are sending out Morse code. Botox. Rufies. Hummer. Saturday night rocks. Jeremy gets so drunk at his birthday party that's he's falling up the stairs, grabbing his crotch and yelling at everyone: *take it all.* He keeps saying he needs to stop drinking, then grabs the nearest beer. Everyone's doing coke in the bathroom, Jeremy says what are they doing? Coke—he's rushing to the door like a little kid. Jeremy, you said you didn't want any coke. I kiss him to distract, and also because I want to kiss him. It works for a few minutes, but then he's back at the door, I turn him around and he heads down the hallway.

By 3 a.m., I'm way too tired to continue pretending I'm having fun. Jeremy says I'm sober now—see, I don't need coke—and then he's drinking another beer. I kiss him goodbye—love you—I'm disobeying my own rules by trying to keep him from the drugs, I always say that never works. In the cab, I'm sketchy, eyes rolling back and I'm craving coke for the first time in a while—the rush—it's okay to let it roll just as long as I'm not actually rolling.

The next day, Jeremy calls to say thank you for taking care of me and keeping me from the coke—well, at least I was successful. We go to the Powerhouse and some guy squeezes his come into my mouth—damn that's hot, though Jeremy misses it and immediately I worry about STDs. Jeremy says I love watching you suck cock. Jeremy's already jerked off twice today and I don't understand my libido, for a minute I was rock hard and then I drifted away, there's some fear there. And performance anxiety, or is it just exhaustion? I try to get Jeremy to go to the Power Exchange, but he's ready for bed. He drops me off there because I want to be horny. It doesn't work. Cab driver says eye candy or eyesores? At home, I just want to get in bed, but my sheets are in the washer, have to wait until they dry. I call Jeremy, but is he on the internet? I keep hitting redial, but it goes right to voicemail. Why am I obsessing?

Don't call me an internet sex addict, but I've been off and on craigslist for the last three hours—gotta get some more photos for the comeshot archive. First guy is so damn hot, beefy muscular guy with shaved blond hair—I can tell he's sweet by how softly he touches my head. He starts pumping and just lets it all loose in my throat. So much for the photo. Next guy is prepped-out to the Abercrombie nines, but cute and skinny and nervous. I take it all over my face, he snaps the photo—send me one, okay? I can still smell his awful cologne, funny how my face feels stretched where the come landed—forget green clay! Now I'm waiting for a third guy to call. I guess I should get off sometime too, but really I just want more photos.

A vice cop comes over for an appointment. The funny thing is that it doesn't make me nervous, but let me just look outside my door. Wait a second. A vice cop just came into my apartment—well, at least we didn't have sex. He was shaking, I asked him if he wanted some water, the ice was shaking—but why do I feel sad for a cop who can't express his gay desires? Maybe my brain synapses are wired wrong.

Chrissie calls, she can't stop shitting 'cause of the jail food. Honey, when were you in jail? She says I took a sleeping pill and woke up in a hospital bed, fell on a cop and got arrested for assault. What? She says Luke and I got in a fight and he called the cops, I took a sleeping pill and went to bed. I say: now you're back in his house again? She says it's either here or the street.

When I wake up, never mind: I'm not awake. Chrissie calls, she says I'm painting the walls. What color? Oh just white, I'm covering up the graffiti. Did I tell you about that? It's what happened after I talked to you last night—this whole house is falling down I need some glue. Don't worry about me, Mattilda, I'm going to a clinic—I'm getting a job in a clinic, it pays $22,000 an hour.

Horny, tired. Horny. Tired. But wait here's the horny part—at least, for a few minutes. I'm trying a new yoga studio—they keep the heat at 95 instead of 120. On the phone, they say they keep the windows open, so you can breathe, because that's what it's all about, right? After yoga, my asshole is pulsing with the rest of my body and I want Jeremy to fuck me. But yoga's too hot; I wake up in the morning with holes in every single sinus. Help, date rape! Today's the anti-war demo, a social event if there ever was one. Too bad it's aimless choreography through the abandoned streets. Thousands of people marching with a permit on a Saturday instead of getting on a bridge and refusing to leave. Or doing anything more confrontational than holding signs and babies.

Jeremy's rubbing my calf muscle during the movie! It's these little things that drive me wild, leaning into him, hum. The next day it's beautiful, basking in the alley cat sun, then to Jeremy's bed for a nap—no, sex—which is all about grabbing his head and gazing into his eyes. Going wild when I come 'cause that's the only way, a sunny day, his come all over me but no camera, a nap and a sinus headache.

Wow, it's already dark. Jeremy and I are holding each other in so many different ways, days and days and days and days. Someone drops a tea ball in one apartment, a zipper goes down, piss, up. Outside, it's still almost warm, but wait: this is the East Bay, I love Jeremy, this is the East Bay, I love Jeremy. Then I'm in my father's office for the first time since I left, everything looks taller, and can he really be that well-preserved, thirty and tanned and muscular? He's enraged then curious, he says what do you think? I say stop by my bedroom after you're done with your patient. This strange game that I've been playing in my dreams: I'm taking control back from my father by sexualizing *him*. Instead of the same old split-me-in-half and check to see how I can possibly be alive.

Tweaked-out trick says I can't come down to let you in, I'm getting a blow job. I get another cab. The next day is a day of car alarms, trick says are you open-minded or do you play safe? It must be flake season, because the next guy wants me to go across the street and get him two six-packs of Bud. At therapy, I'm crying about two kitty cats, they killed them and made me eat them? Or ee—for Easter, bunnies? But no it's cats, dropped live into a fire pit, do cats have souls? I keep saying Allison's so scared, she's just a baby—holding my hands eight inches apart and cry cry crying for the kitty cats so sad. I'm trying to feel all of it and not worry about what actually happened versus what is also real, but maybe didn't happen.

The next day's adventure begins and ends out on the fire escape in the sun with my shorts rolled up and oil all over my chest, I'm a porn movie just waiting to happen. In the fake condos across the street, this guy leans out of his second-floor window to smoke, but pretty soon he's staring up at me. I try not to notice until the right moment. He waves, then runs inside and re-emerges with a camera. I pose with my plate of food. Later, I wave him over, but he has to go to work. Maybe another day is what I'm thinking.

Jeremy calls before bed, he says I've got two words and only two words: Marina. Safeway. It's that game we play in bed—our two favorite locations are Fontana West, posh '6os condos on the water, and, of course, Marina Safeway itself. We dream of the chilly produce aisle on hot summer days, the old ladies with Vuitton purses from way before it got trendy again, the straight men with manicures.

This guy comes on my face, and when I ask him to snap a picture, he says: evidence to live by. Throwing together my outfit for the anti-capitalist fashion show—why don't I do this more often? I wake up manic about Prada, Prada, nothing but Prada. Jeremy wants me to dress him up but he's scared—oh honey, don't be worried, I'll hug and kiss you, and if you need heroin . . . We photocopy the Prada label onto hundreds of sheets of paper and onto huge labels that go on everything. Garbage bags, Santa slippers, stuffed flamingo—we're gonna rule every runway from here to Miami and back to Tokyo.

Jeremy and I are too gorgeous to even describe; let's just say it's all about minimalism. Mullets, visors, layers and layers of gowns and bathing suits, smeared lipstick and black glitter, stuffed animals beneath our clothes to help our figures, and the rest is art. We pick up Brodie, on the street someone says where'd you get those outfits? Prada. We're late to the show, but we are the show. Everyone's working anarcho chic runway damage: striped T-shirts, ties with cut-off dress shirts, asymmetrical hair. I say if everyone isn't wearing Prada, how come they're all wearing the same thing? I guess it's anti-capitalist, but not anti-fashion. Every time someone stares—which is every time—I say: it's Prada. If someone says I like your Prada, I say how'd you know? Oh—the cut, of course.

Brodie disappears and the place is more than packed. Kirk's one of the few people who fully appreciates us, his whole face lights up—he says Sahar just told me you'd be wearing Prada suits. Jeremy needs pot, so we go to the car and I get bitchy—everyone's so tired, they look at me like tourists, I always feel like I'm wasting my outfits. Then Jeremy gets bitchy—I don't know what to say to these people, this wig itches—I just need the right mix of drugs and alcohol and people and it isn't happening.

We sit it out, which is what I like about our relationship: we're drama'd out but we're not having drama. We go to the Castro for runway, and I want to engage and enrage, but Jeremy wants to hide. We eat at Bagdad, where at least a couple of queens praise our Prada—do you know how much this cost? At my house, we take showers for hours and then Jeremy leaves, but let's fast-forward to two more showers—that's five for the day—four tricks, well that almost pays for the ergonomic desk chair and the air purifier!

Sometimes I get up in the morning, and even though I'm a mess, or maybe because I'm a mess, I need to talk to someone now because the world's going to end. I call Allison because maybe it's a good time to reach her. Then I call Rue. Rhania's at work, Jeremy's sleeping, I'm not ready for a long conversation with Andee or Ananda, Zan's out of town, I'm not in the mood for Chrissie, I need to eat before Socket or Jaysen, okay forget the phone I better eat, that's what I need: to eat.

Emergency: it looks like they're starting construction next door, what am I going to do? I go out to look at apartments, reminds me how nice my place is. Even if the building's a dump and the owner will only give me a rent adjustment, not a rent reduction. On NPR, they're interviewing the woman that invented new ways to slaughter cows. She knows how they feel, which moo means they're happy. She's autistic, once she was incapacitated but now she's a success story: every day she gets up to perfect the methods of murder.

The good news is that the construction next door won't start until 2003, the bad news is that they're planning a thirteen-story building. After all the times I've tried to get Jeremy to go to the Power Exchange, she goes alone. Bitch.

I'm obsessing about the boy across the street who took a photo of me. I think he's in hiding, but tonight there are two buff guys with their shirts off, watching the internet. I get so horny that I go downstairs to watch their internet too, but they've pulled the blinds. I go to Frenchy's and suck off some tweaker. The radio announcer says don't pathologize, mythologize, but a Palestinian boy's first word is "shooting." In therapy, four personalities emerge. The best one is Marie, who says: oh Mattilda, she's tired. Marie's more me than me. Everything starts with choking, choking, choking—Latin is the language of torture, stop putting needles in me, I don't even do drugs. Then back to the little boy, who says: why do they want to kill me? The twelve-year-old is enraged and desperate, internalizing the dying part, unaware of any other possible history. And then there's the point where everything goes white, and I'm floating floating floating—it's not just the dissociation, it's the drugs, I guess they drugged me.

This guy comes over from the phone sex line; I'm always surprised when they show up. He's cute, fucks my face until I'm bored, plus there's something scratchy in my throat. I keep getting distracted by some awful smell—is that his ass, or his breath? Finally, I realize it's his feet. I open all the windows after he leaves, but it still smells. The word that comes up over and over: release. Jeremy's entering a diving competition and I'm going to a synagogue at a hotel where all these different parties are happening—one of the rooms is for rich hasids, then later people like hasids but they wear stylish red sun-hats and dresses like bibs. Then it's every warehouse I've ever been to, except it's Bloomingdale's, it's the Power Exchange, it's my house, it's Berlin. I'm trying to clear people out because I want to go to bed. But then I figure I might as well dance, so I change into tight, bright floral shorts and do this move where my feet don't touch the floor for 45 minutes. Finally, good exercise that doesn't hurt—I'm weaving between cocktail waiters and high-end security guards, feet don't stop pumping until the bath-and-body section, where there are lots of glass bottles on glass shelves with mirrors.

When I land, I'm looking for Jeremy, through an area where someone's trying to pull a curtain—for a back room? But it's too crowded, actually it's a wrestling ring but I'm not going in there. I'm trying to slide through and some guy starts to rub my chest, but not until I find Jeremy. There's Jeremy—he's got a new haircut with tighter curls, I rush over to hug him but he turns away. I know it's because he's flirting with some boy, he looks really angry with me, saying *not now* and acting all cold too. I turn to the boy and smile: hi, I'm Mattilda. I can't believe Jeremy won't kiss me because he's flirting, I'm boiling and the boy says I don't live in a didacticism because this is Berlin where we have neighborhoods. Jeremy disagrees: didacticism is a neighborhood. Oh no—they both like those conversations!

The boy turns to leave; he's the kind who can't deal with boyfriends. And Jeremy still looks mad—I yell after the boy: you can have sex with him! This is where I realize it's a dream because Jeremy's so angry. What's so good about having a relationship is that tired boys don't matter to me; there are so so many tired boys and only one beautiful Jeremy, though that doesn't answer the question of why this boy mattered to Jeremy. I go back into the dream because I still want to tell Jeremy that it was only the kiss, I was so excited to see him and there he was so cold over an even colder boy, because, after all, it was Germany. When I get back, I realize they're selling office supplies—postal scales for one Mark—that's too cheap, they must not work—I find one on the floor and I start bouncing up and down on it, readying myself for takeoff. Waking up again, I feel so calm, because in the dream my legs were wings, pumping toward the sky.

MOTHER'S DAY

⊙   ⊙   ⊙   ⊙

I hear the most horrible conversations in yoga studio locker rooms. This time, it's a hatha studio but the owner of the Bikram place is there, bragging that the way to keep employees working hard is to get them to invest their life savings in the studio. Another guy starts talking about opening a factory in China—I'm serious. I want to say: slave labor or child labor? But the guy says something to me and I even smile. Why am I invested in his good will?

Today there are 67 pigeons standing in a row on the façade of the demolished laundromat, plus 33 more perched on the sign. An even hundred is as far as I can count. Only one pigeon is brown. Every time I meditate, I start to nod off—is it the liver detox pills? On the radio, Jennifer Stone says: Medea is a suicide bomber, she takes no prisoners.

I go to the new Ethiopian restaurant that took over Maye's, Seafood Since 1887. It's all about the teal booths, photos of old San Francisco on the walls, worn-out Oriental carpet—the only problem is the Trekkie techies arguing about who's figured out the most complicated computer language. At home, I crash. What is wrong with the radio? First it's taking care of Mother Earth like she's your own mother—hello, have you met my mother? Then it's an announcer finding his voice while covering Little League. And finally, *Car Talk*: I was driving my girlfriend's Bronco and suddenly it was a tropical rain forest. No, Mary—that was your pants.

Jeremy's great-aunt has closets and closets full of things she's ordered from the Home Shopping Network, a whole attic filled with zip-front caftans and collectable figurines, but Jeremy says: you're not the kind of boyfriend I could bring home. I'm insulted—I can't imagine going to see Jeremy's family in Minnesota, even if I got to try on all the great-aunt's caftans. Actually, I hate caftans. But what does Jeremy mean? Jeremy says: you know, you're just not the family type. I say: you're just worried they'll see who you really are. All this tension in my stomach, I'm wondering whether Jeremy's ashamed of me—I'm not so sure I want to know. He says maybe you're right.

How many times in one day can I meditate, each time more exhausting than the last? I'm not mentally ill, I'm mentally still! An old woman walks on the bus wearing a T-shirt that says Gray Matters. It's Rue's birthday, honey are you feeling thirty-five? Ninety-five—well, you always have been ahead of your time! Later, I'm sucking my mother's cock and a piece of it comes off in my mouth—gross—and the crazy part is that up until that moment, I thought I was still awake, lying in bed misunderstanding everything. Jeremy tells me it's Mother's Day. Zan's mother dies and he feels numb, doesn't know what to think and I guess that's how I'd feel too.

This trick is driving me crazy, everything he does makes me cringe so I'm sucking his cock and my jaw starts to hurt, it's the new pain from the new yoga like half of my face is going numb. Job hazards: if I can't jerk him off or suck him off, then what can I do? Finally I get hard, so I fuck him. Afterwards, he says: this may sound weird, but you're the best sex partner I've ever had in my life.

Jeremy says some people like pets, and some people like their feet—and you don't even have to feed your feet. We drive to Orr Hot Springs, Jeremy wants the windows closed but then I can't breathe. He closes my window while I'm meditating; hello it's about being hyper-aware, not brain-dead. All I can think is I'm sweating, open the fucking window, I'm sweating, open the fucking window— until I give up, and open it.

We get to Orr, the redwoods and the stars and could there be anything more beautiful than looking up at all those white things? And holding Jeremy in the steam room, he doesn't want me to suck his dick there because it's against the rules. Bitch, whose rules? After a few joints, though, he's shooting his load all over my face in the hot tub, then running back to get the camera and I'm still there, posing for the world. The cold pool is the best, hills sloping upward into sky and those stars, so many stars, we're stars!

In the warm pool is where I grab Jeremy's head and start to shoot, but he pulls away and damn I'm shooting shooting darling I'm a shooting star! Jeremy says was there a big turtle in the water? Turtles live in shells, I say—if you were a turtle, you'd have a pretty shell and I'd come live inside.

There's so much air, but I'm still learning to breathe: diaphragm, belly, chest up, into neck and head, down to the earth and up to the sky, more sky here too and maybe someday, everywhere, when everything will be easier. Sometimes, fighting all this pain I get from trying to take care of myself, I forget that maybe I'm still getting there, everywhere I want to be. Even though my head hurts, my neck is going numb, back muscles burning.

In the morning, I feel like a demolished parakeet and Jeremy's aggro, I used to hate that word but it's grown on me. The springs calm us both down—as long as I can meditate every hour, I'll be okay. Jeremy hurt his finger and it's swelling up, a lava lamp waiting to happen. In Guerneville, they won't let me in the bar without ID, which is just fine with me. Jeremy jokes: such derivation is not alien to the syntax—he's studying for his linguistics finals.

In the morning, I stay in bed for two extra hours to try and feel relaxed. I end up with a sinus headache and an attitude problem. I think there's lavender in my eye pillow because my eyes are burning, the 400-dollar air purifier doesn't do a damn thing. If I keep the hood of my sweatshirt over my head, will the day fade away? Oh

my head my head my head, ache! At least my handwriting looks
good. On my way home, "Pretty Woman" is blasting out of some
bar and two guys start singing to me. I am a pretty woman, I swear
I am! I wake up thinking how loving Jeremy is opening doors,
though one door leads back to how all my friends were always trying to kill themselves and I was afraid of bridges because what if a
gust of wind came and blew me off?

Opening doors to my heart and that's a scary place, mace—no, pepper spray, it can make you blind and cause panic attacks—you
definitely cry, maybe die. That time Zan and I got bashed after the
March on Washington in '93, which is where we met. We got bashed
right after a million gays in white T-shirts packed their bags and flew
home, leaving a lot of trash in the streets, including the preppy Georgetown University students who asked me and Zan what we were doing.
Kissing. Their parents had probably given them pepper spray to keep
them safe from muggers and black people. Or fags, I guess.

They sprayed it directly into my eyes, such a burning pain I was
screaming into a restaurant where I splashed cold water in my face
so red I thought it was spraypaint, the restaurant where I used to go
late at night in high school. They said take this outside. I took it to
the hospital for saline pumped directly into my eyes through tubes.
They said it was a good thing I came right away because I might
have lost my vision. Afterwards, a cop prevented me from using the
snack room—not your kind. Meeting my parents for dinner the next
night, they asked: why did you have to be so overt?

Benjamin wants to kill his mother and my trick is all about frottage, but after three couples arguing on Maury Povich about
whether the child is his, my dick is sore. Frottage can be painful. The
trick points to the TV and says black people are crazy. He's black,
but maybe he doesn't realize I'm crazy. Later, phone sex is funny—
all these tweakers playing games. This one guy wants to know if I
was molested—well, yes, actually. Then he says I must be on some
crazy drugs. I want to go over to this other guy's house but it's 4
a.m., my dick is jumping for side-stroke, back-stroke, fancy diving
too—but what about the crawl? When I shoot, there's so much come
on the floor and I wonder who Jeremy is fucking.

The next day is only the usual garage sale: babies, rabies, and scabies. Your pick—a million dollars! Having experienced not only the glamour but the misfortune of celebrity over the years, Danielle Steel nonetheless does not park more than one or two of her twenty-something cars on the street at a time. It's true that she's lost count of all the cars, but since someone else writes her books, she spends most of her days with kids who've tried to kill themselves. Her maybe-gay son succeeded, she doesn't want these kids to join him. Sometimes, late at night, Danielle Steel gets dressed up as Jackie Collins and stands out in the rain yelling TAXI!

Postmodern terrorism: the next target is the World Trade Center at Little New York in Vegas, and you thought gambling was a joke! Memorial Day and fighter jets are flying overhead, yesterday they arrested thirty people at the permitted anti-war demo. The protesters agreed to march on the sidewalks, without signs or noisemakers, but apparently they were still going too slow for democracy.

Well, I finally figured out how to use craigslist successfully. Posted for sex in Lafayette Park, just below Danielle Steel's magnificent driveway, and then rushed over. The guys weren't all that hot but damn I was fucking this guy in the dirt. And the fog was surrounding us with romance. Except that when I came, I felt disgusting. I don't like the feeling of coming in a guy's ass, even with a condom—I think it's the physical sensation, like I'm trapped with nowhere to explode.

On the walk home, there's this guy I'd die for, but stop dying, okay? He's so clean-cut, it's sick. I almost turn around and follow him home 'cause I'm disguised as clean-cut and sick too, but I figure I just came, it won't be that fun to suck cock. Even this preppy blond jock boy's—well sure I'd take his load if he offered it, but I'm not going to run back uphill stalking him. Though he did have his hands near his crotch, inviting me to watch, watch!

Rolling out of bed and into my sinus headache, oh it's my fucking birthday! Everyone comes over late and we're going to the beach, here come the clouds. I just love waking up ready to vomit, thinking why don't I drink, why not? We get there and it's freezing—

and ugly, really—but I'm calmer. We visit the sea lions at Pier 39 and they're so cute, Rhania strips for the tourists and I just love hugging people like the sea lions. At Golden Era, I'm exhausted and everyone leaves after dinner except Jeremy, Rue and I on my sofa. Should we go to a movie?

We get to know the sofa, actually we all know her well already—can you believe this trick called her worn out? Rue leaves and Jaysen arrives, then leaves. Jeremy and I go on a walk and then I'm exhausted again—we hug for a while and at least I feel happier in my exhaustion. Jeremy leaves to pick up Sarah from the airport and I'm wired again, guess I'll go to Cala and buy greens.

Jeremy gives me a stuffed-animal cat for my birthday, and he didn't even know about the flashbacks I've been having—cats burned alive or strangled. I pet this cat in bed and I feel like that little kid, struggling to endure. At the bank, Alex stands in line listening to this woman scream about her offshore bank accounts with hedge fund international high-interest yield checking plus savings option, finally Alex says: could you just shut up? The woman whirls around and looks Alex over—you're just a fucking dyke hiding your tits. Alex says you better watch your back, because there are a lot of us out there, hiding our tits.

GAY PEOPLE

◎   ◎   ◎   ◎

There's something so satisfying about pretending to shoot in the condom in this trick's ass—he gets all excited, I'm moaning and my eyes roll back—just like coming except I don't feel like shit afterwards. Later, I feel like shit. I meditate, which helps me feel better for five whole minutes. Looking at a flower—oh how pretty!—and then boom it's back to bed. At 1 a.m., I decide to be horny, rushing over to Lafayette Park. A few runarounds and then I'm sucking some guy's dick, but pretty soon I realize I'm not horny. I rush home for another night of worthless sleep.

On the phone, Jeremy wishes I could feel better—oh no, he's starting to pity me. When I say I miss you, he doesn't say anything. I get so tired, I can't think, trying to fight sleep. Finally I get in bed, or at least I wish I did—this conversation with Jeremy is too much trying, we're both trying the wrong things. I guess he's trying to empathize and I'm trying to sound better than I feel. Then I'm trying to get back in bed. Earlier I was thinking I'm dying, someone's killing me—but really I'm not that paranoid. My accomplishments for the day: I ordered a replacement water filter; I went to the chiropractor.

More news from Andee: Larry King interviews Kitty Kelley about the Royal Family, it's the Queen's fiftieth year on the throne—how is that possible? Kitty says it's good to see some beauty after 9-11. This trick tells me he's going to open four strip clubs and his bodyguard is waiting next door with a machine gun. Don't let me forget to mention the bubble gum lube—hello LA! Smog and stretch marks, pass the lines. Aaron says he's not sure anymore about the line between casual crystal use and addiction. Lately, he's been struck by the resemblance between Bremerton, where he lives, and quicksand. His birthday is on the same night as a bartender friend's, he tips her twenty dollars and she promises a treat. But when he asks her for it, she beats him up—and Aaron's so appalled by violence of any sort, rushing to the peep show to vomit. He says as much time as I've spent living with and observing people on the wrong side of the tracks, I realize I have no picture of what it's like to live there.

Ralowe calls three times with ideas for Pride. First call: rainbow clown outfits, naked bottoms. Second: the evil gay-gay-gay. Third: genetically modified dog made to pour beer for the gay-gay-gays, but it wants to become a real dog.

Jeremy gets all excited about making plans with Randy, who Zan fell in love with for a few weeks and maybe Jaysen slept with him too or was it Benjamin? Small World Syndrome. Plus all my neurosis about Jeremy finding someone to fuck and then leaving me—bitch, your asshole's too tight! My voice gets all hollow and I can't think, why did I call him before eating?

When I'm sad, I like petting this stuffed cat that Jeremy gave me. I wake up at 6 a.m., oh no the sun! After a sleeping pill, barley, a bath, and I guess sleep—or something that resembles it—I practice what to say to Jeremy if he's late because he had to cruise the bathrooms. Not, I *figured* that *would* happen but I *thought* that *might* happen. He's late, says it's because he had to wait in line to fight his parking ticket and lose. I hug him over and over.

Waking up at 8:30 a.m., I feel so incredibly rested and ready to face the world. Just kidding. Later—or was it yesterday?—I spend two hours cruising the internet, even though I'm not horny. I just want to escape all that amazing rest. Needless to say, everything gets worse. Where's Jeremy? It's been weeks since we've hung out alone for more than a few hours. Today's her date with Randy, well actually they don't have plans yet but they might hang out so Jeremy can't hang out with me. I love his priorities.

Turns out Ralowe didn't say rainbow clown outfits, it was rainbow Klan outfits and the evil Gay Gay Gay, the gays wearing couture hoods to protect their well-coiffed hair. Chrissie wants to celebrate with a pretty little rainbow bomb. Rhania's combining new wave and no-wave in a neue way, so we don't get to the beach until 4:30 p.m., but when we get there it's still hot out. Of course I start talking about awful Provincetown—oh the beach, the beach—what's the point of going anywhere else? I call Jeremy and he's too stoned, I feel like we're acting. I say well we have plans on Tuesday, he says it'll be good. Don't patronize me. Later, I remember why I like him to tell me everything: because otherwise I don't believe anything.

I feel like I've meditated myself to an amazing place, then I open my eyes and everything's still the same. Trying to channel the energy from the back-center and top sides of my head, picturing my hands flying side-to-side and up, twist, turn, down—hips shake shaking, knees bent and feet sliding back and back. I'm weightless, I'm weightless—look honey, sweat glands!

At Whole Foods, this woman's in a panic, holding up the tamales and saying: I just can't taste it if it's not organic—but I can't cook, I can't! Jake interviews Miss Kittin, who says that eighties look—I won't do it, I won't! Then why are you doing it?

Did I mention my conversation with the boy across the street? He was so boring, it was painful. Then he had blue hair with a big blue T-shirt, today he has red hair with a big red T-shirt. A thrilling expression of individuality. Okay—so maybe I'm in a bad mood. This trick pretends I'm tied up and begging him not to touch my pecs. No—not my pecs! It's exhausting; he smells. After my shower, I walk all the way up Columbus to City Lights, just in time not to find anything I'm looking for. It's nice that there are so many people out on the street in North Beach at midnight—if only they weren't all ready to kill for America.

Do you do the kissing thing? Summer in San Francisco: I swear it was ninety degrees yesterday, but today it's fifty. Petting Jeremy in the car, will you purr for me? The sea lions on the pier make me so happy, the way they look like they're resting even when they're fighting. Afterwards I want to buy a sea lion stuffed animal. Jeremy says maybe you should wait—I decide to wait, and see if he gets me one.

At first I think I have a disease, because the fucking hottest boy shows up from gay.com, then when I come I still feel sad. The sadness disease. Luckily it fades and I actually feel calm, Steve and I take a shower—that's his name, Steve—he asks me about my books. He says you have a lot of cool things here.

At Whole Foods, it's all about the guy with baggy over-dyed jeans, a fleece pullover with a collar, and the frat mod hairstyle. Then, in line it's the guy I catch staring at my earrings—how do jocks get such big lips? But there's a conspiracy against me: all of my tricks wear the same awful cologne!

News Alert: my six-month anniversary with Jeremy! We go to the beach and of course it's freezing. Jeremy's my mermaid all cold in the sand, and I warm him up by getting on top of him and licking his face. He gives me the stuffed-animal seal, I just want to pet it and pet it and pet Jeremy. I give him this pincushion plant with red berries in a porcelain pot with red flowers on it. Plus a collage of the two of us making out. Our sex is great, the relaxing moments that interrupt the frenzy. The Tibetan food is so good that it doesn't even matter that the dance performance we want to see is sold out. I piss in a windstorm in Alamo Square Park. Back at my house, Jeremy's rolling around in my new ergonomic chair that hurts me. Of course I need to piss again, bitch it's been six months and you haven't gulped down my piss yet! Then there's my come in yellow sticky gobs all over his face, and wow it smells, I rub my face against Jeremy's and we lie down. His note says: I can't wait for the next six months.

This guy's so big from steroids, he's almost like a weird animal— so hard in some places and saggy in others. I'm worried that his dick will never be one of the hard places, but then he pulls it out of my mouth and shoots. He moves over to the computer and shows me a picture on the screen, some guy's jerking off. Who's that? You. It's not me. He doesn't believe it.

The cab driver is eating the smelliest pizza and asking me too many questions. I get so tired and then of course I'm depressed, then I want sex to take me out of it—even though it never does—and then I'm more tired, and more depressed. On a radio health show, an announcer says you need to change your lifestyle, but I've already changed everything, what's the next step? The yoga teacher hugs everyone goodbye, which is sweet, though final relaxation makes my whole body hurt again. At Whole Foods, this woman comes up to me in line and says I used to do what you do, for a living. How does she know I'm a whore? She says I've been listening to the intercom and they're onto you. I realize she means stealing—I mean bargain shopping—and everything sinks down inside but the floor's not moving. Thanks, I say, and scan the store, making sure that I'm yawning. The security guard's not even glancing my way, no one looks ready to jump me, but what if this is it? Or what if that woman's undercover security?

I decide the woman's wrong, wait casually for the elevator but my heart is thumping—is shoplifting really worth all this stress? I almost jump because someone's waiting at the door, but it's just a customer reading *Yoga Magazine*. Outside, it's extra-foggy and I'm kind of hoping the woman comes out to talk to me, I want to know what she did for a living. Whether she was really trying to help me. Whether they were really following me on the intercom. Or whether she just got paranoid because everyone was staring at my unconventional fashion. She was the only other person there who looked out of place—a black woman who wasn't particularly bourgie.

Rhania tells me she's feeling a little disoriented, painting murals in the bathroom at the Lexington for eight hours a day—paint fumes and piss, not to mention all the free cocktails. I pick up the charger for my electric toothbrush and roaches come pouring out of it, dammit the roach motels keep filling and filling, but so many of the roaches can't afford it! I hate being sick—I'm exhausted enough already. With my great luck, I wake up wired at 8 a.m. anyway. Chiropractic makes me calm, but does it help for more than five minutes?

In preparation for Gay Shame, we make a Budweiser Vomitorium—a six-foot-tall cardboard structure that people can go inside to vomit out their Budweiser Pride. It looks real. Wheatpasting every night for two weeks and now stenciling, official Gay Shame vomit bags—we're going to be devastating. Jeremy's thinking about taking e the night before at 2 a.m., maybe he'll show up late. Bitch, there is no showing up late—we're interrupting a million people!

I jump in bed for three hours of sleep and wake up into a world of headache and nausea. Suddenly I'm wired, ripping apart jeans to make daisy-dukes and it's hard work, definitely not helping my repetitive stress injury drama. I keep ripping and ripping—more ass, more ass! Then I'm high, taking deep deep deep breaths and digging through my closet for prom dresses to rip apart.

Everyone's partying and I'm sick, don't want to party anyway but Pride is the most depressing time of the year. Except for Thanksgiving, Christmas, and July 4th. I keep saying tomorrow I'll feel better, tomorrow I'll feel better. The daisy-dukes get me so high that I'm worried I'm not going to be able to sleep. Then I start coming down: breathe, stretch, breathe. My forearms are burning, why am I so fucking fragile? I'll give you three choices: a. incest, b. incest, c. incest.

One a.m. and I'm putting together my outfit, Socket says I've never seen you with this much energy before. Trying out the runway: Modesto thinks she's New York, Modesto thinks she's New York on a budget. I just keep ripping and ripping the daisy-dukes. Well, they're already ripped but I'm still ripping until the back is just a denim g-string, front a cock flap over rainbow fishnets and my ass looks juicy. Two lace teddies and then just the bows and shoulders off a red velvet prom dress. The frosted mullet wig sprayed to the sky and yes honey the Budweiser visor, rainbow barcode that says Be Yourself. Of course the slippers made of Prada labels and oh the jewels and glitter over smeared lipstick, lovely lovely lovely lipstick, well that's tomorrow.

Okay, tomorrow: I really get up at 7 a.m. Did I mention the burnt

U.S. flag hanging out of my back pocket? I stick a huge 2(x)ist under-wear label on my ass, the makeup, Socket borrows some accessories and we're out of here and into what, the heat? 10 a.m. and it's already hot—good thing we're prepared with sunscreen. No cabs while we're waiting for the bus, luckily the detour goes right to Alex's house.

Brodie's so hung-over he's demolished, everyone's a bit sketchy but gorgeous—Rhania on stilts in a dress made of garbage bags; Karoline in an outfit made of Gap, Starbucks and Abercrombie shopping bags; Ralowe with a huge black wig, pig's nose and fatigue short shorts. Fast-forward to Ninth and Mission: we've got a crowd, a brass band, George Michael and Rosie O'Donnell buttons, a KPFA reporter, shopping carts full of food, the van filled with sofas to install in the middle of the parade, the sound system, the vomit bags. Are we ready to confront the rabid monster of assimilation? Are we ready for a devastating mobilization of queer brilliance? We try to burn rainbow flags, but they melt because they're plastic and every-one yells BURN BABY BURN anyway.

The band plays, we march, it's festive, I'm high—but shit, every-one's left the sofas behind, how are we going to block the parade? I'm gathering helpers, but people are already at the barricades. Then suddenly it's the cops pounding us and everyone backing up, cops dragging someone off but I can't write anymore because my hand burns, never learns, yearns and yearns and yearns! I wake up in the middle of the night wired like I couldn't possibly have gotten up at 7 a.m., what are you crazy?

But the point is that pretty soon I'm thinking about this random guy who pulled someone aside and said if you hadn't shut the door for the cops, our sister would still be out here with us. Because everyone was fighting the cops, they were dragging Everly into Burger King through the crowd shouting Whopper Copper! At the time I was just amazed that we could actually fight the cops with-out getting beaten bloody or shot dead à la New York. But when I wake up in the middle of the night, I start crying because I think this guy really meant sister.

I don't mean to suggest that activism appears out of nowhere, like Jackie Collins in Lafayette Park. Of course it also takes all those dark nights crouching in the shadows. Back when I was nineteen, I discovered David Wojnarowicz's *Close to the Knives*, which was the first time I found writing that held my overwhelming rage combined with a sense of maybe a little bit of hope in a world of loss. David was already lost when I found him in an obituary, perhaps this allowed me to treasure him more. He knew that activism meant driving feeling into meaning.

I knew Jeremy wouldn't show, but I'm really angry about it anyway—it's what I've been working on for months. I tell her she's tired and she agrees and I feel better. Someone leaves a message: I'm an old lady now, but I want to thank the young people of today for still carrying on what needs to be done. Chrissie calls: I need to go to the beach, I know I'd be terrible company, but I need terrible company.

Jeremy and I get it on in Buena Vista and it's fun, except that I get 64 bug bites. Yes, it's the same place in Buena Vista where this book starts, but this time it's all in Jeremy's mouth, yum. Even though I saw the bugs biting me, and there was nothing green in sight because it had all been cleared away to keep out the fags, I still wonder if I have poison ivy. There's no business like show business!

At therapy, I'm my mother screaming Di-loaded, get me some of that loaded Dilaudid! The weirdest things come up. Some of it makes sense and some of it I've never even imagined, which means it makes more sense. I don't even know what Dilaudid is. Rue says it's an opiate.

First cab driver says pussy's cheaper in Reno. Second cab driver says that Carlos Santana, fuck man! In between is the trick who's a lawyer. He doesn't remember me, I play along, he tells me about his book again, I pretend to come in the condom in his ass, he comes twice. Then he says I lost track of time, I'll give you $200. Lawyers don't lose track of time. I say you're cheap, squeeze out an extra twenty—he's so rich, it's a joke—I run to Carlos Santana. The next trick is moving out as soon as he comes all over his sweatshirt.

Zan says he went to the new bar in New York's financial district after the drag march and two guys fucked onstage. I want to know what Zan wore to the drag march, but she says of course I washed it all off before I went to the bar, I'm not a bimbo. I say you mean a hero. She says I know how to get laid, I can be a hero some other time.

Rhania's Party Like a Hooker actually turns out to be fun. Everyone's joking with me because I'm the hooker and they want to know how to party. You arrive, get a call, leave. On my way out, some random woman wants me to buy her a cocktail? Crazy lesbo. I've come to see Rhania's S.C.U.B. Manifesto—Society for Cutting Up Boxes. One bathroom is before—cardboard. The other is after—birds flying beyond walls.

At hatha yoga, I can't do anything on my hands, but it's still better than nothing. Afterwards, I feel stronger until I get outside and depression sets in like hair dye. Permanent? The bus driver makes me pay because my transfer has expired, bitch this is San Francisco! I want to kill him. Zan says he's moving to New York, a vortex opened up after 9-11 and people finally treat each other well, all these amazing things are happening. Is she doing drugs?

The St. Francis has fallen on hard times—the lobby chandelier looks grand, but the carpet in the hallway looks like a bad flashback from the seventies. The bathroom in my trick's room is a disgrace—scratches on the floor, chrome peeling off the handles of the cabinet, shade missing from the window, which is—gasp—black-framed. In an all-white bathroom! Can you believe the security guard at Whole Foods has started following me around? In therapy, I'm crying about my mother, all the little animals that can't take care of themselves—seals and sheep and mice—they never meant anybody harm! Pearls: they're beautiful, but entire coral reefs are destroyed for them. All the little animals and me, my mother's claws digging in. The smell of her period in my face, I don't want to get graphic here but here's graphic.

Did I mention last week's therapy, where I became my mother? Saying: I don't know what to do about those brats, I think he does something to them 'cause when they come back upstairs, they're dead—just give me some more of that Di-loaded. At home, she actually calls me and why do I talk to her? End up becoming her therapist; she says sometimes I get so depressed about you that I don't want to live anymore.

Rue calls me on my cellphone, his voice is so tense. I say: are you high? He says: no, but there's a lot going on, can I come over your house, I'm nearby. I say: I'm at Cha-ya with Jeremy, do you need me to come meet you? Rue needs me, Jeremy drops me off at the BART and then I start crying because Rue never asks for help, what if he tested positive and I don't want to cry right when he says it. Some healer-type person on the BART looks at me and says we are all born two-legged creatures; our goal is to become human.

FISH TANK

◉   ◉   ◉   ◉

I'm kissing Rue's ears and forehead and he starts sobbing softly, tears running down his face I'm kissing them it feel romantic. Maybe that's the wrong word—I'm wondering about the way beauty accompanies sadness and whether that's scary. I look at Rue's eyes, so much softness and yearning. All that glassy green and why do I look away?

I hold Rue and he says sometimes I just wish I could spit it all out, all the horrible things in the world—I've just been so stressed, I need to find what's going to give me the most meaning and I'm just not sure. In Rue's dream, he was worried about a fish tank, how it needed a certain kind of water. He says I've just been so busy, all the doctor's appointments—I've decided not to drink or do drugs at all, it just doesn't make sense when the alcohol and the psych meds were so much a part of what got me to where I am. I mean, I take full responsibility, but there were just all those nights when I blacked out and found myself wandering home at 6 a.m., no idea what I'd just done.

Rue says maybe I stayed negative for so long because I wasn't on any psych meds. I'm glad she brings up the meds because that way I can talk about them. I say honey, you were scary when you were on the highest dosage, you'd get that crazed violent look in your eyes like that time on the beach when you started talking about how wouldn't it be great to know how to kill an animal with your bare hands? I mean, you said that to me and I thought it was the meds, but then I thought maybe you were becoming scary. I didn't want to take away your right to choose. But then your dosage went down and I thought good, she's back.

In one of my dreams, there are hundreds of cops in the kitchen, a naked Latino hustler with a hard-on and I worry that the hustler's going to get arrested. We're in the center of a dark city like Warsaw, above it all in a fetish bar/hotel-for-Pride but it's also organized crime and dangerous red chandeliers. In my second dream, there's a huge cop, towering over the rich straight couple that are accusing me of stealing the woman's purse on the beach, before I even get to my trick's house. How am I going to defend myself?

I wake up to a message from Jeremy saying I can't wait to see you. I go over to meet him in the East Bay and we eat at Cha-ya, and then go over to his house to lie in bed because he's tired from doing K all weekend. It just feels so great lying there with him, especially hugging him from behind which is the way he likes it, even if it makes my shoulder hurt. I want someone to come in and snap a photo.

We go to Aquatic Park because Sarah's home. I want to have sex in the apartment anyway, but I guess there is only that sheet separating Jeremy's bed in the closet from the rest of the apartment. We walk out on this dock to a pagoda and etch M + J into the railing because Mattilda + Jeremy is too hard to write. A woman walks her dog as the sun goes down and the fags start arriving, Jeremy says does she know what goes on in this park? The mosquitoes are biting my legs while Jeremy's sucking my cock—which he's become an expert at, seven months really helps—then he's holding me from behind while I shoot deep into the trees, and the woman throws a ball for her dog with one of those ball-throwers, and a few guys sort of watch. Jeremy hugs me and says I love you and it's so sweet. I always resist saying I love you after sex 'cause I'm thinking that's cheesy, but it's weird to resist—it's not some random person, it's beautiful beautiful Jeremy who makes me feel little and strong.

Later, I'm holding Rue outside some terrible party because it's way too smoky for me inside, she says I just want you to know that you're such an inspiration to me, you're so calm and healthy and clear. I'm not sure if I feel calm or healthy or clear—I just feel like crying. I say you're an inspiration to me too; she brightens like a little boy, really? Of course you are—you know that—you always have been. For ten years. We're hugging outside, and when the cops arrive to shut down the party—straight indie rockers and suburban jocks and bad bad music—we're still hugging.

I wake up from a dream where Jeremy wants to die and then he does, just from willing it, and when I wake up I'm scared, even though I know it's just superstition. I call Jeremy anyway and leave a message. Then I get all hypoglycemic and worried about losing him, which happens so fast, my stomach clenches up and I feel nauseous, what if he met someone else? I know it's stupid but I can't help feeling it. At therapy, I close my eyes and picture the exhaustion, my skeleton with blood and guts everywhere, standing in front of me with huge fangs, ready to cut out my heart and eat it. Karen says what do you want it to do? I let it eat my heart and then I'm dead, that skeleton on the ground with bugs and people stepping on it, cracking my ribs. Even though I'm dead, everything still hurts.

Then there's a part of me floating away in a flower basket, seals in a pool but that pool's not big enough for seals. Mountains and lakes for the seals and I'm playing with them, it's so much fun. Then people arrive and kill the seals for their fur, I keep seeing the image from the zoo of seals cut open and their bellies filled with the pennies people throw in the water.

EVERYTHING
SHOULD BE EASY

⊙   ⊙   ⊙   ⊙

Globalization at its worst: someone on the subway in Paris asks
Andee if he knows CeCe Peniston, you know that terrible house
diva. I can't remember what she sings. Then, when I'm on the subway, someone asks me if I was on TV. He means: were you on one
of those talk shows in the mid-nineties about club kids? I say yeah,
I was Farrah Fawcett in *The Burning Bed*.

I get a hot trick—I just love watching his facial expressions and
pounding out grunts. When I say *look at me*, and we come together,
he says that doesn't even happen in the movies. Afterwards, he gives
me a ride home. On O'Farrell, four cops stand over a homeless man
they've hog-tied on the sidewalk. The trick says that's the worst—
having to arrest a dirty person. So much for our connection.

Benjamin says to Ralowe: this stream-of-consciousness thing has
gone too far. We're on our way to a movie at the Four Star. At the
Vietnamese restaurant, all these white yuppies are staring at us. It's
like they've never heard faggots talking about sex in a restaurant
before. Or maybe they're scared of Ralowe's Afro, my earrings, and

Benjamin's makeup. Or my inappropriately gendered and loudly mismatching thrift store finery, Benjamin's professionally coiffed dreadlocks styled into a Mohawk, and all 600 safety pins clinging precariously to Ralowe's threadbare jeans. Or Benjamin's scolding, Ralowe's scowl, and my cackling. Maybe these customers don't like race-mixing or clunky shoes, or maybe they're just listening carefully for the ticking sound of suicide bombs—our bags are big. And Benjamin is loud—sometimes I wonder who she's talking to.

I make the mistake of stopping at the Dore Alley Street Fair. On the way there, this circuit monster is having a seizure from I-don't-know-what scary drug combination, his friends are holding him up against a wall while another friend runs away to party some more. They're all so tan and buff and tweaked, and I'm worried the guy's going to die, but I don't know how to help. My mood goes so low, I keep saying I need to go home and commit suicide. Ralowe says this is more embarrassing than going to see any Steven Spielberg movie, 'cause I'm always making fun of him for that. He's right; it's so depressing what gay people are. Ralowe hugs me, but I'm still ready to die.

I rush home in a cab, tear off my clothes because really I feel dirty, and Jeremy arrives just as I'm getting dressed. I'm sketchy, we get in bed and it actually works, just resting my hand on his hip makes me so calm.

I show Jeremy how I fuck my kitchen counter, and he holds me from behind—I use olive oil because it's there—I come in a sticky pile instead of the boom-boom-boom. We hold each other in so many ways, days and days and days. My cellphone rings, this guy wants to know if I have a discount for married guys with kids. Yes, of course your straight privilege applies even when you're hiring a man to fuck you. On NPR, involuntary treatment helps people with mental illness to regain control of their lives! First trick wants me to come, and I get hypoglycemic. Thinking: I hate you. I hate you. I hate you. While I'm kissing him. Maybe this isn't so healthy right now, but then he pays me. Second trick is more fun; I like the way his dick beats in my hand after he comes.

After acupuncture, I feel kind of high but crashing, like everything in the world could lift away and I'd be left walking on the side-walk. Rue says he went to the Powerhouse, there was a guy gnawing at Rue's pants like he couldn't figure out how to open them, the guy was so fucked up. I meet Jeremy at his new place in the Mission; he's so excited about it. He says isn't this the best apartment—I could live here for the rest of my life. It's a railroad apartment that's been fixed up since its tenement days: new light fixtures and kitchen appliances, and very shiny pine floors—I wouldn't want to pay $1800 for it, but I wouldn't want to live with all the hipsters and yuppies in the Mission, even if it was free—I'd get too depressed and have to move to another city. I keep this to myself. Jeremy and I lie in bed for a while and then I take him out to Millennium—on our way, we're holding hands on Eighteenth St. and it's funny, flashbacks of Zan from years ago—the Mission, holding hands. Jeremy looks so cute in the blue shirt with brown tie, and the sparkly blue hoop earrings I got him.

At Millennium, this woman says to her friend: we meet in the most exotic places, remember Uruguay? But otherwise it's so fun, eating slowly and enjoying it, sharing blueberry blackened tempeh and marinated chanterelle mushrooms with Jeremy, and staring at him until he gets nervous and starts to talk a lot. We go back to his house and of course he comes on my face, then he's drifting off while I'm hugging him and slowly grinding into his side. I keep asking: is this okay? He says yeah, it's lulling me to sleep. I keep grinding, and the pressure on the top of my dick feels so good, slowly faster then harder, hugging Jeremy tighter and tighter and even panting until I just love that I'm screaming and I'm here in bed with Jeremy. He turns around to kiss me, those lips and hands and sweet sweet droopy eyelids. Afterwards, I'm just so fucking high, watching the reflection of the lamp on the ceiling while Jeremy tries to sleep.

When Jeremy gives up on the nap, we talk about one of his linguistics terms—bilabial slips, or is it stops? I think it's when two consonant sounds are different because with one you use the vocal chords and with the other you don't: mmm and nnn. We practice them. At Whole Foods, this old queen in tweed says I love your outfit, the patterns and the colors—how sweet. It's one of my contrasting plaid days, and at least the security guard isn't following me—I get free condoms and passionflower tincture, and only spend $9.

Rue says he feels like there are six hamsters in wet suits doing goofy-foot in his intestines. And why can't Wylie have an easy conversation, Rue's tired of being reminded he has the AIDS. I'm worried that we're not connecting, but Ralowe says: seeing you two interact gives me hope in the world. On the radio, Roxanne Dunbar-Ortiz talks about a class she's teaching called The Sexuality of Terrorism: most of my students were involved in the military, they taught me a lot of what I know—they didn't like what was happening to them, and they wanted to figure out how to stop it.

But I can't remember: am I always this depressed? There was a window of opportunity after I got a massage, but it was a closed window. I throw a book off my fire escape because it's boring. Help! I can't rearrange the clothes and papers on the sofas, papers on the table, papers on the desk. My hands hurt too much to write, my head hurts too much to think. Oh the sadness, pure madness! It's too early to go to bed, and I never sleep well anyway. Why are there hills in my floor? After my nap, this guy comes over and I suck his cock, it puts me in a good mood, then Adam X is taking me to the dark electro techno dance floor, but there's my sinus headache—pulling my eyes into caves.

This guy asks Jaysen and me for money at the BART, then as soon as Jaysen drives away, he says: you're gonna burn in hell for being gay. Doesn't even raise his voice—just the facts, ma'am. Rhania says she licked someone's nose that had a lot of coke in it, and got a stomachache. Help—somebody vacuum up the leftovers before the roaches arrive in V-formation like seagulls locked up! This trick wants to spank me but he can't afford much, then he just wants to meet me and thank me for my time. The bitch makes me miss Jeremy's call, I get so upset and angry with myself that I'm screaming and hitting a book against my head. Okay, so I haven't eaten yet. I spend the whole day taking naps, winter in August and I love the way the right side of my jaw goes numb—retro-futurism at its finest! At the end of the movie, a plane drives up on the beach—just another runway, silly. Get in.

The Palace is always impressive, with its endless lobby of chandeliers, but what is this crap they have as shampoo? At the Palomar, they serve only Aveda—the bath bar and rosemary mint shampoos are my favorites. I'd never buy them because I'm sure they have tons of preservatives, but I love my luxurious shower. Can you believe they sell every item in the rooms at the W? The bed is $700, or maybe that's just the extra pillow top—the desk is $1400. I'm sick of seeing that cheesy photo in the bathroom: "Datura and Stone." I guess a Datura is something that looks like a calla lily.

The W has Aveda products, but not the bath bar. The blue light in the elevator is cute, but the chrome walls are scuffed, and why are people drinking cocktails in an elevator? Back at the Palace, everything except the toiletries is absolutely perfect and posh, old money but not falling apart like the Fairmont, though the Jacuzzi doesn't work. I take a bubble bath.

I've tried everything to get rid of this jock itch. First, the anti-fungal powder with grapefruit seed extract and tea tree oil. Then chaparral tincture, which Rue suggested—it burned! I diluted it, but that just made my fingers sticky. Then I tried some anti-itching lotion for all areas, but honey that was so painful I had to jump into a cold shower and scream. Tinactin didn't work either—I don't know what to do, when the trick in the Palace rubs my balls, I almost bite my lip. He says: the hardest part is saying goodbye.

So much powder in my crotch, is it affecting my sinuses? Clouds in my apartment—the fog has moved in. But these are dust clouds; Vegas in my heart and my balls still itch! I thought maybe this homeopathic florazone cream was working, but the burning wakes me up at 9 a.m. Jock itch is my payback for being such a jock, I guess, though I can barely tie my shoes without hurting something.

I meet Rhania and Erica in the Castro, where I get that wonderful desperate-longing-for-something-I-hate feeling. What's great is that I have Jeremy, beautiful Jeremy—last night he put noodles on his head like a wig, do I look weird this way? No, you just look special. Later, he wasn't horny because he'd just had sex in the bathrooms. I was kind of annoyed, but I asked him how that made him feel. He said I don't like talking about my feelings. Either way,

I kissed and kissed him until I felt like sleeping there, but had to leave because of today's 2 p.m. trick at my house.

Later, Jeremy's sketchy and we have one of those annoying conversations. He says ginkgo biloba—it doesn't help your memory, natural health is a niche market ploy! Why do I argue with him? Later, we have a second annoying conversation—is San Francisco a progressive city? This one's ongoing; today Jeremy thinks SF is progressive because homeless people can still get general assistance, even if it might get taken away at the ballot. $370 a month—how progressive!

I get so exhausted that I can't possibly function, we go to my house and Jeremy wants to leave. I thought we were going to take a nap together—that's one of my favorite things. But this time Jeremy doesn't want to take a nap, or leave and come back either—he wants to go drinking with someone he doesn't even like that much. I get all dramatic, catch myself changing my expression when Jeremy looks at me, so I'll look okay. I tell him that. I feel really vulnerable. I ask him to stay. I say: I just feel sad right now—and you make me happier.

Jeremy leaves. I take a nap. When I get up, I want drugs so badly that I can't leave the house. I talk to Jaysen, then Zero, then Rue, then the phone sex line for way too long, and then I go to bed.

The next day I've got it all figured out, so I'm in a better mood. I ask Jeremy if he'd come over if there were an emergency. He says of course I would—he didn't realize how important it was for him to stay. I need to make sure that he understands. I say: then if it happens again, you'll stay? He agrees and I'm okay, then I get all dressed up, cab driver asks if I'm heading home. It's 4 p.m., and the cab driver means are you heading home from a long night? I get to the Gay Shame meeting, which way is the club? You know, the club. Later, I'm dancing in the street for the tourists, then at Jeremy's housewarming, where straight women and gay boys point to guys and ask each other: is he or isn't he? My plaid shirt and fuchsia hair match the plaid cellophane on the wall—photo op! The best part is that Jeremy keeps saying you're so sexy, hands on my thighs, just between the bloomers and the thigh-highs.

As usual, I love waking up at nine in the morning—with a headache this big, I could take over the world! Heat wave—at Rhania's party, it's so hot that I take off my clothes and put on an apron that says More Time For Misbehavin' Since I've Been Microwavin'. Blake, Annie and I play word games and everyone else sort of gets it, maybe. I'm the first person to arrive and the last to leave—as long as I can sit on this sofa, I can interact with anyone. And share my jock itch powder.

On the 22, this white guy almost falls over this black woman, he says well I guess it is the Fillmore and then he mumbles something about everyone on the bus being black. He says I'm the minority here. I ask the woman what he said, she doesn't know. I say: obviously something offensive. He says: I fought in Vietnam. The woman next to him says so fucking what—you're right, you are a minority here, and we'll take you down—the three of us laugh together. It's a beautiful moment.

At 7:45 a.m., I wake up and every muscle in my face hurts. At 8 a.m., they start the construction next door, feels like my sinuses are filled with every single grain of the debris—how'd they pack it all in? Then come seventeen different fire engines and an ambulance—an ode to city living! I just want to go back to the innocent days when I slept forever and never felt rested.

At 12:41 p.m., I get up and check my voicemail. There's a message from my mother, sent at 12:41 p.m. There's a fine line between awareness and Tourette's syndrome—I call a trick and say hey this is Mattilda. Aaron says your friend Candy from the 7-11 says hi, she's the Pakistani woman who plays folk music when she's working. When her son with red-and-blue hair is working, he plays hard rock. When they're both working, they alternate.

Anyway, Candy told Aaron I reminded her of a friend back home, a dancer. When they first met, she thought something was wrong, so she asked a doctor. He said it's perfectly normal, a certain percentage of babies are born predisposed to be dancers.

In the bathroom of my dream, I piss into the spout of the tub—will it go back up? The bathroom is larger than I thought—three tubs and at least six urinals—I should unlock the door, but in the yard there are these weird animals, like fat cats with big hammer heads. They come running up and I'm scared, they're butting my legs until I lean down to pet them—they just want affection too! At this fancy French restaurant with a trick, there are so many waiters it's ridiculous. I have to put the melon gelée in my napkin because it's the first course. Fruit gives me indigestion. The trick tells me service stories—good service, bad service. Doesn't he realize that I'm in the service industry too? Next to us, this old couple holds hands—it's their thirty-ninth anniversary. Just after dessert, the woman says: you shouldn't have said that we couldn't expect her parents to contribute to the college fund because she's dirt poor. They're not holding hands anymore. He says I didn't say that, I don't even know that phrase. She says yes you did—remember, I was that way too when we met.

In my dream, I'm meeting two people, but I don't know how to say hi to the second one. She's a metal box with arms of steel. Her friend starts pushing her buttons but she doesn't respond. She's a tank with two levels, upstairs is where she is and her friend goes up to see what's wrong. First, the top half of a body comes floating down, but it's Styrofoam. Then the second half, also Styrofoam. There's a garbage bag filled with discarded organs—we've been tricked, this person has bought someone's body to house her own organs and now she's escaped.

I wake up from the dream because fighter jets are flying overhead, one after the other and I'm just going to keep sleeping. My building's shaking and then I get scared—what if this is the end of the world, the anniversary of 9-11 right around the corner and all? I look out the window and it's hundreds of vintage motorcycles driving down Polk Street—what the fuck? I call Rue because the discarded organs are her dream imagery—she sounds all manic, but then she says she was getting shivers down her back, because sure enough—she's been having that dream for months.

Rue says stop stealing my dreams! I say stop invading my consciousness! Jeremy and I have the conversation I've been dreading, delaying, trying to avoid.

It starts because he's smoking in the car and I get in, say oh you don't even bother to open the window when I'm not in the car. I say it in a joking way and I even kiss him first, but he says it's my fucking car; I'll smoke in it if I want to. He looks really upset and angry and full of hate. I say don't talk to me like that—is something wrong? He says maybe something is wrong. I say let's get dinner, and then we can talk about it afterwards.

I get really scared, I think: as soon as we're done with this conversation, I'm going to do coke. Just once—I've gotta feel that high.

We get dinner, I try to taste it but I'm too nervous, afterwards we go to Dolores Park. We're sitting on the staircase at the bottom, or I'm sitting and Jeremy's standing. Jeremy's telling me that he wants his emotional independence. He says he doesn't want to change or question anything about himself just to grow closer to me.

I wonder about my faith, that's the word I think of. Faith that Jeremy will open up to me, if I just keep making myself more vulnerable.

I want to feel vulnerable—I just don't want it to end up destroying me. Jeremy keeps talking about transitioning from being boyfriends to being friends and I'm kind of in shock. I just want to continue holding Jeremy and going to visit the sea lions—friends or boyfriends, whatever. But Jeremy keeps insisting that we need two weeks without talking, to start the grieving process. He's got it all worked out. He keeps saying we have to meet again like we've never met before.

I don't like people who I've never met before—especially when I know all their faults ahead of time. I thought this novel was turning into a love story, but now Jeremy's fucking that up. Did I even mention that our conversation started with Jeremy declaring: we're not having good sex. Sex for him is that aggressive, charged, orgasm-focused activity that's all drive until the comeshot and then it's naptime. Maybe I should have paid more attention to the first time we had sex—at the height of it, he was trying over and over to slide his dick into my asshole without a condom, without asking. Later, when I confronted him about it, he said it was good that I kept angling away.

Jeremy doesn't want to hold me when I feel triggered, or lie in bed petting me for hours—that isn't sex to him. He keeps saying: everything should be easy. Everything should be easy. Everything should be easy.

I don't even know what that means.

WILLPOWER, MINK COATS, HUMANS, CITY ENTERTAINMENT, A DEEPER RELATIONSHIP, SHEEP, RAW KALE, LEFT FIELD, PINWORMS, LAURYN HILL, AND MY SOUND FACTORY MOMENT

◎   ◎   ◎   ◎

Imagine my all-too-common predicament: sweating on my bed as the sun pours in through my window, and this trick's balls smell like fish, but I'm sucking his dick anyway. Every time he touches me, my jock itch burns. I feel like a hooker in a movie—save me from my degradation!

As soon as the sun goes down, it's cold out—what a relief—I was sick of that SoCal realness. If I want LA, I'll fucking move there. Finally I get to the clinic, balls burning and they're playing *The Matrix* in the waiting area. I get an adrenaline rush from all the killing but no gore—maybe that's why people watch these movies. Though some people like the gore too. The doctor says I have contact urethritis—whoops, I mean neuro-dermatitis, 'cause the fungus is gone but it's in my brain—pain pain pain pain PAIN—no, he means I itch and it erupts, I itch more, it never goes away.

Bedtime feels like "Willpower" by Kate Bush, even though I haven't heard that song since I lost the Greenpeace benefit album in high school—don't scratch don't scratch don't fucking scratch.

Jeremy thinks you can't change anything by willing it—look at me now, bitch. She's got Whiteboy Syndrome—doesn't want to work on anything, doesn't want to feel vulnerable. Oh no, the sun's coming out—turn it off!

At the Power Exchange, I'm sucking this guy's dick, he's shoving it into the back of my throat, I can feel the skin stretching—internal yoga. This other guy says, to the guy I'm sucking: that's a great blow job, you better come—and the guy pulls his dick out of my mouth and walks away. Doesn't matter because I'm shooting, though physical contact might make it better. The second guy watches and then walks away too. Ah, the community!

In the bathroom, this guy's taken the wrong combination of drugs. First he's banging his head against the marble stall walls, and then he's struggling to do something at the sink—anything—while his whole body lurches out of control. Eyes bugging in and out, he keeps lunging—definite seizure material, one step away from the guy at Dore Alley. So much extra pain but still no weight gain—flawless! Outside, there's a line-up of oh-so-sexy smoking teeth-grinders, cab driver asleep at the wheel. I'll take the next cab, thanks.

Why do they tell you to take antihistamines before bed? I take this one for my itch and then it's heartburn city, like I didn't already have palpitations. When I wake up—wait, I can't wake up! It's like someone shot a hole through my forehead 'cause there's no center, all around is just pain. Nothing works except maybe my brain. I can hardly even piss. If I keep this hooded sweatshirt over my head, will the world go away?

In therapy, I'm two years old, looking at my sister and she's so cute but so scared. She doesn't like being naked; they do things to her when she's naked. They do things to me too, but I'm older.

Then I see all the cute seals that are killed for mink coats, and the lobsters people boil alive, and then all the little kids on buses who aren't protected and you can see it 'cause their eyes are rolled back, and no one does anything. Then I'm crying for all these little kids, I mean bawling like I haven't done in months or maybe even years. I hate humans so much, I'm crying and crying because what can I possibly do? When I leave the office, I don't quite feel hopeful but I feel like more of myself.

I go to Ralowe's show at the End Up. The doorman throws away my eye-drops and water—at least he lets me keep my food or I'd be tweaking with the rest of the girls in this legendary speed den. Salim says what's a tweaker? My favorite part is when Ralowe pretends to have a fit, like a seizure but he keeps on rapping, going from really fast to really slow, and afterwards we head over to City Entertainment, but it's way too boring for me—standing in the hallway waiting for action, reaction, distraction, traction—forget satisfaction. Though I must admit that I'm enjoying the giant poster of syphilis sores, Health Department love just oozing out at us.

I know I'm living in the Tenderloin, because it's 3 a.m. and an alarm in some building has been going off for five hours. In the morning, I feed the pigeons dandelion greens, scallions, shiitake mushroom stems and onion skins. It's hard to write about Jeremy because I talk about him so much. When will I stop feeling hopeless? On the phone, I have this sudden insight that if Jeremy would open up about his emotions, then maybe we could have a deeper relationship—I could hold him while he cried and cried, every tear intensifying my love! Then I remember he doesn't want a deeper relationship.

This guy comes over from the phone sex line, what a chore. Was I this compulsive before I met Jeremy, sitting at home all day just trying to hook up? Outside, this guy says who are you—Little Bo Peep? Why yes, of course—but where are my fucking sheep? The guy who collides into me says stop fucking following me. Benjamin wants to know who's in my support system. I drink four glasses of water.

One minute I'm desperate to come, the next minute I can't even imagine it. The taxi driver is quitting smoking in twenty days. He says: the New Century Theatre is always so crowded because it's practically a brothel, they do nasty things at Mitchell Brothers too, but they don't go that far. I'm wearing Jeremy's underwear, first I think I don't want that bitch's underwear, but then I think: that bitch isn't getting her underwear back from me. Do you know what I'm saying? No—do you know what I'm saying? Thank you.

I think the pigeons prefer raw kale to steamed kale. Personally, I can't eat kale unless it's cooked. I get a trick at the Travelodge down the street from my house, it's two guys and I'm supposed to suck them both off. The first one's cute and young and Latino and the second one's the usual. They're from Fresno. Finally the first one comes and then it's daddy's turn, he says: I won't take as long. Gold chain under wrinkled neck and too much tan, but at least he powders his snatch. He comes and is that really blood? Oh no, it's a horror movie remake! I go in the bathroom to check my mouth. It's time to go back to the clinic.

Talk about nurse! The young one's out to get Diet Coke for daddy, who says we don't have sex, I'm old enough to be his—father, well—grandfather. And mine too, sweetie, except that if daddy had given me an STD in the good old days of my so-called childhood, well maybe that would have tipped someone off. Though if they're willing to ignore everything else, pinworms piling up like dried potatoes in the wrong cabinet—well, maybe not.

Another sunny day in San Francisco and I'm ready for winter. Though then I have a trick with graffiti on his walls, he hired someone to paint it, and I almost want to fuck him longer. Outside, it's the right night, foggy and damp and not too cold. There's a cute cat outside of the Hayes Street convalescent home. I feel so close to this cat, its strong head and all those lost cats from my childhood, cut open never pasted back together. But this cat is here, living for the sidewalk. In Alamo Square Park, the moon is just past full, trees relaxing upward with me, the dark sky. It's the right kind of night, when suddenly I can breathe, I feel calmer—I'd even use the word "happy."

Table tennis in your eyes, honey—they only call it table tennis after 7 a.m., before then it's just ping-pong. For some reason, I always wait until every restaurant in the city is closed before I go out for food. Hypoglycemia strikes and this girl is crying behind the scaffolding across the street, I want to invite her up for tea. I follow her, dark sunglasses and a dark bob, dark skin and a red top that shows her broad tranny shoulders. I wait too long.

Did I mention my dinner with Jeremy? Just dinner, we're only allowed to have dinner. There's a car parked nearby, with planters attached to all the flat surfaces, and not cactuses but what do you call them? Succulents, growing out of the planters. Jeremy hugs me and then we're off to dinner, I'm nervous. He wants to know why. I let him think about it. He asks me what else I've been doing. I say it'll come up. He's so afraid of the silent spaces. He surprises me by saying that yes, he does want emotional intimacy, though later he qualifies that: to a point. We talk about his new roommate's eating disorder, is it anorexia or bulimia? What can you do?

When Jeremy comes over to my side of the booth, that's when I really love him—and when I really feel sad. His touch feels too powerful. He says I've missed you and that's sweet, really sweet. He says in six months, we can re-evaluate if this isn't working for you. Always on his terms. At home, my jock itch starts burning again. I wake up from a dream where I squeeze my foot and a stream of mud comes out, then a pebble, then—is that shit? When I get out of bed, I twist my ankle.

Cala Foods at 2 a.m. and every drunk is trying to buy liquor. I get gum from the machine, my last occasional drug. I chew it and then crash, think about reading Jeremy—just tearing her apart—bitch, do you know who I am? Really I just miss holding her hand at movies. I'm at Espresso Brava for the Gay Shame meeting and Jeremy walks by, big smiling doll-face. Did everyone notice how fake that was? The good news is that there are a lot of people with the capability of getting online while watching TV at the same time.

Benjamin says: I was in the bathroom at City College and these white boys there, they take a look at my black cock but they're too scared to do anything. This black boy though—he was just as fine as any of these white boys, actually finer. He knew what he wanted. That's what I need—someone who sits down on it like he's not gonna let go—I'm not gonna give it up, this is mine. Forget the white boy bullshit. She says it a couple of times. Forget the white boy bullshit.

Speaking of aspirations, why on earth do I go to the Power Exchange? I just want to walk around for an hour and a half without any hope of getting fresh air. I want to hang out with tweakers; one of them whistles at me so I turn around—my friend thinks you're hot, he says. Something about the place actually calms me, and it's not the circular pattern of my walk, how Zen! It's the music, but why don't I just go out dancing once in a while? I'm worried about the pain in the arches of my feet, but it doesn't really help to walk in circles.

This woman on Geary says I like your colors, you have to be brave to wear those colors, I wish I were that brave when I was young. Crying while listening to the radio—the U.S. demands immunity in international criminal court, 400,000 protest war in London, half a trillion dollars spent putting people of color behind bars in the drug war, stiffening blood-caked corpses lining the streets of Sierra Leone. I know I mentioned that the pigeons prefer raw vegetables to steamed, but I'm not sure about the roaches. The good thing about being really tan at one point is that I can go out in the sun late in the day for a half hour and boom I'm golden.

Jaysen quits smoking, says he went out the last few nights and he felt like his soul was being rubbed out with an eraser. At the restaurant, I get a New York flashback—it's because it's so crowded and they're playing Lauryn Hill, plus everyone's drinking fancy cocktails. Maybe I should just have a few cocktails. Three a.m. and I can hear someone choking and vomiting down below, my contacts are off so all the lights blur. I want to have a contest for worst night of sleep in my life, but there are just way too many contestants. And I don't know what to do about the seal stuffed animal Jeremy gave me. Before, it made me so happy, now it's just another loneliness death wish. Benjamin says can you help me write my bio—I know you can't type because of your pain, but maybe Ralowe could type and you could write. I just need help; I'm asking for help, I need help.

My chiropractor goes to the Folsom Street Fair with his girlfriend; he says there were two interesting things. He leans in to whisper: this guy had the biggest dick I've ever seen, I looked over at Elaine and her mouth was hanging open, I said close your mouth Elaine. Later on, there were these two bears just going at it, sucking and fucking and sucking and fucking—two bears!

Billeil's got a new slogan: I'm okay with homelessness, as long as they keep it in the bedroom. Every time I see a VW convertible, I think of Jeremy—I never realized it was such a popular car. Paper failure—I feel like a failure too. Rue says did you fan your paper before you put it in? That's so *Paris Is Burning*. This trick says I'm an older man but I still have all my hair and most of my teeth, and my tastes are roughly the same as Oscar Wilde.

A trick right on Buena Vista Park—how convenient! I'm not gonna come, I'm not gonna come, I'm not gonna come. He collects telephones in boxes—until the late '70s, you could only rent phones and you had to pay extra for colored ones. The first guy in the park pulls away before he shoots, three shots—is three my magic number? He says I haven't come in a month. The second guy approaches me with a big smile, touching my French cuffs: I thought you had carpal tunnel. I do have tendonitis, but these are just sleeves. We hold hands. No boyfriend and now I'm back to wanting romance from anonymous sex. Just a smile brings back my libido, I'm craving more but not in a desperate way. Just like I feel good and I want it to last. Walking downhill from Buena Vista destroys my feet, later on a tweaker trick fucks me and the condom breaks. Polyurethane condoms are shit. Another VW convertible drives by.

Ralowe, Benjamin and I hang out at Taqueria Cancun for way too long. There's so much mold it's unbelievable—in the front, it's rotten flowers and in the back, it's salsa from twelve years ago. Co-ed bathroom and the seat is covered in piss, Benjamin tells me I have gender guilt. So? Ralowe says the only art is activism. Benjamin says all art is amoral. Oh, no!

A drunken straight boy sitting outside of Cala Foods tells me I'm sexy, that's how I know he's straight—a faggot would never say something so nice. We can't go to his house because of his roommate. I say let's do it in the alley. He starts with kissing—what a novelty! He's Benjamin's usual pick-up, closeted but he knows what he wants, ravenous for my cock. His roommate rides by on a bike, but doesn't see us.

Fighter jets flying over my bed—please no war, please no war! Allison's kitten dies and so does Sonia, our childhood cat. Benjamin, Ralowe and I just can't stop talking, I make them quinoa and we have a 2 a.m. family moment listening to the Fugees "Killing Me Softly" because I think it's the only good thing Lauryn Hill ever did—and then Kevin Aviance, because I think she's genius, or at least she used to be. I mean, my Sound Factory moment was when I saw Kevin Aviance do the Noon runway, gold stilettos and short-short metallic dress with a huge Afro, every step it was like she was going to fall over—but she never did. Then the climax was when she threw off the Afro, head shaved to the skin and I almost gasped. My ecstasy was over, the K had faded, but I was enthralled.

I get wired talking about electro and minimal house with booming bass, Kraftwerk and Save the Robots, every backroom bar in New York and why not here? Benjamin used to live in New York too and Ralowe's curious. Then I put on "Everybody Dance Now" and it's just what we need. Benjamin says she's going to make a goth metal opera version and I can't wait.

DIAMOND BRACELETS

⊙   ⊙   ⊙   ⊙

You know those tricks that've had 50 years of practice sucking cock—and I do mean 50 years—and still it's sandpaper city. What's up with that? This straight boy on the street says you remind me of Alice in Wonderland, how sweet! Though I think my father molested me during that movie. Alice just kept falling and falling.

Three a.m. and of course I'm wired—remember the early nineties? Tweakin' and tweezin', tweakin' and tweazin'. Every time a trick hangs up on me, I gain a renewed faith in humanity—someone really cares! Looking worse in the mirror, do you believe in insurance? Aaron says there's an online community called pneumothorax.com—his collapsed lung finally has a home: Donna Karan Donna Karan Donna Karan.

Fighter jets and fire engines, oh it's my mother's birthday! She leaves a message; did she really say I love you? More sirens. I'm so dehydrated and Congress authorizes President Bush to wage war against Iraq while fighter jets just keep flying over and over. Everyone in the street stops to stare. But where are all those jets going?

The U.S. government is already talking about post-war occupation of Iraq, and the tendons in my feet and hands are burning. The sky is still so loud—is that a bomb? So much pain in my head, everybody's allergic to war. But wait—there's good news: the stock market is up 7.8 percent in two days and you've been invited to celebrate Disney's 100th Anniversary with a four-day, three-night vacation stay in Orlando, Florida, near world-famous Walt Disney World. Plus, you'll enjoy three days/two nights on the white sand beaches of Daytona—all for $99 per person. The confirmation for your invitation is Magical 752.

News brief: someone on the phone sex line used the word tender! Apparently the roaches enjoy the base of my electric toothbrush, a safe warm home for the fringe. I hate it when I get so exhausted that I can't function, and then I get depressed—wait, that happens every day. My trick loves this weather—we have this weather every night. If I stayed in bed for two months, who would feed me?

This trick says wasn't it fun to watch the Blue Angels? A taxi driver tells me air shows are America's number one pastime. The toast at 7 a.m. is so dry, and I can feel my depression creeping up on me—HELP! There's a good luck penny in the hallway—okay, everything's going to be fine. Sick, sick, sick, sick—kick!

My next trick has such pale skin, reminds me of when I was afraid of the sun too—was I that pale? My favorite moment is when I tell him his hair is soft; he says thanks, I work on it. Felix's mixing takes me out of depression, through nostalgia and into the border area. Like I could cry, or fly. Which do I prefer—using a dildo and fucking up my hand, or using my dick and inflaming my jock itch? The bride is arriving soon, and I must please her. Over the phone, he says: I just got in from Paris and I feel like shit, are you up for fucking? I just got in from Paris and I feel like shit, are you up for fucking? I just got in from Paris and I feel like shit, are you up for fucking?

As soon as the trick walks in, I know I'm not going to be able to fuck him. He's working the receding hairline with gooey gray ponytail and blue contacts to contrast his leather tanning salon skin, Fila jumpsuit and big silver rings on all his fingers, round tortoiseshell eyeglasses. This girl is married, with kids—and now she needs tea, then a shower. But God Save the Queen, he comes while I'm jerking him off. Then the best part is when he tells me about his town, he says the racial composition is twenty-five different shades of white, and the architecture is like Taco Bell designed heaven.

In the depressed area of the trick's town, the houses go for $500,000, but to really fit in you need to own not only a pool, but an indoor pool, a North-South tennis court and a two-story garage for the $500,000 RV. It's not just a gated community; they've got armed guards on patrol. Everywhere there are blue-haired ladies in designer jeans wearing enough diamond bracelets to get a hernia.

Did I mention the trick's umbilical hernia, a bubble of mushy skin oozing out of his belly button like a force field? Rich people are so glamorous. The next trick hands me a glass of tap water—the bitch doesn't know if she can get money out of the bank, but her apartment must be worth three million, and the doorman has to unlock the elevator. This is just the San Francisco apartment.

Dreams of new houseplants, changing what it says on the computer screen, and stress, stress, stress! Did I mention Ralowe's show? We performed together at this hipster nightmare, he finished the night with layers of noise, drums that were just another instrument on top of the machines and then Ralowe shaking his body and shouting rap vocals over the commotion. It was delicious. Everyone left.

Today the sun is filtering through the clouds, and I'm rooting for the clouds. Shit—here comes the sun—and is it really 4 p.m.? All the little memories loading me down—like I'm eating tom kha soup with Rue, and Jeremy introduced me to that soup. Buying plants together, going to visit the sea lions and I can't bring myself to get rid of the stuffed animals, even though they just make me think of petting Jeremy, sweet Jeremy. I want to call him and tell him I miss him, but I don't want to call him.

I know it's dangerous to get all teary-eyed about the time when my white boyfriend introduced me to a Thai specialty, but that's how nostalgia works—nostalgia is dangerous. Kayti remembers when she used to say she was Persian, so people wouldn't know that she was Latina—people thought it was more glamorous to be from Persia; we both had a lot of Persian friends. Kayti says they were really from Iran, right?

Dreams that they've changed my front door, can I get out? I'm thinking about how many pairs of eyes we look into each day—there's this guy on the bus with beautiful gray eyes, I can't stop looking. I catch another eye in the back, just one, a blond guy. The bus arrives. At home, I jerk off so I don't have to think about hooking up.

I'm telling Justin and Owen about Jeremy, and then all of the sudden ten people show up at their house, I guess it's 2 a.m. Owen says you switch so easily into social mode. I don't know what mode I'm in, suddenly I've got so much energy, and Xylor says I saw you earlier and I was telling somebody about your outfit—it was the most preposterous combination of colors I've ever seen, I even remembered the red socks, though it didn't make sense. The person I was talking to said yeah, Mattilda likes red socks.

Ralowe starts freestyling and I'm dancing on top of the ottoman, it's all about the hands and body twisting and tensening, breathe in, out. Almost falling off and recovering. I have so much energy, it's crazy—and too late, really. Xylor says I wonder why. I say no, that's not why. She looks at my eyes. Well, maybe you're just a night person.

I'm so glad everyone goes outside to smoke, Billeil even checks to make sure. Ralowe and I leave; I'm looking at the doors in front of the apartment. The apartment's so long and thin, was it made for immigrant workers or did they subdivide it? Then I'm looking into the funeral home, and wait the doorframe next door is gorgeous and Ralowe says he's exhausted. I'm getting exhausted too.

Just as I'm hailing a taxi, the bus comes. Ralowe tries to get on the back and the bus driver calls him out—get off the bus, he says. Ralowe gets off; I'm waving him to the front and the bus driver speeds away. This woman says just because they're black, they think they can get on for free. The bus driver, who's black, says shut your mouth already. The woman looks at me, she says your daddy raped you and that's why you're a faggot. I say my daddy raped me, but that's not why I'm a faggot. She says your daddy raped you and that's why you're a faggot. I say your problem is that you tasted shit, and then you just kept eating it. She gets off the bus.

I call Ralowe on his cellphone: honey, you should have asked me for a dollar. Ralowe says I'm gonna walk home—all the way to

North Beach? He says: I'm gonna work on this song. I say well I'll call you when I get home, 'cause I've got a story for you. He says don't call me because I don't have any minutes, I'll see you tomorrow. I say I might not get up in time. He says then I'll see you Tuesday. We're all crazy, holding it together with such fine threads. I'm waiting for the 90 at Van Ness and Mission, and I'm getting all emotional—it's not okay for a bus driver to make you walk home because you don't have enough money for the fare—and does the 90 ever come? Finally it pulls up, I can't believe it, and just as I get on the bus there's a 10-foot-high ad for Tommy Hilfiger, the whole ad is this guy's abs and the stars-and-stripes. It's sickening and suddenly I'm horny in that desperate way.

LAYER CAKES

◎   ◎   ◎   ◎

Asked on the BBC how she feels about the sniper who shot and
killed three people in the D.C. area, a Virginia woman says: I don't
think he has any regard for human life! Benjamin says make sure
you quote me—but honey, you already asked me to change your
name! News bulletin: Thai food that I'm not allergic to, and it's
right across the street! A 3 a.m. screaming fight outside, and three
cops arrive within ten minutes—how charming. This guy on the
phone sex line wants me to stick my cock inside his foreskin; he'll
be over in ten minutes. I watch the strippers in velour jumpsuits
pick up their cars at the parking lot across the street, bodyguards
on lookout. After I come, I just feel terrible—maybe I shouldn't
ever do that again.

I wake up crying because is there hope—there is hope—or is there
hope? Talking to the stuffed animals Jeremy gave me, and I try not
to look at the picture of us hugging. Forget about that bitch—I'm at
the Gay Shame demo; we bring a Haunted Shantytown of cardboard
shacks to Gavin Newsom's posh Marina district. We're protesting

his ballot measure known as Care Not Cash, which would take away homeless people's welfare checks, and replace them with—"care." We make a sudden decision to march up the hill into ruling-class Pacific Heights because the cops won't let us stay in the Marina—it's such a beautiful moment, pushing the sound system up and taking our festival further. The cops won't let us into the temple where Gavin's speaking, even though it's supposed to be an open forum. We circle the block, and when we return in small groups there's news: now we're too late to attend.

The Chrissie Contagious update: at the Castro Street Fair, she's breathing fire and the crowd is cheering, the next thing she knows there are six cops tackling her. Twenty-four hours in the padded cell and then twenty-four hours in the psych ward. It was just a waste of time, she says—I haven't been partying and playing as much. Just partying?

I get out of bed thinking it's late, but really it's only 11:30—that's what I get for stopping myself from looking at the clock. On the radio, they say it's the biggest anti-war demo since Vietnam, over a hundred thousand in the streets but I can't get up this early.

It's going to be a great day—the only thing I have to eat is barley, which I'm allergic to. I end up going to the anti-war demo, late. I wasn't going to go because those big demos always feel pointless, but the news coverage gets me excited. The best thing I see is an older woman with her daughter, or maybe granddaughter, hand-painted sign that says WAR IS SO LAST CENTURY. And a bus with a Jean Cocteau quote: "Film will only become art when its materials are as inexpensive as pencil and paper." A few thousand people are left; at least things feel better than usual.

I'm telling Jeremy about Kirk's cat, and I feel like my sister—how excited she gets about cats. But I don't like it when Jeremy tells me about sex—stomach pain. I drag him to the beach in the darkness and cold, the cops shining their lights into everyone's cars.

Seeing Jeremy makes me feel like a little child, wild with anticipation and vulnerability, but lonelier afterwards like it's all just empty. What does he give me back? A hug, just one hug—my kingdom for Jeremy's rug! My trick is a sloppy drunk, he keeps whining:

you don't want to fuck me? I don't want to fuck you. I walk all the
way to the Castro for the parking lot orgy area by Collingwood. The
gate is locked.

I sit on the stone bench outside Starbucks, and this guy asks me
if I've seen the moon tonight. On the beach, there wasn't any
moon—new moon? No, he says. I stand up to look: oh there it is, a
tiny sliver, a shiver—delivery! The pizza place across the street is
crowded; I guess they're open 'til three.

Later, my feet hurt. But the political funeral is gorgeous, torches
on Castro Street—what more could I ask for? Well, that everything
burns down, but at least everyone is screaming and pounding drums
and I almost start to cry right away, so why the fuck do I stop
myself?

Jeremy opens his door to look out, but activism isn't about hating ex-boyfriends who don't join you. We march to the police
station; the cops are scared. Later, Benjamin calls to say she woke
up to turn the heater off, and started crying. She had two conversations with people who were at the action—they wanted to protest
for Gwen, a Latina teenager strangled and beaten to death after she
was exposed as a tranny, but not for Jihad, a black man shot to
death at point-blank range by the SFPD. Jihad was waving butcher
knives, does that mean it was okay to kill him? Benjamin says I'm
worried that we might not have gotten our message across.

In my dream at Fontana West, the apartment is so large that the
floors move like elevators. Andee calls, I say I was just singing a
song: I miss him, I hate him, I miss him, I hate him. Andee says that's
not a song, it's a broken record. Chrissie says I think I ate a fly, I
didn't know what to do—it was in my soup. Says she has an infected
spider bite on her arm and it's swollen up, maybe she was in the
woods or something. Oh no—are you going to get an abscess on
your arm again from shooting up, another week in the hospital?

Don't work my nerves unless it's working for you. If you're working for my nerves, then you're still working. Everybody hates work. If
it's you're wife, then at least it isn't your life, turn. It's all about 11:37
p.m. Alex says I heard your walk and I looked upstairs—there she is!

Why do I always know when Rue's going to drink? It's not like

I'm clairvoyant. If she wants to lie to herself, that's one thing, but don't drag me into it. At least tonight she doesn't get totally smashed. She and Benjamin—who is smashed—ride the BART back with me and they're having one of those earnest conversations that's half as smart as it would be if they weren't drunk. They're saying: fags are so awful—no, people are awful. Benjamin needs a blow job and Rue is sick of sex.

We get back and Rue gets off with us, he's going with Benjamin to some sex party—honey, why don't you go home? She says she's not going to drink anymore; she's just going to get sex. I lose it—bitch, why are you lying to me? She starts to rationalize. I say will you stop arguing with me unless you don't think I'm right. Rue doesn't know what to say, Benjamin's there so Rue sort of defends himself. We're downstairs from the party, Jeremy's upstairs so smashed that he can't walk, and having sex with everyone around him. I say I can't be seen here. We kiss goodbye and my runway is beyond high hypoglycemia, it's pure solid polar ice. Before global warming.

Sure, I'm wired in bed at 4 a.m., but at least I have the most amazing orgasm ever—it's all about my finger in my ass and running out of bed to turn on the lights and watch myself. I don't eat my come because it's too late at night to digest protein. Afterwards, my whole arm hurts from sticking that one finger in my ass. See, masturbation will kill you.

Every Sunday, I want mail. In my dream, my mother introduces me to Gretchen—we're in Russian Hill or some San Francisco postcard, Gretchen lives in North Beach and pays $3,200. She shows me her book, it's the same publisher that did *Memories That Smell Like Gasoline*, I thought they went out of business. I open it up—two dirty band-aids—is this part of the book? Gretchen says yes, pulls at the band-aids—AIDS—and there's a whole tower that falls out, all the people who have died. Each of my cries is a cross between a shriek and a whine, my eyes like two water bottles upside-down and then squeezed shut. My mother goes to look at other books, I'm just downpouring salt water in gasps and then when I wake up, my throat is so dry, legs almost too heavy to walk.

Waiting in the lobby of the Emeryville Holiday Inn, I'm staring up at the '60s chandeliers—upside-down castles, sixteen of them—or layer cakes. The hotel is playing really bad overwrought elevator music—I guess it's lobby music because of the overwrought part.

Beforehand, Jaysen said what do you think he looks like? I said I don't guess about that. Later, I tell her: he's six feet and maybe 250, ruddy or drunk, receding hairline with a long brown ponytail, goatee and scratchy beard. There's a sweetness about him, and I want to give him love and beauty and so many other abstract things like maybe even hope.

LITTLE HEART SHAPES

⊙   ⊙   ⊙   ⊙

It's all about *Details*. The cover story asks, "Can we ever forgive Justin Timberlake for all that sissy music?" The banner headline at the top reads, "Forget Feminism: Why Your Wife Should Take Your Name." Inside, Justin poses in tight tan pants that could be Wranglers but they're Dolce&Gabbana, seventies-style cowboy belt, and black 2(x)ist underwear.

Justin's growling, water bottle in hand, shirt off and six-pack tightened, hand grabbing his crotch. I'd fuck him, but then I do have a straight boy fetish. Not to mention a flamer fetish. In the table of contents: "American Idol—Justin Timberlake, boy-bandom's reigning prince, is making a grab for Michael Jackson's king of pop mitten." And what's he grabbing again?

Inside *Details*, almost at the end: "Jake's a nice guy from Colorado. Has a girlfriend. Has a baby. Has a high-paying career. Of course, the career involves giving blow jobs and taking it in the ass, so that's kind of a drag." And the best quote of all, from Jake: "I always have it in my head that if my girlfriend finds out, it's over, she'll take the baby."

I ask Rue what he thinks, would he recognize this guy with his head turned down, if he was the guy's girlfriend? Rue says yes, but I'm ready for a survey. We're in the magazine store and the first guy is the one who was flirting with me, curly hair with the hint of a faux-hawk, he's not sure—but one thing I'm sure of now is that he was only cruising my fashion. Next guy can't even answer, he's so scared, out the door. At least the salesperson is amused; she's talking to someone on the phone but taking a look at each of the details I point out.

At midnight, I'm about to go out for Thai food, but I don't want to get sick from the oil, the MSG, the chilies, or whatever else might destroy me. I cook pasta, but what can I put in it? I throw in a bunch of scallions; tamari, rice vinegar, lemon; and then kidney beans—honey, kidney beans are the answer! It's a vegan break-through, because it's almost like meat sauce—it's much darker than just tomatoes, staining the pasta the color of a gory movie.

Even with all the new lofts, South of Market is still beautiful, late at night. I do a tour of all the alleys I've had sex in, then I walk home. There are six cop cars in front of The Century, so I turn the corner at O'Farrell and this guy says: finally someone attractive out tonight. I like the attention, but he's not in my dimension.

Right outside my building, this trannygirl yells for me: you don't remember me, do you? I used to be more boyish. Destiny—she holds out her hand. She invites me over to her house for pot; well if you don't smoke pot then I guess we don't have anything in common. Unless you want to fuck. I go home, but then I'm thinking about Destiny. Maybe I should've gone home with her.

The NPR announcer asks: what was going through your mind when the car slid off the highway, and you were lying upside-down, trapped in the car with your neck broken? What a smart question. Rue says he hasn't eaten yet today, except for chocolate cake. Benjamin says she had a night of threes—three bumps of coke, a three-way, and three orgasms. It was horrible, she says.

Every day, some new part of my body hurts. Right now, it's the sides of my ankles—is that my shins? Why is it 4 a.m. again? The laundry machines deposit brown spots on all my favorite T-shirts, and I can never memorize the repair number long enough to call.

Zan flakes on me again and I'm through—when I call him, he says why did you take so long? I say I was too annoyed to call you. He says I had to get work. That's what yuppies say to their freak friends—I have a job, girl—even if Zan is talking about porn. I say well, you're always flaking on me. He says I can't hear this right now. I say well, when you've been flaking on me for ten years, you're gonna have to do something to regain my trust.

Afterwards, I feel so cold. Rue comes over and I'm upset, and then exhausted. We go on a walk, and then we're both exhausted. On NPR, they're playing Chanukah songs sung by a chorus like Christmas carols, how charming. More good news from the news: being Chinese still affects Chinese identity.

There's a real mouse in my house—it wasn't just big roaches, after all. Is the San Francisco Center really the center of San Francisco? Honey, of course it is—Abercrombie Abercrombie Abercrombie. I just love it when I open a cabinet and roaches come tumbling down, how biblical! But will I ever see the sun again? My straight boy fetish is out of control, I see them walking down the street from my fifth floor window and beckon them inside with my eyes. It never works.

I figured out what's wrong with the world: people get up too early; they go to take the trash out at 7 a.m. I realize it's 11 a.m., and most people would call that late—but oh, people wake up to alarm clocks! Coffee. That's what's wrong.

I'm lying in bed with Rue, we're hanging out but I'm so tired I can hardly keep my eyes open. I get scared like I'm little and I'm trying to tell Rue something, but it only comes out in a whisper, he can't hear me. What I finally say is: all those cats and dogs and they were so cute and my parents made us watch them die, why did they have to die? When I close my eyes I see a ritual with a fire-pit and everything, faces obscured with dark masks and it's so hard when everything gets even scarier than I've ever imagined. We were so young, what did those animals do wrong? And I'm sobbing and sobbing from saying it aloud, Rue's hugging me and I'm sobbing. He says: you've been through so much. I think: no, you've been through so much. I guess we both have.

So that's why I think Allison wants to become a veternarian. General Tommy Franks, on the war in Iraq: every time we go from Microsoft-something to Microsoft-something-else, I go through a new training process. Benjamin gets stopped by the cops for jaywalking outside her house: um, why yes, officer—I am black.

Everyone's always holding something in, and I'm sick of it. I leave beans cooking on the stove when I go out, don't remember for four hours. It would be fine if they were in the expensive pot, but the fire department comes, the building manager climbs up the fire escape so that they don't bust down my door. That way I don't have to pay for it. She's in my apartment with her girlfriend when I get back—I've never met her before; I actually didn't even realize we had a new building manager.

At Cala, they're playing Christmas carols. Two fake cable cars turn the corner, full of screaming drunken yuppies in Santa outfits. Then they're back, they just went around the block. Jeremy flakes on me 'cause he doesn't want someone else to think he's a flake. Tragic mixed with tragique—how'd you know that was my favorite cocktail? Damage control: I come with a trick so that I don't go to the Power Exchange. Afterwards, I feel just lovely.

I haven't seen the sun since the '80s, but there are so many interesting stories on so-called public radio. There's this one about selling Christmas trees, and how the market is really tough this year, sales are up for artificial trees. This one place sells live trees, meaning you can pick your own tree to chop down—then you know it's fresh. Another place gives out free candy and eggnog. Afterwards, a reporter asks: when was the last time you prayed?

Hot sex with someone I met on the phone line—are you crazy? He's from Austin, I ask him what to do when I visit my sister. Ice cream, he says. I don't like ice cream, what about thrift stores? He doesn't know of any cruising parks. He lives about seven blocks from where Jeremy used to live in Oakland; the Walgreen's where Jeremy and I got harassed is his Walgreen's too.

I test negative for syphilis, and they still try to convince me to take antibiotics: public health over personal health, how thoughtful! Jeremy and I are sick at the same time—it's not fate, I swear it's not fate. I'm in bed for thirty-six hours. In my dream, I'm trying to get the saliva out of my mouth—I'm pulling and pulling, it's a solid object. I'm worried I'm going to pull out my tongue. Finally it comes out, straps at the very ends like what keeps a saddle on, or maybe the reins? I let the straps hang in my mouth, and I wake up to what sounds like sheets of glass shattering on the ground outside. Christmas? Never heard of it. If only Nixon were still in China, bringing on all that détente! My name is Luka, I live on the second floor. My name is Luka, yes I think you've seen me before. This tweaker calls, he says: are you part God? Stop soiling my corduroys!

What to say when Walgreen's security catches you stealing a pen: I was just testing how it feels in my pocket. Ralowe says he watched the second *Lord of the Rings* and there was a walking tree, he can't wait to get a Game Cube so he can play "Zelda"—the scary part is that Ralowe's serious.

Burdock root for the birds, I hope they appreciate such delicacies. It's hard to believe that I can do anything at all when I wake up feeling so awful. Watching the pigeons eat the burdock—they like it! My apartment still smells like smoke from the fire, which luckily only damaged the pot. I steam kale for way too long—more food for the pigeons. I just want to go back to bed—it's so nice in there. More on NPR about prayer—the same program on two stations— I just love the holidays! South of Market: I can't believe these people still exist, going to the same awful bars. Benjamin says she got so frustrated on the phone sex line that she called suicide prevention.

Finally something interesting on NPR: someone's dog was drowning in the river, the owner couldn't reach it because the tide was too high, then all of the sudden a seal emerged and pushed the dog to the safety of the riverbank. This trick calls, he says I saw your picture, and you look like the kind of guy who'd appreciate some herb I grew at my home in Lake County, so I thought maybe I'd swing by.

I get a real trick; he lives in that weird condo in the back of the Safeway parking lot on Geary. The doorperson says I've heard all about you. I say I've heard all about *you*. The trick's cute enough, I push him up on the kitchen counter, I'm grinding against him and he says let me ask you a question: are you gay? These people. Later, he says: what do you do for a living?

During the previews, every movie looks like it has great cinematography and a horrible script—maybe I should move to LA. Sit
by the pool and do line after line, cocktails to take away the taste
and food on silver trays—just get me a hospital room with a view!
Like in the one good scene in *Boogie Nights*, line after line and they
can't leave the room—why do I think that was Julianne Moore, was
that Julianne Moore? Anyway, Rollergirl looks at the older woman;
she's not thinking about whether it's Julianne Moore because her
eyes are red and tears well up—MOMMY! So many nights like that,
when one room is the world and you never escape.

In the new Almodóvar movie, someone says there's nothing
worse than leaving someone you love, and I think about Jeremy,
who I'm sitting with. But I don't feel dramatic about it. Jeremy asks
if I've had any good sex. That's when I'm more dramatic: I feel like
there was a time, a number of years ago, when I felt a sense of so
much possibility in sex, in sluttiness—and now it seems like everyone's so compulsive about finding dissatisfaction, and it makes me
so depressed that I stop thinking about sex. I don't really have a
libido, either—except at random moments when I'm on the bus or
walking down the street and unfortunately it's not those random
moments that are scripted to lead to something.

I always think I'm going to get some amazing mail—today I get
two credit card applications and a missing persons postcard.
Remember: jumping out the window is not good exercise, exercise,
exercise! Everything hurts, no not everything—just fingers, wrists,
arms, shoulders, neck, jaw, head, feet, back. Zan goes to a New
Year's party in New York to check his email: no, honey—put that
line back in the road where it belongs!

More bills, get me some pills. I want to go to Buena Vista Park,
but I'm worried I'll hurt my hands carrying my bag. Then hurt my
feet getting down. But where else can I go to suck cock with the city
below my lips? So that's where I go, I suck cock; the guy tells me
he's the Mayor. Of the park. He shows me his favorite spot, which
isn't my favorite. Then he walks me down, so I don't get lost—
chivalry is still alive! At home, I feel less exhausted. As soon as I get
out of bed, the fire alarm goes off.

Next Thursday, I'm getting on a plane to visit Allison in Austin, I'm worried I'll get so drained from the plane that I'll never get out of that dark DARK depression. I just need the answer. Zan calls my cellphone, why my cellphone? Neck, forearms, or wrist—which will hurt the most? Zan says you don't want to talk to me right now; I'm an example of all the worst New York has to offer. Is she coked-out and waiting for the Gucci store to open in Williamsburg?

Illusions will only get you so far. Now, delusions . . . What's the difference between blasé and bla bla bla? Parfait touché, farfait flambé, parfait with hay. Some guy on the bus says: engaging with this planet is essential. Zan goes to Steamworks in Chicago, she says: I was trying to stir up some action in the glory hole video room, and I walked into this hot torso on the screen with cock in hand, then the camera pulled back and it was your lovely face in full faux ecstasy.

While I'm waiting for the bus, this homeless guy asks: what's the difference between murder and killing? My mood swings when this boy at Whole Foods keeps looking at me. He's the hottest thing on earth. I thought he was straight, but then I always think the boys who cruise me are straight. Did I mention he's the hottest thing on earth—shaved head but it's growing out, and big eyes, maybe even chubby and that tattoo on his arm makes me swoon? Corporate health food romance.

Ralowe thinks he's the only person who doesn't relate to anyone else in the world. Keys, kikis, keys, kikis. The boy from Austin isn't calling me back to give me the thrift store story, what a bitch. I call Jeremy 'cause he's forgotten to call before leaving for Paris. It's 4 a.m., no one answers the phone. Why are they cleaning the streets in the rain? Watching the cops harass the trannygirls from five stories above, I feel so powerless.

Wow, the cops let the girls go. I've already thought of what I'm going to write on postcards from Austin: Texas is Texas. But here's what I'll remember most, even though it could happen anywhere: it's Monday, first day back for UT students. I'm on the main drag outside of the campus, giving high hypoglycemia runway drama—nothing out of the ordinary. I'm walking fast, getting all sorts of comments—are you gay?—intellectual sorts of things, outside the university. Though this one cute straight boy does look me up and down like he's in awe of how many mismatching pieces of clothing I can throw together, transcending everything. Anyway, after a few blocks, I spot these two fags. I'm excited, I smile hello and these bitches start giving me shade. Imitating my walk, saying *girl*.

If I had a gun, I'd pull it out and shoot them: euthanasia. Back at home, I'm jetlag soup—more radiation please, pass the sea salt. There's another anti-war demo on Saturday and I'm feeling the new P'n'P: powerless and paranoid. Benjamin says she went to the Stud and she felt like that scene in *Stand By Me* with the leeches crawling all over her. The bus driver says to me: I haven't seen mittens in a long time. This trick comes over for a blow job—when we're done, he says it's 25, right? Huh? He says that's what it says on the Internet. I say I charge 200, it must have said 250. He says no, shows me a listing on cruisingforsex that sort of sounds like me, some guy who literally charges 25 for a blow job, supposedly he gave the trick my number.

The trick only brought 25 dollars—I just want him out of my sight. I go back to the listing that's supposedly me, there's a picture of someone's dick and it looks like Jeremy's. I'm probably just paranoid, but it really does look like Jeremy's dick. Someone's playing weird games. I email the guy in the listing: what's going on? He emails me back, his name's Jeremy Lapolla. Jeremy La-pole-ah. I'm freaked out.

Jenna comes over and we talk about the war protest, the splinter demo of anarchists and freaks—how disorganized it was, how much potential but no planning, so of course it wasn't realized. I get Thai food across the street, they're showing a video where four Asian women jump into a pool to fight like goldfish for a piece of food; a blond woman with huge breasts in an insane gold '80s sequined dress fights a Don Johnson impresario for her life, leaves on a motorcycle with a Volvo and a Mercedes in extra-hot pursuit.

Jeremy gets back from Europe, he says Paris is great, but don't go to Amsterdam, everyone is so aggressive—they get right in your face asking for change, and all you can do is smoke pot and sit on wooden benches eating meatballs. This trick calls, he says I talked to you the other day, and you sounded really nice—I just got authorization from my cat that if you do dishes, it's an extra 40 dollars. Rue and I see a movie where they're dancing in Ibiza to just about the hardest techno I've ever heard. I'm confused, whatever happened to bad Baleiric happy-house?

Is there a cure for waiting for the bus? I just want to have sex with someone I want to have sex with. Jetlag jetlag jetlag jetlag. I'm looking at CDs at Amoeba, and my wrists start to burn so much, I jump into a cab and race home to soak my hands in ice water. Now what am I going to eat? The beat, we got the beat!

The roaches are just living it up in the electric toothbrush—home, sweet home. I wonder how effective it is to tell them they don't belong. I hate getting so tired that I don't want to go to bed, ever—just turn the music up and dance! But I haven't seen piranhas since the '80s. Aaron says are you taking street drugs again? I don't need street drugs—I am street drugs! What's manic plus manique? Manishamba! My new strategy for trying to get some sleep: when I wake up thinking yayayayayayayyayayayyayahhhhhh, I just repeat the same sentence over and over again, to try and stop my brain from moving moving moving. How to structure a novel: eviction, conviction, nurse!

Jock itch itch itch itch itch ITCH! I go to Frenchy's at 4 a.m. There's no one there, the security guard kicks me out because I'm not in a booth. Outside, there's the drug dealer who always grabs my hand and says hey honey, I like your colors. Tonight he says: you're out late, something's gonna happen. I'm delirious and calm, walking downtown on Geary, looking for what's going to happen. All the pimps are out, Thai Noodle House is still open, there's a tweaker who asks me for a leaf. A leaf? Yeah, isn't it fall? I walk home.

Rue says he keeps buying things on eBay, selling things on eBay—so many ways to explore the American dream. But he drank absinthe at Balazo: expatriotism! Andee calls me on my cellphone while I'm at Rainbow—your answering machine says you're paranoid, and you haven't answered the phone all week.

At Benjamin's show, she pulls apart the top half of the mike stand and wields it like a hot poker. Zan and I are supposed to watch the sunset; she's coming over at 4. I call her at 5—she says oh, were we supposed to get together? She says you know I'm crazy. I say honey, we're all crazy. There's crazy, and then there's crazy flakes.

Back to Benjamin's show, it all comes together when Benjamin gets audience members to scream STRANGULATION, and Eliott's keyboards are making spooky tinny sounds. The next band keeps going to the bathroom to chew gum. Valentine's Day is only two weeks away, and I've got pink rock salt, I'm gonna pour it on the counter in little heart shapes, no girl that's not cocaine! It's 4:50 a.m., is that cop car outside—five floors down and half a block away—waiting for me? No, really—I don't need a ride—thanks!

Here's how I'm feeling today: I step up onto the toilet seat to brush the dust off the plants in the bathroom, and I have this image of falling in, first one foot and then my whole body sucked into the abyss. Does sleeping cause cancer? 'Cause I think I got some last night. A rubber band in my toaster: will that increase my chances of survival? Andee says: after seeing Belle and Sebastian at the Royal Albert Hall, everything else is just whipped cream—when I die, if I can't be reassigned to some other dimension, I want to be a tree that gives cover for gay men having sex. She's drunk. I go out on my fire escape for the first sun of the season, it doesn't reach me during the winter.

I give Benjamin a pair of my contacts, because she's been wearing the same pair of disposables for a couple years. Later, she calls me to say: your gift has changed my life and you will be rewarded for your Christian generosity. Rue says I can hear hypoglycemia in your laughter, the bravado is abbreviated. Someone from the phone sex line swallows my come and then tells me about mortgages: fifty-five percent of all U.S. mortgages are in California.

Now I know why people feed pigeons—just seeing them fly down to eat that kale makes me so happy! What does it mean when a taxi driver waits for you to go in your front door? Does it mean he loves me? Does it mean you love me? Rhania calls: how long do you soak your adzuki beans? A long time, considering that when the cops throw me facedown into the middle of the street and someone catches my fall, it's Zan, he kisses me, I'm crying. Then there's a pile of people on top of us until we're handcuffed and dragged into a police van. At 850 Bryant, the guard says: you respect me and I'll respect you. How original. I ask him to loosen my handcuffs, because my wrists hurt. He tightens his grip.

We were protesting Gavin Newsom's Hot Pink fundraiser at the beautiful new LGBT Center, dressed in our own color-coordinated finery. The Center called the cops to prevent us from going inside. When Gavin arrived, the cops escorted him in and immediately started bashing us. Devon got clubbed in the face by a police baton, tooth shattered, blood dripping down her face. Matt ended up in a police chokehold. Center staff just stood there and watched. They kept saying: it's not worth it. It's not worth it.

What's not worth it? I wake up crying in the middle of the night. Picturing the blood dripping down Devon's face even though I didn't see it because I was already in a police van—I just saw the photos afterwards. All because of the Center, our center, the fucking Center!

At the Nob Hill Theatre, it's all about this guy with a pink-and-white-checkered shirt, that's what makes me go into his booth. Okay, there's this girl Mattilda, right? She always leaves the most amazing phone messages. They're kind of a cross between complete insanity and absolute clarity—and what's the difference, anyway? Well, I'll tell you the difference. Complete insanity is when you just talk talk talk talk—and you don't even know what you're doing. Absolute clarity is when you just talk talk talk talk—and you know exactly what you're doing. Well, maybe not exactly, but you know what you're doing.

I eat a fortune cookie and then there's this rotten taste in my mouth, I guess that's my fortune. Alex isn't sure polyamory's a good idea. Zero's still waiting for her records to arrive in Mo's cross-country caravan. Chrissie calls to tell me about the mainstream anti-war demo, do I want to go to a planning meeting? To plan what—I have something to plan—did I tell you about my three counts of battery on a police officer? 'Cause they threw me into oncoming traffic, Zan caught me, I was crying in his arms because what else was there to do? The cops pulling my arms back, I was worried about my hands, my wrists, my link to the world of doing things. My hands hurt, honey my hands fucking hurt!

At a Valentine's party, did someone really say: investment in anti-capitalism? Benjamin's been crying all week, she says if someone harasses me on the way home, I'm gonna ask them to kill me. Because I want to die.

Call me crazy, but this fucking Richard Hinge CD is making my eyes tear. I call Zero so she can listen to the builds. Three-thirty a.m. and—ladies and gentlemen, it's Ms. Mattilda Sycamore, stretch, shake, take and take and take! Wow, there's the scratch and the echo twisted cymbal sound building up and up and up, always in threes, it's always in threes is three still my lucky number?

Okay, so what's the difference between good insomnia and bad insomnia? I can't believe I get up at 6 a.m. to visit Ralowe in jail, she's been there since the last anti-war demo, the one I didn't bother describing because they're all the same. This time a few windows got shattered and the cops went crazy. Arrested something like a hundred people, most of them got out but Ralowe and a few others are stuck. So I get up in the morning, it's all about Richard Hinge on my Walkman, glitter in streaks on my face and a plaid polyester skirt, out the door and into a cab. Outside, I'm asking everyone if they're on the guest list. Inside, I can't breathe.

Everyone keeps asking how Ralowe was, I just couldn't tell. She said the new jail's set up like a food court, with the cops in the middle. Still trying to entertain us. It made me so sad. At the whore social, I'm so tired I can't be social. Or a whore. Just as I'm leaving, Zan asks me to do runway and I'm self-conscious at first, but then I'm living it, loving it—finally I feel human!

An anonymous donor bails Ralowe out—and we were just getting to know the County Jail, our home away from home. Ralowe exits in flip-flops because they confiscated her shoes as evidence. Well, at least she's out—eight days in that place and I'd be over with. On the radio, Ward Churchill's talking about how Wall Street got its name from the wall of the slave market. Talking about U.S. nuclear tests on the Marshall Islands, he says: have you ever seen a baby born without a skeleton?

Aaron's report: at the hospital, someone shoved a tube down his throat for forty-five minutes, shouting BLOW HARDER! I thought I'd solved the lice problem by cultivating jock itch for six months, but now I've got both. So many pets in the house, and not a thing to feed them except me, poor me—will I ever be able to exercise? Learning to hate my body again is so easy, but at least Jeremy finally calls, after I dream that he still thinks I want to have sex with him. Rue and I are in the magazine store, and the cashier says: sorry, guys, but there's no camping here—that's the second camping comment, first one was at 850 Bryant, waiting for people to get out of jail and this cop said: there's no camping out in the Hall of Justice. Did I mention the worst Gay Shame meeting ever? People talking about not wanting to critique the community. I mean, we started Gay Shame to challenge the hypocrisy of gay spaces, and now people embrace the new hipster hot spot like it's salvation. I've done my time getting smashed in terrible gay bars, but I've never thought that was community. Benjamin and Ralowe have been talking about leaving the group for a while, but it's the first time I think about it too.

Finally, a trick: two guys from Alabama, one of them's mad at the other one for not getting hard. We watch porn with subtitles. It's supposedly this Czech guy's first time getting a hand job, but somehow his asshole swallows cock effortlessly. He keeps getting pumped even after coming three times, face twisted into a lifetime grimace: this was fun when it started, but now all I can do is act.

The perils of doing anything before I put on my contacts: I just picked a roach up off the floor—I thought it was a grain of wild rice, I swear I thought it was rice. Luckily this guy comes over to pump a load down my throat, the cure for hypoglycemia.

Outside, I'm kind of laughing. Even the post office is fun. Later, on the Geary bus, I crash. I can't stop yawning; one yawn's so big I almost fall into some guy's lap. What do you mean I'm just depressed? Have you ever been depressed? Is there anything just about it? Jeremy and I get an MSG surprise, I'm talking through a tunnel, but somehow it doesn't get too bad. I'm so calm—I can't tell if it's because I'm with Jeremy or because I'm okay with losing him and maybe still having something that might really be nothing.

But I miss Herb Ritts! With all those photos of neutered, musclebound gym queens, he really changed the face of photography. Richard Gere writes about his dear friend Herb in *Vogue*. No, I'm serious. They shot big in the desert, Perry Como on board, too bad the car broke down and they had to spend the whole trip in the service station. It was the Tour de France, and all they wanted was to dance! Zan calls from the Betty Ford Clinic—they cover that on SSI? Or are you on the work-study program? She says my crystal just kicked in—but sweetheart, everyone knows that crystal doesn't take time to kick in!

Sugar gives Benjamin a pair of glasses, he says with Sugar's glasses and Mattilda's contacts, I can see pretty well. This trick bargains me down over the phone, then when he arrives he's covered in so much sweat it's like he forgot to dry off after the shower, which is maybe what happened because at least he doesn't smell. He wants me to sit on his ass, literally, bouncing up and down, which is kind of fun. Then he wants me to suck his dick. I'm rubbing his thighs; all these red zits and I get paranoid that it's the drug-resistant staph infection. No sucking this afternoon. He comes through the sheet that's covering my sheets. He's wearing a bracelet of glass beads, and I compliment him on it, just to say something nice, because I couldn't be present enough. Afterwards, I feel so depressed.

I can't believe that just carrying a small bag of groceries home from Cala destroys me—the muscles by my collarbone are burning, shoulders of rocks. Next day is a hard day; I don't leave the house until 9:40 p.m. I rush onto the bus to make it to horrible Whole Foods before they close, and believe it or not, I've shopped and I'm back home by 10:10—sometimes public transportation can save your life!

New allergy alert: I wake up and my legs are burning, like so many pinpricks. Court at 8 a.m. because the cops threw us into the street and now we're being charged. People show up for us and that makes me feel better, we go to Ananda Fuara for lunch and look at the book Sri Chimnoy wrote about Princess Di—there are songs in it. After my nap, I'm so strung out that I spill my food all over Kirk's car. Headache in the middle of my forehead that threatens to conquer everyone and everything—talk about empire.

This allergy again, a burning underneath my skin. Is there really a review of the Buzzcocks and the Jam on NPR? When are they going to review my book? News from Serbia: politics and crime are very closely intertwined. All these bills on my table, do I really have to pay them? In the cafeteria at the Capitol, they've removed French fries from the menu, due to France's opposition to the war on Iraq.

Remember when a halogen torchière was an amazing luxury? I look in the mirror; I look like the kind of person who goes out a lot. So I figure I should go out. I go to the Powerhouse and there's a cover, I pay it, everything's awful, I leave. Outside, there are so many kinds of horrible people walking around. Ralowe's on the internet trying to get people to say racist things, so he can write about it. A range of eventualities on the phone sex line: a nice tight hole that needs to be stretched, three big mushroom heads, two work-out-five-days-a-week, two pig bottoms, three raw bottoms, two aggressive tops, two two-guys-partying-and-playing, one virgin ass that needs to get plowed, one guy who gets off on other guys' dicks. Before, I was hopeless, but now that I know there's so much creativity out there, the possibilities for world peace have just increased.

My trick is staying in the upscale side of Beck's Motor Lodge—who knew there was an upscale side? On my way in, this hot guy asks me if I'm Jonah, and the whole time I'm having sex with the trick, I'm thinking about Jonah, I mean the guy looking for Jonah, who even followed me around the corner but I had to work. On the way out, I want to look into all the open doors to see if the guy's there, but I don't want to see everyone else who's there. The Thai restaurant across the street from me hits me with an MSG bomb—I was already depressed, now I'm possessed!

Why do I try to cruise craigslist? All it does is destroy my fingers, hands, forearms, shoulders, neck and everything that's above, including what's in my head. I keep cruising. I guess I just want to be horny so I can have *some* energy. I even try gay.com, which is kind of lucky because this trick catches me there; I say you wanna hire me? And then I'm out of my darkness and over to his house by Buena Vista Park, I figure it's time to come—with him—even though the park is right out there. Afterwards, I lie in his arms and stare at the ceiling, inhale, exhale. Inhale, exhale. Trying to approximate romance. Or even hot sex, lying exhausted and transformed afterwards.

I can't believe the trick only has some crappy grocery store white

bar soap, and Pantene, which is water and twenty different chemicals. Really twenty—I count them—starting with ammonium lauryl
sulfate and then sodium lauryl sulfate. Every fancy trick should have
fancy bath supplies, isn't it written in the contract? I mean, this is
the guy who throws the come-towel into the closet and says: the
laundress will do that, the laundress does everything. Outside, the
trees are so beautiful, everything's beautiful, it's my first energized
and calm mood in days or weeks. Why can't I always feel—like this?

Another trick in the Upper Haight, and I come two days in a row.
Actually it feels kinda good. He has the same Lush soap from London that Andee bought me, the kind that looks like what sea water
should look like—only, if it did, I'd be scared. Afterwards, I'm enjoying the trees in the Panhandle, it's just a one-block-wide stretch of
green, but the air smells so much better. I need to spend more time
with the trees. President Bush is on the radio, giving Saddam Hussein
48 hours to leave Iraq, and I'm trying to eat but I can't breathe. Bush
says every effort has been made to avoid war, and every effort will be
made to win it. It's so sunny outside; my face is reflected in the computer screen.

THE GETAWAY CAR

⊙ ⊙ ⊙ ⊙

Benjamin says to Ralowe: how can you talk about fatal strategy when you're not suicidal? Ralowe says: how can you assume that I'm not suicidal? But can I describe my continuing jetlag bags—valleys of purple and reddish hues, sunset down from a cold cold mountain, rings of semi-precious—no, make that priceless—gems. Only the brightest moments for my raggedy bags! And my hands just feel great, five fingers of invisible bruises leading to nerves for arms. I call the phone sex line, the one where you just say hello, and someone hangs up on you. This one guy says I heard you laugh and I came. We talk for a while, and then I run out of free time and the phone cuts me off.

High on life doesn't even begin to describe the moment abruptly cut short by the sight of a mouse scurrying across my floor. 'Cause really it's just high—the music taking me, well not quite taking me, but facilitating my movement—there—to the heights, eyes up and up. But my travels are abruptly cut short by that mouse in my house; there it really is, peering out from underneath the closet door—a dis-

play of pure audacity. I want to find it cute, but it's in my house—
disease disease DISEASE! If I could just catch it, and release it into
the woods, or at least some park—how did it get all the way to the
third floor anyway? Wait—I live on the fifth floor.

Imagine the journey—I mean, it's hard enough for me to walk up
five flights of stairs, but this tiny creature made the journey of hope
into a new world of unknown perils. How desperate is its rage?
Metabolism so fast it can't sit still, that's what people say about me
though it's really just my brain, pain, say that again! I call Florence;
she wants to know if I get enough protein. Yes, I say, I eat a lot of
beans—with almost every meal. Florence says that's right; I forget
that beans contain protein. I say what do you eat? Florence says: for
breakfast, I have a scooped out bagel with a tiny bit of cheese and I
put it under the broiler. Coffee and I love it. Lunch: tuna. Toasted
English muffin. Dinner varies.

Florence tells me about D.C.'s newly gentrified neighborhoods,
she says oh these were the most depressed areas for fifty years and
now look at them—new condos everywhere, block after block—and
the best restaurants, you wouldn't believe the restaurants, these were
areas where you couldn't even go. I ask about the people who used
to live in these neighborhoods. She says oh, there was no one living
there before, and if there was, then there shouldn't have been.

Florence wants to buy me new clothes for my thirtieth birthday—
something nice instead of that flea market look. And why don't you
take off those earrings, you are so handsome without them. I call
Rose, who says: you're so handsome without those earrings. I say:
why don't you talk to Florence about that. She says you're right; I
have been talking to Florence.

I ask about Rose's art, she says oh there are two whole periods
that you haven't even seen yet, I won't tell you about them because
I want it to be a surprise. She tells me about someone who wrote to
her for twenty years, sent these elaborate letters after she discovered
one of Rose's paintings, and even though they never met, she would
tell Rose about absolutely everything going on in her life—the cancer, the failed marriage, the heartbreak. Rose didn't tell her much.
She wondered about that, because the woman always asked how she

was doing. When Ed died, Rose told her, and the woman hasn't written back since. She used to write every week, Rose says—I think I miss her.

I'm on a roll, so I call my mother. She says you know your father and I are in marriage counseling? I didn't know. She says the therapist thinks I'm too harsh. I say I could give her some perspective, and my mother seems into it, I'm not quite sure why. Rue says the cool side of the room at Mission Yoga is only eighty degrees, but I don't know if I believe him. I call the studio, they say there's no way to measure the temperature, but it's not as hot as Funky Door, where I used to go. I think of trying it out, until my sinuses take over, throbbing me into meditation, then onto the floor with my head on the sofa, into bed and then out of bed so hypoglycemic I can't stand anything! Jaysen calls, echoing my voice—I say is this me? He's in hysterics and I want to go there too.

I can't believe my sinuses are still throbbing, it's been weeks since I got off the plane so calm like maybe this time it wouldn't be a disaster until wait, is that a hole in my head? Rue says you should go to the Oxygen Bar—are you kidding? On NPR: precision bombing, the new feng shui. Alex calls from New York, he was at the gym in the women's locker room and two big guys followed him in—excuse me sir, do you have a problem? New York Sports Club on Seventh Avenue just above Christopher, the same gym that opened without a steam room so fags couldn't cruise. It was the early '90s, and I think people actually protested, but there's no protest for Alex who has to say *I'm a woman*—even if he doesn't believe it.

I go to the Oxygen Bar, but why does the oxygen smell like lavender? I'm allergic to lavender—or maybe I'm allergic to oxygen. That would explain a lot. Outside, this guy's wearing sneakers instead of gloves, how creative! Which is worse: being wired when you're tired, or tired when you're wired? All day long, I can't stop shitting: eat, rush to the bathroom, eat, rush to the bathroom. Next day, I wake up thinking I hate the world, oh wait that's every day. Was there an earthquake, or was that a pigeon rushing under my bed?

Ralowe sees a sign at Mission and Third for the Museum of the African Diaspora, he says: everyone looking at me looking at the sign made me think about what it means to be one of those white people staring. Rue says the pollen count is really high today, so maybe that's why I'm picturing a double-flip five floors down onto the cement floor of the demolished laundromat—see, just because the elevator's not working doesn't mean you have to take the stairs!

The roaches are almost gone, but now it's the mice. In the morning, I hear them crawling through every plastic bag in the cabinets under the sink—any time but the morning, please, I really need some rest! The third week of jetlag is almost over, and my ride to L.A. from craigslist flakes—she's a midwife; I wonder if she flakes on the babies too. I take a plane, does that mean I'm at the beginning of my jetlag cycle again? Did I really just turn thirty? Allison sends me flowers, but they're kind of dried out and they don't fit in the enclosed vase. The magic powder wakes them up, white daisies on my white table—they make me happy. Still haven't talked to Allison—we've been calling back and forth for a whole month but it's just voicemail city.

I'm wearing one of those impossible outfits on Upper Fillmore by the chiropractor—pink-and-red-striped shirt with an argyle belt and the red, white, and navy plaid pants that I never wear because they're too baggy, but today it's hot as fuck so I've gotta wear them. I run into Jeremy, he's with Sarah and his new boyfriend, Sandy. He gives me such a sweet hug, and says you look beautiful. Afterwards I'm high, which gets me to yoga, where I hurt my back. But I feel pretty calm about it. Until I'm watching all the cars on Van Ness and it's worse than the suburbs—because I'm not there, but they are, peering out at me like what is that? When the massage practitioner works on my hand, things fall out: deep worlds that make my mind go dark. Oh please don't ever stop, please—but then it's done.

Who knew that after yoga, I'd have a drug flashback. On the bus I'm so cold, eyes blinking and yes it's that world where I'm beyond what's going on around me. Just don't let me crash—hot flash! I'm glad the pigeons love my black-eyed peas, because I wasn't enjoying them. Rue says you don't have roaches anymore because of the mice—that's a lot of mice. Apparently, they chew so fast you can't see their teeth, but why was that one I saw clear? Rue says you have to kill them, and I get tears in my eyes because as a kid they were my friends, all different stuffed-animal mice under my bed and maybe they'd keep me safe.

One of the few nice moments I remember about my father: he caught a mouse in a shoebox, and we took it to a park to release it. Tears in my eyes and Rue says you can't kill anything, you can sense a roach's sentient being, and he's right—I'd rather move out than kill the mice, cute mice so innocent and small, gnawing away at my foundations.

Rue says there are mice in every building in the Tenderloin, soon they'll be in your food—plastic bags with holes in them and shit everywhere, that's how you get cysts—maybe you should get a cat and it'll eat them up. Rue's got that look in his eyes; he likes to watch a cat batting a mouse around until it's torn apart, and I do like cats but not the litter or that horrible food, and certainly not the idea of them devouring torn-up corpses in my kitchen. I could put the litter box on the fire escape, but then the cat would climb down and get killed—wait I don't want a cat anyway.

Rue's addicted to Bikram Yoga, I'm trying to convince him to practice some other type, but he whines like a little boy: Mommy, I like Bikram's. After he leaves, I'm getting high listening to the Miss Kittin CD that was in *Muzik Magazine*, it's better than the rest of her shit because it's some serious mixing, until—is that Joy Division? That's taking it a little too far. No—it's something else, worse. Not that I didn't sit up many a night at least five years after Ian Curtis killed himself, listening to "She's Lost Control Again"—oh wait, it really is some sort of techno mix with the melody from "She's Lost Control," which is sort of genius, maybe.

I go on a walk, to Union Square and then back—have I ever been this tired? On my way home, a trick calls—are you serious? The only other trick I've had in weeks was the double with the hooker who had stuffed animals attached to his sneakers. Whatever happened to Sudden Infant Death Syndrome? Kayti's worried about Oprah because of the Martha Stewart insider trading scandal, she sends Oprah an email: they're after you next.

The mice are taking over my apartment, but at Original Casper's Hot Dogs in Oakland, it's more than just a hot dog, it's a feeling.

Late night drama: I get so nervous that I'm not going to be able to sleep, then I can't sleep because I'm so nervous. Andee says there's a scandal in her house, she went to do a nasal lavage and her half-filled bottle of distilled water was gone. She says: I think someone doesn't like that I do nasal lavages at four in the morning. But there's progress in Berlin: A TGI Friday's in Alexanderplatz, and three times as many trendy shops on Kastanienallee—everywhere you go, alterna-yuppies with strollers!

Everyone wants to tell Andee the latest news from Iraq—see what your country is doing? The latest news is that they didn't lock up the weapons factories, and people used the empty barrels to carry water—birth defects for the next three generations. But is that Chrissie pulling up outside? She says: I just got back from seeing Crystal Waters at San Jose Pride—are you serious? Jupiter is with her, she says Crystal Waters had backup dancers who did full splits, she didn't have to do that to get paid.

The next day, there's something wrong, like the molecules in the back of my body aren't connecting with the front. I get back in bed at 7 p.m. and actually sleep, though it only helps for about a half hour after I'm awake. Meditation, medication, meditation, medication. I figure out why the mice are coming to my house, instead of some other apartment where it's just pizza boxes and beer cans all over the floor. It's 'cause of the flour under the counter, they've gnawed through the plastic and paper bags to get at what's inside. Then they've also devoured the baking soda—flecks of black in the white wedding—oh no, it's the toxic shit! Sponging up the flour and what's inside it, I'm having nightmares about disease, even if it's morning.

Magdalena says you're so sensitive; it's amazing you can get out of the house. Jens, Andee's boyfriend, makes Andee watch *The Day After,* and then he talks about how it felt growing up fifty miles from the Iron Curtain, always worrying about mutual assured destruction. This woman on the bus is obsessed with her split ends, and so am I. But the new sliding-scale therapist doesn't want me to eat in the room—don't you realize I'm going to lose it? After therapy, I crave coke for the first time in a while—maybe a cocktail or two wouldn't be that bad of an idea. Jeremy and I go to a movie about the anti-war protests—holding hands is still my favorite part. The movie makes me wish I could throw myself in harm's way and not worry about a few bruises and sprains. Yoga: so many ways to hurt myself. But when I get home, everyone on the street looks so hot from five floors up. I'm the broken windmill at the end of the beach, so lonely I suck men in from miles away—to keep me company, right—company—that's what I need: more company! A new mattress wouldn't hurt either, then I wouldn't have to wake up in a hole—help, dig me out!

What do you want to do—connect to the internet, continue working off-line, or exit the program? If only there were more choices. Chrissie comes over at 1:30 am: I'll do anything you want—clean your house, do your dishes, type for you—I just need you to play me one song. What is it? "Mack the Knife." Oh honey, I don't have that. You don't have Ella or Louis, Billie didn't do it—who's the fourth one—Ella Fitzgerald, Billie Holiday, Louis Armstrong . . . not Dizzy Gillespie—you know. I don't know. That guy—the other one.

Chrissie says she's in her Warhol drag: blond wig with a suit and women's shoes. Did Warhol wear heels? At the Tibetan restaurant, Jaysen and I sit next to these two straight couples that talk about buying houses, and how hard it is to get the hang of it. One guy says something about being fertile and the other woman says no—*you're* potent, *she's* fertile. In my dream, I'm on so many drugs it's ridiculous—I guess when I wake up, I'm supposed to think well, at least I feel better than if I did all that. Instead, I think: in the minefields, what does the golden wasp say to the golden butterfly?

I want that Christina Aguilera wig—bleached white dreads that fling quickly to the side when I turn. I'm complaining to Socket, on the corner of Valencia and Twentieth: I'm so over being a whore. But wait—seven hours later and I've turned three tricks: why would I ever do anything else? Just sit at home and count twenties, hello.

Here's a snapshot of the glamorous life: this guy's shit pouring onto my mint green sheet—um, I think you need to clean up. Afterwards, he still wants to get fucked—you can't have your baby and eat it too! Aaron tells me about riding around Bremerton looking for drugs—for someone else—he only did one symbolic line, but there was no burning or anything. Kirk calls: was fatalistic the word you were looking for?

I decide to come in my food—Jeremy never did it for me. It's 3 a.m. pasta, and I'm on the phone sex line, whoops I got disconnected. Over to the other one, and this guy can't do it right, but I'm playing anyway. I shoot right into the pasta while it's sitting demurely in the sink: scallions, string beans, bean sprouts, cilantro, lemon, tamari, rice vinegar—and come. I can't really taste it.

Every day starts with the three d's: disappointment, disillusionment, and devastation. Rue says he was done editing his video, and then everything went out of sync. He says: I spent hours and hours and hours and hours on it, and now I have to erase my hard drive and start over—I hate computers, but now I've based my whole life around them; I just want to go to the woods and eat bark—I went to get my blood test results, and I've lost a hundred T cells—I'm down to 483, a hundred more and the doctor says I'll have to start thinking about meds.

Rue says everyone's crazy, you're completely crazy but at least you're rational. I cook a pot of lentils, and every time I eat some, I can't think—I'm allergic to lentils and I can't think. Chrissie says it's yin and yang, what you get is what you take, are you going to the benefit for the Faerie Freedom Village at Pride? More repressed and less depressed, or is that more stressed and equally possessed? Ralowe says he came twelve times yesterday, all over the place—the bathrooms at UC Berkeley, downtown, seven times on the internet when he was supposed to be making music. On the radio: a guy who runs an animal shelter in LA talks about nurturing this cat dying of cancer, he says at that time they're perfect because they know about here and beyond, and what we're doing between the two.

In the morning, I always want more messages, someone's voice to keep me company. I have a sore throat; I just hope it isn't an STD because then the antibiotics will make me sick for weeks. Ralowe says they don't do anything, but yes they do: they make me sick for weeks! I have some weird moment when I think maybe my hands are getting better; then they start to hurt. But the real emergency is that I'm beginning to get a tan line from my fire escape sunbathing—

help, take me to the beach! Body image drama: I can't exercise, so the only thing that makes me able to deal is a tan. It makes me look less flabby.

On the way to Whole Foods and there's a chick chirping in a bush—where's your mother? Oh there she is, little black bird swooping in with food and yes of course I've got tears in my eyes at this display of parental duty. But then the bird flies away again, and after the woman in the Mercedes stops staring at me; I put some food up on the mailbox so the bird will find it.

Originally, I started going to Whole Foods for the bargain shopping, you know what I mean. Though recently—ever since that security guard started following me around—I haven't been doing much bargain shopping. Also, I get that panic attack every time, and I'm trying to calm my nerves, thirty years of not knowing how to relax my brain is too long already, right? So now I just go to Whole Foods because it's the closest place with supposedly organic produce and I don't want to hurt my hands too much trying to get home— although 40 dollars for eight items isn't exactly calming, especially when there's no work. Kayti leaves a message: she went to *The Hulk* and it made her think of the good old days; that hulk has really been working out. She says when are they gonna make *The Dukes of Hazzard* movie—I love that car!

On the plane back from LA, Eric gets this headache so bad; he thinks something's going to break. Then he thinks he might die, better go to the emergency room. They tell him he has a cyst in his brain, probably aggravated because of the air pressure. Eric says: I can deal with anything else in my body going wrong, but my brain? Andee says how old did you just turn? I say thirty, she says I knew it would happen to me, but I never thought it would happen to you—well, at least now I know someone else who's thirty. You don't know anyone who's older than you? Well, sure, but I don't know anyone else who's thirty.

Andee says she just bought a shirt on sale at H&M because there's nowhere else to buy clothes in Berlin. Well, you can bet their workers are on sale too! Then she bought some Diesel jeans, but they're cheap in Berlin. Are they the ones with acid-washed asses?

No, Mattilda, they're just regular jeans, I like that they have a stitch on the back of the knee.

This is the best story ever . . . I'm trying to get someone to drive me around to search for rainbow flags to snatch—gotta burn a couple and make an outfit, right? My mother sends me a package, inside there's a fucking rainbow flag from Italy, PACE written in white. She says the flags were hanging everywhere, and I'm confused that I'm touched by this misguided gesture. Well, at least it's made of cloth—here, they're all plastic—it goes right up, hello beautiful. It'll look gorgeous with the burnt American flag, wrapped over my rainbow fishnets and not much else.

Every Pride weekend, we have a heat wave. Benjamin says all the gays who come here from everywhere else probably don't realize this isn't how it is here. The gays, polluting the air until my head is nothing but sinuses, my poor poor sinuses—I should be on *The 700 Club*. But seriously it's HOT, the Walk of Shame is gonna be a long long walk, honey get me a stretcher!

Did you hear that? It's so hot out, I'm wearing shorts. At home, there's dried come on my leg and it looks like a scar. I taste some, crunchy, but leave the rest for realness points. How do I write about activism? My moment starts with burning the flags for my outfit, wrapped around the rainbow fishnet bodysuit like a frat boy realness mini-sarong, the Prada label shoes, new wig-of-all-wigs—purple with all the plastic flowers in the world growing there. But the magic begins when I'm speaking on the bullhorn because the sound system hasn't arrived, and then Karoline comes up with the sound system mike, and then boom from then on it's flawless. I do mean flawless. Everyone's brilliant. Somehow the police negotiators get us a whole side of Market Street, we march all the way to the Castro with only our own interruptions. Of course we give out more awards. Best Front-Row Seat to Watch Police Brutality goes to the Center, with Bagdad Café a runner-up because that's where the cops gunned down Jihad Alim Akbar. Harvey's gets the Auntie Tom Award for supporting Gavin Newsom while making money off the legacy of Harvey Milk. The highlight is when we light an effigy of Gavin Newsom on fire in the middle of Eighteenth and Castro and it burns to the ground, a fire truck arrives to disperse us. Even Chrissie Contagious is there, I think this is the first time she's ever shown up to anything I've ever done.

We move the sound system to an impromptu after-party in Collingwood Park. Spin-the-bottle is the highlight for me—my first time, really. I make out with Benjamin, Rhania, Yasmine and Brodie—ready for more, but for some reason the game loses energy. The walk back to Eric's car through the Castro is a spectacle of its own—all the gays gaping—yes, darling, we are mixing Chanel with Prada!

At Whole Foods, Ralowe says: what I'm attracted to is so fucked up—it's like my desire is still informed by Disney movies—I never get hard about anything in the real world, I searched the internet but couldn't find any pictures of Gore Vidal when he was young, so I found some other porn. Ralowe says everyone's trying to look like Gay Shame—Miss Thing, are you having delusions of grandeur? Then she says it's Tokyo '96, but I put her in her place—Tokyo '96 was just New York '92—club kid realness, please. Ralowe says: but have you seen Tokyo '97?

My trick is jerking all over the place because of alcohol and some crazy meds. Celexa in the bathroom cabinet—that's an HIV med, right? He says let me tell you something, sometimes you're like a psychiatrist—yeah, no kidding. On the way out, he shows me the living room: that's the sofa I'll die in, he says. You'll be bringing me Meals-on-Wheels, and you'll say hey I remember that guy.

Jeremy has Sarah's car, so we go to visit the sea lions—it's been so long. On our way there, some guys yell faggots—are you kidding? There aren't too many sea lions around, but this one dock is covered by wet ones who keep pushing each other into the water, then a closer dock where they're all snuggling together. Way in the back are the big big ones who rarely move. Jeremy likes to talk about what the sea lions are thinking—those two are in love. That one wants the other one to sit on him.

We drive to Baker Beach 'cause I want to see the ocean, but the entrance is locked. Same thing at China Beach. I remember the trick that had his friends kidnap him and then I sucked his dick while he was blindfolded, but he freaked out when he felt stubble on my face, he wasn't ready for faggotry. So Jeremy and I rush to Ocean Beach 'cause I have a trick at 11:30. The ocean is so big, I get that little kid feeling—I just have to figure out how to get there without Jeremy. The sea lions. I tell Jeremy it's weird reading the beginning of this book, because it starts when we just met and there's no foresight at all about anything. Sandy's moved into Jeremy's room. Jeremy says: every two weeks, Sandy has a breakdown about being in an open relationship, but other than that, it's great.

Chrissie calls from downstairs: I've got a gift for you, something you can use to decorate the neighborhood. Knock knock and when I get to the door, she's already back by the elevator and there's a brick on the floor. I can't stop laughing. Andee's on the phone, telling me how she was on Oranienstrasse in Kreuzberg shopping, well not shopping because she can't afford to buy anything—shopping for what she might want to buy, if she had money. Then she heard some commotion and it was a punk-rock record store that'd just appeared out of nowhere.

Andee went inside, and there was the back of Zan's head. Zan said: I just turned thirty. Andee said: I turned thirty months ago, are you having a crisis? Zan said I'm dating someone who's nineteen. Andee said that sounds like a crisis.

Rue and I walk to North Beach, there's a stuffed animal shop and I get excited looking in the window, tears in my eyes and all. Then I see the panda, oh the panda—and actually now I'm crying and I'm not sure whether Rue thinks I'm laughing. I start thinking up plans to rescue the stuffed animals I had as a kid—the panda, the mice, Henry the Hippo. What's the difference between riding a bike and bike riding? Bike riding is what I did with my father as a kid, our time together—he screamed and screamed and screamed. Of course I screamed too, scared of the bridges because I might just fly off.

In the morning, I wake up to the sound of squealing mice. Are they having babies in my cabinets, or is it just the pigeons in the ceiling? I try to convince myself that it's the pigeons, but I still can't sleep. When I get up, there's a roach crawling out of the drain—are the mice in the drain, scaring the roaches? At least when I go to yoga, I know that I'll stop eating for an hour and a half.

I'm having a Provincetown nostalgia moment because of the heat wave, which is over now, but my moment goes on. Thinking about running with sweat pouring down my face, riding a bike with my groceries attached to a rack with bungee cords, walking through the sand on the way to the beach. When will I be able to use my body again?

Okay, so there are plenty of possible reasons why I get kind of high at the Power Exchange, well not kind of high but HIGH really fucking high. Like towards the end, when some song comes on, and the song isn't that good but the beat oh the beat—I just have to do runway, and even if my runway isn't that inspired, it sure is better than whatever else is going on. Then there's the moment that guy with the newsboy hat—well, the one with the newsboy hat who actually looks British, the one whose dick I'm sucking and it curves upward and then he pulls away. But when I get high is later, he holds his dick all the way in the back of my throat and shoots, oh I just want him to hold me like that forever. Even though someone else just came in my mouth, and then I hugged him—that wasn't as good as this, and then the guy punches me like we're on the soccer team together—have a good game!

That almost makes me crash, but then there's the contact high from all the drugs, though more likely it's the actual drugs going through everyone's bodies, into their dicks, through their come and into me. News bulletin: yoga made me stronger! Today I actually did the plow and shoulder stand, two poses that I haven't been able to do in at least a year. But did I really just sign up for classmates.com?

Ralowe says she wants to get a job at summer camp, teaching kids to scream. But wait—the new Abercrombie catalog has arrived. Ralowe says: I might get super-aroused and have to self-suck. But is my jaw ache worse than my headache? One-thirty a.m. comes around and I can't even think: dog-walker or dogcatcher? I take three dropperfuls of passionflower and one of cactus grandiflorus, get into bed and hope for sleep.

But no luck. I lie in bed trying to fall asleep by concentrating really hard on any sounds that might be mice. I figure that might put me into a trance, but by 2 a.m. I'm completely sky-high wired. The exciting part is that I get to make spaghetti with radicchio, fresh corn, basil and scallions, scallions, scallions. Then I mix up a miso dressing with lemon for days, and I'm flawlessing all over the room. But in the bathroom, I hear a gnawing noise coming from the plants—are the mice up there, swimming in dirt, devouring the roots?

I'm still amazed how much kidney beans taste like the idea of meat sauce. News bulletin: I've figured out a way to get rid of my tan line! I've been pulling my boxers down lower and lower on the fire escape, but today I realized that around 4 p.m., the sun shines directly onto my bed—so I can lie there naked and get tan. On the bus, this tranny-boy asks if I think leather bars are part of the gay mainstream. I say well, with a lifelong history of racism and misogyny, and a masculinity fetish that borders on fascism . . . what do you think?

How long does it take to get the brim of your baseball cap to fray, or do you buy it that way? And why do so many blonde women take yoga? On the BBC, they're trying to figure out whether President Bush lied about weapons of mass destruction in Iraq, fabricating evidence to fool the American people. The reporter says—with President Clinton and Monica Lewinsky, the issue was: did he lie? The reporter asks, is there anything of that scale going on now? No—just a couple hundred thousand dead Iraqi children.

My mother sees *Take Me Out* on Broadway, or maybe it's off-Broadway, about gay baseball players and there's a shower on stage. My mother says: I've never seen anything like that, a real shower. I wonder what my father thought of the naked men. Then my mother tells me about the Fourth of July in New York. She says: everyone stopped to watch the fireworks, and tears were rolling down my face because I've never seen anything like that, then Macy's put on a show with really good entertainers.

Kayti says she has the answer to all three questions, starting with number three: yoga inspires women to dye their hair blond. Number two: you purchase hats like that, just like you buy ripped jeans—you're gay, right, it's fashion, I thought you people were supposed to know about that stuff—it's not cool to have a flat baseball cap. Number one: doesn't Britney Spears have a whip in her friggin' videos, and if Britney Spears has it then pretty soon all the sixteen-year-olds will have it. And more importantly, what did you wear to the fashion show the other day when it took you nine friggin' hours to get ready?

Ralowe says it's amazing what your body can do—almost as amazing as what it can't do. I get up in the morning to go to court; I can't believe people get up like this every day. I know I've said that before, but I really can't believe it. When I get home, I'm a mess. The rest of the day consists of lying in bed, trying to fall asleep, and then getting up to shit, my nerves and my useless digestion in a bag on someone's doorstep, an unwelcome mat. Every time I think will I ever fall asleep, something wakes me up and then I realize oh, I was asleep.

Today's the trick who wants a prepped-out photo shoot and I have a zit on my dick, thought it would have healed by now but instead it looks like something between a scab and herpes. At the photographer's apartment, it's full porn formula crap. Every pose hurts, and I can't stay hard in any of them. When I'm on my knees in the bed it's all fine, but the photographer doesn't like that pose. He loves the one where I'm on my stomach with my ass in the air, and I turn all the way around to look at the camera. He says: that's a really cool pose. It's the tackiest thing imaginable, and my back hurts. Three hours later and we're both hypoglycemic as all hell, I can't stay hard worth shit, finally I come all over myself—I mean, it's a lot of sticky come—and I'm not even sure if he gets any pictures. When we're done, he shows me the photos—nothing I can use for an escort ad, which is what I really wanted. I mean I did this photo shoot for free—just don't tell anyone, okay?

Back at home, the kids in the stairwell are arguing: Pinoy food is not the same as Vietnamese food because Vietnam lost the war to America! Interesting theory. I can't get out of the house before 7 p.m., so I miss yoga. I go on a walk instead, and within a block, my neck hurts. Then the right side of my jaw starts to go numb, and pretty soon my hands are burning and I can hardly breathe. Am I going to die? The arches of my feet hurt, what's the point of those fucking arch supports? At home, I stretch and stretch. After I eat, I feel a little better. Aaron says he owes me because I lent him money when he was really poor, but he's still really poor. He says he's been spending so much time reading Plato that his neck hurts. Benjamin calls, she says I'm calling to tell you about this really intense conversation I had with Timothy; my skin looks really good today.

I just saw a rat in my house, really a rat—not just a mouse—it's behind the bookshelf but my hands hurt too much to check for sure. It's late, I'm scared of the rat, like it's going to grow larger than the sofa and when it opens its jaws, each tooth will be bigger than my neck. Shit, I just saw it again—it's fast—and why is it making that scratching noise? I was in denial about the rats in the ceiling, but pigeons don't scurry. Some people say pigeons are just flying rats, but I've seen them up close and they're definitely birds.

The only thing worse than live rats in my house would be dead ones. Thinking of all those animals bleeding and cut open by my father or parents or some people—and every time I see them sliced apart, it's those anti-vivisection ads and I haven't dealt with those ads, I mean those memories. The ones that keep coming up, but not as much any more because I haven't been in therapy.

There's a parasite that eats out a fish's tongue, then replaces the tongue, so when the fish needs to chew, there's a parasite doing the work of its tongue. There's another parasite that's a one-cell organism that makes a rat forget its fear of cats, though I'm not sure that would help me. Socket says a rat chewed through her mother's dishwasher, and Rue says rats' teeth grow an inch every few hours, and that's why they have to keep chewing. Finally a day with three tricks—first one makes sure to take exactly fifty-nine minutes. Second one touches me too softly. Third one wants to cuddle for three hours and treat me like a little boy, which is kind of relaxing, actually.

At the bus stop, there's the cutest boy ever created, he's maybe kind of cruising me and I'm staring into the distance trying to look emotionally open. He's not cruising me enough, so I sit down and study the weave of his jeans. Then I get another call, but this trick doesn't know where he is—the bus comes and I lose my chance at a new boyfriend. I eat Thai food and then another trick calls me, says he'll pay me 850 dollars tomorrow just for showing up, and how much would it take to make me his boyfriend 'cause he likes my smile. He's just come from a business dinner where he had eight or nine martinis, but he could drink forty-eight martinis and fly a plane to New Zealand.

The mice or rats or cats or whatever's in my walls wakes me up at fucking 5 or 6 a.m., sometime before dusk I mean dawn at least because, well, it's still dark out. The clock is dead, so the only way I can tell time is if I turn on the cellphone, which I have to do with my teeth because the button's fucked up and I can't push hard enough with my fingers or they'll hurt. The rats are scratching in my cabinets and just as I'm about to get in bed, I see plastic bags shift, imagining Cujo in my kitchen/bedroom. Rats falling out of holes in the ceiling and onto my heart attack.

I don't notice I've fallen asleep until there's someone talking to me: I'm the exterminator. What—it says NO SPRAY on my door—what are you doing in my apartment, I'm sleeping! He says I'm here for the mice, I say just don't put traps out. I keep my eye mask on.

The five-hundred-dollar trick from last night takes me to Millennium, which is so delicious I can't even explain it. He likes me to call him Daddy while I lie on top of him and pretend I'm falling asleep. He says you feel so safe with me that you're falling asleep. Right. He wants me to stay overnight—he's offering to pay for the pleasure—his pleasure, of course. Because I know better. He says you're already sleeping with rats. Then he wants to know about the senior discount. Sure—that's 300 an hour. The California discount? 400. How 'bout forty dollars? No, just give me four dollars and pay me in pennies, I want some chewing gum. He says how 'bout pesos?

Before, he was telling me that he was Mexican-American, but he'd never seen any need to cross the border—I guess they have pesos at U.S. banks. He's a mortician; he says if I saw a young guy like you on the table, I'd cry. He gives me a couple of gifts from Macy's: a Calvin Klein jockstrap and silk Perry Ellis boxers. See, Daddy spoils you. If that's spoiling, then I need a new fruit!

Is there really a whole half-hour on NPR about a BBC makeover show that helps women to look more feminine and throw all the wrong clothes into the trash? Terry Gross should be ashamed of herself, saying she'd really enjoy going shopping with these women and maybe picking out a neat skirt. This trick shows up and he's so hot, preppy boy with a shaved head and lots of freckles—and he's grinning at me. Right away, we're making out and it's totally sex, soft and hard and warm and connected. His dick is delicious, so straight—I think he said he was straight too, but maybe that was someone else.

I'm on top of him then he's on top of me, so much kissing and frantic jerking off, and looking into his eyes with meaning or feeling really—just giving it all—and when I come, he pulls me up to his face so the come is all over his mouth, white and yellow, why is my come always yellow? Then he pulls me in to kiss, and there's my come on my face, which feels kind of gross, I guess because I just came and so I'm worn out. He comes all over his chest and then we just lie there and absorb everything. It's almost too intense. Afterwards, he says the best part was just looking at you, you're so hot. That's what I was thinking about him.

When I put on the new Freaks CD, it's all about the twisted beats and the vocals that go nowhere—when I'm finished with this novel, I'm going to make that kind of music. Lying in bed, I'm listening to the rats devouring my wall, tapping the wall to make sure they're not going to walk out into my bed. Though I've got so much wax in my ears—do rats eat earwax? Rue says they eat everything—roaches, mice, the glue in the floors. I stay in bed until I have to piss so badly that I'm wired, and then just as I'm about to get out of bed, my headache overwhelms everything. Why does piss bubble so much? Andee says you know the pigeons, roaches, mice and rats don't get along—they eat each other, and if they don't eat each other, they just shit on each other.

There's so much pain in between my eyes that I can't even stay balanced—am I getting anemic? I get back in bed, hole in my head until I wake up because the mice are squealing. How are we going to co-exist if they won't even let me sleep? Blake says: remember, mice are rats. Benjamin says: I'd rather see them dead, but I'm not allergic to everything.

Kayti says why do you always try to be lying—there ain't no fucking pigeons in your ceiling—I mean, I know there's rats—there's definitely bugs, probably bedbugs, probably moths, but there ain't no damn pigeons in your goddamn ceiling, I can tell you that right now because there's no pigeons and there's no birds, definitely no deers, probably some vomit. And nope, they don't all get along—I'm sure the bird eats the worm, the worm gets run over by a car, the car hits a deer, the deer—I don't know what deer eat—the deer eats the grass, the grass pretty much doesn't do shit to anything. So pretty much the grass is very benign, very good, I don't think they have problems with any other living thing, you've gotta think about that some more—if grass has any enemies—as far as I know, it doesn't—except for the lawn mower. Yeah, the grass is a pretty good thing, a pretty good thing.

I remember Kayti used to be allergic to grass. Rue says mice don't squeal, haven't you heard the saying "quiet as a mouse"? He says a rat will walk over your body while you're sleeping; I've lived with rats. How do I get rid of them? Poison. What kind of poison will hurt them the least? Rue says: I think that dying of poison is usually painful. At least he's honest. After I get off the phone, I start crying—just a little—about all of it. Because I can't live with rats, but I don't want to poison them. I wish I could just make a deal: stay in my ceiling and it'll be okay! I'll even protect you. I'll let you have the kitchen cabinets, if you want somewhere else. But you can't crawl all over my house and poison me—I'm sensitive.

I have the sweetest trick. He's just returned from walking the dog, Sadie, so he takes a bath while I talk to him. He was in a therapy cult in the seventies, convinced himself that people were born with the THC removed from their bodies, and so you had to smoke pot all the time, twenty-four hours a day. He took the bar to become a lawyer while he was high, but quit six years ago—not the bar, but the pot. He's converted the garage of his house into his living quarters so he can rent out the upstairs—it's crowded and comfy, the ceiling's low but there's a huge garden outside. He wants to get to know me first, and after he comes, the dog jumps onto the bed and licks it all off.

In the morning, I lie in bed tortured by the rats, shouting get out get out GET OUT. They don't listen. I get out of bed—Rue says he has the worst sinus headache in the world, but I have the worst sinus headache in the world, certified by experts from thirty-three different countries. I have the papers to prove it. Another trick who asks what do you do for a living? I'm a cop, and you're arrested for wearing cologne with baby oil—a terrorist threat. I sit in the house all day and read Steve's book—Steve is the THC trick, his book is about a therapy cult—it's the fantasy of family that's drawing me in, I'm waiting for the ultimate collapse. A bulk email that says Young Teen Wall Papers? My dick's so hard on the phone sex line, aching to come I mean really aching, and then after I come OUCH I'm still aching, ouch and then I'm trying to get pictures of the come on the floor but I don't know if it'll show up with the disposable camera.

Why do so many jocks go to art school—whatever happened to the good old days of limp-wristed sissies? And why does everyone in the chiropractor's office have to ask me about my weekend—I don't give a shit about weekends, I'm a whore—get it—a whore! Shove that fucking weekend down my throat and then hand me a few hundreds, okay? Walk bitch walk bitch walk. Turn. Pose. Walk bitch walk bitch walk. Turn. Oops—forgot to look—swimming pool runway, good thing the collagen is waterproof. Breast stroke or have a stroke? Lifesaver—eight calories—forget it—lifeguard! Up the stairs and it's dripping-wet runway—doesn't matter 'cause the sun's so hot you're gonna burn. Are the rats doing runway in my ceiling?

Sha-sha-sha-bleh, sheh-sheh-sheh-blah. Sha-sha-sha-bleh, sheh-sheh-sheh-blah. Rah rah rah! Rah rah rah! Rah rah rah! Movin' on the freeway, shakin' on the highway—movin' shakin' movin' shakin' movin' shakin' fakin' bakin' makin' my house—in my house—in my, in my—house! I swear those are the lyrics. A trick calls with a subtle yet sensational request: how much? One-fifty. A dollar and fifty cents? How 'bout two dollars—that way, I can take the bus back too. Ralowe says he ate apples and soy milk all day yesterday, and for some reason he felt faint. He says how do you get protein—every time I eat meat, I get all sluggish and can't stop masturbating.

Ralowe says is that a rat tap-dancing in your ceiling, but no, it's a rat-pigeon tango—but which one's the man and which one's the woman? Gender is always an issue, even in inter-species romance.

Bouncing on that diving board into infinity—no wait, girl, that's not infinity—that's the street! I walk into this trick's motel room and his eyes are popping out of his head while he's smoking in the dark. I say I can't really deal with smoking. He says okay, then I won't offer you one. I say no, seriously—I'm really allergic. He says you should have told me that over the phone—I'm out the door—enjoy your fucking speed addiction!

It's 2 a.m. on Polk Street, just across from the Econo Lodge that's getting demolished, and there's that blonde woman playing violin again. I get closer and her smile gets bigger, I give her a couple dollars and ask her why she's on this corner. She says because I live over there, and she points to the demolished motel.

Why wear three different overpriced labels when you can spend three times as much on one label—VuittonPradaGucci. Rhania's back from Mexico and she's already making an outfit, she wants it to be strange but not sta-range. What's wrong with sta-range? Rhania says I don't want to go back to work, the kids say weird things to me. The seven-year-old says: you don't smell good because you don't wear deodorant. Rhania says: different people smell different. The kid says: yeah, some people smell like roses and some people smell like trash. Later, the kid tells Rhania: I wish we didn't have to pay you because our parents don't have a lot of money. Right—with the multimillion-dollar home and the trust fund, they're definitely struggling.

It's one of those days when I wake up feeling like my face is scrunched, so much pain between my eyes and nose—and eyes and cheeks—and everything's dry, I don't want to take the eye mask off, ever again. Did I mention my new strategy: keeping the eye mask on when I go to the bathroom in the middle of the night/day/sleep? That way the light doesn't wake me up too much. Kind of works, but it hasn't helped me to feel any better. Sitting on the sofa thinking about going to bed at 8 p.m. I'm so exhausted that if I listen hard enough, I can hear the rats breathing. Went to get rat bait with Rue, and he pointed out the picture of the rat on the box. I almost started crying; I couldn't get the rat bait.

Eleven p.m. and I finally have energy—there is hope in the world!

I clean all the papers off my desk for the first time in at least two years, then I move the pens to the left side and it all feels so much better. On NPR: a black church that's paying white people five dollars to go to services, because they want the church to look like God's country. How much do Asian people get? Jenna says she hasn't called because she's been so tired all the time—tell me about it, we can hang out and be tired somewhere together. I take a sleeping pill, and it does make me fall asleep earlier, but at 10 a.m. I'm still eating toast. It's dry. Back into my head, bed, and when I wake up again, I'm so depressed it's like a wall between the world and me. More like a ditch—no, seriously, I'm loving it!

I do the craigslist thing to recruit people for Lafayette Park, these people are so skittish! Sure, I suck two guys off, but it's not even fun because they're so nervous. At least it gets me out of my exhaustion for an hour, until the walk home, which is eternal—like hope, right? Right. At home, I try to figure out which walls the rats are eating—please just stay out of my food.

If the pens on my desk started dancing, I'd watch. They don't, but I still wait for miracles, blurring my vision to focus on each color. I just got out of bed, I don't want to go back—it never fucking helps! The U.S. military spokesperson says we got Saddam's sons; we'll get Saddam too. He says the only question is who will get the $25 million reward, and move to another country. Is the $25 million part of the $80 billion Congress appropriated—anything to get control of that oil! You're wondering about Chrissie—has she died? I'm wondering too, but I can't bring myself to call her.

I take the 38 to the beach because no one wants to drive there, I always forget which 38 doesn't go all the way there. It's always the one I'm on. I discover Sutro Heights Park, where long-ago Mayor Adolph Sutro used to have an estate—there are people playing croquet and so many little black birds! I watch the birds and then I'm tired, have to go down a hill to get to the beach and my hands are burning and the bottom of my right foot is burning too—I shouldn't have worn the insoles! I feel like an invalid walking down, and then when I finally arrive, everyone's laughing at my spectacle and I'm way too exhausted. I sit down in the sand and watch the surfers—

with the humidity, it's actually still warm out. I take my shoes off and everything feels better.

I watch the sun, as it becomes a circle—almost white really against the gray-blue clouds, and as it sinks closer to the ocean, I picture my hands falling off into the sand—if only I could bury them and new ones would grow back! The sun gets brighter as it goes down and I'm watching it closely, this ball of yellow with pink and blue fading in and out. And everyone's watching now, as it starts to sink into the clouds that are right above the water, and everything's pink and I need to piss. As soon as I leave the beach, I'm exhausted again. I try to find the area by the windmills where the cruising takes place.

Craigslist is such a terrible thing—I'm always thinking it's going to rescue me, but instead it keeps beating my poor tired hands, my hands—will I ever rescue my hands? But wait, there's an actual hook-up. Rushing over to his house, I'm high—anything to bring me out of that deep dark despair in my chair—help, Tony Blair! I get to this guy's house, and let's just say I'm not cruising craigslist for at least six months—it's a promise. Not that he wasn't cute or anything, it's just that horrible feeling of having sex with someone who's trying so desperately not to connect on any level at all. Kirk calls it two-dimensional sex—it's worse than a trick because at least a trick wants passion, or the illusion of passion. Rhania calls to ask what I do to stay in my body, which actually brings me into my body.

The story of my life: I wake up, I break up, I wake up, I break up. I love heroin in the springtime, I love heroin in the fall! At least my air purifier covers the sound of the rats. Of course, there's everything that sounds like rats, and then there's the sound of claws—or feet—or whatever they have, scurrying across my kitchen floor—at least I hope it's the floor. Eric wants to know if I have any new crushes—what do you mean? He says it's funny; you'll talk about absolutely anything else. Then I start talking about the come-on-my-face photo project, so I guess Eric's right.

The elevator in my building is broken again, and I have crabs. It's another day when I don't know how I'll stay up, but then 3 a.m. rolls around and I'm wired—it's so predictable and strange. There was a fire in the building two doors down, and a whole charred apartment is in the street. Ralowe's getting her wisdom teeth removed at General tomorrow, and I'm worried that I'm going to need a root canal. Two years ago, a dentist tried to give me one, I said give me another dentist!

Ralowe wants to know if his music is full of purposely obscure and arty references. Is that a serious question? Jeremy and I go to Golden Era—just after we arrive, a table of seventeen sits down, so we're rushing to order but no one's rushing to take our order. Wednesday night and it's completely packed, what's going on? Tenderloin gentrification for sure, but the food is extra-delicious because I haven't been there in so long. Jeremy's taking a Greek and Roman mythology class this summer. The teacher gives these multiple-choice tests where she tries to trick you into picking the wrong answer; Jeremy says: does it really matter if the monster had a thousand hands or a hundred hands? Though he got that question right—he says you can have a hundred hands, but you can't have a thousand. He's talking so there won't be any quiet spaces. I wait for one, look him in the eyes. He goes to the bathroom.

When Jeremy and I get back to my house, someone who looks like Rhania is at the door—oh wait, that is Rhania. She says I'm just buzzing my friend Mattilda, but she's not here yet. She comes up and we all sit down on the sofa—Jeremy and I are exhausted, and Rhania's wired. Jeremy goes home and Rhania and I end up talking more about how to stay in our bodies. I say you're definitely way more in your body since you haven't been doing so many drugs. She says well, if that doesn't help, then something's really wrong.

The pigeons enjoy celery, they love beans, collard greens, and kale, but they're not particularly interested in cilantro. And they don't even touch lemons or kombu seaweed. I'm afraid that the rats are not as particular, chewing away at every plastic bag underneath the sink. I just wish they wouldn't make so much noise. This morning, I was actually having a restful dream, Ralowe was squeezing cloves into a stew like cloves of garlic or maybe they were chestnuts. And all of the sudden I heard this scurrying behind my head: if this novel is about parasites, then how will it end?

I call Rue and ask him if he'll go to the hardware store again to get bait, just don't show me the picture! I don't want to kill the rats, but I don't want them gnawing away at the electrical wires until BOOM—there goes my apartment. Or feeding me allergies until my head is one big cocoon. Andee says you need to go to the country, and when I excavate the stack of bills towering over my desk—I don't want to live with money, wait I mean without money—I mean I don't want to give them any more money. That's where the country comes in, starving to death on some farm because I can't pick anything, my hands planted in the soil. Reap and sow, honey, reap and sow!

Oh wait—the pigeons are eating the cilantro—they just like to let it cook in the sun for a little while. Rue's been working sixteen-hour days doing cinematography for a movie she doesn't really like that much, she says this is gonna kill me much faster than the AIDS. On our walk, she starts to get a fever. Everyone's getting impetigo, this rash that spreads all over your face. Jaysen, Jeremy and Rue have all had it, and the corners of my mouth keep getting redder—is it the impetigo? In the morning, it's the same old mantra: I don't want to get up, should I get up? I don't want to get up. Should I get up? I get up to see what time it is—12:47, which means I guess I should get up. I thought maybe it would be eleven-something, and then I'd have to get back in bed.

NPR says the mini-nukes are almost ready! I guess there's always something to choke on, if it's not a ham sandwich then it's Hammer time. Later, I'm choking on this guy's cock and he still pushes my head down, he knows just the right time to pull back and then I'm back on it. It's Buena Vista Park and when I come, I'm so crazed that the guy holding me says breathe, breathe.

I breathe, kind of twisting my ankle as I'm walking down the hill, but honey it sure was fucking worth it. The first guy I had sex with was wearing Jeremy's blue jacket, and he had spongy hands, too. The second guy was smellier, but damn I just loved the way he held my head like a football. On the bus, there's some tweaked queen who asks me if I'm still living at the President Hotel—no, I live a few doors down. But how does she know I live on that block? She says: in the building that had the fire? I say no, two doors down from that one.

Someone on the radio says you can't die from heartache, and then this trick comes over with a bag of three different kinds of poppers. He says: shit, I left the thing in my car—the thing. I'll be right back. Can't I just go back to bed—street cred: hole in my head? In my dream, Ralowe has the heat on and I'm sweating, there's a plant in a glass jar inside of another plant's pot—it needs company. In real life, I talk to my mother's therapist—no kidding. It happens because of that time when my mother said something about her therapist not understanding her relationship with Dad. I said I could tell her a few things.

So—really—I tell my mother's therapist a few things. And it's fun, until the therapist starts talking about how my parents are crushed, destroyed by what they did—the therapist wants to talk about the four of us getting together. I say first, he has to acknowledge that he sexually abused me—that's the first step—it's been seven years since I confronted him, and he hasn't even taken that first step. I think the therapist realizes she's pushed the wrong button, but then my trick arrives. I have to go.

It's summer out, but I'm still cooking for winter: beans with root vegetables, collard greens, teff. I feel like hell. Zero says sorry I haven't talked to you lately; I don't know what my problem is. Ralowe tells me the nerves in my ears will die if I don't put the headphones on a certain way. He's playing his music for me in the Indymedia room at the Redstone Building, distorted craziness and when I get bottled water across the street, it tastes like flat 7UP. It's the brand of water that's owned by 7UP. Ralowe says maybe there was a strike at the factory.

I go on a date, yes really a date—with that boy Jonah who I've thought was cute ever since I met him when I got out of jail after the Center escapade. We go to see *The Discreet Charm of the Bourgeoisie* at the Castro, everyone gets gunned down at the end and then we walk out to these kids forming a crowd around one kid beating up another. In seconds, the cops arrive to drag people off—they know who they want, and everyone else leaves. These fags say:

does this happen every day? We're from Portland, and nothing this exciting ever happens there.

Tourists have so much insight. Jonah and I make out in the kitchen and it's fun, the best part is just rubbing my face against his. He says he wants to take things slow, and that's fine. What do you think—I'm a slut? Rue calls on the hottest day, he says it's awful, Mattilda, it's awful. I get wired, decide to walk to Rue's house, but she says it's too polluted out. I walk up to Russian Hill in the new shoes I accidentally bought on Haight Street, seized by the demon of consumerism and they're not even as comfortable as I thought. My pinkie toes start to get chafed, but I keep walking. I've gotta get some kind of cardio exercise. Fifty minutes and I'm back in my apartment, it wasn't as hot as Rue said—there was a nice breeze— but it's later now, and I'm not in the Mission. There are big blisters on my toes—these shoes don't even fit right.

Eric says: did you have your date yet? I say yeah, it was fun. Eric laughs—you didn't tell me about it, I'll have to keep bothering you. Andee runs into Zan in Berlin again, he says one thing we agree on is that it's scandalous you're not drinking cocktails—you don't really feel any better? After two miraculous success stories, the Power Exchange is back to normal—everyone I'm hot for isn't interested. I can't believe I stay until closing, it's so depressing and I don't even get a good orgasm out of it, just light trails in my eyes. When I get home, I smell, even though I barely touched anyone—the cooties probably jumped off and landed on fresh meat. Matt calls to say are you ready for court tomorrow? Yeah, I have to bring a measuring tape this time so I can measure the fluorescents in the hallway ceiling and then replicate all that beautiful light.

Of course the judge isn't in the courtroom, so it's time to watch the Hall of Justice runway. My new boyfriend is working the Brooklyn Italian thug look, but today he's got on a three-button suit and his shoes are freshly shined, burgundy shirt, and his eyes keep looking in my direction. I know he just wants me to hold him in my arms while he sobs heavily and I say: I'll visit you in jail. For some reason, though, he won't sit on the same bench as us. His suit is slightly wrinkled, even though it fits right, and that's how I know he's not used to wearing it.

The sweatshirt with half a word written on one side of the zipper—and the other half written on the other side—is very popular today. FRI-SCO makes several appearances, and baby-phat spends her share of time in the ladies room—lines? It's all about stripes and solids for the formal set, patterns are a rarity, though Ms. Sausalito '78—or maybe '82—when did Sausalito go from counterculture haven to tourist trap? Ms. Sausalito is wearing lots of turquoise jewelry and a silk pants suit with yellow palm trees on blue, and the extra-extra-wide belt cinching it all together. Apparently, she needs to powder her nose quite often in the privacy of the bathroom. When she comes out, she leans over to us and says: are you driving the getaway car? Did she just come from the Weather Underground movie, or did she do her own time underground? Eleven a.m.—two hours late—and the judge has still not arrived. Ms. Sausalito asks me if I'm the judge. I say yes, everybody is dismissed—and she leaves.

THE NEW TOASTER

◉　　◉　　◉　　◉

I play Diamanda's "My World Is Empty Without You" for Rue, and
I keep having to rewind it to the point where Diamanda goes from
a growl to softness. I close my eyes and yes, I think of Rue dying—
and whether my world will be empty without him. I know that's
dramatic, but we *are* listening to Diamanda. Then I play David
Bowie's version of the Jacques Brel song "Amsterdam," because I'm
a sucker for any ridiculous song about hookers. What's the line?
Something about giving up their bodies for a thousand other men.

Rue says a thousand—I think I'm up around five thousand. And
five of them were fun. Later, there's a report on NPR about tourism,
17 million visitors to San Francisco is down to 13 million, seven billion dollars is down to under six. Did they really just say seven
billion dollars? I go to see *Party Monster*, where Macaulay Culkin
plays club kid Michael Alig chopping up Angel the drug dealer and
dropping him in the East River. It's supposed to be the early nineties,
but they're playing Stacey Q and Miss Kittin—fuck that shit, I want
club kid realness! Plus, we only get a few shots of the outfits—it was

all about the outfits, right? And drugs, of course, which of course I start to crave, even with some of the worst acting combined with a script written by a not-so-creative ten-year-old.

My trick at the W wants me to stay over—when I tell him I've got to go, he says what, there's someone else? That's the funny part—play-acting—but then his personality suddenly changes, he says: you're stupid. Why am I stupid? Because you're not staying here, in the Heavenly Bed. That's the bed's official name, I remember that from another trick. The trick starts patting the bed, he says come over here—you haven't done enough for me to pay you yet.

It's a totally different culture out there in the East Bay, luckily Jaysen picks me up at the BART and we go to New World Vegetarian. There are two burn-outs from Burning Man counting out six hundred dollars in ones at their table. They got spotted by the feds smoking pot, and were issued a four-hundred-dollar ticket, but then they made six hundred in an hour of panhandling. Jaysen says he's been working all the time, but he's still broke. And since he started doing massage at Eros, his sex life is totally tied up with work, since he meets guys in the steam room on his break—he doesn't like it. I say: I don't have any idea what you're talking about.

I come home and my whole apartment is filled with flies—where did they all come from? Ralowe scans the *BAR* and spots a new sex club—333 Linden—the ad shows a guy with his clothes on! Ralowe thinks that means it'll be extra-bourgie, but I'm just looking for any new place where I can have bad sex.

Ralowe calls me in the morning—he actually went to 333, there was no one there, but the guy working sucked him off. Actually, Ralowe doesn't say that much, she describes the setting but not the sex. What did the guy look like? I don't know. What did you do? Stuff. Was it fun? Yeah—it was great—but not worth ten dollars.

Actually, I go to 333 two hours before Ralowe, at night the alleys in Hayes Valley almost feel like alleys. I hear the house music and see the steel mesh door, when someone exits I ask him how it was. He says there's no one there, but the guy behind the counter is nice. And you know what—I think of going in and asking that guy if he wants me to suck him off. But Ralowe will be ready soon, and I'm not horny anyway. The walk home is endlessly filled with fatigue, not to mention this sketcher who follows me for three blocks—Hey mister! Hey mister!

Mister Mary, Sir! I call the phone sex line—maybe I should be asexual. The new sea salt is not nearly as salty as the old, I just keep piling and piling it on until maybe there's a little food with my salt, thanks. Would you like some fresh-ground pepper with that? Chrissie calls, she says I bought my plane ticket, and I'm leaving next Tuesday for West Virginia—I'm gonna live with my godmother for six months and get off drugs, then I'm gonna apprentice as a chef with my mother's cousin in Vegas; I haven't seen my godmother since I was four—and I'm not sure I'll see another fag for six months—so I'm kind of nervous.

On the phone sex line, this guy doesn't believe I haven't come in a week—he says don't you masturbate? The next guy wants a magical time, but then he's worried that he knows me. I guess I care, because I study his voice for clues. I talk to some guy, who's supposedly bisexual, but by the end it's full gay porn talk—he wants to breed me—I come anyway.

The new toaster is amazing. Not only is it red, but I don't have to flip the toast over three times—and I can toast two pieces at once, pure luxury! But what is going on with my sinuses? It's like New York all over again—collapsing on stoops, gazing at any hot guy thinking maybe he's the one to drag me out of all this pain. Staring into space, I'm so tired I want to kill myself just for being alive.

I think about cruising craigslist, even though I've banned myself—how am I supposed to have bad sex without craigslist? I try Lafayette Park—it's the first foggy night in months, and there's some crazy shit going on. I'm staring at what looks like someone's bags on a bench, but when I get closer I see it's this guy lying down with no pants on, boots sitting on the ground below his feet, ass in the air, jerking off. He's got long gray hair and a beard, kind of a lumberjack type and the vacuum cleaner salesman standing next to me smells like a closet full of moldy laundry and moth balls.

Then there's the guy on the tennis court, sticking his dick through the fence, and a guy outside the fence sucking him off. The guy's really pumping away, I come closer to get a good look—he's the same guy I ran into on one of the benches in the clearing, a black guy with a white hoodie that obscures his face. When he sees me, he pulls away to button up. I say you don't have to stop, and he grunts—he's got an aggressive limp like a straight guy who gets in fights, but what kind of straight guy would be working that faggotty jailhouse fantasy?

Then when I circle around again, the lumberjack guy has moved to a different bench, but same scene. Something's really weird, because then I spot the guy from the tennis court, on the other tennis court, and the same guy is sucking his cock again. There are some drunken straight guys in the dark above me, just standing around waiting—I'm wondering if it's some bashing scenario because I think I hear them say something about faggots. I stand there below them, trying to figure it out. Then I walk around the circuit, there's a homeless guy on a bench who sits up and says: I couldn't get a taxi I couldn't get a taxi.

When I'm back around, the bashers are down below, where it's even darker, standing there sort of swaying because they're so drunk but not touching or saying anything. It's really eerie. I figure I better go home. As I turn to walk through the tennis court, some guy hurls something into the trashcan with a loud boom, and walks quickly towards me. I walk faster, trying not to look like I'm running away. But I'm running away.

THE LABORATORY

◉   ◉   ◉   ◉

When mice chew, they sound like someone's cutting my nails. Or maybe that's the sink dripping, the hot water screeching, the ceiling caving in on my sinuses. It's the anniversary of September 11, a Korean rice farmer and labor activist stabs himself to death on top of a police barricade at the WTO protests in Cancún, yelling WTO KILLS FARMERS. I'm stretching on the floor, collapsing into sobs as the Mexican government spokesperson says they may deport the Korean contingent for conducting a singing vigil at the site of the suicide.

My trick smells like that combination of liquor and cigarettes that everyone I used to sleep with smelled like—kind of rotten and not quite comforting. Sort of makes me want to vomit, but not nearly as much as earlier, recovering from the oil in the vegan pizza I ate at Rue's last night. I thought that for some reason the oil didn't affect me—a miracle—until I got out of bed and had to shit seven times. Then I went out into the heat, all nauseous and shaky.

Karoline's showing me around this mall where the front is posh stores, but then you step into the back and each story is half as tall—and there are yoga studios and daycare centers. In the front, Karoline says, it's rich fags and yuppies, but punk kids live in the back. Only in Santa Cruz, I think, and then I wonder where the ocean is. I'm wandering around in the stairways, but I can't figure out how to get to the front. Finally, I find a door that leads outside, but into an old crumbling graveyard with lots of little kids and tourists. I don't want to step on the stones or the plants or the kids, so it's hard to walk.

There's this really steep area of just slate that feels like it's going to crack, and when I get to the top of that, there's a café. An old woman is smoking so many cigarettes that she has a silver football helmet full of ashes and butts. She pours the helmet over her head, laughing, and then drops it. When I reach over to hug her with my legs, I notice a spider on her head. Then I look closer, and it's maggots. My father's somewhere. When I wake up, it's so hot that I'm sweating under just a sheet, something is terribly wrong.

I'm not sure how much of the mouse problem is my imagination, and how much is theirs. I finally figured out that the nail-clipping sound isn't the rats eating my walls, but the pigeons talking. Now I'm thinking that all the noise is the pigeons in the ceiling, not the rats under the cabinet, but what's that scampering across the floor? My wrists burn, but before the mall or the maggots or the rats, there's the parking lot. I'm waiting for my sister in the car, and I decide to move it, only I'm not at the wheel and I almost hit all the homophobic kids screaming at me. There's a huge headless man on top of a truck, asking for change, but then I realize that he's not headless because he's got his head in his hands. He's a machine that comes out to chase me, and I'm trying to move the car. I leave my bag on the side of the road, that's how we know dreams are just like reality.

I wake up with a beautiful cool breeze blowing the curtains up almost to the ceiling—honey, that's no breeze, that's a windstorm! Whatever it is, it means the heat wave is finally over and I don't ever want to move from this place of wind in my covers. When I get up, I realize I should have stayed in bed—because I'm still in bed in my head. Eventually I go on a walk, to avoid a terrible nap.

I decide to try the Turkish restaurant with Magdalena because otherwise I'll have to get steamed vegetables at the Thai restaurant again, since everything else makes me feel like I'm crashing from acid because of the MSG, or shitting non-stop because of the oil. I bite into a stuffed grape leaf and at first it tastes great, then my head's so stuffy I can't even open my eyes. I'm serious—it's like someone just gave me a sleeping pill. On the bus, there's this big straight guy in leather pants, grabbing his crotch, actually he's just scratching there. He's leaning back and staring at the women in the front or maybe out the window, pumping his crotch up into the air a few inches, over and over. This goes on for at least ten blocks— I'm totally enthralled—is that really his hard-on pointing back towards me? He's not cute, but I can feel myself getting hard anyway. Just as I'm about to get off the bus, I catch the eye of a woman behind me—she's got the same perplexed look I have on my face. She meets my eyes and we start laughing, I can't stop laughing, across the street and into everyone's eyes with giggles.

So I feel good for a few minutes, then it's back to the usual. When Chrissie takes off her sunglasses, it looks like someone hit her, and the bruises aren't wearing off. She says no, it was makeup, but I guess it's just the color of her skin: too many bones poking through her face. Black marks all over her knuckles, and she asks if she can shoot up in the bathroom; I can't tell if she's serious. I say: me first.

I ask Chrissie if she's going to quit everything—she says well, of course I'll go out on the weekends. I say you're just going to West Virginia to get to the source, your own bathtub of crank and pretty soon you'll own the whole town. She says it'll be like three farm boys in a movie. She means a porn movie, but I say I hope it's not *Boys Don't Cry*—don't end up like Brandon Teena, honey—well the tina's a given, but skip the beatings, the blood and the bullets.

Chrissie has taxi vouchers, so we head over to the Tibetan restaurant, but they're closed because it's Monday. We're in the Marina with nowhere to go—it's like the Connecticut suburbs, right in the middle of San Francisco—four tiny blond women in waistless khakis love my pants, no they *really* love them. Thanks.

We end up at Fuzio—I went to the one at the Embarcadero once with Thea, and it was okay. This one's pretty good too, except for my bloating stomach, expanding over my belt and under my jacket—I hate my body. I take my jacket off. Afterwards, we walk to Van Ness and Chrissie holds my hand, well my mitten over my hand. It's the first time in a while when I really feel like I love her, like we have this shared history and I hope maybe one day she'll get better. When we stop holding hands, Chrissie says her headache is so bad that half her head is numb, and the other half is being hit with a sledgehammer. Rhania has a dream where she can't take her elephant in the rich elephant park, Yasmine jumps over the fence and hits her head. When Rhania gets back out, her elephant is waiting in a cab. Andee says ever since I moved to London, my hair is all dry and limp, I don't know what to do—sometimes when I get off the bus, I can't stop choking from all the fumes. Sounds like LA—you walk outside and there's only one choice: suicide. These people wake up and they think that's air. Ralowe says: you slept? Well, I mean— you know. Oh.

Chrissie calls from Parkersburg, West Virginia. She got a job at Chi-Chiz and there's a fag who's the host, plus there are two gay bars there. But actually she sounds okay, isn't slurring or mumbling all her words, so that's good. Socket says the way she decides whether to go back to bed is by looking at the bags under her eyes— if they're worse, she goes back to bed. Today the bags under my eyes are more angular than usual, red mixed in with the dark and I'm scared because I've been in bed for the last three hours trying to sleep. First, I was too tired to get up to eat, then I got up to eat, then back in bed, then I was too wired to get out of bed. Tired, wired, tired, wired—just get me a sledgehammer and some mayonnaise!

I go to 333 Linden on the night before the Folsom Street Fair, just to see what it's like at the busiest possible time, but there's hardly anyone there. And how can I still be the youngest person at a sex club—I'm thirty now, it's been over ten years of going to these terrible places. My home away from home, the apple in my eyes—that's why they're dry, it's not my contacts. Donuts without holes in them—wait, that's not donuts, unless maybe they're filled with cream, right cream. But no one's showing holes or cream, they're playing a porn video with the guy who bought a house from one of my tricks in Provincetown.

Outside, there are people waiting to see if there's anyone inside. This one hot guy is giving Santa Cruz straight boy, ruddy cheeks and long blondish hair and stubble, pants cut off below the knee with a white T-shirt tucked in. He wants to know if it's worth going inside, I say I'd be glad to suck your cock in the alley, but he says he's drunk and high, it'll probably take him a while to get it up. He says are you going to the Power Exchange—I hate the Power Exchange. Doesn't everyone hate the Power Exchange?

Benjamin says Friendster's the answer, so many virtual friends and so little time! Which would you prefer: not breathing, or suffocating? Um, I'll take an Alka-Seltzer and some stolen art, SweeTarts and a biodegradable toothbrush, thanks. This trick arrives and I think oh no, how do I do this? We're hugging and I'm trying to obey my own advice: find something hot about it, stay present. After he comes, he falls asleep. I let him rest. When he opens his eyes, he says how do I get you to fuck me now? Gross—why did you have to ruin it? When he pays me, he gives me 147 and says I'll owe you three bucks. He has three more twenties—why do I let him get away with that?

Eric still wants to know if I have any crushes; Jonah isn't gonna call me back. Just as Eric arrives to pick me up, a trick calls from the Ritz-Carlton and I rush over there, feeling the rush in a cab and then walking through the lobby. It's that high again. The floors of the bathroom are marble, but the room isn't impressive otherwise.

I'm watching Maya Deren movies outdoors, and I feel so good because they're almost making me cry, and then I notice every muscle in my body hurts, feet and jaw and wrists are burning. Maybe it's the way I'm sitting, but maybe this is what fibromyalgia feels like. That's what the doctors say I have now. What do I do about it? Well, there's a hot pool with more chlorine in it than a gas chamber, you can do exercises. Any other options? I'll send you the bill.

Chrissie calls from West Virginia to tell me about the ads on TV, images of bathtubs in different chaotic lighting: IF YOU'RE COOKING METH IN YOUR TUB, YOU WILL BE FOUND. At the donut shop, there's a cop behind the counter, helping himself to various items until he disappears to the back. Ralowe thinks he went into a trap door, but I spot him exiting through the kitchen. The cashier acts like nothing is happening, especially when the speed freak leans over to ask if there's any trouble. No, the cashier says, come back later.

Outside, Ralowe wonders about the fashion victims with pants way too short for fall, and way too long for last season's last season, but it's 1:50 a.m.—the runways are pouring out of Tenderloin hot spots and Frenchy's looks packed. There's some guy outside with a really big face—put your pennies in here and I'll turn them into rainforests, pirate ships, seascapes, volcanic eruptions, sunsets on beaches, a monsoon, a coral reef, natives in grass skirts, skyscrapers, the Taj Majal with Stonehenge, a safari, women in bikinis, mudslides, the Cathedral of St. Fill-in-the-Blank, the end of the Palestinian-Israeli conflict, the world's tallest man in heels, cruise ships in the Bermuda triangle, Art Deco hotels, shells in your ears, a river of tears.

But back to the fashion victims, did you see the ads in *San Francisco Magazine* for Gucci babies? Although these models are post-infantile—or permanently infantile, depending on the angle and lighting. Everybody at the Edinburgh Castle has a shag of one sort or another, and of course a Burberry bag, and a striped rag—no, honey, that's not a rag—that's my boyfriend! Ralowe says when you work, you feel like you have less time and so you hang out at awful places that make you feel terrible about yourself. He should know; he used to work at Wells Fargo and eat at the steakhouse.

I'm enjoying the dark window against the green plants in the shower, until I realize that means it's night out and I haven't left the house—hello, seasonal depression! In Sara Shelton Mann's show, there are so many moments of intimacy and violence between men that send me into previews of tears—I shake but don't pour: Don't call my eyes naked! Later, my trick in Concord cancels—well, actually he doesn't cancel until I call to confirm that I'm on my way. He says I was trying to call you, some guests surprised me. Then it's the wired tired phenomenon, stronger and stranger and faster than a speeding rhinoceros—that's twenty-seven miles per hour, which isn't really that fast these days. Get with the times: the new Jaguar R series starts at only $31,230. Sure, a rhinoceros has horns—a Jaguar

R series has a mesh grille and larger air intake, not to mention a tiny cat jumping into infinity.

It's late at night and I throw some food out the window, into the shell of the demolished building next door—nothing new, except that I look down. I look down at the rats devouring the food—huge white ones and tiny white ones, who ever heard of white rats running wild—is my building a laboratory? Then, of course, the gray ones, large and small too. There are at least twenty huge rats—I mean HUGE—I'm never throwing food down there again, I don't care how many bags I waste for trash.

Are those the rats in my ceiling, scurrying around to devour pigeons? I'm not sure it's okay to leave my windows open any more. I definitely shouldn't leave food out on the counter. In the morning, the pigeons are back, scouring the same exact area where the rats were last night. I wonder if pigeons eat rat shit. On my way to the bus, the junkie who's always collapsed against a wall is holding a pigeon by the wings, staring it in the eyes. I'm disgusted, but I rush on the bus and then I'm more disgusted—at myself, for not intervening. I hope she didn't kill it; people can be so evil. This guy on the bus is giving LA film industry realness, with the black suit, black shirt, black-rimmed glasses and reddish curly hair. He's holding a Frommer's guide to Shanghai and talking on his cellphone, the sentence I catch is: treat him like a big developer. Actually, the suit is charcoal—maybe he's from New York.

Benjamin keeps going to after-parties to look for sex. But all she can find is drugs. Lines and lines for lines in the bathroom. On the card table. In the Mercedes. By the pool—it's just so cool! Benjamin's not really doing the lines—well, a few every now and then—but that's just so she can have a fascinating six-hour conversation with some straight boy about art. Ralowe says I wonder if Schwarzenegger will keep making movies if he becomes governor. Advice of the day: you can't smoke yoga. The BBC at 1 a.m.: crack houses in Nottingham, England, cocaine producers in Putomayo, Colombia, Italian cooking—149 of their cheeses are recognized as rather special. Geometry on the bus: six people talk on their cellphones and six people listen to music on headphones, two people have visible face injuries and my headache begins. Rue sees a mouse scurrying under my bed—so much for my fantasy that they'd left me alone. I go to Golden Era, where everything's good except the fried onions and why'd I eat that indigestion Buddha bun? Then of course there's the sweat pouring from my pores underneath my green pants, activating my jock itch loveliness.

Did I tell you Benjamin's story from a few weeks ago? This guy on the phone sex line wanted to suck her big black dick through a glory hole. Benjamin went over and the guy didn't answer the door. Later, on the phone sex line, there he was again—glory hole and all. Benjamin said: didn't I just go over your house? The guy said: are you transgendered or something? Benjamin thought about it: no, I'm not transgendered, but something?

The bra providers for the Queen of England are asked on BBC Radio what feminism means to them—it means that there are different bras for different occasions, all here in this store. More important information from National Public Radio: the moons are in alignment for a Cubs–Red Sox World Series. I call Rue to see if she wants to go to the beach, but she cancels on me and then I call ten people. Really, ten—Jaysen, Magdalena, Blake, Ralowe, Karoline, Liz, Rhania, Eric . . . well okay, eight—and not in that order either, in case anyone's sensitive.

Waiting for the bus, I can hardly stand up, and the sidewalk is so dirty it's making me nauseous. Finally the bus arrives—the driver does that trick where he stops extra-early so no one can get on, even though there's no other bus in sight. But his plan is foiled with a rare moment of bus-rider solidarity, as someone holds the middle door open and we all rush in. The beach is freezing, but there are these amazing chunks of foam blowing out of the ocean like plastic bags. When the sun sets, it's like a genie going back into the bottle in the fog. I've never seen it like that. Afterwards, every part of my body aches—is it because of the cold? I try to cruise in the park by the windmills, but there's no one there—I don't understand, that spot is legendary. So much for legends. I go home and sleep for three hours, get up to wait until I'm tired enough to go back to bed. Which happens pretty soon.

At the bus stop, this boy-girl is staring at me until finally she says you're so beautiful. Then our eyes meet for too long maybe, and she says yeah, I never see anyone who I'm so impressed by, even the way you're standing—where do you get your clothes? On the bus, we have a romantic moment together on the plastic seats. I think she's a straight girl from Quebec. We kiss goodbye and I feel better, for about three minutes until I'm exhausted again. Though I channel full runway for the walk home—the guys outside the building across from Frenchy's are whistling at me, and yelling to each other in Spanish. Back at my building, I take down the NO TRESPASSING sign.

On the radio, this guy who was in a coma says: it was not like being in a dream, it was like being awake in a strange new place—a comfortable place to be—it wasn't until I woke up that I began to realize how sick I was.

BARBARA

⊙   ⊙   ⊙   ⊙

Julia says: with all these people eating so healthy, pretty soon everyone's gonna be dying of nothing. Diamanda and I are really getting
to be friends, it's that amazing transition between bluesy almost-
moan to the operatic trill where just listening to the flow from low
to high and deep to soft is enough to make me cry, except that I
don't, as usual. I just sit in that space and listen to Diamanda's amazing control over her vocal chords, the piano and me.

Then I play it again—it's the sixth or seventh time today, and I'm
just listening to the intro, while the rats or pigeons crawl in the ceiling but pause just before "babe"—it's almost comical until
Diamanda brings her voice up and her fingers take the piano forward, and she's back and forth from hope to longing and are they
the same thing? I'm still wearing my jeans from the trick at the
Argent who really wore me out, and Diamanda's saying: "I need
your love—more than before." Should I listen to it one more time?

The trick from Kentucky who has that huge apartment on Russian
Hill calls, and I'm dreading it, but standing on the side of the bed

while he slides his ass into me feels very Zen, I'm almost upset when he wants to stop. But the worst part about the heat wave is the sinus headache, stretching around my head until it's a rubber mask or actually it's plaster that's cracking. At the Van Ness and Market bus stop, this guy sits down next to me. Hello officer, he says. I ignore him. Hello officer, he says. I'm not an officer.

Well, you never know, he says, you never know—I really don't want to do this but I have to. He takes out his crack pipe and starts smoking. Then he's yelling at the top of his lungs: I'm gonna fucking KILL you, you fucking faggot! And then, softer: I've been approached so many times and I've always turned them down, but when someone's between your legs—what does it matter if they've got a cunt, right? He looks me in the eyes: I'm not calling you faggot, I only call straight guys faggot, since the seventies.

Rue asks me to meet him at Esta Noche because someone's paying him to make a video of some fashion shoot, and he doesn't want to drink. I get there at exactly five, like Rue asked. The music is pounding, which is kind of amusing because it's so bad that it makes it better, and there's Rue in the back. I kiss her and she tastes like liquor, I say you've already started drinking? She says I've been here an hour, I just had one drink. I say there's no way that you've been here a whole hour, and only had one drink. Her eyes are glassy and she's kind of swinging like a doll, she says how did you know?

At home, I can smell cigarette smoke coming through my kitchen from the apartment next door. My mother leaves a message: I'm wondering about the fires in Southern California, I know that's not close, but I'm wondering if they're affecting you in any way. She says it twice. This trick wants me to jerk hard, harder, and all I can think about is how much my hands are going to hurt afterwards. Then he's rubbing Eros lube all over my body and it feels good, but that shit never comes off—I hope I don't get a rash. At least he provides Aveda toiletries in the shower, I'm always ready for that rosemary mint shampoo!

In the morning, it's freezing and Daylight Savings is over, I'm already worried about getting out of the house before dark. Sure, Daylight Savings ended over a week ago, but now that the heat wave is over, the darkness is really hitting. I've started to use a neti pot to clean my sinuses. I pour salt water from one nostril to the other, but sometimes the water gets in my ears—I'm worried that this is going to affect my hearing. Like that one winter when I basically couldn't hear anything, I thought it was because of the ear candle, but I was doing nasal lavage then too.

Rue says she's glad she's positive, because now she can have so much fun barebacking with tweakers who want to kill themselves afterwards. On Geary, this super-tall tranny is coming towards me, she looks like she's nodding off but also she's smiling. People don't usually smile when they're nodding off. She holds out her arms and I give her a hug, which feels good. She says are you going to the Castro? Hell no. Halloween and at least I get a trick, in the Upper Haight—the cab driver says I've been lucky tonight, no one's asked me to go to the Castro.

After my trick I take another cab to the top of the hill by Buena Vista Park, and then climb the rest of it. Pretty soon, I'm out of breath. At the top, there are the same eight people for over an hour. The only ones who are the least bit interesting are the two guys fucking at the end of the stroll, behind a tree. They're both in the indeterminate messy middle age area: one of them's a tweaker on a bunch of AIDS meds, and the other's a drunk bending over to get fucked. That's as hot as it gets. Other than that, there's the huge guy in all white with a big backpack, and the tweaker jerking his limp dick in the shadows. He's very excited about his limp dick.

I walk around and around about fifty-seven times, listening to all the commotion in the Castro. The cops were supposedly shutting it down at midnight this year, because last year there were five stabbings and one guy got knifed really badly. But it's 1 a.m. and it's still going on. I'm hoping for a riot, straight guys with baseball bats smashing gay store windows, but I don't hear any glass breaking. Though I'm hundreds of feet up and half a mile away, so who knows?

There's all this hay in the park where the bushes used to be, some of it's in bales—I'm ready to sit on a bale and get my face pumped, but no such luck. Just as I'm about to leave for the seventh time, I see this really hot guy with a baseball cap. I follow him. When I catch up, he's already got something started with the limp tweaker and some shaggy guy who's just appeared. There's a new crowd because I guess it's getting close to 2 a.m.

The hot guy's a tweaker too, but his dick is rock-hard and he smells so clean, like he took a shower five minutes ago, and I'm kind of hugging him while I'm sucking his cock, and he leans over to kind of hug me while he sucks the limp tweaker's cock. I can't imagine why, but he's really into the limp tweaker. I stand up, because it's getting hard to suck with this guy leaning over me, and he stands up too, gets behind me and I've got my pants up, but I'm already thinking about him sliding it in.

I've never been into gambling; life has always seemed dangerous enough. Once, with Andee in the Las Vegas airport, I let go of a roll of quarters. Every few years, I buy a lottery ticket. When Jeremy and I decided not to use condoms, after we got tested, we agreed to use condoms with everyone else. That's what made me safer—my promise, Jeremy's desire.

Where does responsibility start, and where does responsibility end? Jeremy never liked fucking me, because I could never fucking relax. I wanted him to hold me in his arms and tell me everything was okay. He held me in his arms, and I believed everything was okay. You notice the difference, right?

The best part of the legacy of my relationship with Jeremy is that now I'm so safe—I'm not going to let this guy fuck me and then there's a smelly crowd and the guy's zipping up, I say wait a minute and watch me come. The crowd leaves and he holds me, I shoot almost immediately. Then I'm holding him from behind, squeezing him tight and that's the best part—see, girls like us just want hugs, really, just hugs.

Walking downhill, I'm finally in a good mood—sex was worth it, after all! At home, I open a cabinet and a roach comes flying onto my face—it's a big one, so it hurts my cheek. Ralowe and I go to Aquarius, and I listen to the new Peaches album on the listening station. The beats are good, but the lyrics are embarrassing. I listen to the beginning of each song, just to make sure that every song is awful—so I don't end up buying the album used at Amoeba. The worst song is when she's telling the guys to shake their dicks, girls to shake their tits. I mean, who does she think she is? I thought it was going to be guys shake your dicks, girls shake your dicks—so she'd at least be acknowledging the butches and the trannyboys, but no such luck.

Ralowe shows me his new room—subsidized housing, hello. They've got a lot of rules, but in the lobby there's this queen telling us how she's got the biggest room in the building—six windows. She looks at Ralowe: how many windows do you have? Ralowe has two windows. The queen says: I've been here for twelve years, and I can guarantee you that I have the biggest room and the best view, will I see you at the End Up on Sunday for tea dance? After we leave, Ralowe says why was she trying so hard to make me feel bad—we're both living in subsidized housing, why does she want to compete about windows? I guess I've been around more shady queens than Ralowe—I just thought she was trying to be friendly.

Another hotel lobby after turning a trick—I could stay in that place between leaving the elevator and walking out the lobby door, for the rest of my life. Soon it's 1:37 a.m. and it's time for The Mattilda Show, fifteen minutes of thinking I'm going to take over the world until the inevitable: I crash hard. There's a mouse crawling across my kitchen counter, and I can't do anything but gasp.

It's the time of year when the sun only shines onto my fire escape for about twenty minutes a day; I have to rush out to catch it. I don't even understand why this happens—I guess it's the angle of the earth in relation to the huge '80s monstrosity on O'Farrell and the 1000 Van Ness theater addition—the ugliest building in San Francisco, except maybe the senior housing on Ellis near Larkin, fourteen stories of poured concrete with a rocky finish. When I wake up, I'm so tired I literally start crying. I want to go back to bed, but I'm not sure if I'll fall asleep, so I just keep walking back and forth from the kitchen to the bathroom. I turn the radio up way too loud—it's about Found Magazine, and it hurts my ears. Handwriting is a huge part of it; at least you think you know something about someone by his or her handwriting. I cut my nails—they look good. I'm sick of walking around acting like I'm okay.

I decide that today's the day I'm going to find a chi gung class—

if I don't get some exercise soon, I'm going to have to start jumping off buildings. I call all the acupuncture schools, then ten or fifteen acupuncturists from the yellow pages, plus all the practitioners I've seen. Every class isn't starting until next year. Can't they see I'm desperate, the sides of my stomach turning to blubber for the first time in my life, and the only energy I have is in my head, waking me up at all the wrong times.

My mother calls, why do I pick up the phone? I have caller i.d. Actually it's okay, though I was about to get out of the house before dusk, for the first time in a week. She wants to know why I'm so tired. Then she tells me about seeing *Taboo* on Broadway, the show about '80s London club culture where Boy George plays Leigh Bowery. She and my father got an upgrade at their hotel so they were in the penthouse for the first time ever, the view was great but the alarm kept going off at three or four in the morning. The hotel said it was a technical difficulty, but my mother thought it would be hard to get downstairs if there were a problem, like terrorists on the roof.

My mother wants to know why I haven't called Barbara, her therapist. I'm just so tired. She says Barbara's really upset, she felt like she was connecting with you and she's confused about not being able to reach you. Will you call her?

My mother claims she's trying not to obsess over things as much, but then she asks me over and over again if I'm going to call Barbara. Barbara would really like that. I say it sounds like you would really like that. But no, she's just worried about Barbara.

LOVE POTION #9

⊙　　⊙　　⊙　　⊙

Voicemail on my cellphone: we met on bareback city or bareback—whatever. You had it. I wanted it. I'm calling to let you know that it finally took.

I play the message again, somehow in disbelief at this horrible world—the whole world first, and then the more specific world of guys searching out HIV infection and the scarier world of the guys who want to give it to them. And give them my number—ha ha—I'll breed him with my poz load, and then give him some hooker's cell!

It's hard to stay present in so much hopelessness, I mean way more than the usual despair, burning out my lungs and replacing them with air. Why lungs? Because heart would be too painful.

Blake calls; he says an eight-year-old boy set our house on fire—twice—so we're having a benefit. Rue says: I'm at the bottom of my everything right now. But I want to emphasize his illusions and finesse them into delusions. What about a ten-day land-and-sea vacation? Meanwhile, Ralowe wants to know if *The Hulk* made back all the money, or if there are warehouses full of green oreos.

173

How many amps are in your breaker, how many breakers to get to your maker? I'm dressed up, Zero and I are frantically trying to hail a cab in the rain and this guy says what do they call New Yorkers who used to dress like you in clubs? Club kids? That's right, he says—club kids. I spend the next day recovering from sleep, Ralowe says we need to start a group for people who don't do drugs, but feel strung out anyway. Benjamin and I talk about the tension between us, because she doesn't see herself as a queen; she constantly needs to tell me this.

Benjamin says: I don't identify with that culture, everyone wants me to perform that role and it's disgusting. I think she's just in denial; she's the queeniest person I know. She says: I'm not invested in that identity in the way you are. I think about it. I realize she's right, I want her to be a queen too because she's been around East Coast girls doing 4 a.m. runway, she knows that culture. I miss it.

I call my voicemail and it says I'm sorry—all three access lines are busy. Oh shit—that's not my voicemail, it's the phone sex line. Before, she was an institution—now she's in an institution. At 4:30 p.m., I rush outside to get some sun. There isn't any. My trick says: ever since I moved into this new apartment, the cat has been throwing itself at the window. What do you mean? All the sudden, the cat leaps off the bed and throws itself at the window.

Benjamin says: I haven't been able to sleep, whatever you have is contagious—I'm not used to this, I'm emotionally melting down. Benjamin was on the bus and this guy met her gaze, so she followed him to the Marina. When she got off the bus, she followed him further, and when he came out of a store he seemed surprised. Oh hey, you're from the bus—see you later, I'm going to Sacramento.

Benjamin walked all the way to the beach—that's a long walk, were you wearing your platforms? She says it was okay because I came twice, but then on my way home I went to Mission News to cruise more—my whole life is tragic—drugs are ruining my life, even though I don't do them; everyone in my life is strung out on drugs.

I get in bed at 1 a.m. because I just can't function, everything hurts. As soon as I lie down, I'm wired—alarm clock! I get up to take pills. At 9 a.m., there's a pigeon dying in my wall. I make toast, and take another pill. I talk to the pigeon: I wish your friends could help you, I hope you won't be devoured by the rats.

It's the twenty-fifth anniversary of the Jonestown Massacre, and one of the cult survivors says it's hard to tell what's insanity and what's keeping people together. Ralowe wants to know if she could live on nori seaweed, just nori seaweed. She's vegan now, and trying to figure it all out. This is an actual Marines chant: blood makes the grass grow—who makes the blood flow? A trick calls, he wants to cross-dress at my place—well, that shouldn't be a problem, not like I usually do that kind of thing around here, but . . .

Rue says in Northern Europe, a standard treatment for seasonal affective disorder is a homeopathic dose of gold, three times a year. I'll take a suitcase full of gold, skip the homeopathy, thanks. Blake is moving to SF and we're going to start a free door-to-door sleep deprivation clinic—Sleep Deprivation: You Want It, We Got It! Today, I feel like there's a piece of particleboard between my eyes and my brain. My head is filled with distance. When I exit the bus at the same stop as this snooty British woman, she says from ahead of me: some days, it's just not worth it—getting out of bed, or getting on the bus. I say especially the first one, and I go into the Relax the Back Store, just to see what they have. Everything's so expensive. When I get in bed, I can't sleep because everything itches again—is it the dust mites or am I allergic to sleep? I take a pill.

In the morning, I lie in bed staring at a piece of string rising off my sheet like a hook, it's shaking slightly due to the air purifier. I look at it closely from all different angles, but I can't figure out what it's trying to tell me. What are the barriers between a chainsaw and a child? Benjamin sees the London anti-Bush protests on TV, she says there was this huge effigy of Bush—like fifty feet tall—with a bomb in his hand and they toppled it, it was beautiful. You don't have a TV, she says, but maybe it'll be in tomorrow's newspaper.

I go over to Eric, Matt and Jason's and we watch *Circuit*, about, well—you know. This guy's a cop from Illinois and he moves to LA, within minutes he's smoking crystal and trying to kill a cat in a tree. There's someone in the movie making a documentary about circuit parties, there's the cop's childhood friend—a woman!—who's a comedian, there's the porn star, and there's a high-priced escort. The cop can't handle his drugs, the movie-maker hides his, the comedian cleans the house, the porn star injects Caverject into his dick to get hard, the escort can't feel. The climax is when the escort gets paid to kill the porn star with poison disguised as drugs, or pure drugs which are poison, but instead the escort takes the poison drugs himself 'cause it's his thirtieth birthday and his cheek implants are slipping. The former cop, who was in love with the escort, rushes in after the overdose and then the guy who set it all up is confused, the cop chokes him for a while to teach him a lesson.

Afterwards, Eric talks about panic attacks—he thought someone was going to kill him—and I talk about incest flashbacks: I thought someone was going to kill me. Eric eats more vegan pie, and I taste it—it's delicious, but it makes me shit. I think about everything that I want to do if the new herbalist helps—I want to exercise and feel better about my body, I want to go dancing and feel amazing afterwards and even the next day, I want to sleep.

At home, I wonder about queers who've never experienced tacky gay culture, and I wonder what they've missed out on. Outside, someone's honking their horn at me, and I figure it's the usual homophobia drama so I ignore it. But it's some woman screaming at me: do you know where the RR Bar is, Polk and Sutter? I say Polk and Sutter's two blocks, she says you wanna come? I get in the car, she's this super-posh tiny white woman, coked out of her mind on the best coke, I can tell it's the best coke because she's not biting her lips or anything, but her eyes are open wide to possiblity. You're so cute, she says, can I buy you a drink? I'm okay. She says I don't care if you're okay; I want to buy you a drink. I walk her to the bar and we kiss goodbye, I really want a drink.

I think my apartment manager's a tweaker, because he's painting psychedelic clouds on the ceiling in the lobby, and he has the same hours as me. Lately, I can't seem to get to sleep before 5 a.m., then I'm struggling to get out of the house before dusk. Like today, focusing on the blue of the darkening sky while waiting for the bus and everything hurts. I do mean everything.

I hook up with someone on craigslist—have I broken my promise? But it's actually fun. He shakes when I lick his balls. Ralowe describes his first overnight: I still feel like I slept next to a trick, his breath smelled like a toilet and all night long, he kept belching—in the morning, I had to pretend I liked him, I kept jerking him off and jerking him off and he kept getting close to coming, but not going all the way there, and then I knew I had to suck him off. Andee says she wishes she could visit me, but I live in a fascist country. What about Germany? She says if there's any country that's done its share of soul-searching, it's Germany.

Zero and I listen to Carl Cox to find out what he does with the breakdown, Zero says there's one in every track. It's all about the pounding bass, heartbeat—oh that fucking bass, do we have that here in San Francisco? When Carl Cox fades out, there's still some beautiful beat in the distance, waiting to take us home, sweet home to all that bang bang clang clang glory! It's Thanksgiving, on NPR there's a special about a turkey farmer who's researching what kinds of music turkeys like best. He says they like the wind whistling on the moors, and the Tibetan monks, but they don't like whale sounds. He doesn't tell us what they like when their heads are snapped off.

The building manager is vacuuming again—he just vacuumed two days ago. I use the neti pot, but my sinuses feel more clogged than ever, like my nose just stops at my head and nothing goes through. Well, pain, of course—that gets through. On Polk Street, this tall stumbling boy with glitter on his face stops me with a hug, you're so cute! He's smashed, and his friend with blond hair and the same glitter is embarrassed.

They're probably in high school, drinking cocktails out of Pepsi bottles with the spout cut off. I say you're cute too—I'm already getting hard with all the rubbing. He wants to go home with me, but he's supposed to go to a rave at the self-defense studio on Bush, which is a block away, even though they're pretending to be lost. I walk them in that direction and the boy pushes me against the wall and we make out. He grabs my dick and says to his friend: look at this! She says you two can have anal sex all night long, but we have to go to the rave first—come on! I don't want to be another tired fag who grabs the boy and ditches his best girlfriend—which is this boy's plan, I can tell—so I make him go with her. In the morning, there's glitter all over my face. I get the fancy full-spectrum seasonal affective disorder light in the mail, and at first I think what is this horrible heavy metal box? The light's fluorescent and not even that bright, how can it possibly mimic the sunshine at Noon? I sit with it anyway, and within a few minutes I get that clear, fun feeling in my head—oh, I have a new friend, he's awfully square, but he makes me feel special.

These days, I usually ask someone to carry my bag for me, so I don't hurt my hands, but on the way to see the herbalist in Berkeley, I'm all on my own. It doesn't feel too bad until later on, back home, after stopping at Socket's house where they're having a sing-along and I can't deal. At my house, everything burns, until I go on the internet to look for sex—why?—and after that my wrists feel like they're going to split. I soak my hands in ice water, but then I'm hungry again so I have to cook. I run out to some boy's house two blocks away, he sucks me off, I run back to make pasta. My hands feel better, but my sinuses are ruined because the guy who sucked me off was smoking and all the windows were closed. I use the neti pot, and then everything feels clogged, the pasta is overcooked, it's 5:30 a.m. I go to bed.

Zero and I go to Millennium, since she's moving back to Provincetown. Of course I think about Jeremy—I think about Jeremy every time I go into just about any restaurant, it hits me all the sudden like oh I guess I still miss him. But I'm feeling the Love Potion #9, which is pomegranate and lemon juices with mystery herbs in a martini glass. The chestnut ravioli is one of the best parts, though the crunchy vegetables in the stuffed squash and the maple smoked tempeh are pretty amazing, not to mention the pickled onions that taste like oranges, and the persimmon—I've never had a persimmon before. Zero gets the chocolate dessert and I'm already crashing from Love Potion # 9.

Late night gas drama: unfortunately it happens in bed with a trick, he says did you just pass wind? Yes, darling. It's the guy who likes me to call him Daddy while he talks about raping my ass— what an exciting new idea! I have an ad out that says Ty instead of

Tyler, and the photo's different—the trick says what happened to that nice little boy, now he's mean. Then he says: I think I'm falling in love with you. I say: open me a bank account.

Ralowe presents the new Sunday tea dance for men: Casual-Tea. Didn't I see you there? Speaking of casualties, there's Patrick, the trick who's called me ten times and asked me if I'd shit in his mouth. Last time I said don't call me anymore; you're too much of a tweaker mess. He said I have a great job. This time he's rented a hotel room at an SRO on Market, I get upstairs and he's yelling at someone inside the room: can't get the door open!

I end up with a crumpled twenty-dollar bill. Don't ask. Luckily, I don't have to spend it on a cab, since the 19 Polk appears out of nowhere to rescue me. I'm home just as the clock moves from 2 a.m. to 2:01. Then it's 4 a.m. and just when I've convinced myself that I was imagining the rats in my walls—it was really just the pigeons in the ceiling—I hear something gnawing. There's no way that's a pigeon. It sounds huge, like one of those cat-sized rats, just on the other side of my flimsy kitchen cabinets. The bottom cabinets are rotting away, and they don't even shut—I'm afraid the rat is going to swallow my kitchen whole, that means me too—help!

The next day, it's sunny and I actually get outside for a little bit of it, since I have to get to the chiropractor by 4. Later, it's the first night in months when I have two tricks. First it's the Palomar, leopard pattern carpet and clouds painted on the ceiling. These clouds look better than the ones in my lobby. The trick tells me I won't smell the poppers while I fuck him, because he'll hold them close to his nose. Right. The next trick is the story; he's got the mirror and the razor blade out on the table.

His bed is so comfortable, I don't know how he ever gets out of it—and I tell him that, which he thinks is funny. He wants to cuddle, at first it feels forced but I relax into it once I'm giving him a soft massage and he's grabbing my thighs. When he sucks my dick, I make him do it slowly. Every time he moves his hands, I put them back where they belong: one hand under my balls, the other above my dick. Softly on the balls, really softly. I'm holding off, letting the tension build inside me until it almost isn't there anymore, and then building it back up again. When I come, it's so intense that I can't possibly open my eyes.

Well, okay—it's possible. I look out the window and into the next room, I close my eyes. He says how are you doing? I open my eyes, stare at the chandelier on the red ceiling while I lie there next to the trick and he lets me. The chandelier is in three layers, but it's kind of simple too, and the music is a cheesy circuit mix but then the vocals fade out and the music is just those minimal beats that I live for. I'm staring at the chandelier and breathing, wondering if somehow I got some coke through the trick's mouth. If the coke is this good, I'll never be able to stop.

I just keep staring at the chandelier and the ceiling, squinting my eyes so that light pinpoints me and I'm wondering, really wondering how I got so high. Everything is here, in this bed—in that chandelier hanging from that ceiling. Everything. Then there's a horn in the ceiling, in the music, just a tiny imitation car horn, honking over and over with the bells ringing and the beat, of course the beat and then everything drops out. I'm waiting for what's next.

SHARKS

⊙ ⊙ ⊙ ⊙

A blonde woman who looks like she could be on *Sex in the City* answers the door. I'm always worried I'll ring the wrong doorbell, but this woman doesn't seem confused, she even asks if I'm Tyler. I go inside.

The trick's on the sofa and the woman's name is Amber, she's the trick's daughter. Her boyfriend broke up with her tonight and then she started drinking belly-button shots off other guys, he told her she was a slut and now she's ready to go to the strip clubs with the guys she met, they're already there but she's going to meet them. She tells me: if you went both ways, then I'd be interested.

The trick's daughter leaves and we go into her brother's room. The trick says: she's not really my daughter. I'm not sure what that means exactly but the room is huge. The trick tells me he wants to please me, loves that I'm ticklish, smells like brandy or some gross liquor and keeps insisting on kissing. We finish, there's a pumpkin-scented cleanser in the shower that's amazing. The trick is sweet and uncomfortable, he pays me and I go into the lobby, which looks like some rich person's living room. I count the money, and sure he paid 200, but don't I deserve a tip for chatting up his not-quite-daughter?

On my way home, I look at the pictures of rescued dogs and cats at the Pacific Heights animal shelter. The place is immaculate, even elegant—all the adopted pets in the pictures are adults and that's nice because it's harder to find them homes. They all have stories and names. My favorite is a cat named Shadow who has long whiskers and likes to cuddle with his best friend Casper. Somehow I end up going over to see that same guy who pumped my face like two years ago, and then asked if I'd had stuffing for dinner. He was an asshole, but we talk on the phone sex line and I'm not even horny, but he wants to fuck my face and then I'm walking over to his house at 2:30 a.m. instead of getting ready for bed. I can't fall asleep before 5 a.m. anyway. There's nothing more amazing than City Hall Plaza deserted and glowing at 3 a.m., except maybe how many homeless encampments are nearby. But that's a different kind of amazing.

Ralowe and I are walking by Gavin Newsom's campaign headquarters and every press van in the city is there, what's going on? President Clinton is arriving in half an hour, Ralowe and I plan a demo in fifteen minutes and we get ten people screaming Napa Wines and Big Fat Lines, Kill Bill, and RACIST—it's fun! Chrissie says she was sucking this guy's dick and he said yeah suck that cock bitch, Chrissie said if you wanna call me bitch then that's another fifty. He actually gave her another fifty.

U.S. troops admit to mistakenly bombing a house in Iraq, killing nine children—six months after the war supposedly ended. In Cincinnati, the cops kill another black man and the city responds by deciding to issue the cops non-lethal weapons, in addition to the lethal ones. So now they can tase people after they shoot them. But in Paris there's a McDonald's that striking workers have occupied for nine months. Meanwhile, Rue's on the internet for six hours researching flashlights for doomsday. Ralowe's quote of the day: this guy looked like he was gonna pull out his inheritance and hit me with it. I wonder what I'd find if I had a secret camera inside the ceiling—rotting corpses and shit from so many different animals. Chrissie calls to cancel our dinner plans and she sounds tweaked, she says: I went in for a gonorrhea swab and they took a whole chunk of my ass, it still burns—now I'm sure you know about conspiracy theories, about plenty of tests like this before like when gay men thought they were being vaccinated for hepatitis but they were being injected with AIDS, I don't even know what I need.

Gavin Newsom gets elected; I didn't think it would depress me this much. The worst part is going to his victory party to protest and there are only about twenty of us. We congratulate the attendees on electing a racist mayor, but it isn't really fun. Standing out there in the rain, we're yelling at blank faces while trying to spot the bigwigs. Our signs are soaked, and it feels totally disempowering. Ralowe gets arrested for mooning someone, but luckily we get him out. I sleep so terribly my eyes hurt, and then I sit in the house all day feeling like I'm going to cry, and staring at the walls until I get hungry, then eating and staring at the walls.

The closest thing I get to outdoor sun exposure is gazing into the deep blue sky at dusk. Today it's raining again, and every car wants to hit a pedestrian, any pedestrian. I go to the post office, and I'm enjoying my runway back down Polk Street when Jenna calls to cancel our dinner plans. There goes my structure for the day. I go home and try not to get back in bed, actually I get in bed but I try not to get under the covers.

Rue doesn't believe I've got rats in my walls, but then he's over the house and there's one squealing. We both jump—Mattilda, he says, that was a rat! Oh yeah, it's in the walls. Are you sure it's not in the house? Honey—let me have my denial and eat it too!

Rue says she's gaining weight and none of her pants fit, that's after I say if I can't exercise soon, then I'm going to have to start wearing layers at all times like junior high, sweating in the sun and Mattilda, how come you don't take off those six layers? I want to tell Rue that none of my pants fit either, but I can't. I know it's ridiculous, but it's scarier than talking about incest, or maybe it is talking about incest—hiding and hating my body, poor helpless body.

The first chewing of the day and I feel like my jaw is stapled to my face—relaxation exercises don't work! Am I allergic to the air purifier? I can't tell if the full-spectrum light is hurting my eyes, but something is. Looking outside, I'm having a Seattle moment because you can see the sun through the clouds today—high clouds—oh, how pretty! On the news: U.S. soldiers slaughter Afghani children while attempting to root out terrorists, Queen Elizabeth has surgery on her face to remove some benign lesions.

Okay, say there's a roomful of guys jerking off on my face and then there's a golden retriever—who gets the come? Well, I get it first, and then whatever falls onto the ground, the golden retriever can lap up. Though I'm scared of kissing people when I think they might have been sick recently. I'm standing on Mission, waiting for the bus, and I just lose it. I know that if I eat I'll feel better, but I've just walked eight blocks up Valencia, with my bag—high hypoglycemia, plus I kept running into people but now I'm left waiting for the bus with burning hands. There are no seats at this stop, so I can't eat—I don't want to hold my food because it will hurt too much.

I go home and I'm a disaster, pacing around, craving lines, wondering if I should get dressed up and go out, but where would I go? I call everyone; no one answers. When I hang out with Rue, she talks about not fitting into her pants again, and I say I can't fit into mine either.

Benjamin tells me how her sister is trying to get out of an abusive relationship, and how Benjamin's afraid the boyfriend's going to kill her. The boyfriend's totally brainwashed Benjamin's sister into thinking she's worthless, and she cooks for him, gets him more beer. And she's a feminist, Benjamin says, she's just totally internalized this idea that as a tranny, she's worthless—and she's worried that if she leaves her boyfriend then she'll have no one to deal with but the tranny chasers—and we know how bad they are—gay men are awful, but they're nothing compared to tranny chasers. Tranny chasers mix fetishism with unbelievable amounts of denial and then act like you've asked for it.

The U.S. captures Saddam, so there's no evil left. Benjamin's talking about all her friendships with white upper-middle-class intellectual academic types, the other day I asked her what she got from them. She says she really likes the theory, how to a certain degree they can understand things through these discourses, she uses that word on purpose. I say the only problem is that they don't apply what they learn, on any level. Benjamin says yeah, I feel like they study these critiques of anthropology, and then they enact the same fucked-up shit on me—when my sister was in danger and you were decomposing, I called Ralowe and said: tell me you're all right. Maybe I was being melodramatic, but he called me back from the bathrooms at UC Berkeley, started talking about a hot boy he'd just cruised. I thought: you're not all right, but you don't know it.

The good news is that I've figured out that it's not the full-spectrum light that's giving me this horrible headache, deep underneath my eyebrows and up through my skull, because today I haven't turned the light on, and the headache is worse than ever—must be the dust mites crawling all over my bed, or the mold growing underneath the sink. But what's the bad news—well, you know the joke. Somehow, when I'm heating water for the nasal lavage, the water doubles in volume—is someone adding water to my water?

On the radio, a portrait of Rivercrest, a town in Texas near coal-burning plants, where thirty percent of children suffer from birth defects due to mercury poisoning. The mercury gets dumped into the river and the fish absorb it. A local woman talks about going to a fish fry and saying what are you doing—you know what's in these fish! The response is always the same: we've been eating them all our life, we're gonna die anyway—and we have to eat something.

Chrissie comes over at 2 a.m. to give me twenty dollars, she says well I can't do any more speed, I've done it four times since I've been back, but I've only shot it once! I just can't do any more speed, Mattilda—I hit my Saturn return and now I want to get to a point in my life when I can take care of myself, and maybe other people too instead of just relying on everyone; I just hope someone's at Luke's when I get there so I can say no thanks, I don't want any of that—you can snort it or shoot it or whatever and I'll just fuck you all night.

Eric and I drive out to the beach around midnight and it's beautiful, so much foam and so many stars. Eric walks faster when we pass a group of people and I look toward them to say hello. They look away. Eric talks about going back to Virginia, and how his brother's in the Marines, and Eric caught him looking at gay porn—but his brother doesn't know that, though he showed Eric a picture of his best friend who got discharged. Eric looked at the picture and the guy was a flamer, Eric said why did he get discharged? His brother said can't you tell—it's obvious.

Outside on Christmas Day, there's some guy giving homeless chic with a derby hat and a coat with a fake fur hood, what do they call those? Anyway, he's got all this luggage, and he's certainly not homeless, but then the luggage isn't Vuitton either. But what is he waiting for?

For me, obviously, ready to fuck his face until next Christmas, but that's another story—and anyway, I need a libido first. Speaking of cash, no one's calling my new hooker ad; new because the *BAR* lost the old photo, which really was fucking priceless. I need to get the photos that guy took six months ago, I asked him to send them to me and he said he didn't have the four dollars. Don't you work at Wells Fargo Bank—take a cash advance, Lance! He really is a Lance, black guy working some kind of white boy realness; only I'm not exactly sure what kind.

There's no business. Right? Like show business. Okay—I see where you're going. There's no business—none? Like we don't all know that one. The point, Ralowe says, is that once you're on the inside, you're always there. But what movie is that from? *Sister Act II.* Outside, a woman wearing a white, white cowboy hat smacks a woman wearing a sideways trucker cap—my hat is bigger than yours! A boy rides by on a bike; he's wearing all tan—fully giving tan-ness. Ralowe wants to know if people are taking it. They are.

Walking outside into the glory of 4:45 p.m. winter sunshine, I catch the bus like a tennis ball—thrown, not hit, darling. Everything's wonderful until the sun goes down, which doesn't take long, and then I'm losing it, again, on the MUNI. But what are you losing? Everything. Potato, po-tah-to, Escondido, Escondato. A fake cable car drives by, with a tour guide announcing the sights: "San Francisco is a mecca for homeless people." It's the first time I barely notice New Year's, except for all the police cars driving by right around 2 a.m., and everyone screaming around midnight. I go to

Lafayette Park and suck some guy's dick. He's not touching me enough. Afterwards, I look at the stars.

Aaron says I'm sorry I've been out of touch, my father died in November and then I had nightmares for a month and a half; I stopped taking Dalmane because I was sleeping all the time anyway, so why take sleeping pills—I've been coughing up blood again, and it's not good when you have a slow drain. I finally cleaned it out with a plunger, no chemicals, but there's still blood splattering the mirror. Did you know that the word paradise comes from Farsi, literally it means mud walls? Every year there's a list of banished words put out by the University of Michigan in some small town, this year they started the list with "metrosexual."

Okay, so it's 4 a.m., I'm completely wired—I've already taken a sleeping pill, so I get up. I look in the refrigerator and something smells rotten, I mean something's smelled rotten for several days, and I've been worried that somehow the rats were in my refrigerator laying eggs. Anyway, so I'm looking into all these plastic containers, and there's all this rotten shit in my refrigerator—so, at least there's something to snack on, right?

The next night I talk to Eric, who's still in Virginia visiting his parents, he says he's been going to bed at 9 a.m. and getting up at 5 p.m.—the workday schedule is ingrained in all of us! So then I don't feel so bad; when I get up, I'm not as much of a mess as I expected. Until later, when I'm sitting at the restaurant with Ralowe and Liz, head in my hands, or not quite in my hands but I'm rubbing my hands, all over the side of my head because it hurts so much. I go home and listen to scratch djs who are brilliant but the music's crap, but why on earth did I get the fucking *Party Monster* soundtrack?

I wake up at some horrible horrible time in the morning, look at the clock and—oh, no—its 1:20 p.m. Today's public radio warning: terrorists could use almanacs to cause harm. Don't let your child outgrow the stroller until you've got the right leash. Meet the man who invented the Cosmopolitan! But wait: are you a low-level associate of insurgents? It's one of those days when I'm trying to harvest energy so that I can harness it—do you know what I mean, even with all these farming and energy and maybe even livestock metaphors? I finally go to a chi gung class—it's all right, but I hurt a muscle in my right foot.

Why does every mattress I get cave in within two weeks? I guess I've only had two, but it's happened to both of them. The other one I kept for three years anyway, because it was non-returnable. This one I've had for a couple months now, but I can exchange it at any time, I made sure of that. But I keep trying to convince myself that it couldn't really be caving in—maybe the floor is tilted, or the frame isn't attached right.

Preventative medicine: today I've bitten my lip at least five times, inside there's a small swollen sore with pus, but I'm craving the Power Exchange. Not a good idea, so that's where the preventative part comes in—jerking off on the phone, after this guy tells me he wants me to sit on his cock and milk the load out. Or maybe that's what I want. He's got a familiar voice, soft and masculine and I'm eager to shoot my load in the sink, which isn't really that fun.

I know this is going to sound weird after I just jerked off, but I think I used to have a libido. I mean, just now I jerked off so I wouldn't go to the Power Exchange, where I was going to go to see if I had a libido. Maybe I would have found it, though instead I bite my lip again: more blood.

THE ANSWER

◉　　◉　　◉　　◉

There are so many things I used to do that I can't imagine anymore. I used to sleep with sunlight streaming in through the window. I used to sleep with people talking, they would just keep on talking and I would sleep. I used to sleep with the lights on, shining right onto my face—no eye mask. I used to sleep on my side, and I'd wake up without every single part of my body hurting.

Do you know about the New Economy Depression Syndrome, or NEDS—that's when the career professional spends more than five hours a day online, and loses the ability to connect with people face-to-face. Most people I know are suffering from No Economy Depression Syndrome, or NoEDS. But now, thanks to the accessibility of the internet, people with no money can spend more than five hours a day online. Unfortunately, this sometimes leads to No New Economy Depression Syndrome—cure unknown.

Every time I turn around, I eat another pot of beans. What's that over there? Another pot of beans—oops, I ate that one. Rue says: I was talking to Blaine, my new AA friend, about alcohol and seroconverting and sex and it was the first time this whole year that I really felt it, I wanted to cry but I couldn't, it's stuck between my heart and my throat and I just feel this ache. A message from Benjamin: I just left this after–Phone Booth party and it's 6 a.m. but I'm in a great mood, I'm enamored of Cameron—the boy I met on Friendster—I'm feeling artistically creative, and yes I did two lines of coke earlier and that's informing my mood, but wait this woman says she knows me—I don't think I know her, but maybe I'll fuck her.

I see a mouse on the counter, just sitting there, scared of me. It's the cutest thing I've seen in a long time, and I really wish we could just be friends. All the little mice in my apartment could crawl everywhere and I would pet them and leave food out for them. There must've been some time when mice didn't carry disease, and I want to go back there.

Ralowe says he lives on the toughest block in the Mission—every time he leaves his house, he's afraid he'll get run over by a faux-hawk. Or a mullet. But should we put the laundry in the dryer? Should we put the car in the garage? Should we put the airplane in the hangar? On the radio: one-seventh of U.S. troops who've died non-combat deaths committed suicide. Someone mentions "our people in Iraq," and I start crying—I'm actually sympathizing with them like any TV mother. Allison comes back from Costa Rica, where she got parasites, and Allen, her boyfriend, got dengue fever—they kept delaying their return because they were so sick. But there were monkeys on the beach, she says—they cracked coconuts and then came right up to you and stared.

Allison tells me about something called a Swim-Ex pool that they have at her gym in Texas: it's a one-person pool, with no chlorine, and maybe some sort of current, so you can exercise even though it's tiny—I've gotta find one. On my way to chi gung and the bus driver takes away my transfer because I don't have the extra quarter now that the fare's raised. I'm so angry, I make him let me off the bus. But chi gung actually works; afterwards I can feel the bottoms of my feet.

Okay—so it's Thursday night at 2 a.m. and I'm completely wired—what's there to do besides walk up and then back down Polk Street?

I go to the Power Exchange. I know what you're thinking: why does she break her own rules—it'll only lead to disaster, and it does, honey, it does. I can't even describe how boring and awful it is, but I'm a writer—that's my job. At one point, I walk into a room and there are four guys jerking off, but not interacting with each other, just the porn. It's like they're straight except there's not even the tension. I'm looking at these four hard cocks, and four empty gazes—well, okay, two hard cocks and two limp cocks and four empty gazes—and there's nothing sexual about it. All I can think is that I want to hit them, I want to kick them, I want to spit in their faces.

JACQUELINE

⊙ ⊙ ⊙ ⊙

Benjamin's on her way to see Cameron in Marin, she's taking the bus this time, so Cameron doesn't have to pay the five-dollar toll, twice. She says it's all going so well, it must be a lie—I got all my STD tests, and I don't have anything, but Cameron's a bit paranoid because I've had a lot more sex. Cameron likes underwear, and you know I don't usually wear underwear, but Lacey hooked me up with some that are kind of fetishy, and I thought I'd surprise Cameron with them. I'm going to meet him at his parents' house, they have two dogs and two cats, you know how much I hate cats but I hate dogs even more—I'm more nervous about the animals than the parents. Parents like me, I just don't know if this is all going to end tonight.

What my trick says about his cat: she's such a slut; she'll get in bed with anyone. Are you trying to tell me something? It actually ends up being fun, I tell him about my hand pain because he likes to be squeezed hard, and then he says I'll just do the squeezing. It's actually an incredible orgasm, the cat arrives just in time—she's not throwing herself at the window any more.

London calling, I mean really calling, it's Andee—three times in a row on my cellphone, that's nine minutes of talking time, I don't have one of those fucked-up phones that cuts you off after thirty seconds. First message, summarized: I'm totally disgusted by the fact that you're not answering the phone, I even dialed the wrong number and got Orion's Organic Wagon, tonight's my night to give advice to the real people, the cat lovers of the world. I had a transfumal experience tonight—through the fumes—I saw this awful choreography, I thought why isn't Mattilda choreographing for the girls in London? I'm crossing my fingers and my legs, I'm here to tell you that you need a vacation, that's it—just take a fucking vacation and it will all go away. Just break it down and take a holiday, just go there and get it, girl! But I'm not Chrissie Contagious with my messiness. Hmm . . . no, I'm not. Just take a vacation! Go on a cruise, I don't care, Julie McCoy, though maybe you're more like the Captain or . . .

Message two, actually this one's short: You have got some fascist . . . is she real, is she not . . . I can't believe she cut me off. I'm sorry for interrupting whatever it is you're doing . . . Message three: this is the third installment, there's two points—one is that I'm not Barbara Hershey . . . And a fourth call: I hope I'm not off the list, am I off the list?

I'm on some horrible internet connection site, and someone emails me—you look familiar, but guys downtown don't usually come up to Haight Street, they're usually pulling taffy. Very funny—turns out it's Marc, the guy who I used to talk to on the phone line, we had sex once and then he'd call me when he was drunk, and pass out on the phone. It was kind of romantic, even though he freaked out when we went on a date—was it the mayonnaise in the Vietnamese spring rolls, or was I just not butch enough? We talk for three hours, turns out we've had good sex with the same awful guys online—Vince and Jordan—why can't anyone deal?

Eric, Matt and Jason are getting a dog. I don't really like dogs, mostly because they're so dependent, I'm like—get a grip. I like cats, or dogs that act like cats. Eric likes cats that act like dogs, though he grew up with four cats and three dogs, plus a few lizards—and possums who'd lost their mothers, and he and his brothers would try to rescue them. Eric didn't like his brother's lizards; one of them had a head that you could see through.

Muscle spasms in my right hand—I hope it's not from chi gung—my latest, greatest hope for ever feeling better, maybe just a little better? But wait—the Ethan Allen catalog has arrived! You can get a new country family room set for just $127 a month, for sixty months! Sixty months—is that a joke? I guess it's better than a car.

This happens a lot. I wake up, go to the bathroom and look in the mirror—no, don't do that yet! Later, when I'm putting on my contacts, I look in the mirror again—oh, no, the bags!!! Lack of sleep and endless allergies and discontent deepening the blue and red—actually they're kind of purple—creases. I walk into the kitchen just as the beans are about to overflow—for once, perfect timing.

Today's radio crying: this guy was a hospital chaplain who fainted a lot. But one time he didn't faint, Jacqueline was a two-year-old who fell off a high chair and split her head open. Her father, Nick, was covered in Jacqueline's blood. The chaplain took the man's hands, even though they were covered in blood. The man said it was an accident, and that's when the chaplain knew. Until I met Nick, the chaplain says, I always believed in the possibility of redemption.

HEAVEN

◎   ◎   ◎   ◎

Jason's doing a night at Vertigo, the yuppie bar that replaced the next-to-last hooker bar on Polk Street. For some reason, Ralowe and I go over there, I guess because it's two blocks away, and we want to be supportive. I get dressed up because I'm feeling my music—fuschia wig with sunglasses and hot pink fishnets pulled over my head and enlarged lips. When we get there, I feel like an animal in a zoo, except everyone's trying not to watch. It makes me even more alienated that I'm hot for some of the boys, their snide disapproval framed by understated trendiness. Ralowe says he wants them to die.

Air pollution brings me to my senses. There's a separate smoking room at Vertigo, but it connects to the bar and the whole place smells like smoke. Smoke makes me want to kill people, I want to bring drywall and seal the smokers in that room.

Ralowe and I have the same trick, Room 610 at the Maxwell. Ralowe says did you fuck him? I did. How did you do it? I don't know. Walking home, a straight couple asks me if there's a bar nearby—I guess I'm passing. I go to the video booths at the Nob Hill

Theatre, just to walk around in circles for a little while. Zan's back in town, she says why didn't you call me? Because I didn't have your new number.

Whenever Rue comes over here, she spends the whole time lying on the sofa. At her house, she seems to have more energy. We always lie in bed a little towards the end, because her bedtime is 9 p.m. these days. I like lying in bed with her the best. I feel like myself, which I guess isn't always the case. So, I have to admit it—even though I'm sick of being a whore, I'm completely over it, I've got nothing left to learn from it—I still enjoy nothing more than the cab ride home after a trick that was fun enough, his apartment was interesting, I liked sucking his cock, I liked the view, I even liked coming. And then on the cab ride home, the driver plays, "In the still . . . of the ni-ight. I-I-I held you. I held you ti-ight . . ." And I just feel great. A little lonely, maybe, but not as lonely as usual. A little tired, but not as tired as usual. The air is cold and refreshing and I feel clear in this overwrought musical moment at 3 a.m., that beautiful time when the sky contrasts against the buildings, and I guess I'm really not so over it—certain parts of it, being a whore.

I guess I could just be a slut, and have those moments too, but somehow that feels like more work. Jeremy and I visit the sea lions—there's a new sculpture of two of them kissing, and I start laughing and almost crying and laughing and almost crying. But there aren't too many actual sea lions around. There's one group, but they're on the furthest dock. We go into the marine mammal store to ask about them, apparently it's different ones every time we go, because they're constantly migrating, and this is just one stop on their migration. The so-called males migrate and the "females" stay in the Channel Islands and have babies.

It's fun hanging out with Jeremy, I like hugging him, it feels soft. Afterwards, I'm tired, but that's to be expected. I meant to buy some new sleep herbs, but then we're driving back to my house. That fucking herbalist still hasn't called me, I've called him four or five times, and we met a month ago. I guess he must be a mess, but can't he at least call me to tell me that? I pet the sea lions in the postcards I got at Pier 39.

There's absolutely no way to explain this, maybe it's just walking out of the Ritz Carlton at 2:30 a.m., it's just completely empty and it's *mine*. That shouldn't really get me so excited. My first trick, before the Ritz, is pretty hot—an Asian circuit boy—I come, he gives me 150 instead of 180. I don't count the money until I get out in the hall, because it's too dark. He doesn't answer my knock, and I can't really deal with causing a scene.

The guy at the Ritz tells me I'm giving him the best head ever, which is always great to hear, and I love the marble floor in the bathroom—all the blue in the white! Then the guy says you didn't give me anything, right—if I get anything, then I'll hunt you down and kill you. How romantic! Then he says: you have a great personality, I'd like to get to know you but I live in Georgia. Is he kidding? Afterwards, I'm walking home and why do I feel so completely calm and alive—loving everything except the poison some guy's squirting out of a hose to clean the sidewalk.

Someone catches sea lions in a dish that's way too small, they keep jumping up in the air to get out, but there's not enough water. Where is the nearest ocean? The dish keeps getting smaller, until it's barely bigger than a soap dish, but no one notices. That's what waking up is for—if you can't save the sea lions then you might as well wake up.

Another trick that wants to know if I have any diseases, he doesn't want to bring anything home to his wife. I have leprosy, lion bite fever, and ebola. I suck his cock anyway. It cures me. On the way home, I'm walking down Polk Street practically jumping up in the air, wait I am jumping up in the air. Until I see the cops, and I'm waiting by a red light even though the street's deserted, which probably looks more suspicious than just walking, but I guess I'm white and dressed like a prep, so I can do practically anything. Not like the time they were going to arrest me for walking too fast, they even confiscated my bag of groceries. They were sure I was a tweaker. In this terrible world, tweaking is illegal while preppiness reigns.

So at the Ritz Carlton, all five door people just smiled and waved me in. For some reason, there were six or seven cops in the lobby too, maybe someone important was arriving. Oh, right—

me. The thing to remember about the Ritz Carlton is that the lobby is on the fourth floor, so when the trick's on three, you've got to go DOWN.

Benjamin, on the state of the world: I love my new shoes, but I hate my life. There's one point in chi gung class when the instructor, Suzanne, looks at me and her eyes stay in my eyes, and I can't tell what she can tell. We're supposed to exhale the sadness and grief, inhale life and energy—I'm suddenly surrounded by the sadness and grief, flooding my sinuses so it's almost hard for me to see. The best thing about my 4 a.m. walk down Polk Street is the Latina tranny-girls on Post, singing songs in Spanish, practicing dance moves, and hugging each other in the rain.

You know those times when you take a photo of yourself in the dark, and you just hope the flash works? So I'm sitting here, I'm getting ready for bed and I'm thinking: what does it mean to feel rested? What does it feel like? The best thing I've heard about this whole Democratic primary election drama is in this interview with a guy in South Carolina. He says: I have to decide what's best for my two mortuaries.

A momentous occasion: over a million people gather at a rally in Boston—to celebrate the Super Bowl victory. Three a.m. and I'm so wired, I'm licking the inside of my teeth. I'm so wired, I'm shaking my head back and forth. I'm so wired, I'd be doing back-flips if my hands weren't so fucked up, or at least I'd be going dancing, or on a long long LONG walk back and forth from here to Atlanta.

I call Rue because she went to some horror movie so she's up. She keeps trying to tell me about the horror movie, but I won't let her— I don't need nightmares! All day long, it's just pull it together, pull it together, trying trying trying really trying but it's so hard, and then 2:30 a.m. comes around and suddenly it's all okay, only it's not okay because I'm just wired, it's just a high, I mean exactly like a high like hello, my ecstasy's kicking in or yes, that first bump, I mean really really like a high dammit I know I'm going to crash and then still sleep like hell and wake up thinking: pull it together.

Rue makes fun of me for getting all teary-eyed every time I think about sea lions, even while I'm talking about the postcard with the two sea lions hugging. But then I'm all teary-eyed, so Rue stops making fun of me and instead he sits on my lap, like a sea lion.

Today's proof that liberals are a mess: Al Franken, current pundit-of-the-moment, talks about doing an ISO tour for the troops in Iraq. The radio announcer asks how the troops reacted. Al says they loved it, but he didn't tell them they were dying for a President who didn't care about them, he asked who was from out of town, made Saddam and Osama jokes. He says: I was there to boost their morale.

Today's inspirational moment: Cesar Chavez's daughter, responding to questions about an artist's depiction of Cesar and Che kissing, says she thought it was beautiful. I go to a make-out party, where everyone likes watching me and Deacon, probably because we're the only fags in the spin-the-bottle circle. Though there's this hot trannyboy outside the circle who looks like the ideal blond young not-quite-jock. He comes up to me and asks if we can make out—delicious! Madison gives me a tour of his room, with a mid-nineties theme—but who are all these people on the wall with feathered hair? And that sequined shirt on the wall? Madison says he wants to play spin-the-bottle with me, so we make out. He tumbles onto the bed, and so we both do. Then the floor, so I go in the hallway. Pouneh steams carrots and chard for me.

Outside, I'm ready to go and Deacon rides up on his bike—he says: I've come to warn everyone that the powders are arriving, the other party just got shut down—the coked-out one. Sure enough, two taxis pull up, plus a few scooters and the most ridiculous fashiony people from everywhere. The girls on the Vespas both have frosted shags, and their denim skirts look like they were cut with the same scissors, but they probably bought them at Gucci together. All the women have huge plastic hoop earrings, and the boys look faggier than any current fags.

It's a high-fashion take-over and I'm loving it—everything's right here to see, all this money and coke and attitude and bad hair. Benjamin arrives and I'm jumping up and down, of course she's chasing one of the boys—he's from Santa Rosa but he's giving I've-been-in-London-since-the-sixties. Konstantina shows up in some elaborately hand-crafted suit with matching hat, I say this party just went from low-end to high-end to high-end giving low-end to low-end giving high-end. Konstantina's a bit wired, and everyone else is upstairs except some really scary coke-heads, so I go over to 24th Street and catch a cab.

Billeil calls to tell me the gays are lining up outside City Hall, in the rain, to camp out and get married in the morning, since Gavin Newsom said they could hitch. Billeil says he was riding by on his bike and saw all these people, he thought maybe it was a protest, but it was midnight and the gays were passing around wine and egg salad sandwiches. What could be more depressing?

On the radio, this guy says he was homeless because he was trying to find out what was truth. Sure, I'm looking for new themes or beams of light shining down from the not-heavens, nowhere near heavens NO. But let's contextualize, elaborate, contemplate—which isn't the same thing as dreaming: blight, flight and hand-held light, flickering on the walls of doom in my gloom room. Actually the walls are okay, it's just that flickering in my head until it's out.

There are these few minutes after chi gung class and ear acupuncture, when I'm on the BART chewing my food, or wait no I'm already on the bus because the BART was so quick. But the point is that then I'm on the bus, chewing my food, and I actually notice the texture of the rice, soft and smooth and silky and rough, all at once. The beans taste good, even if they don't have much flavor. This is what it feels like to be in my body. By the time I get home, I'm exhausted again and my brain's fogged up, but I'm excited about that window of taste and desire that didn't quite feel like longing.

Later, I'm just tired, cruising for sex on the internet, which is great, really great. I send a letter to my man: So I know people on the internet are an inferior breed, but is that like some hot fucking fantasy . . . dude, I'm gonna send him an email, get him excited, tell him I'm gonna call him, and . . . ha ha ha . . . here I thought we were gonna get married . . . sob . . . though really, show some manners, I'm sure it just gets your pole rock fucking hard to do rails of tina in your sultry internet abode . . . but really, humans can be fun too, maybe you should meet some.

I'm in this old German train station with my father, we're on a trip together and all the sudden someone starts shooting—I'm hurled to the ground by fear, the man in front of me is whimpering and I'm trying to position my head behind his ass, so that at least the bullets won't hit my brain. I wonder whether that's ethical, but the drive to survive brings me there anyway.

Six, seven, eight, nine bullets—I think that's all there are, but actually I don't know anything about guns. I get up anyway to run, and realize I'm heading towards the guy with the gun, because he turns back with it, and then I'm running the other way. Then I say it— Daddy!!!—that's when I know it's a dream because I don't think I've called him that since . . . way before I stopped calling, I mean like maybe when I was five or six. But still, the way dreams are sticky, that's me, running through the Berlin train station yelling Daddy!

We get outside and there's no one around. I'm in a panic, pulling my father mentally around corners until we get to the subway, even though it's so far above-ground that we have to climb a cliff to get there, and since it's a dream my hands work but my father's not in such good shape, someone helps him and then this Dutch boy with short blond hair grabs him in an embrace, like he's the next big thing.

In this dream, it's not the usual terror of my father, it's like we're on a trip together and I'm taking care of him. He and the blond boy go into the bathroom or the conductor's cabin, and I think, well— I'm going to have to at least tell him to take my needs into account when he goes into bathrooms with boys. I try to look under the glass door, but I don't want to scare my father.

That's the beauty of the dream—and I know it sounds crazy, but it's my desire and awareness that my father's afraid of. This is the part where I'm slightly more awake, and so I wonder about the blond boy falling for this sixty-year-old man. Obviously it's a Daddy-boy thing, except that my father somehow looks like he did when he was my age, his usual beard and moustache but that's kind of trendy these days.

Then they come out, too quickly, and I want to say GET HIS NUMBER, because of all those missed opportunities in my life, but maybe this one's missed too. When I wake up, I think: I have to remember this dream—but I don't want to write it down, so I piss in the sink—that's so I don't wake up too much—and then I move the glass of water to the back of the kitchen counter, so my memory will be there when I get up again.

There's some music that's just so good that you could live in it, like when the bicycle horn comes in and out of the song that moves through samples and all these different melodies on toys, and then back into the beat, which is cracked, all the while sampling various men saying various things but still the beat, and Kevin says: is the narrator a music critic? What I love is when the whole song stops, just for a beat or two and then boom it's back and almost backwards until the car skids, the record inside the music skips. The music almost slows because of all the talking with various records going so fast that everything else becomes scenery and still the horn, the horn, the horn and then back to the melody—or is it the harmony?—whatever it is fades out and there's static.

When I fall back asleep it's weirder, because I'm on my way back to the Berlin apartment and I find Rue on her way back from drinking at Heaven. Why did you go to Heaven, the tackiest club in London, of all the terrible places in the world? But I already know the story. Rue is fixated on who did the talking. I just want him to know that he doesn't have to lie to me, I kind of want to know the details—what my father's dick was like—oh no, Rue had sex with my father? Is Rue the blond boy, or did Rue have sex with the blond boy?

From the BBC: our reporter reflects upon the turbulent times unleashed upon South Africa following the release of Nelson Mandela. Then on NPR, there's a guy talking about pitchers and catchers, but I don't think he means what we mean. I take a sleeping pill at noon, well just a part of one. It's after the screeching of the hot water wakes me up, what is wrong with the pipes? Then when I wake up—or at least get out of bed—there's a sudden hailstorm, and when I get out of the bathroom, there are all these tiny balls of ice in the windowsill, and everything smells like vinegar.

Rue wants me to tell him how much more comfortable his bed is, now that he covered the futon in magical foam. No—it's not magical, it's memory. I'm lying on top of him, which is the most comfortable position for me, but then I'm crushing out all the air in his lungs, so I move over. It's 9:30 p.m., so Rue's decomposing. He holds his hand up in the air—what's this? I look closely. It looks kind of like a lobster claw. Rue is giggling—and I'm laughing—and his roommates are walking by in the hallway, you can hear the creaking of the floor. Rue holds up his hand again: I'm five, he says. I'm thinking: I'll be five with you—I want to try it all over again, sort of.

Waiting for the bus, there's some preppy boy with a thick red hooded sweatshirt, I can't stop thinking how comfortable it would be to be inside it. With him, sure, and I guess that's some of what Ralowe feels too—wanting that ease. The safety disease. Though Ralowe's fetish is a bit more over-the-top, or maybe I just keep mine quieter. On the bus, the preppy boy is looking away and I'm studying his white white calves, lips a bit too red, redder than the sweatshirt, which is really pinkish in its softness.

I go to a movie where fifteen-year-old boys plot to jump off buildings, it's about the dark side of Singapore and the boys who are forced there by the smallest acts—like tattooing or piercing—acts that grow larger, into murder and suicide. It's about longing, mostly homosexual, though the director claims he only filmed what he saw, since these boys are non-actors acting like themselves. In one scene, this boy swallows condoms filled with pills, to smuggle them across the border, and it's so clearly sexualized by the camera, even though and especially because of all the pain when the boy has to get the drugs out. Later, the director says: these kids had to do that every day, and if they didn't get across in two hours then they could die when stomach acid went through the condoms.

Everything in the movie is surreal and you never see the boys do drugs, even though they're always supposed to be on them. I wonder if that's because of the law. In one scene, a schoolgirl jumps from a building when she fails her exams, and the boys look down at the blood dripping out of her mouth and walk onward. Later, they're making music videos, rapping over techno and doing everything femme. Apparently they shot a lot of these scenes themselves, after the director gave them cameras so they could get used to them. In the end, he says, they got too good at acting, and I had to edit those parts out.

ECSTASY THERAPY

◎   ◎   ◎   ◎

On NPR, a commentator wonders why baby boomers hate rap music—it almost seems like he's going to critique the way the music industry creates corporate rap as a fake counterpoint to white power, but instead he goes on to explain that rap music doesn't have a conscience. Actually he uses the word hip-hop. At one point, he says something about June Cleaver, and later in the week I'm going to see Kathleen Cleaver speak—I thought she was married to Eldridge Cleaver and they were in the Black Panthers together, but maybe that was June. Oh wait—June Cleaver is on *The Simpsons*.

Ralowe calls: what is that flavor-enhancing seaweed? Kombu. And what kind of mushrooms did you suggest for lentils? Crimini—are you at Rainbow? No, I'm at Baker Beach and there's a man in a van, maybe I should get in the van. Later, Ralowe calls to ask why there are eight helicopters flying over. It's because if there were seven, they'd get confused with the days of the week. I realize that June Cleaver can't be married to Homer on *The Simpsons* because her name's Cleaver. Oh—June Cleaver is the wife on *Leave*

It to Beaver. It takes me six hours to figure this out, which is pretty exciting.

Sometimes everything's terrible, and sometimes it's worse. Of course I can't fall asleep, I get up to eat toast, get back in bed. The rats are back in my kitchen, one of them is dashing across the floor and making skidding sounds. Is it a rat chasing a mouse? When I wake up, I feel like I've been fighting someone all night and there are bruises all over my body. The highlight of the day is getting my hair cut, 5:30 p.m. and then everything's downhill. Actually, it's uphill to sell CDs on Haight Street, where the guy will only give me twenty-four dollars for fifteen CDs. I think it's because I left the store tags on them, saying they were bought used. Then I'm eating at the noodle house, and I feel like I'm going to nod off. That's pretty much how I've felt all day long, for the last week at least, like at any moment I could just pass out. Everything, absolutely everything, is a challenge and I'm sick of it.

Oh wait—2 a.m. is around the corner and suddenly I can hardly breathe, my eyes popping out of my head. I check in the mirror to see if that's really the case, and what's really the case is that my eyes are surrounded by wrinkles when I smile—oh well, that's thirty to you—but the wired part is that my pupils are tiny inside the rest. I guess I'll have to go to the Power Exchange, unless I can think of some club that would be bearable.

Okay, so the next day is just hell, I can hardly even get out of the house I'm so exhausted and depressed and hopeless. Chrissie calls to try and sell me something from her new job, an entertainment card with discounts in Vegas or LA, Chrissie gets paid seven dollars per sale and there's no hourly wage. Today she's made one sale. Well—no reason to outsource telemarketing to India when you've got tweakers in San Francisco!

Later, Chrissie gives me the news: I'm looking at teenage fitness number seven, which is the number of the whore I think we can relate to this but what I'm talking about, eight is eternal, six is the beast, seven is the whore, then there's magical four—we're talking astronomical—raise yourself on parallel bars and then dip down as far as you can, you got to get some bars, go to a bar and push yourself up—but this is for teenagers and we're old—I want what Britney Spears has, she can find out what each and every molecule needs and they give her that.

Fashion alert: Vuitton driver wearing MUNI! But wait: I actually meet a hot guy over the internet. He's so nervous and maybe even straight, cute and preppy and so hard when he takes his clothes off. I suck his dick so I don't come too quickly, and after we're done, he's still nervous. Went to Georgetown University, and he says the area's even scarier now than how I remember it, just an outdoor mall full of Abercrombie stores for the college kids. This is when I realize the world's more and less complicated than I ever imagined, because here's this preppy guy who lives by the new ballpark and calls that an interesting neighborhood, but he's giving a critique of Abercrombie even while giving Abercrombie. Though I didn't check his labels, the girl is fully working Tevas.

Mabel Williams says something brilliant about taking up guns in Monroe, N.C. to defend against the KKK. She says: then the KKK members had to decide whether to risk their superior lives for our inferior ones. On the radio: democracy is a cleansing! But here's how depressing my sex-and-romance life is: I'm already thinking about the boy from last night, wondering if he'll call. You know the answer, from previous research. I check my email anyway. Then I get my first trick in a few weeks. I meet him at the Hot Tubs and I'm on, despite the nap that left me with a sinus headache—no, this is a hole. He's into my hole, but I'm not feeling that. After he comes on my stomach, I lie in bed with him and I realize something about how sex can bring this beautiful intimacy into the room.

I ask him if he's okay. He says: nothing, I'm just thinking. I don't ask what he's thinking about, because I can tell he doesn't want me to know. Suddenly he gets up, dresses and leaves me in the room. Luckily, he paid me first. I take a towel on my way out, because I need to get back into stealing things—and because it says Hot Tubs, which makes it a great souvenir.

At the last minute, I rush to the breakaway march at the anti-war demo, food in my hands. There are these weird conservatives over by City Hall with signs that say things like, "I Don't Support War—Unless a Democrat Is President." And, "Vote Green—So We Can All

Be Stupid and Poor." There are cops everywhere, so it takes a while for us to find a place where we can break away.

The march is the usual, except there are so many cops that we can't succeed in doing much, trying to march this way and then that way—the straight anarcho guys screaming like they're in the military, and ordering people around. The annoying thing is that most people follow their orders, like when they say RUN, everybody runs like it's a good idea or something. Pretty soon, we get to Market and I guess we're too close to the Abercrombie store, so the cops surround us. We're not allowed to be in the street or on the sidewalk—democracy in action: people get clobbered and dragged off. There are a lot of us, though—I'd say a thousand at the peak—so it almost feels empowering. Afterwards, Pouneh and I get food at my house, and then we take the 49 towards Market and it takes forever. Those goddamned anarchists—fucking up traffic!

A trick. A what? A trick. Oh, a trick. He's in the penthouse suite at the Pickwick Hotel, which is funny because the Pickwick isn't fancy. The suite is nice, though—the furniture's a bit worn but the old paneling on the walls and the grand marble fireplace are beautiful. I'm sure you haven't noticed yet, but I have a hotel fetish. The trick hasn't gotten fucked in two years, so it's kind of difficult. I'm so present it's insane, and then afterwards he rubs my body while I jerk myself off, which is kind of fun because I haven't come in a while—his hands feel good, plus I have complete control. Which is what every hooker wants, I mean needs.

Outside, it's cool and damp and foggy—I'm so glad. I always think the heat isn't going to end, but then it always does, 'cause thankfully this is San Francisco. Eric leaves me a message about what happened to Eldridge Cleaver, he came back to the U.S. from exile and became a Republican, ran for Congress in California and then got addicted to crack, died in '89.

Another dream where I'm going on a trip with my father, we stop at a gas station and the line is so long it goes out the door. It's because we're on the border. We wait in line forever. Afterwards, I ask my father if there was a Phish concert or something. He doesn't get the joke; I mean he doesn't know who Phish is.

When I wake up, every muscle in my body hurts. I try self-massage, which makes everything worse. When I get out of bed, there's so much dust in my room. I read *From Fatigued to Fantastic*, a 440-page book, in one day. Afterwards, I'm exhausted. Actually, I'm exhausted the whole time. Socket comes over for beans and rice. She watches me using the foot massage tools under the table. She says: you're so good at taking care of yourself—too bad it doesn't work. I walk four blocks to the post office, but it's closed. I'm exhausted. I go to Walgreen's to get a new prescription sleeping pill, but it's sixty dollars. I leave it there. I walk home. At my door, I'm so out of it that I think of lying down on the carpet in the hallway, a spectacle of collapse. I figure I can do that in my bed, too, which is caving in even more—pretty soon, I'll hit the floor—Bingo/Fish/Uno!

Perhaps a new album by Wynton Marsalis will make it easier to put the children to sleep at night. But now I present to you: The Unborn Victims of Violence Act, fire engines in the rain, and a lifetime's supply of grapefruit-flavored packing peanuts. Rue says those aren't packing peanuts, they're pomelos—but they taste the same. I keep thinking no one's calling me back because it's Friday, then I realize it's Thursday, then I keep thinking no one's calling me back because it's Friday.

Kid Koala rescues me from oblivion, with that crazy maudlin moaning and groaning only possible with amazing feats of turntable madness. Wait: is it maudlin or melancholy? I don't have a clue what he's doing, but it sounds like a trumpet, and one of those big string instruments, mixed with a foghorn in the rain, I love the foghorn.

But then I'm sad, just like that—the sentence ends, and then I'm sad again. Should I still go out for a walk? Okay, now Kid Koala's got dogs barking into violins as the records skip and the melody becomes a marching band in tandem with horror soundtracks backwards. Anything is possible, until my stomachache—well, that's what you get for eating beans at 2:36 a.m. On NPR: America is one of the most complex and vibrant brands I've ever met—someone actually says that. She's a former State Department official—or something like that—her job didn't work out because she moved in right after 9-11, and no one liked her. The best part of the Medea Project performance is this dance number one woman does, falling and collapsing in high heels—I want to gasp, but I almost can't breathe it's so good, reminds me of what I would want to do if I wasn't so injured. Afterwards, there's a dyke who moved here from Chicago, talking about looking for the other black people, and she didn't find many until she worked at the jail: there they were—San Francisco natives, all of them.

I wonder if I'll ever find exercise that doesn't hurt. Rue comes over and I have a breakdown about everybody's inconsistencies, then we go on a walk for seven blocks until I'm completely exhausted. At least it's fun to lie in Rue's arms, and hope to be saved. An NPR reporter on the BBC: I still think of England as Mother England, we're all English in one way or another. Pledge drive—it's only 33 cents a day to support Mother England. Peter Ustinov died today—he won his first Oscar for training slaves to fight as gladiators in *Spartacus*! James Bond says: when Peter and I fucked, it was like a train hitting Mother Teresa.

The U.S. government admits to killing two Iraqi journalists: we regret that we didn't like what they were saying. Ralowe's strung out from eating too much sugar with the hipsters yesterday, she keeps saying I don't know why I went to that party—you said you'd be there. But I never said I'd be there, you should have called me. She says: why did I think you'd be there—it's the sugar, I have to call people and warn them about the sugar, everybody just lives that way, Mattilda—is there any hope?

We go wheatpasting, which is fun, except that when I get home I feel good for about one-and-a-half minutes and then I get the full fibromyalgia drama—everything aches, from jaw to heels. Writing checks hurts more than just about anything else—I guess I should stop paying bills. For some reason, I get up at noon—I think it's the earliest I've been up in about a year. There's a whole different variety of radio programs. I don't like any of them. I go back to bed. Ralowe thinks maybe he was a crack baby. Sure, why not. Because I was adopted, he says: is there a test I can take to find out? Maybe you should call your parents.

Ralowe realizes he was born in 1975, that's too early to be a crack baby. Then he drinks a bottle of kombucha tea, and starts twisting his body side to side, and shaking his head with his tongue sticking out and his hands in the air. Well, if you weren't a crack baby then, you certainly are now. But it's okay—Ralowe and I are gonna move to LA and meet the woman who made so much money selling Avon that she started *Hairless Cat Magazine*, just to do something good for the world.

Benjamin calls, she says I was having sex with this guy and he turned to me and said: you remind me of the guy that gave me HIV. Speaking of romance and death, I go over someone's house for a hot internet hook up, and here is the lovely response I get: "I think we'll pass." Pass me the machine gun and I'll give you a facelift.

I walk to Lafayette Park, and some guy who I'm not attracted to gives me a terrible blow job, but first he asks yet another romantic question: is it clean? Walking down the hill into the lowlands of Pacific Heights, I'm screaming I HATE THE WORLD, which makes me feel much better.

I always thought that people who became celibate were a little crazy, but now it sounds awfully appealing. If only someone would pay my rent! Even though I used to feel more despair about life in general, I did feel like I belonged to a sexual culture of faggot freaks who loved and hated and dated one another. Don't get me wrong—we would never have used the word dated. We cultivated sluttiness and painted our nails, hung out with dykes because we scorned the larger world of fags, which we were also a part of. But we didn't think so.

We believed in dreams, even if we didn't think they'd come true. My heart is still broken from the first guy who didn't call me back—we met at an ACT UP meeting, he was from Pittsburgh. Benjamin leaves a message: I think I called you recently, but I'm not sure why. Ralowe comes over to help me with my life, and I'm having trouble getting off the floor: do you think everything's getting worse?

As Easter approaches, we take a look at the historical uses of crucifixion as a means of execution. But what about the price of oil? Some pigeons are beautiful, with bright eyes and shiny feathers, then others look like they've been through a car crash. But they all hang out together, preening and poking each other during the quiet moments.

I read Samuel Delany's *Heavenly Breakfast*, about living in a commune in the East Village in 1967, and it's too distant in tone and even content until the end, when the commune collapses and I'm left with tears in my eyes, trying to figure out how to cope. Also, thinking about their commune—twenty people in three rooms—and how I could never do that, I wonder what I'm missing out on.

Earlier, I was thinking about what drug addicts have that I don't, or what I have that drug addicts don't. I got confused.

I wonder what would happen if I met someone who was the head of Football Research at Liverpool University—marriage! But what would I wear? How 'bout a dark blue cap with the BBC lettering, it looks so official that I could get into 3Com Park for free—I mean a 75-dollar pledge. But sweetheart—that's U.S. football.

The April Fool's Day Pro-America Parade turns out well—everyone in their red, white, and blue finery, and I have to admit it is awfully fun to scream U-S-A like a frat boy and then yell KILL KILL KILL. The climax is the smashing of a cardboard cow in front of Neiman Marcus, as red paint pours all over the sidewalk, though it does end up getting people arrested. For some reason, the organizers didn't plan legal, media, or police negotiation. A sixty-year-old tourist gets knocked over by charging cops, and four people get arrested. Everyone's in panic mode as someone rides off with the sound system and the genuine police billy club I've snatched from the ground. A tourist screams at the cops, with cocktail in hand.

After people get dragged off, a police officer tries to talk to us about why he's right. I go to Macy's to use the bathroom, they've got a Marc Jacobs shirt stenciled with something about rock 'n' roll—$160. Though I prefer the vinyl jacket for $865. Outside, everyone's still there. Some people go to the police station; I go home and try not to lie down.

Chrissie leaves me a message: I need to end our relationship because I'm tired of hurting you, and tired of being hurt by you. What is she talking about? Benjamin watches some TV show about ecstasy. What do you think about ecstasy therapy, she says—I've never done ecstasy, do you think it would help?

I did plenty of ecstasy therapy. It didn't help.

BACK TO THE FAMILY

◉   ◉   ◉   ◉

There's a fire across the street, I go out on my fire escape in the cold—yes, it's cold again, really cold. The air smells charred, which is strange because there's so much of it between here and there, so the fire must be large—or somehow the charred air is getting stuck on my fire escape. I go back inside. Ralowe says she likes the new awkward delivery of my answering message. But the message hasn't changed. My sweatshop-free organic underwear finally arrives—it's not so stylish, but it's awfully soft. On the radio, Jennifer Stone says: the cross is a weapon of mass destruction, imagine wearing an electric chair on a string around your throat.

I go to a movie at the Castro, where I run into Hektor and Mark at exactly the same time. Mark's just walking by, he's working in corporate something or other, which I guess he tells me so I'll be scandalized. But I already know. Hektor and I go into the movie with his friend who seems sweet. The movie is hilarious—it's not supposed to be, but I can't stop laughing. The main character clutches his heart at the end, on the bridge where he picks up guys,

215

and then he just collapses into heaven—everything's bright and he can finally feel intimacy. I'm cackling and almost choking—I think the audience knows it's funny too because no one says anything. I can't breathe, I get a pain in my belly from so much laughing, but it's worth it—afterwards, I have so much energy that I even think of going out.

Meanwhile, there's pot smoke blowing through the walls and into my apartment, but I can't stop thinking about Tom Cruise's hardest break-up ever! Huge roaches on my counter—they went away for a while, but they're back from a healthy trip to neighborhood restaurants, maybe they even ate the rats. Several people have revealed their deep fears of roaches versus rats to me recently, maybe when I've opened a cabinet and a prime specimen has tumbled to the counter—oh, there you are.

Now that I know it's the pigeons in the ceiling, and the pipes that make the screeching noise, the only time I worry about the rats is when I hear that weird tapping sound while I'm in bed, it sounds like the rats jumping down to a lower level in the wall. Sometimes the electricity flashes a little, so maybe it's the refrigerator—except the refrigerator isn't in the wall.

It's a freezing, foggy night and I go on a 3 a.m. walk. I decide to figure out where Polk Street stops being Polk Street, and it's not until around Washington, which is pretty surprising, actually—that's fully Nob Hill if you're over a few blocks. I'm having such a good time looking at all the old buildings and neon signs, some on and some off, the people crowded into the 24-hour donut shop. A lot of scary, speed-destroyed faces on the way back, and of course the cops, but it still feels calm.

Around Sutter, there are these two white guys hanging out in an alley, one of them points drunkenly my way and yells hey, you fucking faggot—get away, I need to get some pussy. I turn around—bitch, I live here, you don't. Then there are a couple groups of weird straight guys who aren't white and aren't as interested in me. I wonder why all these straight guys come to Polk Street on the weekends and walk up and down, like me I guess. It's not the yuppies who were in the bars earlier, it's an entirely different, rougher crowd that might be scarier in the physical violence way, but it stills feels better than yuppies. Especially now that the last sketchy dive bar on Polk Street, Katie's, turned into Blur. I think that really might have been the last one. Except the Rendezvous, with a lease that runs out in May.

Though what are straight guys getting from Polk Street? Speed, I guess. Or they're supposedly pimps. At home, I feel better. Doctor says: more walks. Actually, doctor says more sleeping pills—they're not addictive—just take more. I don't think so. It's the next night, I get in bed but I'm wired. I get out of bed—maybe tomorrow I'll actually take the sleeping pills, but tonight I'm going to read the newest autobiography in my '70s radical explorations: this one is H. Rap Brown, who says, "there's only one party in America and that's the party of white nationalism."

On the phone sex line, this guy who announces he's 100 percent Italian tells me he's gonna pump five tablespoons of come down my throat when I'm not looking. Florence calls to alert me to the fact that the real estate market in D.C. is hot, she's only selling properties in her building but that keeps her busy. She tells me about the condo my parents bought, and how if I'd just make up with them, then I'd have a great place to stay—you'd love the restaurants in the neighborhood, and oh the furniture stores—though the condo won't be ready for a year because it isn't built yet. She says: your life would be so easy if you'd just make up with them, think about it that way—will you think about it?

Then Florence wants me to think about getting new clothes. She doesn't mind if they look gay—just none of that flea market look. Will you think about that? I think about whether my beans are ready. Florence wants to know if I got the invitation for Rose's art show. No. Well, she said she sent you one. I didn't get it. Well you should call her, she's home today and she was asking about you. She hasn't called here to ask. Well, you're so hard to reach.

I get up from not sleeping to realize I was sleeping. I know because I was thinking, over and over again, that I needed to make it to the meeting to plan some sort of '70s covert action that involved elaborate wigs and an endless array of maps. When I wake up, it's not the '70s but I am in some flashback state, not a world of bell-bottoms but a world where the holes in the toast are scaring me. I have to turn on all the lights to make sure no one's behind the shower curtain, in the closet—and then I shield myself from the brightness, eat the holes in my toast, get back in bed.

In Ralowe's dream, he goes to Golden Era at 9 a.m. and runs into me, he says what are you doing up so early? I say I don't want to talk about it; I'm having a confusion attack. Someone on the 9-11 Commission starts his questions to Secretary of Defense Donald Rumsfeld by saying: thank you for your fulsome testimony. I look it up, but yes, I was right—fulsome means offensively insincere. Ralowe and I listen to President Bush's press conference on the radio—Bush can't even answer the simplest questions, I can't believe he hasn't figured it out yet. Someone asks if he's made any mistakes. He pauses, stutters, says: I wish you'd given me that question ahead of time.

I need a real dictionary; I'm still using the one I borrowed from Kinko's in Boston nine years ago. I call Rose, she wants me to get the operation for carpal tunnel. But I don't have carpal tunnel. What do you have? Fibromyalgia. Oh that's terrible, I wonder if there's a cure. So do I.

Of course we've already talked about fibromyalgia, but this time Rose thinks maybe it's because of my earrings. She just wants me to take them off. Then she asks an interesting and thought-provoking new question: when are you coming back to the family? Chrissie calls: I love you!

I say: I love you. Chrissie says: did you get my message? I say yeah, was I supposed to call you back? She says just negate it—I was going through my process.

Benjamin calls from downstairs—sorry I didn't call first, but I'm having an emergency, can I come up? Turns out she has a trick at the Days Inn on the corner in five minutes, but she has to call the guy and her cellphone just went dead, she doesn't have the number 'cause it's on her phone—can she charge her phone? I've always wondered about that Days Inn, because I've never had a trick there. Sure, it looks sketchy, but there's a huge clock you can see in the not-quite lobby, and the best thing about the hotel is there's a portion that's just the frame of an old building, in the middle of two sections that are '60s modern rundown ugliness. There's some kind of balcony on the other side of the old façade—like it's an amphitheater, and I've always been curious about the view from inside.

Of course the trick's flaking on Benjamin, and she's upset about the trucker cap she's wearing to look like a man. Plus, her electricity got turned off and this was the trick that was going to pay to turn it back on. We need to start a club for all the people who wake up at 1 p.m. and can't face the world—we can talk to each other on the phone until the radio makes us cry at the same time. But Benjamin doesn't want to cry. Advice for skipping stones: to get it to skip a lot, you need a flat stone about the size of your hand, and you need to throw it hard, down as well as out. A can of tuna doesn't work as well as a bagel. Anger helps.

I call Andee. For an hour, I'm a mess and she's talking, then all the sudden she's a mess and I'm talking. My headache takes over. My hands hurt. On the radio, I hear about the law that went into effect banning the killing of baby harp seals for fur, but it defines seals older than three weeks as adults—so much maturity before a seal hunter bludgeons you into someone's hat!

I get my first trick in weeks, just after Ralowe and I go on the internet to place new ads—maybe it actually worked. But no, it's from an old ad—the tragic thing is that I'm actually looking forward to it, because I haven't had sex in so long. This changes when I arrive—the looking-forward part—the sex happens, I can tell he wants to get me off because his dick isn't going anywhere. I lie back. Afterwards, I walk home, through Union Square and then up Geary. The weirdest thing is the new café that's going to replace a Tenderloin gay bar with hardly any windows—the Hob Nob—yet another gentrification casualty.

Vocabulary from my dreams: a Montenegro cocktail! It all happens in Provincetown, each house on Commercial Street has a cage that rises behind it like a stadium. I try to go to yoga—a huge building of packed rooms—I accidentally knock someone over who's doing final relaxation on the top of a door frame, then step on someone's hair in one crowded class. Needless to say, everyone hates me. I find the teacher I like, but then lose her in the hallway, and when I get to her class I'm trying to explain my injuries, but then that class is overflowing too.

Crying, I go outside, onto a beach filled with redwoods until some punk kids are screaming WATCH OUT—Montenegro cocktails—and the cops, drinking cocktails in a boat-size Hummer with glass walls, are hurling gallon-size bottles of gasoline into the woods—Molotovs might have started the Russian Revolution, but Montenegro started the First World War! Somehow, nothing is on fire but I'm running far and fast. When I wake up, the bottoms of my feet hurt.

Someone calls from downstairs—this is Monica, remember me? No. I'm from City Clinic; I have some medication for you. Huh? Did you get the message? No. She comes up, I look out the peephole just to make sure it's not an FBI agent, ready to take me to Guantánamo— I haven't even eaten yet! Luckily, it's a friendly woman who tells me I have gonorrhea in my throat. She gives me a pill. I ask about side effects—none. Of course that's a lie, but I take the pill anyway—it's so small, hopefully it isn't arsenic.

Sometimes it's just too hard to write, like today I walked around the Tenderloin for a while, and when I got home there was an octopus in my head, wrapped around my brain and I still can't get it off. I remember when my father would order calamari at Minetta Tavern on our visits to New York, and I always thought it was so gross, even though it looked like pasta. Or maybe because it looked like pasta—he'd always try to trick me. In bed, I bite off a piece of a fingernail and then chew on it until I can't remember where it came from. When I pull off my eye mask, the sun's so bright. I'm not sure if my headache throbs, I just know that I want to hit my sinuses with a sledgehammer—splat!—there goes my brain.

You know it's a bad day when I start singing, "What is love . . . baby don't hurt me, don't hurt me . . . no more." Waiting for the bus, I decide to befriend the woman next to me, because she's eating too, but then I look over at what she's eating: Burger King. On the bus, there's that hilarious queen who moved here from New York, she used to wear a huge hat covered in branches and fake grass and flowers, maybe some of them real. Today, she doesn't have the hat, but she has fake grass in her dreadlocks, and she's wearing a vest with no shirt on, hello heat wave! She keeps turning around on the runway. Then, as usual, she's yelling—Happy Earth Day!—or maybe it is Earth Day. Everyone on the bus is laughing, and we're all probably laughing for different reasons. I'm laughing 'cause it's beautiful.

While I'm on the phone with Andee, I notice there are roaches crawling all over my food—they don't usually come out so much during the day, but they love the fucking heat. At someone else's house, I might be freaked out, but at my house I just brush the roaches off and keep eating—it's not like I'm going to cook an entirely new dish.

But did I tell you about the trick who brought me an apple? It's still sitting on the table, a week later—of course I can't eat apples because of all the sugar, but he didn't know that—he just wanted to keep the doctor away. When I was a kid, I knew it wouldn't work, but I ate apples to keep my father away, since psychiatrists are doctors too.

It's so hot when I wake up that I go right into the shower, to cool off, after the toilet overflows and I wonder how much it's going to hurt to mop it all up. Probably not as much as typing. The soap is melting. The shower doesn't work—I'm still sweating. It's so hot outside that the fire escape feels like it's going to burn my feet. All of my morning voicemail messages are boring.

My new sleeping secret: at 10:10 a.m. I take 5 mg. of Sonata, just before the fire engine drives by. It's supposed to be fast-acting and have a short half-life, or is that what they say about a nuclear bomb? Just when it finally kicks in—about an hour later—the construction vehicle with every hinge permanently rusted—that monstrosity that drives by every day now, shaking my whole building—makes its appearance. Then two amazing runs of the screeching pipes. Two p.m. and I feel just like a duck living in a contact lens case, only dryer. But don't forget the $330 glass Easter basket at Aunt Bill's Antiques!

I take Rue to the Tibetan place for her birthday, she tells me she was in the bathroom at City College and some hottie was waving his dick at her, she opened the stall door and . . . guess who? Jeremy. The food's delicious, except one dish tastes like it was cooked with rancid oil. I don't say anything.

Sometimes when I'm with Rue, I feel like I'm going to start crying because I love him so much and I wonder if that's weird. She's trying to decide whether to go to the trick who fucks her and smells, even though he's clean he just smells. I wake up at 7 a.m. and I've turned on my side on the new mattress, which is too hard, so my neck feels like it's attached to my body with rusted twine between thumbtacks. I guess this isn't a hard mattress for a normal person, but I'm certainly not normal. My nose is glued shut by allergies, and I feel so awful that I start crying. This guy on the radio talks about jumping off the Golden Gate Bridge, the water was like a brick wall and then it pulled him under. Later, but not much later, he felt a fish and that's when he knew this wasn't a dream that he'd survived.

I spend all day craving sex, even though I'm so exhausted I can't think, or maybe that's why. When I can't sleep, I jerk off with the covers around my dick, such a soft playhouse! In the morning, I have a sore throat. From coming? Yeah—from coming. Not to mention the horrible screeching pipes. I call the building manager. He doesn't answer.

Everything is saved by good sex—it really exists. The first guy I meet on craigslist isn't the one, luckily he leaves before I have time to find him attractive. The good thing is that I clean my apartment for him, so it's clean. I decide to meet the next guy in Lafayette Park and it's amazing right away, first he's up against a tool shed and then a tree. I'm kissing his neck and he seems unsure about it, but pretty soon we're making out, over and over again, and my favorite part is rubbing my face up against his, really softly until I feel his cold ears. Then I want his come down my throat but I know he's freaked out about safety, because the first thing he said—after hi, I'm Andrew— was: are you clean?

That's *Mister* Clean, Mary. He's one of those gays who's been playing at straight for so long that it almost feels like it. Except for the passion, which is why it's good sex—thank the fucking Lord for all the spots of come on my coat afterwards! Is it his come or mine? I don't know because we jerk each other off so we'll come together, and afterwards we're both dripping in strange places and we're trying to wipe it off with the toilet paper I brought. It's not quite working.

Andrew's from Seattle, he gives me a ride home and tries to shake my hand goodbye. Sorry, honey—you just sucked my cock—I think we can kiss. I get inside and it's only 11 p.m., there's still time for the rest of my life. What exactly is that, again? Well, there are the rats in the walls—I heard one again last night—the screeching pipes, the pain, and the mattress that's too hard, but what seems even harder is calling the mattress store to get another replacement.

But, more importantly, are you wearing your AIDS ribbon upside-down for Vaccine Awareness Day? News from the future, always stuck in the past: that bitch Mattilda had a ghostwriter; everybody knows she couldn't even type! Now that she's made millions, I hope she does her part by sponsoring Coors Beer Busts for all the little starving children—this is what democracy looks like: shoe polish in an elevator. But what happens when the elevator cable breaks? Silly girl—who has cable in an elevator?

An adult entertainment survey: Do you watch videos? No. Do you rent or buy videos? No. How often do you watch videos? No. When was the last time you watched a video? No. What do you think of adult entertainment options?

Ralowe wants me to be friendlier to the telecommunications specialist, though she won't even say hi to anyone who doesn't look her in the eye. Meanwhile, everyone's looking at Brad Pitt's tits—but where is the milk, there's gotta be milk in here somewhere! Ouch—you got something in my eye. Ralowe says there was some scandal a few years ago at UC Berkeley in a men's sexuality class. It was a student-run class, and the first class was a circle jerk. Ralowe says can you imagine—all those frat boys in a circle jerk? But honey, no frat boys are going to take a men's sexuality course. Ralowe says: but can you imagine? Yes, honey, I took the adult entertainment survey.

In the Bayview: a sting operation by the state police, detaining and arresting hundreds of black people guilty of driving. In Iraq: sifting through plastic bags filled with bones. In Massachusetts: gays and lesbians partying all night in the streets—we can finally get married! Walking outside, I get shooting pains in my neck. I look on the internet for fibromyalgia resources, and then my back hurts too—and I won't even tell you about my wrists. After a sleeping pill and a few hours of something in my bed, I'm assessing the situation. Until the pipes start screeching, and I'm wide awake trying to soothe my brain but thinking about calling a plumber, calling the building management company, shooting the building manager who keeps telling me it's just because people don't turn their water on all the way.

On the radio, I listen to a bunch of guys getting sworn into the army in a dead-end town in Texas, where there are eight prisons. This one guy calls up his father, his father was in Vietnam and tries to dissuade him, but the son says: now, soldiers are respected. Then his dad cries, once he's won over. I cry too, though not because I'm won over—the music becomes overwrought or maybe that's just me, sitting straight in my uncomfortable ergonomic chair and wondering if there's any hope.

The announcer asks the recruiter: do you ever think anyone you recruit might get killed in Iraq? No, says the recruiter, I don't ever think about that. Then we get an announcement from Wal-Mart, which invests in neighborhoods, and advice that parents who monitor their children's behavior starting early on have a good chance of preventing drug abuse.

I call Rose to find out about her show, she says when are you coming back to the family? Oh, no. Apparently, teenagers do stupid things like confronting their fathers about raping them, no one can remember anything from when they were three, it didn't happen, why am I hurting them, it's sad the way I see the world. The cicadas have arrived on the East Coast this year—it's once every seventeen years. I remember the last time—they covered the trees and hummed over everything.

Just the screeching pipes make my day so hard, as Israel kills more Palestinians and the U.S. kills more Iraqis and I read about Vietnam, read that it was impossible not to stand up against that war—to take every risk—and I wonder if that's possible now. The risks. I wish I could go to jail and grow stronger, but I don't know if I'd survive. Nothing to eat and so much pain, it's hard enough to sleep in my plush bed. My whole neck feels like a bruise, a huge bruise I carry around with me from the time when they'd tighten that rope around my neck, bag around my head, I think I mean literally. When I'd float up above while he was doing things down there—to us—the kids—and they—the adults—were out there burrowing themselves in. And my grandmother says: how could you do this to us?

Rue calls: it's hard to walk because my back's out, the chiropractor wouldn't do an adjustment without X-rays and now I have to wait until Monday. Rue's futon feels worse than a rock because who would sleep on a rock? The worst thing about the shrieking pipes is that I think that otherwise I might actually be sleeping, because lately they wake me up from something deep, and then I have to get up and eat toast, take passionflower and pulsatilla, and then pour some of the powder from a sleeping pill into water and drink the bitter fruit.

When I wake up, it's the pipes again and I call the building manager. Now I have ammunition from a plumber who says it's a broken pressure regulator, or the chambers on the pitch valve—and either way, it can be fixed. I get back in bed, then I get back up and that's actually when I take the flurazepam, which puts me into a haze until I wake up feeling like I swallowed the dust out of a vacuum cleaner.

I feel like I'm always rushing onto the bus, hot, at the beginning of the day, and then waiting for the bus, freezing, at the end of the day. Colin Powell's favorite quote: I serve at the pleasure of the President. Hmm . . . slavery? But thirty-year-olds are now renting yachts to celebrate their birthdays! What's better—romance or rejection—wait, is this a trick question? If you hate the world, yourself and your life, things may be more difficult for you than others, who may hate only one, two, or two and a half of the three choices. Vivacious or vicious—you decide!

I'm not suggesting that you can't choose both. Everyone insists that it's always foggy in San Francisco, but I swear it's been sunny for weeks—I just want some fucking clouds! I wake up and I've actually got my wish, but I can see the blue sky underneath, and—sure enough—the sky takes over within five minutes. So long, gray day.

Ralowe wants to talk about the ways in which our work—that is: my work, his work and Benjamin's work—relates because of the ways in which we're all oppressed by power under late capitalism. First, he has to watch more porn. Ralowe says: if you and I had a falling-out, what would you change my name to? The Sustainable Foods Expo at the San Francisco Aquarium: that shark may look tough, but wait until you bite into it! Outside at 2 a.m., I barely need my scarf and mittens—something's wrong. Precarious or vicarious— well, that's an easy question.

Gina's done with school, so we can be friends again. She wants to know if I'm still soaking my wrist guards in boiling water, just in case there are any lice. Here's what I learn from sleep: the Lord is the last piece of information. I make it into a chant, trying to put myself back into dreamland, but pretty soon it's the end of the night and I'm talking to Jaysen. He says when he was three or four, and his mother was on welfare, she'd leave him at daycare and forget to pick him up. She was getting drunk, Jaysen says, but now I'm at peace with it. I say who are you—Featherblower Lavender Sunshine Intention Blessed Be?

There are two roaches crossing the kitchen wall together—they keep bumping into each other, and I wonder if they're in love. I'm talking to Andee about Zan, she goes right up to the people in bars who we'd run away from as fast as we could, the guys who are kind of hot, but you know if you had to talk to them for one minute they'd suck all the life out of you, and you'd never be able to get it back—she goes right for those people and dives in. But last night I went to Rudeboys, Andee says—I danced the whole time, I only went into the darkroom for a second—they were playing all the songs that I don't even remember what they were called, like "Everybody, everybody . . . everybody, everybody." Then there was this guy who I just loved for the way he danced—I wish you were there, though—because then I could have busted all my moves.

Andee realizes it's 10:30 a.m. in London—shit, she says—I have to go, I'm gonna sleep for at least two days. I look outside and the moon is so low, just barely above the Monarch Hotel. Florence says she'd love to see me in D.C., but there's one condition: you can't dress with that flea market look. Why is she obsessed with flea markets? She just wants me to wear khakis or jeans—or something new, anything.

I wear khakis to my tricks these days, but Florence doesn't want to know that. Not that I'm interested in telling her what she wants, but her hearing's not so good these days so I'd have to repeat it too many times. In my dream, Ralowe's afraid of the alligators in a pond by a construction site near where I grew up, but I think they're cute—though I'm not sure how big they are. We're walking on the side of some horrible desolate suburban road with construction all around, though in the dream it just seems normal, like it seems normal to have alligators in a construction site in suburban D.C. I haven't been there in so long, I wouldn't be surprised.

It's a rare night without squeaking pipes, so why do I wake up feeling worse? Actually, I can't wake up, I just walk around standing-up-sleeping. On NPR, the latest research shows that kids are different from adults! Ralowe, Liz and I take the bus together just at the moment when I crash into some hole, and Ralowe is performing 77 flavors of stupidity—why does she needs so much attention? Liz seems all right with it, and I'm trying to get there, though really I just need to get home.

Nothing's better until I get an email from the guy in the park a few weeks ago—says he had fun but he's been traveling, hasn't checked the email—tonight he's horny, though he's just gonna jerk off, it's gonna be a huge load. Whatever. Should I go to the Power Exchange?

I decide to take a sleeping pill and go to bed, then I decide just to take extra mind-numbing sleep tinctures. I really hope tomorrow's better. At the last minute, I add a sleeping pill to the mix, just in case, then I get in bed and sure enough I'm wired. I get out of bed and call the phone sex line 651 times, which is great for my hands, neck—oh, my neck. Did I mention that as soon as I got in bed, my neck started to burn? It's the horrible new mattress—it's killing me! One of these days, I'll get a replacement for the replacement, but right now the store keeps telling me to talk to customer service, and customer service keeps telling me to talk to the store.

I have this fear that I'm going to be chopping vegetables, and then suddenly I'll chop off a finger or poke my eye out—so, no, I didn't sleep well. With so many tinctures and a fucking pill, you'd think I'd sleep past 12:24. But no—wired as all hell, with the added comfort of a head filled with asbestos—so that's where the cancer's coming from! I'm standing on the corner of Church and Market, waiting for the bus, breaking down—help, too many gay people with leases on their partners, partners on their leases! On Van Ness, there's a bar of soap shattered on the ground, and I draw hearts with the pieces. At home, it's 7:46 p.m. and I'm desperate to get in bed—hopefully I'll feel better afterwards, though I'm not expecting it.

When I wake up, I'm bikini-perfect. Ralowe says: why is it that whenever anyone cruises me, it has to be someone wearing a SECURITY T-shirt, like this guy at the Virgin Megastore, I was at the listening station—I figured he was in inventory control, upset that the black person was spending so much time listening to the CDs, but he kept nodding at me. Rue calls to cancel our plans—he's tired after doing yard work for some rich guy. I crash, well actually there's nothing much to crash from, so I just fall. No one to call, so I go to used book stores until I'm too hypoglycemic to function, then I return home. Later, I'm laughing about all the bad vegan food I've eaten at restaurants lately, that's what puts me in a good mood.

Another morning of screeching pipes, I get up and decide not to cruise the internet anymore. It's my birthday—I'm 31 on the 31st! Rue comes over with freshly made Vietnamese spring rolls, and then we visit the sea lions. It's Memorial Day on Pier 39, so it's packed with tourists, but there are a lot of sea lions, and pretty soon Ralowe, Gina, and Liz show up, too. I love watching the way the sea lions lie on top of each other and nothing matters, one of them focuses intently on mastering yoga postures—first sun salute and then what's that one—the bow? A tiny one is busy figuring out how to get out from underneath hundreds of pounds, then suddenly they all start yelling and sneezing in each other's faces, pushing each other off the docks and into the freezing water and then after a short swim they get back on the docks and go right back to sleeping.

There's one enormous one—she must be about 800 pounds—and she's got a whole dock to herself. Any time someone else tries to join her, she just shakes her head—no, no, no. At the marine mammal shop, I get postcards and Gina gets a fake tattoo. We go to the Inner Richmond for Burmese food, but end up getting an MSG surprise instead, because we miss our place in line and the kitchen closes, we have to go down the street to the MSG factory. An unforgiving experience and an unforgettable topic.

In the morning, what's in my head? Sawdust, cotton—the kind of cotton that hurts to touch—windshield wipers that are broken and rusted open, dying pigeons that don't quite smell yet, an olive tree with roots, an airplane hangar like the one that collapsed in Paris though actually that was a terminal, a broken air-raid siren that doesn't even make the sound I like, dandruff on flower stems, venomous snakes, radio waves, the enteric coating from 6,000 bottles of aspirin, plastic recycling fumes, rabies, a CAT scan, Marie Antoinette's head, better off dead, lots of glue that burns, photo-developing chemicals, toluene, broken light bulbs, a deer's head with antlers poking out, 700 bags of cat litter, 200 different toxic perfumes.

And more: chlorine from every pool in Texas, construction vehicles, a fire hydrant that doesn't work, weeping weeping willows, so many crumbling walls, rocks and boulders and cliffs that don't just jut—especially when you fall off—the Grand Canyon—potted plants that didn't make it, berries with thorns, more glue, so much glue and maybe mildew dried out too because it's all dry in there, even the berries aren't colorful they're gray.

I go to bed again—the pipes don't squeak, but it doesn't matter because I sleep like shit anyway. What's in my head in the morning? Hollow-point bullets, Marriott hotels that fell off the chain, demolition debris, paper cuts, mint-flavored hacky-sack choking my eyeballs. What? I push at all the pain to see if I can find the center, but it's all pain.

OH BEAUTIFUL . . .

⊙   ⊙   ⊙   ⊙

Ralowe says he's been on the internet for eight hours, and it just keeps getting worse. But there's good news: Ronald Reagan is dead! Jaysen goes to the war demo, he says I just wanted to see what they were like now, but I had to leave because I realized I could be doing something more important, like folding laundry.

You don't want to know what NPR has to say about Reagan's death—they bring out Margaret Thatcher. George Bush says: his work is done, and now a shining city awaits him. I call Andee—11 p.m. is 7 a.m. for her, but of course she's still awake. She tells me about when she took valerian and there was sweat pouring down her back, she thought it was snakes. She says: maybe you should try cocktails for a week, and then your fibromyalgia will go away. Um, maybe you should try valerian.

In the morning, I open the spices cabinet and four roaches fall on my shoulder—why do they like living so close to the edge? Or maybe it's in their genes—hard-wired for danger. Blake says: have you seen that book *Rats*—it might help. Benjamin calls, she says I just had the most disturbing conversation with Ralowe—he's probably told you about it, but I don't know.

Ralowe calls, he says I just want to kill myself, I don't have any friends—I was talking to Benjamin and she's just not interested in connecting with me in the ways that we always have. I used to feel like Benjamin and I could have these conversations about race and identity and living in the world. I felt like we had this closeness because we've experienced trauma and alienation in similar ways and now she's telling me that never happened, she said: I'm not interested in that, you're making assumptions—I was just interested in your artistic process. I don't know who I'm going to have those conversations with—I know you have all your own problems, and I don't want to burden you, but I go out on the street and everyone's talking to each other, how do they do it? What does it all mean?

Benjamin says: it was like a break-up conversation, he expressed the need for certain things from me, and I expressed a disinterest in those things. It became much more dramatic than it needed to be. I don't want to be another person who thinks Ralowe's too difficult to deal with.

A survey for the world—what do you think is making those scratching noises in my walls: is it pigeons or rats, cats, mice, lice, rice, dice, or a flotation device? If it's rats or pigeons—well, we already know all about that! If it's cats, I hope they're not rabid. If it's mice—same old story. If it's rice, then when am I getting married? If it's dice, what's my lucky number? If my lucky number is seven, isn't that a cliché? And what do I win, anyway?

Decompression advice: I go to the Nob Hill Theatre and eat more come. It tastes good, but afterwards my throat feels raw and I start worrying about STDs again—welcome back to gay life! This new going-to-bed-at-7-a.m. schedule is not working—all day long, I feel like I'm drifting inside of a wall. Chrissie wants to come over and cook a stir-fry—sure, why not? She doesn't show, and I actually end up going to bed by 3.

Of course I'm awake at 9 a.m., ready to start a macrobiotic hair salon—I eat toast, get back in bed to wait for funding. At 10 a.m. I'm still awake, but more desperate. I get up to look at a postcard of the sea lions—they just sleep, in any position at all! I take part of a sleeping pill, get back in bed for another hour of pounding on heaven's—or wait, it's knock knock knockin'—fuck it, just LET ME IN, I swear I'll even become a transaction documentation specialist or a hedge funds advisor or a Louis Vuitton attaché or just strange and blasé, touché, outré.

I get a few hours where I'm looking straight up at bright lights and thinking how can I be dreaming when there's so much light? Aaron tells me there's a new anti-depressant coming out this summer, he figures he can ride out the Paxil withdrawal long enough to try it, but not until after his mother visits. Rue tells his therapist he's having trouble staying awake for more than a few hours, and the therapist gives him another bag of Strattera—the new ADD medicine—I wonder if that's the same one they give U.S. fighter pilots to stay up and shoot Iraqis.

Here's what my life has come to: I need to get curtains so that I don't see the sun rising before I go to bed. Rue and I go to Jefferson Park to watch the sunset. It's pretty, but the five-block walk wears us both out, my back feels like it's going to crack off and then there's no possible way to sit on the bench without hurting everything. We try sitting in the grass, but then my back hurts even more because there's nowhere to lean. Rue's day is coming to an end—9 p.m. is almost bedtime, but I got up at 4. There's a state police officer patrolling the park to make sure no one's sleeping there. When we get back to my house, my whole neck hurts, like I have bruises right up against the cartilage.

Ralowe says he had a trick last night, and it was like a whole year of working at Wells Fargo—some tweaker who inherited his house from a cop who died of cancer and the tweaker needed to re-install Windows on his computer, which took six hours and he was sweating so much that there were puddles on the floor and the dogs were licking it up. These were the dogs that the dead cop made his friend promise he'd take care of, but that was before he was dead.

In the morning, the trick's shooting up . . . vitamin C. He keeps saying, over the course of the twelve romantic hours he and Ralowe spend together in the sweat-drenched sheets of mystic memory—wait, isn't that Meryl Streep in *Out of Africa*? But don't get distracted—the trick's just doing Ralowe a favor, that's what he keeps saying.

News from the laboratory: Paxil might not work for children! News from the Southern Baptist Church: when you have a big tent, with all different kinds of people in it, sometimes the tent collapses. News from Ralowe: the cruising bathrooms at Macy's aren't as crowded as they used to be. News from the Army: a new and improved battlefront uniform hits the racks in stores early next year. News from the hallway: did you order pizza?

News from the garbage chute: there are smart pigeons, hanging out in the stairwell, and when I walk in they fly right out the crack in the window! Benjamin visits the sea lions with her new boyfriend—somehow I can't really picture that. She says it was really beautiful, well actually it was really beautiful seeing the way he reacted. The new mattress arrives, and I swear it's already caving in. Maybe it's some sort of scam: selling caved-in mattresses to faggots with body drama. At least it's softer.

What is this headache, taking over both sides of my head like high-pressure headphones with sandblaster attached? I finally catch someone walking through the demolished building next door—I always suspected that it happened, but I never actually saw anyone doing it. I see this person because of their flashlight. They're looking for something, and not finding it.

News from the BBC: Africans love globalization! My mother calls, for some reason I'm meeting her next week and she sounds so excited, I feel like crying. Kirk does a performance where he appears dressed as Nancy Reagan at her hubbie's funeral, leans his head on the flag-draped coffin, takes a knife out of the coffin and asks the audience to scream YES while he screams NO, chopping up the flag. I wake up to piss, and break a glass. It rolls off the dish rack like magic until it's shattered all over the floor. I sweep it up, and miraculously don't cut myself. Rue tells me scientists just discovered a deep-sea fish that's as old as the Tyrannosaurus Rex. It has teeth like a shark, but it looks like a rat, a five-foot-long rat with wings. Maybe that's what's in my walls.

My trick is so smashed he can't really speak. He wants to suck my dick, but he's biting me and gagging. Just when I think he's hating everything, he says: you're wonderful. I know I shouldn't be turning tricks anymore, because I want to cry, lie down and die.

My new phone sex boyfriend wears baggy jeans and doesn't like having sex outdoors too much because he gets nervous. He's my phone boyfriend because he's staying with a friend in an SRO, can't get back in after 10 p.m. He has a sexy voice and he likes my voice-mail greetings, keeps getting his friends to call and laugh. He's a social worker who's about to get SSI for bipolar and PTSD but he watches *Fox News*.

Benjamin loves her new recording and her new boyfriend, but she's exhausted—she wants to know if I was more tired when I went out with Jeremy. She's wondering if all this intense connection is tiring her out. I call my phone boyfriend, he's not there. It's past his curfew anyway. Maybe tomorrow we'll finally meet.

Gina's thinking of moving to LA to get a film job—oh, no! Just when she's done with school and breaking up with her girlfriend, and we've actually been seeing each other. Andreas, my phone boyfriend, comes over—I don't think we're going to be boyfriends. We're lying in bed, he's rubbing my chest, which feels nice, but not in a sexual way really, he wants to know why I'm not attracted to him.

We lie there awhile, maybe two hours, staring at the ceiling and cuddling and at one point it reminds me of the first scene in Hal Hartley's *The Unbelievable Truth*, which was my favorite movie when I saw it in high school. In the beginning, two girls lie in the grass and talk to each other while they look at the sky. Maybe that's what Andreas and I are doing. I wonder if I know what I want sex to feel like.

Though really I'm afraid of bridges, afraid I might fall off. Ralowe says: I was all nervous going to probation and so I was up all night on the internet, then I went to the jail and at the last minute, the lawyer shows up and he says: Ralowe, it's okay. So I went over to Embarcadero 4 and cruised the bathroom for five hours, or I'm not sure, maybe it was six hours. I'm feeling a little out of it because I didn't sleep last night, I'm not quite all there.

Now, I'm not saying that I'm better than you or anything, but usually I actually sleep.

Someone calls. I don't answer it. But is this time special?

It's special because it's my mother, calling me back after I called to tell her I have a cold, don't call me back. She says I'll hang out with you even if you're sick. Yuck—what you'll do isn't the point. Andee calls—I'm in Seattle! What? I'm visiting my mother. Did something happen? She had to have a breast tumor removed, but she's okay. How long are you going to be here? Two weeks. When are you coming down to SF? That's an entirely different question.

My mother shows up, she understands why I like my apartment—there's so much light, the layout is so interesting, you have so many interesting things around. She looks at the '70s porn decorating my kitchen cabinets: does this have anything to do with you? No, I just thought it was funny. She says: it is funny.

We go to Millennium—the moment I've been looking forward to. My mother orders the kombu noodles, but then she doesn't even want to taste them—they're green, she says. She likes my quinoa cake, and the dahl with it, but grimaces at the broccoli rabe. Actually, the broccoli's called something else, something more unusual.

At home, the kids in the hallway are shooting each other with pellet guns, no wait the cooking school students are playing with them? One of the cooking students is hot, busting out of his tank top and tight pants as he runs up the stairs to shoot it. I stare.

Okay, so I know you've been wondering, all those times you find yourself strolling around Fisherman's Wharf, and you look in the restaurants at all those smiling Americans, all those bulwarks of democracy, those future and current inventors and geniuses of the world—the free world—what are all these smiling Americans eating? And the answer: bowls of steaming clam chowder inside hollowed-out loaves of sourdough bread.

Even my mother can't believe it—the sourdough part—it was just so disgusting, she says—now my face is fat. My mother wants to know if I like flowers—she likes plants better too, they don't die and make such a mess. They're renovating their kitchen, she and my father—at least she thinks so, she'll believe it when she sees it.

My mother likes my apartment, except it's so sunny she has to wear sunglasses. I can't sit in here without them, she says—I'm really sensitive to the light, but oh this weather—every day it's perfect. She asks how I'm feeling—I'm a mess. She says you look exactly the opposite of the way you feel. We go to buy computer ink, she's brought me some but it's the wrong kind. They won't exchange it, so she buys more, says: I'll return it at home. The buzzer goes off, she tells the guard: I'm stealing this, but I'm not very good at it.

We go to Millennium again, this time it's too hot inside, and the food's making me sick. It's Pink Saturday, so there are smiling gay boys at the bar from the hotel upstairs, ordering their first Pride cocktails. I stare at my mother, she asks me something—I don't know what it is, really—maybe she's talking about returning the ink. I look her right in the eyes, and say: you can't take everything back. She doesn't notice. When she hugs me goodbye, I have to feel stiff so that I'm not too vulnerable.

But it's Pink Saturday—Ralowe, Liz and I go to see *Imelda*, where Imelda Marcos tells us that her would-be assassin should have used a prettier knife, and at her trial in New York, the Negroes were rooting for her. Everything's okay until Rue calls from Faerie Village at Pride—smashed, of course. She says I wanted to call you because I know you don't like hanging out with me when I'm drunk, and we're hanging out later. But why are you at Pride? Because I wanted to see people. Who? I got a contact for a job, she says. Right.

I get a message from my mother: I enjoyed spending time with you, but I noticed you were staring at me at the restaurant, and I wondered if there was something you were thinking about, if there was some underlying issue. My mother, the therapist. I call her back: don't delude yourself into thinking you don't know what it is, or that you're helping me.

I'm sucked into serious sinus headache heartache and Ralowe calls, I can't function because it's too hot in my house, I made too much cauliflower, I think the 5HTP I'm taking for sleep is killing my houseplants. What the fuck is 5HTP? I don't know, some awful capsule I swallow before turning on the new relaxation CD.

The relaxation CD works—at getting me to fall asleep, though someone's still pumping turpentine into my lungs. In the morning, scientists are protecting endangered plants with genetically engineered insects! But don't worry—consumer spending rose last month because people are spending more on food and energy. Gina tells me that when she was a born-again Christian, she learned that she was filling her heart with all these things that weren't God-shaped, and so they didn't fit, because everyone has a God-shaped heart!

I wake up with a God-shaped bloody nose. The blood doesn't come pouring out, doesn't stain the sheets or stream onto the floor and make me slip and release more. The blood's just in my nose, waiting for me to blow. Blow. Blow. Until bedtime, which comes remarkably quickly. I know I'm sketchy because I'm heating up some food and I see something in the window, it makes me shudder with a little bit of panic—I look closer and it's my reflection.

It's gotten to the point where I can't actually remember romantic sex. I look at a guy on the bus, he has a cute smile—is he the one? I see some straight hipster on Valencia—fuck my face, okay? That's romance? Well, sure—when they examine my body in the street, come and blood dripping out of my mouth, tire tracks all over my back—bicycle tires—they'll know that it was a crime of passion and longing. His passion, my longing. My fashion, his belonging.

More blood: I know that's what I'm going to hear about if I turn on the news. In the morning, it's cloudy! Even if it's humid and disgusting, I'm just grateful there's no sun pouring into my poor apartment and making me sweat. Oh, wait, I can see blue sky getting ready to erase the clouds at any moment—same old San Francisco story—just give me some rain to help with all my pain! I know it didn't help in the winter, but maybe there's something about the reverse nature of the cosmos with respect to weather expectations. That sounds like something Imelda Marcos would say: when it's 12 a.m. in New York, it's 12 p.m. in Manila, the sun never sets in the Phillippines!

I remember—it must have been years ago—when a few drops of passionflower tincture would settle me down for sleep, endless sleep. I never felt rested, but at least I felt like bed was a place to go where I might get something—Hummers weren't on the market yet, so it wasn't the new low-carb Hummer C2. What was it? Something about lying down and getting up feeling better, right?

So here's the problem about seeing my mother: I keep thinking about her, even after I just fucked this trick and my legs hurt, actually they're shaking when I stand up but I'm still thinking about my mother, how I hate seeing her because it makes me feel so desperate, like I've done something wrong by not letting her lie. And then letting her.

Andee doesn't come to visit—he doesn't have the money, and his mother doesn't want to pay. She has cancer. Maybe I could pay, but I'm too annoyed at Andee for getting so close and not making it work. On the radio: telepathy. The story of my life—I'm no soft mattress, but I sure am caving in. One bite of food and I rush to the bathroom to shit—it was just kale, dinosaur kale—why are the dinosaurs getting back at me, poor Mattilda with the weak digestion? Then this trick comes over, he looks a little like Dick Cheney, only shorter.

There are lots of demeaning jobs, and sucking Dick Cheney's cock is definitely one of them. Everything he does is annoying—the way he scratches my rashes, sucks my cock so it bends against his throat, pokes me with his hands. I don't actually suck his cock, because of that smell. He wants me to come on his face—no way!

Blake goes to the hospital for a urinary tract infection that won't go away, they keep giving him antibiotics but it's still there. The doctor looks up at Blake and says you don't have to worry, men don't get urinary tract infections. Blake says I'm a transsexual. The doctor leaves the room to talk to a nurse, rushes back in and says WHAT DO YOU HAVE? Blake says um, I don't know—what do you think? The doctor says no, do you have a penis?

Everything starts itching when I put on clothes—I've already changed detergents three times, all of them hypo-allergenic, so I'm not sure what to do, other than go to the clinic and listen to them tell me they don't have a clue. Oh, no—the toilet's clogged again. I plunge it over and over, with no effect—except that my hands hurt, arms burn, neck feels broken with plants growing in the cracks between my bones then pulling the tendons tight, tighter. Everywhere on my face it feels like there are bruises like stones, groans, loans, lost retribution, pollution, articles of dissolution: my head, and everything that's below; my feet, and everything that's above.

But let's take a break: I'm on the bus, this woman enters with the full Madonna Material Girl look, and eyes filled with pure disgust or drugged-out bliss, depending on how you interpret it. These mod-'80s fashion kids are watching her, I figure maybe they went to high school together, and when she gets off the bus, one girl says: you know who that was, right? And then I can't hear what she says.

Were they former friends and current enemies, or was the Material Girl an honest-to-dishonest celebrity, a star inside some enormous constellation of bright light and fright tights? I listen carefully for their conversation, even think of asking them: who was it? I look outside to see if I can recognize her pale blue eyeliner with a hint of silver glitter pouring into the sidewalk and leaving a glimmer of rope. She's gone, and my stop arrives.

Here's a snapshot from my glamorous life. This trick shows up at the door, smelling like the cigars that I love so much—how sophisticated! I notice immediately that the whites of his eyes are red, and gooey at the bottom. Death has entered my apartment, and I am ready. For the first time, I notice the words to the song I always play when tricks come over: "from happiness to loneliness . . . you realize that love is gone . . ." I always thought it was a happy song.

Death suggests that we take off our clothes. I can see his bones, poking out oh-so-luxuriously. I know I've been in the Bay Area too long, because here is what I think: maybe I can give him some kindness. He wants me to fuck him, and somehow I manage—though his ass is so bony that it hurts my pelvis. When we're done, he says: here is 150, unless I can give you less.

Maybe I'm in love, and love gives you desperate images like throwing tricks off the fire escape, into the abandoned shell of the laundromat, and getting up early every day just to watch the decomposition of the bodies. But luckily, exactly 12 hours later, I have a manic moment with Ralowe just before she's whisked off in a taxi. I'm re-enacting a devastating Boston k-hole on the stairs, then I'm touring the 3 a.m. joys of Polk Street.

One guy's tagging ERASE, over and over again on the bricks of a building, while down the street his friend does something more elaborate. Lots of pimps are out talking on their cellphones about bitches. Someone has glass. Another guy is tapping his syringes against a wall—this is the line, he says, the line is here. He's pointing to the building that's been demolished for condos, only the façade is up—a false pretense of livability.

One trannygirl yells to me from across the street as I'm heading back—hey, girl! I like that. No cops for the entire walk and it feels like a different world, still a dark and desperate world, but one—for a half hour, at least—with a little more hope. Until I get home and my whole body aches, it feels like someone threw me against a wall when I wasn't looking.

Eric says: I forgot to tell you yesterday's big news—about my little brother, who's a Marine in Iraq, the one who I always thought was gay—he came out to me yesterday, in a series of emails. It was very traumatic; it's a little surreal. I keep thinking: did that really happen? So I go back and read the email.

Nuruddin Farah says: interpreting fear is a very difficult thing because when you are completely afraid, you become a completely different person. In Florida, a man receives a twenty-five-year sentence for taking Percoset for chronic pain—mandatory drug sentence minimums. Now he's hooked up to a morphine IV in jail, he says: they wake me up to eat breakfast, and then I go to bed—they wake me up to eat lunch, and then I go to bed. They wake me up to eat dinner, and then I go to bed.

But how do you choose a really nice baseball cap? One that feels good and looks even better, especially on the new twenty-dollar bill? Andrew Jackson, the great Indian removal hero—shaking his maxed-out track-suit in the wind, blowing into a twisted eagle seal. Ralowe says: now I have fantasies of becoming a self-contained unit in my apartment, creating my own language, and when I get SSI I'll have an internet hookup and I can sit inside all day, talking online to everyone who already won't speak to me, and trying out new words.

An ode to the Power Exchange: Oh beautiful, for specious guys, with amber loads of pain . . . for creamy fountain travesties, inside thy brain's disdain . . . Power Exchange, Power Exchange, God bred his grace in thee . . . And pound thy good into brotherhood . . . through seed of desperate need . . .

The kids in the hallway are playing with new guns, these look like machine guns instead of the usual ones with longer barrels. What kind of guns are they? Ralowe says: I don't know, but they look like toy guns. And can you believe that the prescription sleeping pills have a warning label that says MAY CAUSE DROWSINESS. You mean, I'm going to take this shit and it might not even cause drowsiness?

People on cars: this guy jumps in front of his mother to point excitedly at the new Kia. I can't hear what he says. Cars on cars: this huge truck almost slides into a tiny fake-old car, pounding on the horn instead of trying to avoid an accident. Cars on people: an SUV full of screaming black-and-white guys, I guess they're screaming at me to move, FAGGOT. I'm too hypoglycemic.

Ralowe and I argue about trip-hop. Ralowe: trip-hop is what changed the face of hip-hop, giving artists new freedom to experiment with mismatching sounds and uncomfortable juxtapositions, the Beastie Boys' *Paul's Boutique* made it all possible. Me: what are you talking about? Trip-hop was some stupid marketing trend that lasted two years. Ralowe: trip-hop opened up the idea to mix dissonant sound textures and layers of beats with different time signatures to create subterranean soundscapes. Me: that's what djs do, any good dj mixes layers and layers of crazy things that don't make any sense together, until you can't even figure out what's going on and if you have to die right then, then it's okay. Trip-hop is just some over-produced crap that uses dj techniques in the studio.

Ralowe: maybe I haven't listened to enough djs, but I didn't say that part about *Paul's Boutique* making it all possible, I said it exposed new techniques to the mainstream. Me: I don't care what you said, actually it was something even grander, something that sounded like a music critic and now I can't remember. But the point is that trip-hop was just some marketing gimmick. Ralowe: I don't think you understand what I'm saying. Me: I don't understand what you're saying, but maybe we just need to go out and listen to some good djs, that was one of the first things that we planned to do together. Not that there are any good djs here anyway, or not that I know where to find them, but maybe we should look.

Ralowe: I don't like dancing. Me: that's what you said the first time—you don't have to dance. If it's really good, you can just sit there and let your eyes roll back. I can't dance anyway because of all my pain, though maybe I would *have* to start dancing—so maybe we shouldn't go out. Ralowe: I don't like djs anyway.

No, this isn't a joke about car salesmen, a Harley and a handgun, some bubblegum for the run. But I don't chew gum anymore, it's been years full of tears—seven, to be exact. You remember that myth, right? That the gum stays in your stomach for seven years. I used to eat pack after pack of Juicyfruit—packed with corn syrup—then later Trident packed with saccharine, but see—I feel great now!

Activist Tourism Syndrome (ATS): everyone's talking about going to the Republican Convention to protest. Speaking of revolution, there's a rumor that Tracy Chapman sold her house on Liberty Hill and moved into the old antique store at 17th and Folsom, the one that used to be a police station. The original Power Exchange was right across the street—it was called the Playground and they had a gymnastics horse, see how things have changed?

An interesting question from the BBC: will terrorists sell moon rocks to fund their next operation? Rue goes to a brunch that turns into a cocktail party that turns into a Sunday at the Eagle that turns into frozen pizza all over his hallway. He says: I knew I dropped it, but I thought I cleaned it up.

But what about our plans? On the radio: progressive patriotism. The building manager is pouring that awful carpet deodorizer all over the halls again—he's not even the building manager anymore, he moved to a building in Pacific Heights. What is he doing interfering with my airspace? In my dream, I'm trying to escape a woman in a bright yellow vintage convertible who speeds towards me until I'm doing that flying-in-the-air-by-flapping-my-legs thing and I'm just above the woman's head. All this happens after I leave the outdoor market, where Jeremy hands me running clothes. I hit the woman in the face with my bare feet, but she just looks annoyed. I hit her again, but somehow I can't hit her hard enough. When I wake up, the 9-11 Commission Report has finally been released. They say: it was all a failure of imagination!

But I've got a special offer on non-restorative sleep. That's right—one size fits all. One night, or the rest of your life. You want it—we got it.

I call Allison at her hotel, to see if she wants to go to a dance performance. She hurt her foot, so she's been walking around all day hoping it would get better. Now she's worried it's broken, she's not sure if she should go to the hospital. She says: I hate going to the hospital, I've been there four times this year and they always tell me it's nothing—they're not nice, it takes forever, and all I do is sit there in a sterile room.

I meet Allison at the hotel—it's the Hilton, in case you're wondering. She got it discounted on Priceline. She says I wish I'd picked the boutique hotels instead, I knew I should have, but I was worried that I'd get the wrong one—I don't like it here, there were stains on the sheets so I had to get them changed and the housekeeper was really annoyed because she'd just changed them and I know she's probably making less than minimum wage.

Allison and I go to the Tibetan restaurant. Just when I think we're never going to talk about incest, she brings it up. She says I have to be honest, I believe you but I can't understand how it happened, I love Dad and I can't imagine not having a relationship with him. But she was in that house too—suddenly we're crying together, I'm trying to talk about memories—knives and cut-up animals and curling up in fetal position inside burlap sacks—but I don't know how to talk about any of it. Allison holds out her hand, and that's when I start crying and then she's crying too, it's scary but nice.

I say: I have to admit that I have this feeling of loss, because there's only one person who was there at the time, and in the same position as me, and that was you—and I wish we could talk about it together. She says I don't remember anything at all, I don't know if I want to remember anything—it's easier to have both my relationship with you and my relationship with him. I start telling her about other memories, like in therapy that one time when I became a little kid and what was I saying . . .

I start crying again, and it's too hot in the restaurant, we go outside. We take a cab to Fisherman's Wharf to check if the sea lions are out at night. There are a few, but they're too far away to see, really. At home, why does it smell like shit in my kitchen? I hope it's not rat shit, though maybe that's what I'm allergic to, what gives me sinus headaches in the morning, what ruins my sleep and leaves me yearning to slam my head into something else.

Allison's boyfriend, Allen, somehow manages to drive from LA to San Francisco in five and a half hours, I don't know how. We visit the sea lions—there still aren't too many because it's their migration period, but we study them. Allen says: do you have an animal fetish too?

I never get to tell Allison about that time in therapy when I became a two- or three-year-old, saying: they do things to me, but I can handle it—but what about the baby, the little baby so scared? She was that baby, I'm so scared. Eric drives me to the fibromyalgia doctor in Marin. The doctor tells me he wrote the first book on fibromyalgia in 1985, and now there are 500 books on Amazon, but his is still the best. He says: you should go to my clinic—I'll give you a referral—and here's a prescription for trazodone, it's the only thing that works.

But why do I disobey my own rules again, yet again, and cruise craigslist? I take a cab over to this guy's house to suck him off, and when he shoots his load in my mouth, all I can think is GROSS. It's what I wanted, so I come anyway. Afterwards, I can't find a cab until the 90 bus rescues me, I forgot it came down Potrero. Ralowe calls, he says do you know they're gonna reinstate the draft?

But I forgot to describe the new cure: trazodone. Rue warns me against it, but I try one 50 milligram pill, anyway. Soon, I feel a little loopy and light-headed, staring at myself in the mirror until my legs feel rubbery, my eyes burn and my throat starts closing, but at least I fall asleep. I wake up in the middle of the night feeling like I'm going to vomit. I drink some water and get back in bed. When I get up again, I have the most amazing headache, amazing because it's pounding evenly on all sides of my head at the same time, like a metal vise. When I move, I feel dizzy and shaky and nauseous. I sing a song: now I know I'm not alo-one—now that I got my . . . trazo-do-one.

Ralowe says it's trazic, and he's right. This trick wants to know what my ass is like—it's like a bridge over troubled water. NPR takes me to Coventry, Vermont, waiting with all the other Phish-heads for the final Phish show, after 20 years, and there are 75,000 of us here. There's not very much for me to eat, but the roadside diner is open 24 hours, and they're serving carrot sticks—so I'm going to be eating a lot of carrot sticks, though I'm a little worried about the final show, because President Bush said there might be a terrorist attack. And I can't digest raw carrots

Ralowe wants me to count how many people I see wearing cam-ouflage. There's the baby in the desert camo fleece ski cap, the twin teenagers in matching pink camouflage overalls, and are those pink camo bandannas keeping their ponytails in line? Then there's the art student with the discreet, computer-generated grey-and-charcoal camo shoulder bag to shelter his beloved laptop, and three guys giv-ing old school: head-to-toe army green, but is that a hint of burgundy for Fall 2004?

I pick up the phone: static. Everyone knows opportunity knocks, even if there's someone on the other line doing lines. Listen, Mr. Cointelpro, a windy tunnel is always different than a tin funnel.

Dry your eyes, honey—it's only my demise. Looking out the peep-hole of my front door, I rarely catch anything, just the door across from me in some bad movie's fish-eye lens. Opening my own door, I see a hallway just waiting for runway.

ABOUT THE AUTHOR

Mattilda Bernstein Sycamore is an insomniac with dreams. She is the author of a novel, *Pulling Taffy* (Suspect Thoughts 2003), and the editor of four nonfiction anthologies, most recently *Nobody Passes: Rejecting the Rules of Gender and Conformity* (Seal 2007) and an expanded second edition of *That's Revolting! Queer Strategies for Resisting Assimilation* (Soft Skull 2008). She's also the editor of *Dangerous Families: Queer Writing on Surviving* (Haworth 2004) and *Tricks and Treats: Sex Workers Write About Their Clients* (Haworth 2000). She is currently at work on a new anthology, tentatively titled *Why Are Faggots So Afraid of Faggots?: Flaming Challenges to Masculinity, Objectification and the Desire to Conform.*

Mattilda's writing appears in a variety of publications, including the *San Francisco Bay Guardian*, *Bitch*, *Utne Reader*, *Bookslut*, *make/shift* (where she is the reviews editor, and writes a column), and *Maximumrocknroll* (where she writes a column). Mattilda is a delicate mess, but she has a lot of good ideas, or at least she hopes so. She's still looking for answers, and loves feedback and propositions. You can find her homepage at mattildabernsteinsycamore.com, and she blogs at nobodypasses.blogspot.com.